SLOW BURN

''How do you feel?'' Nate asked tentatively.

''Not great, but not lousy either. Thanks, Nate, you're really making this much better than it could have been,'' Claudia murmured, giving his arm, which enfolded her, a little squeeze.

Stroking her upper arm, he pecked the top of her head with a kiss. ''Just a little time and you'll be good as new. Trust me.''

She did.

She trusted everything about the man who held her gently and stroked her arm as they watched the movie in companionable silence together. His touch created a warm blanket of protection that radiated through her body and stilled her once-panicked soul. As he continued to rub her arm, she felt a new awareness of him, a stirring that she hadn't felt toward any man in a long time.

SLOW BURN

Leslie Esdaile

Pinnacle Books
Kensington Publishing Corp.
http://www.pinnaclebooks.com

PINNACLE BOOKS are published by

Kensington Publishing Corp.
850 Third Avenue
New York, NY 10022

First Printing: August, 1997
10 9 8 7 6 5 4 3 2 1

Printed in the United States of America

Prologue

"When did you find out he got married? When did it all happen?" Claudia placed her palm over her sister's clasped hands and tried to calm her.

"Two hours ago, I had to get out of the office. I just came directly here to your place," Loretta choked out. "His *secretary* left a message on my answering machine! She told me that I had an extra week to get in the report since he'd still be on his honeymoon!" she wailed, breaking Claudia's hold and reaching for a cigarette. "I can't believe he'd do something like this. Just walk away and never say a word?" Loretta stopped and lit the end of the long Benson & Hedges. She took a deep drag and continued just above a whisper, "After all we had together, this man goes off on a weekend and gets married? Sure he had women . . . But I didn't know there was another *woman.*"

Claudia watched her sister intently. Loretta's once shrill voice had become quiet now, and her tone very introspective toward the end of her statement. She had never seen her like this before. Ret always seemed so self-assured and confident where men were concerned, and she had always told her to never fall in love—it just wasn't worth it. But now, as she watched her older sister unravel before her, Claudia knew there was something more than just ego rejection going on here. She could see it in Loretta's face. The woman looked positively shell-shocked, and this hurt was deeper than a normal surface wound. It went way down, congealing with the flash of terror that she also detected in her sister's eyes. Something that shouldn't have been there was mixed in with the pain.

"I'm sorry, Ret. This hurts a lot now, but just like you told me about Trevor, it goes away after a while . . . or at least the ache isn't as unbearable. Time. All you need is some time."

Anguish smoldered in Loretta's eyes as she took another shaky drag on her cigarette. "Yeah, baby sis, but this isn't like what you and Trevor had together. It was so much more."

The comment, although not designed to, cut Claudia to the bone. How could her sister minimize six years of marriage like that? Just because she wasn't as sophisticated as Ret, or as daringly successful, didn't mean that she hadn't loved her husband. Nor did it mean that she hadn't loved him with all of her heart and soul when they'd first married. She had meant it when she'd stood before the altar and said, "With all that I have, with all that I own." Trying to force the still-too-recent memory from her mind, Claudia banished her own pain and looked at her sister.

Normally she had the patience to deal with Ret. Today she didn't. She knew that the anger and pain Loretta vented should have gone in Eric's direction, but she was too close to the source of it to miss the snipes. She was getting tired of being the healer, the patient reasonable one.

"I know you were involved with Eric for years," Claudia said finally, after taking a deep breath to steady herself. "But you always told me that you didn't love him, and that he didn't love you. That it was *cool,* as long as you met each other's needs." Claudia checked herself quickly, because the last part of her statement had come out a little more brittle than intended. Softening her voice, she tried again. "Look, you told me that it was a great physical relationship, and it made excellent business sense to be connected to him because he was so connected to everybody else in Philly—and everything was about connections. I know you're hurt, shocked, and angry now, but didn't you figure that sooner or later one or the both of you would find somebody else who really fulfilled that missing in-love portion of your life? Eventually marriage was inevitable . . ." Claudia trailed off, searching through every bit of logic in her mind, yet still not knowing how to calm or comfort her sister. It was bewildering to watch. Loretta was always the strong one, the confident one.

Ret took another quick drag and exhaled angrily, drying her tears with the back of her hand. "Oh, that's right, I forgot I was talking to Miss Goody Two Shoes—no drinking or smoking or fornicating for the church girl who still believes in love and sweetness and light. Give it a rest, sis. Eric wasn't the marrying kind, and doesn't believe in happily-ever-after love any more than I do. It was my fault for ever getting involved with him, and going to those stupid metaphysical classes to try to figure out my karma."

"What?"

"Forget it. The point is, if that SOB got married, it was for a good reason and to his benefit, not love.

"Obviously, you did love him, or you wouldn't be this upset," Claudia ventured calmly.

Loretta looked down at the smoke curling up from the end of the half-smoked butt that dangled between her tapered, manicured fingers. Tapping the cigarette twice with one long red talon, she watched the graying embers hit the bottom of the tin ashtray and adjusted her gold bangle before speaking. "Yeah, I did," she said in an oddly detached tone, not looking up. "I gave him everything I had to give. Nobody ever got that close. Nobody."

Now *they* were getting somewhere. Progress.

"You have to talk to him at some point, and get this off your chest. You can't carry this hurt around with you forever, Ret. It'll become baggage that'll hold you back from enjoying the rest of your life."

"Who told you that crock? Your ex-marriage counselor? Your minister? If I didn't know better, I'd swear my meditation instructor told you that bull."

Claudia accepted that her sister was upset, and didn't take offense at the verbal assault. She had seen this pattern of behavior in Ret for years, and her heart ached as she watched Loretta drop a frosty barrier between the subject and the pain. "Don't do it, honey," she whispered, once again reaching for her sister's hand, only to have it angrily snatched away. "What are you going to do? I mean, how can you two work together if you're this tortured? If you don't find a way to handle it, he could even try to force you to quit, or even try to fire you. It's a small firm, and like you said before, he's well connected. Let's look at this from that side, too."

Loretta shot out of the chair and began pacing. It was like watching a caged, trapped animal.

"I'd just like to see that man try to force me out of Addison Development. I helped him build that firm! It would be the worst mistake of his life." Violently snatching open a cabinet door, Loretta's eyes narrowed on her. "Why don't you ever keep any liquor in this joint? I swear, Claudia, I don't see how you could live in this dump after giving up that four-bedroom house in Jersey." Slamming the cabinet shut she spun back around. "I hate it! Why does the woman always have to loose? Why does she always end up with the short end of the stick after a divorce or a breakup? Where's the cosmic justice in that?" Loretta lit a new cigarette with the butt of the old one.

"Did he promise that he'd marry you? I didn't know your relationship—"

"No. He just allowed me to dream, that's all. I should have known better."

Claudia went still. For the first time in years, she saw a

glimpse of that teenage woman-child who was her sister again. The scene was so eerie, so familiar . . . just like when she was eight years old and her glamorous older sister stood in their mother's kitchen and confided that she was pregnant. Loretta had been standing at the sink, which was full of dirty dinner dishes, clasping a towel, trying to look strong, refusing to cry. And she had stood next to her becoming numb . . . suddenly realizing that her sister had vulnerabilities. That's when their relationship had changed, and they had silently vowed to stand together through it all. Loretta looked at her that same way now and let two big tears form in her eyes without blinking them away.

"I'm scared, Claud," she whispered, still not allowing herself to fully crumble. "I need a plan."

"Honey, I know you're hurt . . . but you'll be more hurt if you try to go after a married man and take him from his new wife. You have to let it go. What are you going to do? Carry on an office affair with him for ten years, and still have nothing? You're free. You're beautiful, smart, with your whole life in front of you . . . There're no ties between you two now, other than work . . . at least none that would make you have to continue this way. Maybe it would be best to start looking for another job."

"You don't understand, Claud."

Loretta's voice was distant and the vacant look in her eyes made the hair stand up on the back of Claudia's neck. Her sister appeared so close to the edge of hysteria that it was frightening.

"Then make me understand, honey. I'm here for you, always."

Loretta smiled. "I know. You always were. You've kept my ugly little secrets, and were the only one who never judged me . . . but this isn't like any *trouble* I've gotten into before, Claud." Loretta cast a knowing glance in Claudia's direction and turned away.

"Claud, this can't be easily fixed like that other situation. I was young and dumb, and much too vulnerable. Eric and I aren't married, but we are most definitely tied together. And trust me when I tell you, I'm not going out like this. I don't intend to get the short end of the stick. He can't keep walking on everybody . . . I won't allow it any more. So what if I have to come back and do this again. I refuse to be a doormat. I can't!''

''What are you talking about . . . coming back again? Revenge?''

''No. Justice . . . and sometimes you have to come back to finish unfinished business. Past lives and reincarnation . . . to . . . Never mind, you can't handle this. Even with all that you've been through, you're still an innocent, which gives me hope. I can't drag you into this mess, I'd never forgive myself if something happened to you. I should've never come here until I had it all worked out and it was done.''

Claudia looked down at the cracking linoleum floor, bewildered. What could her sister do? Approach the man's new wife and tell her everything about their affair? What would that accomplish but hurt Loretta's pride even more? Claudia sighed and grappled with her urge to tell her sister to let it go.

Their eyes met. A line had been drawn, and Claudia knew better than to repeat the words that's she'd said so often about forgiveness being divine. She could tell from her sister's rigid stance that there'd be no talking to her about this again. That was Loretta.

Besides, this whole mess couldn't have happened at a worse time for Ret, especially since she was scheduled to go in for a biopsy in two days. Claudia wondered if this added stress was contributing to Loretta's hysteria. The smoking had to stop, and the doctors had told her that stress would only make her condition worse. She had to find a way to calm Loretta down. There had to be an answer to bring her sister some peace.

Claudia gazed up at Loretta who was rummaging in her purse for car keys. ''Ret, I don't know what to say that will make this any easier for you. But just know that I love you, and God loves you.'' There. It had been said.

Loretta stopped for a moment and looked at her, then expelled another bitter laugh while shaking her head. Don't they say, 'God helps those who help themselves?' I intend to help myself on this one, doll. Anyway, I like the one that goes 'An eye for an eye' much better. People go the hell on and do what they want to do anyway, without any interruption to their lives.''

Claudia controlled her voice. There was no talking to Ret now. ''But you've left out the rest of it. The other part says, ' . . . And vengeance is Mine sayeth the Lord.' ''

''Yeah, yeah, yeah. Well, let's just see how this one plays out. Otherwise, I have a plan of my own.''

Loretta walked over to Claudia and hugged her with new tears beginning to form in her eyes. ''I shouldn't have told you about this, sis. Everything'll be fine. I've just got some things to do. Don't worry, okay? I'll see you the day after tomorrow. You're still coming to the hospital with me, aren't you?''

Claudia squeezed Loretta back and murmured, ''Of course, I'll always be there for you, just like you've always been there for me. And, even if you don't like it, I'll always pray for you, too.''

Loretta shook her head, and left without addressing the comment. When the door slammed loudly, Claudia sat in the silence, listening to the street sounds that now seemed very far off in the distance. The terror that had flashed in her sister's eyes haunted her. Turning to her only source of strength, she bowed her head and offered up a direct prayer for Loretta's forgiveness and for her peace.

''Dear God, please don't pay her no mind. It's just her way. I _know_ she believes. Please take care of Ret. She's a good woman and she needs you now. She's my sister.''

Chapter 1

Burlington, N.J.
Present Day

It was the final anthem to a decade of losses. Claudia could only stand numbly holding onto the pew for support as the choir began the low beginning notes of "Amazing Grace." So much had happened in such a short span of time. This was the same song that they'd sung at her mother's funeral only eight months earlier.

Everything had been so sudden. Surreal. She had spoken to her sister Loretta in the morning, less than a week ago. In her normal self-confident manner, Ret had told her that she was only going in for routine outpatient surgery. They'd found a tiny dark spot on her lung and needed to take a biopsy. Despite Ret's mood, she had gone with her that fateful day, determined to stay and drive Loretta home. She remembered forcing herself to be cheerful, even though she was consumed about what they'd find inside her sister's lungs, but never once considered that Ret would be gone in a matter of minutes.

All she could think of now was how Ret had fussed at her good-naturedly, trying to convince her about how there was no need to worry . . . how Ret had emphatically reassured her that they'd be home before dinner. But that's not what happened at all. Loretta was gone. The facts still battered Claudia as she stood in the first row looking at her sister, her best friend, lying prone and vacant. The realization that Ret was dead slowly sank in. It was impossible to even conceive of how such a bright spirit could be gone forever.

The church ushers watched on nervously, appearing confused that she didn't cry out like the rest of the mourners. How could she explain to them about simply being all cried out, and just too tired? There weren't any more tears. Loretta had been so full of life, so vital. . . . To see her like this was like a bad and hazy dream.

What was real always happened in small increments. Under normal circumstances, the destruction of a once-resilient soul took a long time.

But it had already been a *very* long time. A tiring road of endless heartache that finally entered her once-strong will and broke it. Claudia let her breath out slowly. They'd won. For some unknown reason, The Forces of The Universe, as Loretta called them, had coalesced a war council against her family. Unceasingly, they'd beaten her down to a catatonic pulp, and now she was resigned, too battle weary to continue fighting the unseen *them* anymore. Maybe that's what happened to her sister . . . she'd just gone into surgery and decided to give it up? Who could say?

Searching for a point in the room, any point other than the casket and sprays of flowers to fix her gaze on, Claudia looked past the cross to the large rectangular stained glass window behind it. The bright April sun shone down colored light on the altar, cascading the blues and golds across the shoulders of a swaying choir.

God had been with her, always. Where was He today? Piercing memories shot through her as she searched the sanctuary for Him. Her mind pleaded for understanding.

Hadn't she kept her guard post of faith when He'd taken the only two babies that she'd ever carried? Claudia braced herself against the avalanche of pain that swept through her chest, vividly recalling how she had miscarried. It was easier to find a justification than to become consumed with the grief. She had logically told herself that something was obviously wrong with the babies, that she was still young, and had time to try again. Everything in His own time.

"You okay, baby? You want some water?"

Claudia stared at the dark round matron dressed in a white nurse's uniform. She couldn't get words to form at her lips, so she just shook her head no. How could she be okay? How was a glass of cool water going to stop the unbearable ache of such a loss?

Even when her husband started staying out all night long, she had been able to rationalize that they were just going through a rocky beginning. Ret had informed her that all men run. The first year of marriage was expected to be tough, her minister said. Although she hadn't planned on hell, she'd kept the faith anyway. Through six years of Trevor's various girlfriends calling the house and confronting her, him walking out, his claiming that he didn't love her anymore, the emotional abuse, finally through the divorce . . . she had at least been faithful to Him, her vows, and her husband. Everybody. Trevor had been the one to initiate the divorce, even after she'd prayed against it. But then, another woman had given him a son—the child that she couldn't seem to bring to term and deliver. So, she'd signed the papers and gave in. No need for the child to suffer just because the parents were sinners. God had to understand that, didn't He?

Claudia's mind ricocheted from one problem to the next, trying to find something that maybe she'd done to anger God to the extent that He would take her only sister.

Of course, the three severed relationships that followed

within six months of her divorce hurt. And, yes, she'd slept
with one of the men. . . . But, she'd also prayed for forgiveness
for her weakness. Wasn't that why she'd opted to remain celi-
bate for four years . . . until the right man came along? Though,
one never did. Still, instead of angering God again, she'd wept
from the disappointment and loneliness and the hard-to-admit
physical ache of not having strong arms to wrap around her.
She'd kept the faith and told herself that there was a reason, a
plan.

"Baby, it'll be all right."

The uniformed woman's touch didn't register in her mind
until after it had left her skin. Claudia held onto the hymnal
for support and looked at the sprays of pink carnations that
covered the front of the church. Her mind fought against another
memory that stabbed into her brain, making her swallow it
down with a dry heave of nausea. When Moms died, it had
been quick. The cancer had ravaged her mother's body in four
inconceivable months. While the loss had been devastating,
and she still grieved deeply, she had also thanked the good
Lord that at least it'd been swift. Moms had lived a full, rich
life, and the illness had only burdened her for a few short
months. Indeed, God had been merciful.

Sickened, Claudia forced her gaze down away from the
flowers, trying to erase her mother's torture from her mind and
closing her eyes briefly against the sight of her older sister laid
out two feet in front of her.

The church was too small . . . not enough air. . . .

Thinking back farther to a less graphic image, Claudia shifted
her thoughts to something benign. Today, she would not cry.
She hadn't when the market crashed in the eighties, or when
she and several close friends lost their jobs. Claudia remembered her eternal optimism with bitter detachment. On it's own
volition, her hand raised to her cheek as a smile made her face
feel like it was crumbling. In the distance, she could hear
women's voices. . . .

"I think we need to take her out . . ."

Shaking her head no again, she staved off the eager cavalry of well-intended matrons. No. She was fine. It would all be over soon. There had to be a reason . . . a bright light at the end of this tunnel of darkness. . . .

She had always decided to take a positive approach, the high road, naively calling the events that changed her entire socioeconomic condition a blessing in disguise. Foolish.

When she was still armed with faith, she'd plunged her entire severance package from the insurance company into a small, mail-order gift business. She'd believed what she read in the business magazines. She was going to be an entrepreneur. But, when that venture failed due to sluggish retail sales and a tax law change, she'd begun teaching. Viewing it as a constructive solution to the horrific inner-city problems in Philadelphia, she'd been grateful that she could still make a way while giving back something to the community in the process. It was another tithe of sorts . . . missionary work . . . all of her talents, and most of her energy.

So what that the house eventually had to go up for sheriff's sale because she could no longer pool her income with her husband's salary. When Trevor left, she didn't have a husband. And he wasn't sending anything to help her—unemployed or not. He had a kid. Anyway, things didn't make you happy, people did. So, okay that she had to move into a dingy little apartment. What did money mean, after it was all said and done? She used to tell herself that she still had her health and strength. She had reinforced her position by thinking of herself as *work in progress*. That's how the various ministers said to view her trials. They'd told her to be thankful. After all, she was more fortunate than most of the people she saw on the news. She didn't live in the streets. She had the gift of patience and clarity to teach. . . .

Memories collided against her heart until they screeched and crashed into the year when her dear cousin had taken his life. Everyone expected it sooner or later. They all kept watch and tried to help erase the pain that caused him years of living a depressing existence following Vietnam.

Claudia felt weightless, disembodied, like she could drift with her thoughts . . . higher and higher until she mixed with the clouds. . . . She vaguely remembered feelings. Yes, she had been sad when her cousin died, but she had also felt a strange sense of peace when it happened. Somehow, tragic though it had been, the entire process of saying goodbye was easier than watching him suffer the internal battle that had robbed his sanity and his will to live. It was also a less cruel way for him to die, than for him to struggle against the horrors of full-blown AIDS. A quick painless death by barbiturates and Scotch had been his solution, and she respected and loved him too much to deny his need to let go. Although she had loved Jimmy like a brother, she also loved him enough to know that he couldn't take it any longer. Everybody had a limit. Jimmy had just found his. And she could remember dropping a rose on his casket, then thanking God that her cousin's personal hell was over.

Claudia shut her mind off to her father's sobs as they wrenched her back into the pew and away from the sky. The sound of his pain caused a hurt inside that robbed her lungs of air. Looking around the congregation, she thought of how the gossip mongers had repeatedly asked how she felt about her father's recent marriage. Even after all the other heartaches, there was still more to bear. It was as if everyone was constantly on the lookout for something to go wrong; any piece of discontent in her family that they could sniff out. Their behavior was a disgrace to her mother's memory, and she wasn't about to let them tarnish that with unjustified speculation about his relationship to Miss Dot. Never. But, that was then . . . when it mattered. It didn't anymore.

Sure, watching her mother's house transform under Dad's new wife's hand had been extremely painful, especially during the holidays. But the fact that he had a new start, a second chance, had been a godsend. In a strange sort of way, watching a man of her father's age get a second chance had given her hope . . . hope that maybe God would grant her such happiness one day. And she'd been able to successfully reason away the nagging twinges of resentment that would occasionally surface within her against Miss Dot—especially during the holidays, or when Dot would give her some unsolicited advice. Miss Dot and her mother were two different people, with vastly different styles. But, if she loved her father, then how could she begrudge him such happiness, or a future filled with companionship? Plus, Doris Eldridge was a good, church-going woman, who really didn't mean any harm. She and Dad had known of each other for years . . . had met through the churches.

Claudia cast her gaze toward the graying couple and swallowed hard, touching her father's shoulder. Her mouth formed words that her heart did not believe. "It'll be all right, Daddy." When he didn't respond, she looked at Miss Dot.

Dad's new wife was kind. Her short buxom frame, golden round face, and big-flowered church hats that covered short, tight pressed curls were a stark contrast to her mother's conservative, yet sophisticated look. Her mother had been tall, thin, light like ginger with auburn hair, and possessed a natural stunning underglow that didn't require much makeup . . . just like Loretta. She, on the other hand, was built more like Miss Dot—shorter, rounder, and browner like her father, and often thought that she might look like Dot when she got to that age. Odd, but she looked more like a cross between Miss Dot and her dad than a combination of her tall color-opposite parents. But, the one thing Dot and her mother shared were dark, kind eyes. That's probably what attracted her father to Dot in the first place . . . kindness that oozed from her eyes, and a smile that invited you into her heart.

Dot reached around her father's back and squeezed Claudia's hand. Their eyes met and a tear rolled down Dot's cheek making Claudia squeeze her hand gently before she let it go. Dot was kind.

In fact, Miss Dot was one of the nicest people she'd ever known. Even though no one could replace Moms, this lady was an angel. A truly decent human being. What more could a daughter ask for when praying on her father's behalf? The thought made Claudia grind her teeth in anger. It was also why she'd been so adamant that the rest of the family accept his new beginning, and had refused to tolerate even the slightest hint of impropriety about the timing of the woman moving in and making changes. Her faith had been unwavering. She'd believed that God had His hand in it, therefore, no one should dare question it. Dot had been around for as long as she could remember.

Claudia looked at the casket again and then down at her hands. But what was God thinking of when this happened to Loretta?

Through every tribulation, Caudia knew she'd followed His will and had borne up under the strain. When she'd gone against it, she'd prayed for both forgiveness and direction. For every single disappointment she had forced the crush from the weighted problems behind her, while thrusting her chin forward like a quiet soldier in His army. Hadn't she kindly accepted every platitude, string of advice, all the old wives tales and fables that she could stand? Hadn't she labored on under the congregation's watchful eyes, never commenting, always pushing forward? Even when they *really* got in her business, she had let it go—turned the other cheek.

Although, admittedly, the one thing she couldn't countenance was a zealot. These people wanted her to abandon her friends, even her sister, all because they didn't practice the right brand of Christianity. Before, it was just easier to hide from them than to fight about it. Claudia found herself shaking her head and thinking about how she'd steadfastly refused to press her views on others. She had friends from every walk of life imaginable: Muslims, Catholics, Jews, Seventh Day Adventists, people who lived together and weren't married, some who were gay, some who were militant, some who were conservative, people that had different children by different fathers and not a husband to be accounted for, a medley of different races. . . . Did that mean that God didn't hear their prayers or care about their suffering? To hear the preacher tell it, and the old ladies confirm it, that's just what it meant. If you were different, you got hit with a thunderbolt of lightning before it was all over. They'd told her that she'd be judged by the company she kept.

Faith had always been a terribly private matter for her, and she felt that everyone had to find their own resolutions about the way they wanted to live their lives. She had loved her friends unconditionally, and left them alone to act in accordance to their own decisions. She didn't dispense judgment with her advice, and her caring didn't have strings attached. Judgment was nobody's business but God's. Was that a bad thing? Was that why her life seemed damned?

Glancing around at the sea of grieving faces now, Claudia was glad that she'd stood her ground early on. Despite the disappointment of her congregation, she would only join them in quiet fellowship, then disappear. She'd never wanted to become involved in church politics, or its rhetoric. And she still couldn't understand why people seemed to enjoy interfering or giving heated opinions on personal subjects. Up until now, her way around the dilemma had been to just go along with her own way of coping, and quietly live by her own convictions about right and wrong. But what had she done that was so terrible?

A new wave of fury battered her as she recalled how these same wailing people had made Ret's outrageous existence a veritable hell. Loretta had been effectively shunned by these same pious people who lived in glass houses. Every stinking last one of them.

Claudia's fingernails cut into her palm. She'd always known that's why her sister had constantly needed her there for self-esteem repair after they'd finished damaging it, no matter what Ret said to the contrary, their words hurt.

And they had all taken a potshot at the poor girl since the day she was born. They'd always said her sister was a little too rambunctious, too fresh for her age, acting too grown, knew too much for her own good, thought she was better than everybody, needed to simmer down. . . . *Behave.* But the truth of the matter was, Ret had only wanted someone to believe in her, someone to love her. Even her dear father couldn't escape her bitter scrutiny on that subject as she stood by his side, watching the tears stream down his long, dark brown, stricken face. Why couldn't they have just let the girl be? Now it was too late.

Claudia felt the muscles in her throat tighten, and her vision blurred from what she was sure had to be elevated blood pressure. It definitely wasn't from tears. There were colors swirling in blues and yellows behind her eyes.

Thinking back on it now, that's probably why she'd always been called in as the voice of reason to referee disputes. She had been labeled Miss Goody Two Shoes, and Ret was the headache child. The bad seed. Each time there had been a crisis in one of their large, close-knit, extended family households, she was the one, little Claudia Harris, who got the 2 A.M. call. Everyone, even coworkers, sought her out when there was a problem, as if her patient words could help them through whatever pain threatened to swallow them. It drove her sister wild during those times, and almost drove them apart, because somehow the story of what happened would always get back twisted and altered, with the not-too-subtle suggestion that Loretta should be more like her.

But now, as she watched the casket close, there were no words of faith to guide her. No Ret to stand by her side to hold her up.

There was only anger.

She felt betrayed. He'd struck down her older sister, the one and only person, other than Moms, who had loved her unconditionally, and now that person was gone. All of this heartache, for no apparent reason. Loretta was only forty-one years old, danced like she was fifteen, and had her whole future in front of her. Why . . . ? Dear, funny, sassy, Ret. The girl who once had a fire in her soul, one that burned bright in her belly, and torched everything in its wake. Now that light of effervescent energy had been unnecessarily extinguished. A lethal mistake by an incompetent anesthesiologist had been the culprit. All in a day's work!

There was no rhyme or reason to this nightmare. Nothing made sense, and for the first time, there was no logical or intellectual fallback position. Nor was there a religious or medical justification for it. It was indefensible. It was another demonstrated lack of fairness in the world that could've been easily righted—if only He had a mind to do so. With one swift blink of His eye, snap of His fingers, or wave of His mighty hand, He could've made them give Ret the right dosage. Instead, He sat idly by, and had allowed them to give her sister, her only sister, something that turned that precious girl blue on the table, taking her life in less than thirty seconds.

This time, she wouldn't stand for such hypocrisy! She'd never forgive Him, or the collective them, for this!

The rage that broiled inside of Claudia began with those pinpoints of colored light that had stopped swirling behind her tightly shut lids. She could feel that rage becoming stronger, coming up from a deep well in her soul as the colors got brighter, igniting her quiet scream. . . .

Chapter 2

Philadelphia
Six Months Later . . .

Claudia continued her search through the coat closet with disgust. There had to be some money in one of the pockets, anything left over from her SSI disability check. Finding her good black wool coat hidden behind the jumble of jackets and sweaters, she dug her hand into the side pocket and struck gold as her fingers touched the distinctive paper of a bill.

"Yes," she mumbled, pulling it out for inspection. "Only a buck, but one more than I had a minute ago."

She vaguely remembered stuffing it in there six months earlier on the way to her sister's funeral. Claudia refused to think about that horrible day. She was on a mission, and needed a drink.

Scraping together the nickels, dimes, and pennies, she had amassed a sum total of two dollars and fifty seven cents—which had to last till the end of the week. And that was assuming her check came on time.

It wasn't enough to buy a bottle of anything strong, she thought wearily, looking down at the pile of change on the warped coffee table. How was she going to be able to make it till Friday without a decent drink? And The State was iffy at best. What if her check came late? Then she'd have to go up to the office and pitch a fit, which never did any good and only seemed to make your money take longer to get there.

Calling Dad or any family was out of the question. Sure, they'd been supportive and visited her every day during the six weeks it took her to recover from the breakdown. Dad hadn't even said a word about the fact that she had literally flipped out in church and gone catatonic for more than a month afterward. Yeah, he'd been there the first time she'd lost it right there at the funeral, but when they brought her in again a couple of months later and she was drunk, they'd turned on her. Both him and Doris could kiss her butt, just like the rest of her so-called friends and family could.

The good Deacon Harris had been the model father, with sweet Miss Doris, like a displaced Doris Day, had been by his side, wearing her flowered church hat and dainty white gloves, and trying to act like her mother and what-not—dispensing her sickening advice as usual. Tough love, pulleeze.

Just because she needed a little something now to help her through, just a little nip to take the edge off the pain of losing her babies, her husband, her home, her job, her business, Moms, her sister, her mind, and ultimately her teaching job . . . they'd listened to the damned counselors and their stupid theories of co-dependency, instead of listening to her from the beginning.

Claudia's gaze darted around the room for anything of value that she could quickly sell. Her coat. That stupid, black wool, funeral-wearing, school-teacher-looking coat. Well, she wasn't a teacher anymore, and she didn't need it for a job interview, that was for sure. Even with her once-untarnished work record and degree, who was going to hire an ex-insurance customer service rep, momentary entrepreneur whose business had failed, or a drunken teacher that had had a nervous breakdown? She wasn't anything anymore. Just like her ex-husband Trevor had once told her. She couldn't make babies and wasn't good to anybody—at least not to a man—which meant that she'd been nobody. So who gave a damn if a nobody had a drink every now and then?

"Right, sis?" she called out to the vacant room. "You always wanted to know why I didn't keep liquor or smokes in this joint. You shoulda stuck around. I'm gonna get some more, come hell or high water, today. But you shoulda told me how expensive this stuff was to keep on tap. Remember, I never made your kind of money."

Scooping up the pile of change, Claudia shoved it into her jeans pocket and picked up a rumpled pack of Benson & Hedges. One cigarette left. Damn. Everything was running out on her this morning! Irate, she flung the coat over her arm and headed out the door into the dimly lit hall. A little queasy, she held onto the wall as she maneuvered the narrow stairway. The incline seemed too steep. All she had to do was hold on ... edge her way down one level. Her legs felt shaky as she slowly descended and fought the persistent nausea. Maybe she'd just blow her change at the bar next door. There was always a fellow barfly at the Watusi Pub on Forty-Fifth who would sport for a drink until the end of the week, if the coat didn't sell. In the bar, everything was negotiable.

As she neared the bottom of the stairwell, a blast of sunlight and wind stopped her. The brightness hurt her eyes and she squinted painfully to make out the tall figure coming toward her. Finally adjusting to the glare, she recognized that it was just Nate, the maintenance man.

"Hey, Nate, wanna buy a coat for your girlfriend? Only a few years old, and got it at Wanamaker's. See," she added turning out the lable, "authentic." She tried hard to muster a smile. She had a sale to make. Her gaze narrowed on his dark, expressionless face. She had to size him up, figure out his thoughts.

Nate came up the stairs and stopped a few feet away from her. "Not today."

"C'mon, there's gotta be somebody who could use this? Hard winter's coming, and it gets mighty cold around here."

He just shook his head and tried to pass her. "You're right. But don't you think you're going to be needing it?"

Knowing there wasn't a sale to be had, she kept walking. She was wasting her time. Without looking back, Claudia flipped a curt reply over her shoulder. "Hey, if I could sell this, I'd have what I needed to keep me warm."

Her comment seemed to stop his advance up the next flight of steps, and he turned around slowly to face her again. "What are you doing? Selling your clothes now? Why don't you just get a job?"

Claudia scoffed at his suggestion. "Pulleeze. I don't need a *maintenance man,* oh, correction, *maintenance engineer,* giving me employment direction. All I need is some cash to hold me over until my check comes. Two dollars and fifty-seven cents isn't even enough to buy cigarettes and a cup of coffee. And that sink in my bathroom is still leaking. When, may I ask, are you going to fulfill *your* contractual *job* obligations?"

She really wasn't expecting an answer, but she also wasn't expecting his intense stare either. Nate just reached into his pants pocket without a word and pulled out a bill, raising his hand to stop her as she thrust the coat in his direction. He didn't want the coat, but was still going to give her money. Now she was a beggar. . . .

Claudia cringed inwardly, knowing that six months ago she would have probably been handing money to Nate. Humiliation tore at her insides, but so did her need for a drink. She looked at the tall, chocolate brown man with patient familiar eyes— beautiful eyes that were always half hidden behind the visor of his baseball cap. He had a quiet dignity and resignation that she had only seen in older people before. Strength. Maybe even wisdom.

As he stood with his arm outstretched toward her and the

money between his two fingers, she surveyed his face. It was rugged and handsome, always bearing a five o'clock shadow, and like today, generally very serious. Something in his dark eyes haunted her, forcing her to look away as she accepted the bill. How could she sink low enough to take anything from this man who obviously worked hard for his money? He was probably a decent church-going guy who had a family to care for on the small pittance she was sure he got for his labor, and she was about to blow it on liquor. If she hadn't felt so bad, she would've declined the kind offer. But she couldn't, she needed a drink.

Without looking at her sudden benefactor, she murmured a quick thank you and left, making a mental note to give the money back to him when her check came. It was a loan. Hell, this was an economic depression, despite what the news said. There was no way to reconcile the changes in her life. In a short six months, she had taken up smoking, drinking, and was deep into the social services system, breaking a series of lifelong vows.

But it didn't matter any longer. Nothing did.

Walking swiftly down south Forty-Fifth Street, and stopping on the corner of Walnut for the light to change, Claudia leaned against the smudged window of the Wingz chicken joint to see how much money Nate had lent her. Probably a one. If she was lucky, and for old times sake, not to mention for the few cups of coffee she'd made him when he'd fixed her door, maybe he'd given her a five. Opening her hand quickly, she stared in disbelief at the crisp new twenty that she had crumpled in her palm. Even though it solved her momentary problem, the discovery made her more depressed.

Not about to get all teary-eyed in the street, she looked down the block toward the boarded-up store that used to be the Seven-Eleven on Forty-Sixth to divert her attention. She had to plan, figure out a way to make this last. Her line of vision traveled to where a group of pipers where standing around the periphery of the adjacent gas station begging patrons for money in exchange for assistance at the pump. Like Loretta had told her countless times, everybody had an angle . . . needed an angle to survive.

But, the sight of the ragged, dirty, crack addicts sickened her, and she brought the coat closer to her stomach as if for protection. She wasn't one of them yet, but how long would it take before she sank to that depth for vodka?

Claudia shivered and pushed herself away from the grimy glass that separated her from the best local Afro-Carribean food in her end of town. But after her divorce from a West Indian, she'd vowed to never eat that type of food again . . . regardless of how good it smelled.

Her stomach was churning with the billows of essence-filled smoke that escaped from the vents. She hadn't eaten in twenty-four hours, but the combined smell of spicy buffalo wings, fried plantain, greens, oxtails, and whatever else they were cooking, made her insides lurch. There was an answer. The State Store on Fortieth and Market.

Nate stood in the hallway for a long time looking at the door. Who was she? Why did Claudia Harris gnaw at his gut this way? It didn't make sense.

When she'd moved in two years ago, she had just been a very pleasant lady who was never around during the day. She didn't talk or act like most of the rest of his tenants. He could tell that she worked, had a little education, and she always kept her tiny second-floor apartment clean. She was quiet, petite— a small woman, around five foot four, with even cocoa-brown skin, and sad eyes. Not his type at all. He'd always liked tall, lean, yellow women. Maybe it was her eyes?

Sure, he'd noticed that she always dressed well, not flashy or expensive clothes, just nice and nondescript tailored outfits. But those big, sad, beautiful brown eyes . . .

Immediately shaking Claudia's face from his mind, he went back to the puzzle, using the more analytical side of his brain.

Okay, the one thing that had immediately let him know she worked was the fact that she always wore a skirt or a dress. You didn't see that too much these days. Everybody, especially the students, mostly wore jeans or sweatpants. He remembered enjoying an occasional glimpse of her legs, which were long, even for her height . . . and pleasingly plump . . . ending at the tops to melt into a high, round, firm behind that tapered into a deep sway in her back. The jeans accentuated the region. . . . "Uhmph, Uhmph, Uhmph . . ." he muttered to himself as he began to walk while he thought about about the way she'd twisted her form sassily out the door.

No question, she was curvaceous, pretty really. A couple of times he'd wondered how old she was, but never thought to ask, since she kept to herself, and he had never given her much thought before. At least she was courteous enough to offer him a cup of coffee, or something cold to drink when he used to come in to make repairs. Home training, of the old-fashioned variety.

But now, thinking back about six months, she hadn't been around. And about the same time, her rent money, which was always paid on time by her personal checks, was now being supplemented by payments from the Housing Authority—section eight. It was odd. His office now received money orders for her portion of the rent payments instead of personal checks. Why was she sending in money orders from Seven-Eleven instead of just writing a check from her account? It didn't make sense.

What had happened to this woman?

Shrugging off the question, he turned away from her door, which had again stopped him in his tracks like a magnet, and continued up the stairs. There were eight million stories in the naked city. Everybody had one. He sure as hell did.

It had been three hours since he'd bumped into Claudia in the hall. He wasn't sure when it had come to him to finally get around to fixing her apartment today. Her request had only been on the list for a couple of days, anyway. What was her complaint? Unless it was a toilet or something dangerous, he got to the repairs as soon as he could, never kept people waiting long.

Growing agitated, Nate stood on the second-floor landing. The least he could do was to fix the woman's sink this afternoon, he thought, as he waited in front of her doorway holding the new valve that he'd picked up from the hardware store around the corner. He knocked again for her to answer. It had been hours since she'd left this morning and she should've been back by now. Lifting his hand to knock again, Nate began to feel the familiar irritation that usually nagged at his days. He hated dealing with people and their trivial little crises. There were three more jobs to do before he called it quits. As a favor, he was squeezing her in and she was disrupting his schedule!

Finally, he heard movement and a low mumble as something fell.

"Maintenance. I brought your water valve," he called out in case Claudia Harris was worried about opening the door to a stranger.

"Just a minute. Everybody's always in a damn hurry," a woman's voice slurred on the other side of the door.

Nate froze. Something was wrong. She didn't sound right.

His tenant managed the battery of locks and stood with her hand on her hip when the door was finally opened.

" 'Bout time," she commented as he crossed over the threshold. "It's the bathroom sink, and the water runs like Niagara Falls every time I use it. Gotta keep a bucket under the bend part of the pipe, or the old buzzard who lives on one will be hollering and beating the ceiling with a broom stick. Glad the landlord pays the water bill around here and not me. I really don't care one way or the other if McGregor Realty wants to waste their money, but I don't want that old man downstairs bugging me to death."

Nate just stared at the disarray that confronted him. This

couldn't be the same apartment that had once been so neat, not the one that used to have doilies on the sofa and lace curtains. As he stood in the middle of the living room, his eyes scanned the cluttered terrain. Newspapers littered the floor and cigarette smoke hung thickly in the air of the small quarters like one would expect in a bar. A dirty plate balanced precariously on top of several scattered magazines on the coffee table, and paperback books were strewn across every available seat— along with what he was sure had to be dirty clothes. Half-filled coffee mugs and glasses created an obstacle course on the floor between the coffee table and the couch, and in the background, an old black and white TV blared from a wicker stool, with a clothes hanger doubling as a makeshift antenna. Oprah was on. What happened to the little wall unit and the stereo that had been there? Where were the plants? Shuddering at the thought, he advanced farther into the apartment and headed toward the bathroom.

As he passed through the kitchen, he stopped and turned on the light. Roaches scattered and ran at the intrusion, and it was all he could do not to turn and leave as his mind tried to catch up to the scene that his eyes witnessed. Greasy plates overflowed from the sink and onto the small beige counter. Thick crusty substances were stuck onto pots and pans that still sat on the stove. The floor was a mosaic of splattered food droppings that he was sure the bugs enjoyed. The trash can was lined with an old, soiled, brown supermarket bag that was filled with garbage, and an open Hefty plastic bag sat next to it packed to the top. But the hardest thing to come to terms with, was the half empty bottle of Stolichnaya on the kitchen table that stood next to a short brimming glass. She was drunk.

"I gave you money so you could get wasted?" He nearly shouted as he spun around to face his tenant.

"Look, if I'da known there were strings attached, I'd a told you to keep your damned money!" she spat back, walking over to the glass and taking an angry gulp. "Just fix my sink and mind your bizness."

"If I'd known you were a damned alcoholic, I'd never have given you the money in the first place!"

"Fix my sink," she said calmly. "You'll have your money back when my check comes. What's it to you, anyway?" she added evenly, and poured more liquor into the glass. "I'll share. Want one?" she asked with a lopsided smile, holding up her glass in a mock toast before taking another deep swallow.

"I don't drink," he said between his teeth, and brushed past her into the bedroom to get to the bathroom.

Standing in the middle of the bedroom for a moment, he surveyed the new room with additional disgust. It was as though each room was worse than the last, like walking through the hall of horrors at a carnival. Grayish sheets hung off the bed, exposing a soiled mattress where he was sure she'd probably gotten sick a number of times. The shades were drawn and clothes littered every surface in varying sized piles around the room. Dust had settled on the once white vanity and mirror so thickly that you could write your name in it, and when he flipped the light switch, it didn't come on.

"How long has this been out?"

"Who knows? I'm not wasting my money on bulbs. That's what I pay rent for—maintenance. Hell, I can see good enough from the bathroom light anyway. So why don't you just stop being *nooosy,* and fix my damned sink?" she said sarcastically, while leaning on the door molding and crossing her long legs at the ankle.

Nate took a deep breath and went into the room he dreaded to enter most. Kicking the toilet seat down with his sneaker, he set his metal tool box on top of it and refused to consider the layers of mold and grime on every porcelain surface around him. He just continued to pull out his tools and test the water in the sink without looking around—ignoring Claudia Harris, who hovered in the doorway.

It should have been second nature by now, since he'd been going in and out of poor people's apartments for almost five years. Piles of laundry usually meant a check was late, or had

been already spent before it got there—because it cost too
much to go to the Laundromat, and laundry detergent was so
dog-gonned high . . . just like trash bags and bug spray were.
Piled up dishes and general disarray were just a symptom of
pure mental depression, and of not having the extra few bucks
to buy dish soap . . . or light bulbs, and all of the other high-
cost-on-a-fixed-income items. Everything was relative. Nate
knew that. It went with the territory, the same way that having
a constant angry attitude did, for people trapped in an untenable
position . . . rage, chip-on-the-shoulder, always . . . It was a
defense mechanism. He could spot it a mile a way. Poverty
was more than just a mentality, or a financial reality—it was
a complex blend of both—a butter versus guns decision com-
pounded by the mentality of hopelessness . . . therefore a circu-
lar and hard to break morass of overwhelming circumstances
that impacted the life of an individual. He knew.

As Nate worked and tried to focus on the pipe, Claudia
slipped away from the door toward the living room. His will
to not think about it betraying him, he thought about how he'd
watched his other tenants struggle to scrape up change to wash
their clothes across the street . . . how he'd watched people in
the aisles at the supermarket trying to make a decision between
soap powder and another bit of over-priced food. He'd seen
people at the registers trying to stretch food stamps to buy the
necessary items to live on from the stores they had to walk to,
which in return for their trapped patronage, further victimized
them by carrying higher prices. And, most of all, he understood
how a bottle of vodka, which could have brought all of the
items a person needed, could become a necessary elixir to
drown out the reality of one's condition. In an odd way, it too
had a place in the cycle, like a nonprescription medicine.

But for some reason, he'd never expected this chaos from
the quiet, almost shy, lady that had moved in here two years
ago.

The place was so completely, outrageously, filthy now—
different from all the other times he had stopped by to do odd

jobs for her. She'd reminded him of his grandmother's saying, "Jus' because ya po, boy, don' mean ya have to be dirty . . ." There was even a point when he'd actually looked forward to Claudia Harris's calls, since coming to her apartment was more like a visit to a relative than a tenant maintenance job. It had become his end of the week break, and he used to schedule special Saturday jobs around her work routine, even though he didn't do that for any other tenant. Claudia Harris's place had always been clean and homey. A couple of times she had even offered him a little of whatever she had on her once-immaculate stove. But now . . . he'd starve to death before accepting *anything* from her kitchen, even water.

When he finally came back out into the living room, she was watching the five o'clock news and had moved the bottle onto the coffee table in front of her, glass still in hand.

"You'd better take it easy," he said in a low voice. "You're gonna get sick. When's the last time you ate anything?"

"You finished with my sink yet?" she said in a surly voice, still looking at the television through glassy eyes.

"No, it's not only a valve. I'll have to run a snake through the pipes. There's a lot of junk in there that's also making it slow and backing up water into the bowl. The tub is real slow, too, which probably accounts for the three inches of scum in there. I've gotta get some more supplies to deal with this nightmare."

"Whatever," she said with disinterest. "Just fix it and leave me alone."

"I'm going to the hardware store before it closes. I'll be back in about a half hour. You gonna be here, or should I let myself in with the key?" he snapped indignantly.

"Where am I going?" she said irritably, still not looking at him. "If I don't answer, I just fell asleep, so use the key."

He didn't reply as he left and bolted toward the fresh air. Turning the corner at the end of the block, Nate stood outside of West Philadelphia Locksmith and Hardware for a moment before going in.

Claudia Harris disturbed him. Deeply.

What had happened to this woman was too reminiscent of his own past. Shoving aside the thought, he entered the store and picked out the plumbing supplies he needed to do the job. She was right. It wasn't his business or his problem. He'd just fix her drains and get the hell out of there. No sense in trying to help somebody who didn't want to help themselves. She could just pull her lazy self up by her own bootstraps for all he cared. He had his own problems.

But as he walked back out to the street with additional supplies in hand, he looked down the block toward the supermarket on Forty-Forth.

Heaving the bag of plumbing supplies over his shoulder, Nate headed down the block toward the market. He'd just get her some basic stuff and quietly slip it into her bathroom and cabinets, not to injure her pride. He was sure that Claudia Harris had some pride left. He had pride, too . . . once.

His walk was brisk and full of determination. A little soap, some toilet paper. Maybe some peanut butter and jelly, bread, soup. . . . That's it, just a few bucks would do it, and she'd never have to really know where it came from. Since he didn't deal with church or the Lord too much, it could be considered a tithe, of sorts. Ten or twenty dollars for a fellow veteran wouldn't kill him. Folks used to look out for their neighbors when he was growing up . . . and that's all this was, he told himself. Just being neighborly.

An hour later, Nate emerged from the always crowded store, hauling more bags than a pack animal could carry. What had he been thinking about when he went in there? Ninety-three dollars worth of stuff for some drunk woman! Lugging the parcels back up the street, he cursed to himself as he bustled toward the building. And what would he tell her? If she got real pissed, he could just lie and say that he had to go to the store for himself. Made sense, since he was out already, and her job would probably take a couple of hours any how. Whatever.

He was feeling stupid about the whole thing as he mounted the steep stairs, almost becoming winded before he reached the top. She was not his problem. Damn, there was a sucker born every minute!

Kicking the door with his foot, he banged loudly to get his tenant to hurry up and open the door before his arms gave out. The too-thin plastic bags were beginning to rip from the weight of the food, and were slipping out of his grip. "Cheap bags, too," he mumbled to himself as he kicked again and yelled for her to open up. But there was no answer.

Half dropping, half lowering the bags that burdened the right side of his body, he fished in his pocket for the ring of keys that he had for the building. Before inserting the correct one into the lock, he stretched out the aching muscles in his arm and mumbled a curse, then awkwardly balanced the other bags while he tried to open the door.

Once inside, he heaved his bounty onto the living room floor, and kicked the door closed behind him, yelling out while he tried to stop a can from rolling away as a new tear opened in the bottom of one of the bags.

Where was she? The TV was still on and the lights were all still blazing. Leaving the heap of food at his feet, Nate walked back into the kitchen, and continued toward the bedroom when he didn't see her. Calling out more tentatively, he entered the bedroom and waited.

"Miss Harris, I've got that stuff from the hardware store. Can I get into the bathroom soon to finish up?"

No answer.

He could hear water running and he moved slowly toward the half opened bathroom doorway and knocked lightly. "Claudia, I'm back. Can I get in there to fix the sink?"

He thought he heard a little movement, then a clink like something metal hitting the tile floor. Maybe she had taken her glass into the bathroom and broken it, and was cleaning up the shattered pieces? In her condition she'd cut herself for sure. Without regard to propriety, he eased open the door and stood back in horror.

Quickly crossing the short distance, he grabbed Claudia Harris by both wrists and shook her hands down over the sink until the razor blade dropped from her grip.

"What are you trying to do?" he yelled, pushing her onto the toilet seat and shutting off the warm water.

"I'm tired!" she sobbed back. "Just leave me *alone!*"

Looking around frantically for a towel, he wrapped her badly scraped wrists with the dirty one that he found and kicked the empty liquor bottle away from his feet. "Is this what you want? To kill yourself! Are you crazy?"

He stared at the woman crying on the toilet for what seemed like a long time. Here, this person that he didn't even know, unraveled right before his eyes. It was just like watching Monica self-destruct. How many times had his wife tried to kill herself after their baby died . . . before she was finally successful? His mind screamed for a solution. He couldn't witness anything like that again.

Garnering control, Nate paced in the small room.

"Look, whatever's happened isn't worth taking your life for. What, for a job? Temporary money problems? You can always get another job, not another life. Plenty of people have been getting laid off. Somebody out there cares about what's happened to you . . ." he trailed off, not knowing what else to say.

"Like who?"

He wasn't prepared for her response. Obviously the rough shaking had sobered her up considerably. Now, Claudia's more lucid tone held the same bitter hopelessness that had torn his own life apart.

"Answer me?" she said, renewed hysteria piercing a sob. "How much more can I take?" she wailed again, her voice cracking as she sputtered out the question. "I've lost two babies! Count 'em—*two.* My husband walked out on me and made a baby with somebody else. I lost my job, lost my business, lost my mother to cancer, my father to his new perfect little wife, my sister who was the only person I could trust . . . and finally my mind. Where am I going to work? So now I've got to wait on a check from the state and beg for money to buy a drink and sell my clothes! My stereo . . . the little bit I had left after Trevor kept it all . . . I just can't take it! This isn't me.''

Nate was momentarily speechless, and he stooped down next to the toilet and put his arm across the disheveled woman's shoulders. In that instant he knew. That's what he saw in her eyes. She had been to hell, just like he had.

As Claudia returned his stare through puffy, bloodshot eyes, he could feel a fragile bridge building between them. She wasn't ready to die. Not really. Or, she wouldn't have waited till she heard his key in the door. He well knew the subtle, yet different, signs between someone who really wanted to kill themselves, and someone who didn't—but wanted help. The problem was that he'd learned painfully four years ago that if the cry for help is ignored, it can easily slip into more than just an attempt. His own wife Monica had taught him that, and her grave that he could never bring himself to visit after the burial served as a constant reminder.

But he could tell that Claudia Harris wanted to be saved. Needed to be helped . . . it was just that nobody had heard her before it got this bad.

"Isn't there any family, or friends? Somebody . . .''

Shrugging off his arm she straightened her shoulders and gave a bitter laugh. "Friends and family? That's an MCI long-distance plan, not my life. My friends, the ones who I listened to all the time, helped, you name it—that fair-weather bunch did a hell of a lot of good by trying to get me out socially, and inviting me to forty-five-dollar a plate networking functions that I couldn't afford to attend. But wait, I have to take that back,'' she added angrily. "Sometimes they would pay for my charity case tickets, but I just didn't have an unlimited supply of rags to wear to their little soirees and black-tie affairs. That's what they called *networking* to get a job in the nineties. The other ones, they only wanted me to listen to their problems, which were always much worse than mine.''

He reached for her hands, and gave her finger tips a reassuring squeeze, carefully avoiding her wrists. She didn't jerk away this time, but let two big tears fall and splotch her jeans. Nate understood how any group of people who had lived a self-righteous, narrow, protected existence treated others. It bred a certain level of self-absorbed callousness that ostracized the fallen immediately, as though your pain or dirt might rub off and contaminate them. He had lived it, and hated them, and knew how it felt to have one's pain ignored, one's dignity assaulted. But, at the moment, he had to reach Claudia—to break the strangle hold of the monster that gripped her now.

Nate drew a deep breath. ''Didn't they know you were struggling financially? Didn't anybody try to help you find a job?''

He had to keep her talking, keep her lucid, make her face the anger head on.

Claudia shook her head wearily and let the tears stream down her face without blinking. ''When I went to them for job leads, you know what they could do for all their fancy titles and positions? Zip. Most of them had been perpetrating fraud for years, like they had any real power in their big-time positions ... I embarrassed them by making them have to admit that they couldn't hire anybody, or influence the hiring of anybody. After a while it became clear that they were fighting for their own necks, and weren't about to stir the pot for me. Besides, for the first time, I laid my problems at their feet, and they couldn't handle it. Talking to me was probably too depressing, since I didn't want to hear about their little boyfriend squabbles, or their issues with the boss who didn't want to give them a promotion, or couldn't seem to focus on their lightweight problems of the damned day. Soon, the phone calls stopped, and the visits ended. But not before they visited me to find out how bad I was doing—not to help or comfort, mind you. Just to get in my business and spread it around like wildfire.''

Nate knew exactly what she was talking about. It seemed like they'd had the same so-called friends. The whole scene became surreal, like watching a movie of his own life. But he couldn't give up.

"What about family?"

"What about them?"

It was a stalemate, but he pressed on.

"Can't you go home? Don't you have any relatives that you could stay with for a while?"

Claudia sighed. "Look, I come from working-class folks, okay. My cousins all have a bunch of kids, problems, and crazy husbands of their own. They don't have the resources to feed another adult mouth, much less the space to board one. I told you about my friends . . . and the old folks, hell, they've paid their dues. All my aunts and uncles are on a fixed income. Plus, they'd worry me every day. Didn't I get the Sunday paper? . . . What am I going to do? . . . Why don't I go back to school? . . . What time did I wake up, what time did I go to sleep, why am I crying, why aren't I crying, why am I dating, why don't I have a date, when am I going to come out of this funk, why haven't I grieved long enough, why aren't I eating, why am I eating so much? . . . That's what it's like when you're grown but have the resources of a child. If you think I'm crazy now . . ."

Nate held up his hand and smiled as he nodded in agreement. "I hear you. 'Nough said. Been there. Don't want to ever go there again in life."

Another silent exchange bound them. Progress. She seemed to appreciate his immediate, uncomplicated acceptance of her answer. But the delicate understanding that bound them made him uncertain of which direction to take next. They were teetering on a precipice. One false move could start the spiral all over again.

Finally garnering the ability to speak, he prodded her gently with his words. "You know, Claudia, when you've got something that people are quietly jealous of, they take sick pleasure

in watching your demise. Even family can be that way sometimes. But you can chose your friends, although you can't chose
your family. Those other people—they were never your real
friends. They were just social-climbing parasites that hung
around because you had something real to give *them*. When
you're finally all used up, those kind of people vanish. Maybe
it's for the best, anyway. This time, when you make friends,
you'll know how to tell the difference.''

She looked at him and nodded her head slowly as another
silent understanding passed between them.

''But surely you have some family,'' he pressed on, too
afraid to give up. ''Your mom or dad?''

''Moms died last year. Dad got remarried . . . and he and I
don't see eye to eye anyway. Besides, his new wife lives there
now. They're happy, I guess, and he's lived a long time working
hard for nothing with a lot of sadness . . . he deserves to have
a little peace, which is the last thing I'd bring him these days.
It's just not home anymore.''

Nate stood up and looked down at the tiny woman's tear
streaked face. He also understood abandonment all too well,
and the anger and despair that came along with it. Reaching
for her arms, he gingerly turned over her wrists and took off
the towel.

''I'm glad you were too drunk to do much damage to yourself,'' he said with a sigh of relief, ''you're probably going to
need a tetanus shot between this mangy towel and that old
blade. Though you might be lucky to have enough alcohol in
your system to sterilize even against *the plague*. Why don't
you go lie down, and I'll make some coffee?''

Grabbing the end of the towel, she blew her nose and looked
at him. ''Don't have any in here. Besides, why are you doing
this? You aren't some holy roller are you, doing missionary
work then going to convert me to your church?''

The comment made him smile. Had she only known him
four years ago. . . .

Claudia's expression fluctuated between bitterness and hopefulness. In her eyes he could see a quiet desperation, a small spark that reinforced his hunch that this woman really didn't want to die.

"No," he finally said, "I'm not in the Holy Crusade. I just didn't want to have to explain to Philadelphia's finest about how I left a woman to bleed to death in one of my buildings. Okay?"

"Shoulda known . . . What would old man McGregor say about his maintenance man leaving one of his apartments like that," she laughed weakly, standing up on unsteady legs.

He hated the way she referred to his occupation, and even though she was probably still half drunk and upset, he couldn't let the comment go again. Her words reminded him too much of Monica, and the way she used to think.

"What's wrong with an honest day's work for an honest days pay?"

The question seemed to startle Claudia. "Nothing? I guess I'm just jealous because you have a job and I don't anymore." She shrugged as he followed her into the bedroom.

"I thought it might be something else . . ." he pressed on, for some reason needing to know. "Like thinking such a job was beneath you, because you kept saying *maintenance man* in a slightly condescending manner. It was in the tone—as though there was something wrong with working with your hands for a living."

Claudia appeared genuinely shocked, and shook her head no vigorously. "Hey look, Nate, you're one of the most straight-arrow guys I know. *Nothing's* wrong with earning a living through honest means. Seriously. If more people did that, then we'd have less problems in the streets today. I've never judged people that way . . . Maybe I was just getting on you because I've been so miserable myself. Hey, if you were a pilot, or a bank president, I'd have found something smart to say to you, regardless. Please, whatever you do, don't take it personal— just consider the source." She ended her apology in a whisper, then flopped down heavily on the bed.

He could tell she'd meant what she said. Claudia Harris didn't seem stuck-up, or mean-spirited. This had been the only time he'd seen her that way. His shoulders relaxed as he assessed that his instincts had been correct. She was good people.

Nate stood in the doorway between the bedroom and the kitchen and thought about her words for a moment. ''No harm, no foul. I believe you.'' After hesitating, he added in a low voice, ''Especially since I own these buildings.''

From her prone position on the bed with her eyes closed, Claudia lifted her head slightly. ''What?''

''Never mind. Just get some rest, okay?''

He watched her settle back down, and he closed the door behind him. There wasn't a clean glass or cup to be had in her kitchen. Even the thought of fixing coffee in there was enough to turn his stomach. Walking into the living room, he approached the pile of supermarket bags and tried to remember which one had dish detergent in it.

''Let me fully introduce myself to you,'' he muttered to himself, sure that she was already asleep behind the shut bedroom door. ''The name's Nathaniel Winston *McGregor,* the second. Ex-attorney-at-law, and current owner of Campus Housing, Inc., McGregor Realty, and a couple of Seven-Elevens around here,'' he added with no small measure of satisfaction. ''That's who you've been sending your checks and money orders to every month. So, while you rest, I'll repair my property, if you don't mind. And, since nobody's honest, I do most of my own repairs these days. Didn't use to, but it's an honest days work for an honest days pay. Don't worry, I'll let myself out when I'm done,'' he murmured, still smiling as he made his way back to the kitchen. ''That's the least I can do.''

Chapter 3

Her head hurt. Bad. It felt like knives were gouging out her eyes, and her tongue had become a thick lump of dough in her mouth. Claudia pulled the covers over her head and tried to focus on the darkness, but the stinging pain from her wrists made it impossible to get comfortable again. She had to go back to sleep. Anything to get her stomach to settle down. The smell of bacon, eggs, and coffee from some apartment in the building was making her want to earl. Probably that damned Thompson family with a hundred and fifty kids upstairs. The woman cooked and cleaned and hollered out the window at them all day long.

Finally, unable to avoid it, she raised her body and pulled her legs over the side of the bed, holding her forehead in the process. All she had to do was walk ten feet to the bathroom, do her business, then make it back to bed. She repeated this fact in her mind until her body could respond to the command. Just ten feet.

Sitting on the cold seat, she covered her eyes with her hands. Too much light. She hated mornings. Unable to avoid the task, she cringed at the sound of the toilet flushing. Everything was too loud, too intense. Maybe if she just put a little water on her face . . . thank God Nate had fixed her sink so Mr. Jones downstairs wouldn't start banging and hollering.

When she reached for the towel, and buried her face in it, she stopped and opened her eyes. It smelled good. Fresh. Washed. What happened?

She painfully forced her gaze around the bathroom. It was clean, had a new shower curtain. A new bar of soap was in the tub dish, and a pump bottle of Softsoap was next to her hand. There was even a new toothbrush still in its wrapper on the outer rim of the sink. Cautiously opening the sparkling medicine cabinet mirror, she stared mouth agape at the new tube of toothpaste, large bottle of Advil, new box of Band-Aides, and unopened bottles of Pepto Bismol, Scope, and perox-ide. She was hallucinating.

Still clutching the clean towel to her, she went back into the bedroom. Where were her clothes? The ones that she had flung over the chair and onto the floor? Where were all of the glasses and dirty plates? How had her vanity gotten clean and rearranged? On a hunch, she tested the light. It worked.

Fear stung her mind, and she quickly slapped off the switch as though not being able to see would change things. She had crossed over to the other side and was obviously having another nervous breakdown. Or worse, maybe she had actually killed herself last night, and now she was destined to be a ghost trapped in this apartment for eternity. Dear God, there was divine justice in the universe! At least He had been kind enough not to condemn her to the previous filth that she lived in.

A light tap at the bedroom door startled her, and she drew the towel up to her throat as her heart pounded wildly within her chest. Air forced its way from her lungs and a cold sweat broke out over her body. Someone tapped again, and her voice squeaked out, ''Come in . . .''

It took a few moments for her to focus on the tall figure that stood in the too-bright doorway. It was only Nate standing over her, shaking her by the shoulders and looking worried.

"Are you all right?" he said nervously.

Pulling it together, Claudia sat up slowly and looked around. "Did you do all of this?"

"What are neighbors for?" he said smiling broadly. "How about if we get something substantial in your stomach? The bacon and eggs are ready. I hope you can keep a little bit of them down."

She stared at him. He had a nice smile, an honest smile that he rarely showed.

This man who she didn't even know, had cleaned her filthy apartment, obviously cared for her during the night, and was making breakfast in her kitchen. Dear God, her kitchen . . . that pigsty that would have shamed Moms Harris into the ground if she wasn't dead already. What had she done? No, more specifically, what had *he* done while she was out of it? What did he want, or, better yet, what had he already taken? Nobody helped anybody without wanting something in return.

Her focus narrowed on the man that stood before her.

Nate laughed, as though reading her mind. "Trust me, I didn't *want any* under those conditions. I know you probably think all men are dogs, but even this canine has his limits."

Now she was offended. What was he trying to say—that she wasn't good enough for him? Irrational resentment uncoiled itself within her. Just like Trevor, he didn't want her. So, why was he helping her?

"Woman, I see you getting evil on me. And don't get all offended either, I was just being a gentleman, is all."

"So why'd you have to compare me to being something that not even a dog would want?"

"Girl, c'mon. Don't even go there. You know that's not what I meant. All I was trying to say was, I'm not in the habit of jumping on top of a woman who's passed out in a coma. Damn, give me a little credit."

Nate's smile was becoming infectious, and even she had to begrudgingly smile at the thought.

"You gonna come on, or what?"

He held out his hand and she placed hers in it tentatively, suddenly becoming serious.

"But for real, why would you go to all this trouble for somebody like me?"

"Because it's somebody like you," he said plainly, still smiling.

He had a nice smile, a warm and genuine one. Before, she hadn't noticed how much farther it went beyond honest . . . yes, it was indeed genuine. Nate's perfect straight teeth flashed white against his mahogany face, and she realized that most times when she'd seen him he had been pleasant, but mostly very serious—hiding his wonderful smile. She wondered for a moment why someone as giving would always seem so serious. She wondered about those unspoken parts of his life as he stood before her now. Who was Nate, really?

"Want a grand tour before you eat?" he asked, helping her up and ushering her toward the kitchen. "You won't believe your eyes, even if I do say so myself."

When they entered her small kitchenette area, she stood in the middle of the floor with one hand over her mouth. He had stripped the floors, put away every pot and pan, there wasn't a dirty dish in the sink, and he had even washed the curtains. A new beige trash can with a lid on it sparkled in the corner, and a new can opener and several duck magnets stuck on the front of her newly white-glove cleaned refrigerator door. The table was set for two, with a bowl of fruit overflowing, and there were even supermarket carnations in a plastic vase.

Tears brimmed in her eyes and fell as he flung open the cabinets, proudly showing her the neat stacks of clean dishes. Then he pulled open the drawers to display his arrangement of the silverware and cooking utensils—just so that she'd know how to function when he left was his excuse, but she knew he was proud. He had every right to be.

As though he were a magician, Nate laughed, took an exaggerated bow, and stepped toward the refrigerator.

"And now . . . for my grand finale," he said with a chuckle. "Voila!" He flung open the door.

Claudia gasped as she stared at the endless rows of food. He had brought milk, juice, butter, yogurt, vegetables, cheeses, hot dogs, bread, rolls, and chicken. Before she could catch her breath, he opened the freezer and began showing her frozen packs of fish filets, hamburger, steaks, french fries, and even ice cream—just so she'd know how he'd packed it and she could plan to eat right, he'd told her.

Then without a word, he spun around like the mad Wizard of Oz, and opened the double cabinet over top the fridge, waving his hand before row, after militarily ordered row of canned goods. There were enough staples inside to feed her all winter. Red beans, pork & beans, white beans, black eyed peas, boxes of rice, jars of tomato sauce, packs of spaghetti, elbow macaroni, dried Cup-of-Soups, bullion cubes, Velvetta cheese, Cheese Whiz, popcorn, cooking oil, jars of Welches' Grape Juice, crackers, Aunt Jemima Pancake Mix, jelly, syrup, and peanut butter. And then in the next cabinet over, he revealed the spices—everything from Louisiana Hot Sauce, to Lawry's Seasoned Salt. You name it, it was in there.

Bustling her into the next room, Nate waved his hand and took another bow. "You like it?" he said sheepishly, motioning to a small wall unit that now contained a nineteen-inch color TV and a stereo combination unit. "I don't stay in much, and don't watch television . . . it gets on my nerves."

Claudia looked at the unit, then at the man, then around the tiny room that now had two small fig trees and a large defanbacci plant, with awe. "I can't let you do this . . . How could I ever pay you back? I—"

"No payback requested," he said firmly, holding up his hand and cutting her off. "When you're in my line of work, things have a way of 'falling off the back of the truck,' so to speak. I didn't come out of pocket that much, and I didn't rob anybody.

A lot of second-hand stuff was already in the basements of the buildings . . . repos and what not, or stuff that I don't really use, plants that I don't water and will eventually kill. Just promise to take it one day at a time, and be good to yourself. No more dramatics with razor blades. Ever. Then, I'll consider the debt paid in full. Deal?''

"But all this food, and—"

"Got friends in the supermarket business. Didn't cost as much as it looks. Wholesale."

Claudia sat down on the freshly shampooed sofa, and let her feet sink into the brand new mauve carpet under her feet. The smell of fresh paint still hung in the air, and her vision blurred again when she looked at the soft-lemon-colored walls. She covered her face to stop the new tears from rolling down her cheeks, but found herself sobbing uncontrollably into her hands anyway.

Nate sat down beside her and put a strong arm around her shoulders. It felt too good. Had been so long. Never had she been able to depend on anyone coming to her aid like this. And this time she didn't care about how it looked, what he'd think if she cried. . . . It was complete freedom to be who she was, however imperfect that might be. Instinctively she turned her face into his chest and cried harder. She had needed to cry this way, being held as she did so, for so long. . . . But there hadn't been a soul around who would just let her do that. He had made it better. For just one day, Nate had made it all right.

He stroked her knotted hair and rubbed her back as she let the hurt inside come out. It was a deep down-home wail, the kind that lets out the darkness and brings back the light, freeing a trapped spirit. She wasn't sure of how long they sat like that, him half rocking her, as she rocked herself. But he didn't try to stop her, or say something trivial that would make her stop and check herself. Somehow, this gentle, strong, quiet man understood—in a way that no family had, no minister had, and no therapist had. This man was real, and human, and cared. That's all she'd ever wanted, was for someone to validate the pain. Just somebody, like her mom would have, to say that it was all right to hurt, all right to be angry, all right to cry. . . . All right to be Claudia Harris, and need a little help.

When she finally lifted her head, Nate spoke in a low, calming voice. "Why don't you go get a hot shower? I'll keep everything warm in the oven. You'll feel better afterward. It'll be okay, Claudia, you'll see. All you need is time."

Claudia nodded, and kissed the kind man's cheek. He was a friend. Slowly moving back toward the bathroom, she thought about what he'd said. "Time. All she needed was time." That was the last thing she'd said to Ret, just before she'd died.

Nate stood and walked into the kitchen, and began putting aluminum foil over the breakfast platter. As he slid the food into the oven, he heard the shower go on and he took a deep breath. It had been a long time since he felt anything. Feeling always hurt too much. Claudia Harris had brought it all back with a vengeance. He had cared enough to help her.

The torment that swept through his heart when he saw the expression of raw appreciation on her face did something to him. Just as the desperation in her eyes, and the pain in her voice, had the night before. He'd seen it all, and felt it all—too vividly in the past.

He was reliving the nightmare. . . .

Nate shut his eyes against the memories. "Don't even go there, Nate McGregor," he whispered to himself. "They're all gone, and it's over."

For the first time in over three years, he wanted a drink.

Opting for a cigarette, he watched the clean, damp woman come back into the room. Claudia was smiling shyly, and was wrapped in the newly washed robe that he'd left hanging on the bathroom door hook. He appreciated the vision before him that wrenched him away from the creeping nightmare. Her thick mass of dripping hair that sent rivulets of water down her cheeks and her throat and down the deep V-cross of her robe, the warm reddish-brown undertone that peeked through her skin to bring her once gray complexion back to life. The way her large round eyes crinkled at the corners with the hint of a smile, her mouth, lush, full, ripe. . . . With just a little attention, this wildflower had come back to life. But Claudia's blooming had thorns, thorns that made him wonder maybe if he had been this kind to his own wife . . . he could have saved her. But that's not what happened.

Instead, when the events of his once-ordered married life where whirling out of control, he'd hidden himself away in his work, and made up the excuse that his law practice couldn't stand for his absence. Everybody had told him to go home, even his partners. But he had stayed night after night until he fell asleep at his desk. If he had only been honest with Monica. . . . just admitted to her that he couldn't bear to watch their two-year-old son lying in a burn unit ward under an oxygen bubble, locked inside a steel crib. . . . Maybe, just maybe, Monica would have been able to cope knowing that he hadn't abandoned her as well.

But he did abandon his wife, and Claudia's wails had brought it all to the surface. Steadying himself, Nate sat down at the table and took out another cigarette. "Want one?"

Claudia looked mildly surprised and wrinkled her brow. "I didn't know you smoked? Sure, thanks."

Nate passed her a Salem, and lit it, staring down into his coffee mug as the fire caught the end of her cigarette. He couldn't get the two women's wails out of his head. Nor could he shake the screams of a baby in excruciating pain from his mind. He shut his eyes briefly and tried to stop a violent shudder.

Memories continued to bombard him until he felt like he would scream himself. The child had been burned over 50 percent of his tiny body. He was there when they brought Jason in. A code blue sounded throughout Crozier Chester Burn Center, and it was his son on the livery as the doors flung open. Then came the dressing changes. The pain that must have racked that small little boy when they scraped away his smoldering clothes, taking up skin and flesh in the process. . . . And he, big strong, Daddy, stood there helplessly, while the child looked into his face—no longer able to cry from the agony, imploring him with his eyes to make the pain go away. Nate felt himself heave at the thought, and he pushed himself out of the chair and headed toward the door.

"What's wrong?" he heard Claudia call behind him, as she quickly followed his pace.

Tears threatened his composure, and he swallowed them down as his throat tightened. "Nothin'. Just need a drink."

"Wait a minute. You don't drink. And if you did, it's ten A.M. You sound like me, needing cheap anesthesia."

"I'll be back. Will even bring you a bottle."

"Uhhh, uhhh," she said shaking her head no, and standing in front of the door. "Something's spooked you. Nate, when's the last time you had a drink? What's the matter? I've been there before, okay?"

"Get out of my way. I don't have to explain anything to you. You've got food, a clean apartment, and you didn't die. So let it rest, and let me out of here."

"When's the last time you had a drink, Nate," she asked again more firmly. "You don't have to tell me what just crashed in on you, but I know you're in some kind of recovery. I can tell by the way you understood how to help me."

A fiery little woman stood resolute before him without blinking as she folded her arms over her chest and thrust her chin up at him. "It's a quiet code ethics—a kind of recognizable honor amongst thieves. You know when one of your own has spotted you. Now, with that said, I'm not letting you out of here to fall off the wagon. Not after what you just did for me. So, go sit your big, stubborn butt, down, and smoke another cigarette, or something. I'll get some more coffee on, okay? We don't have to talk, just eat."

Nate felt the tension ease away from his body, and he moved toward the kitchen. It had been so long since anyone had cared enough about what happened to him to challenge him.

Claudia made him walk ahead of her, eyeing him suspiciously when he passed in front of her as though he might bolt for the door at any moment. He had considered it. But, somehow, he knew that she understood him, just as he understood her. They were cell mates for the time being, and that was okay, even if she was now the one playing warden.

"Three years," he murmured as he sat down and lit another Salem.

Claudia didn't answer, but began pouring coffee with her back still turned to him. He was grateful that she didn't start in with the usual heavy artillery of rapid fire, female questions. This woman had walked a mile in his shoes, and knew better.

"My son, Jason, was only two years old when his grandmother, my mother, was taking him with her to the supermarket four years ago. It was January, around four o'clock in the afternoon, and the roads were icy . . . A drunk driver came out of nowhere, blew the light, and rammed into their car. Mom died instantly, but the baby was trapped in the car seat when the fire started . . ." he whispered hoarsely, taking a long drag from the cigarette.

She didn't respond, but moved toward the table and sat down slowly, pushing a fresh cup of coffee in front of him, then took out one of his cigarettes and lit it carefully. When she looked up, she still didn't say a word, but held him in her gaze. Steadily. He needed that. Silent understanding.

"I saw everything . . . They called me on my car phone. I was already on I-95 coming back from a major client in Wilmington. I almost beat the ambulance to the hospital. Monica, my wife, was at work and arrived later, thank God. I can't even tell you what I saw. I can't deal with it even four years later."

Nate felt his voice quaver from repressed sobs, and he took out his impatience with a deep gulp of coffee, followed by another quick drag. "It didn't take long, Claudia. Within two weeks they had amputated his left hand . . ."

He couldn't go on.

Claudia reached across the table and squeezed his fist, never letting him out of her gaze. Taking a deep breath, he removed his hand crunched out the half smoked butt and lit another cigarette, inhaling deeply. "Every day the boy's condition got worse, and my wife slept in a chair at the hospital . . . slowly losing her mind. I abandoned her. I just couldn't watch it with her. We had tried for five years to have children, lost three to miscarriages, fought through the fertility process, until we made Jason."

Nate let his head hang down and the cigarette dangle loosely between his fingers. The flowered print of the table cloth was getting blurry, and he felt hot moisture consuming his eyes. He could only shake his head at this point, and he took several deep breaths, finally following them with a number of quick drags from his smoldering Salem. He didn't know why he was telling this woman his sad story. For the first time, he felt like he was in the presence of another veteran. A fellow POW held hostage by tragedy. Somehow he knew Claudia would understand without hating him if she heard the whole story.

"Two days after the funeral, I went back to my law practice, and Monica went into the bathroom and slit her wrists. I couldn't watch it again. I found her," he choked out, as a sob stopped his words despite his will to contain it.

Standing quickly, he dropped the cigarette on the newly cleaned linoleum floor and stamped it out with his sneaker, then bolted. Claudia Harris was on his heels. Turning back fast to yell at her to leave him alone, he was surprised to see tears streaming down her face. She neared him and reached up and hugged him hard.

"It was not your fault, Nate. Do you hear me? It was not your fault."

She hadn't let him go as she whispered urgently to him. It was a life raft. A port in an emotional storm. She knew he was drowning and had thrown him a safety line. Hugging her back, he buried his face into her damp hair and let out the pain. Bitter sobs of anguish tore through him, and he stood trembling as the tears mingled with the water in her hair. Soon he became aware that she was rocking him against her. . . .

"I thought I would die from the pain . . ." his voice broke through the sobs. "I couldn't practice law, I gave up everything, since there was no justice in the world if God had taken my son," he croaked angrily. "He was only a baby. Just a baby!"

She just nodded and continued to rock him.

"I nearly drank myself into a coma, until one of my partners forced me to sign myself into rehab, and I gave him power of attorney to sell everything."

She just nodded and rocked him some more.

"When I saw a woman like you, drunk, I knew something had snapped. I just wanted to help, Claudia . . . to save somebody nice from turning into somebody like me."

She just nodded and continued rocking until there was no more to tell, and no more tears to shed. He just held onto her for dear life, breathing heavily, wanting nothing more than to lie down and sleep. Claudia Harris even seemed to sense that, and she moved him gently toward the sofa and pushed him down on it. Without his resistance, she took off his sneakers and lifted his legs, and left the room—returning with an old crocheted comforter to cover him, shoving a handful of tissues at him. Then she left him alone. She was truly a friend.

Chapter 4

Not since the disastrous forty-minute fight in her father's kitchen that they'd all endured six months ago, had she even thought about reading Loretta's journal again. Claudia listened to the low-toned snores coming from the living room sofa where Nate slept like a dead man, a man trying to forget under the merciful cover of sleep. Everyone, it seemed, had a cross to bear. . . . Who would have thought that he'd lived such a tragedy, yet, still had room in his heart to give? Nate's brand of strength reminded her of Loretta's—another well that ran deeper than most people could imagine from the smooth surface.

Closing her eyes as she fished for tiny book in her lingerie drawer, she could recall how she'd bitterly fought with her family for the right to read a portion of it to the congregation during the funeral.

The vivid picture immediately lept into Claudia's mind as her hand made contact with the leather covering. Declared too irreverent and too controversial, the elders had stood their ground, unmoved by her rarely defiant protests. Obviously, her father would never be up for a challenge against the matrons. Ever. Not when he couldn't even bear to hear it read at the kitchen table, let alone at church. He'd advised her to let sleeping dogs lie, to not stir up anything unnecessary, and had even demanded that she give him the book at one point during the feud. Miss Dot had been overly cautious, too, and both her father and Dot seemed too eager to read it, so she put it away lest it get destroyed out of some misguided sense of Christian duty.

Eventually, Claudia had been forced to give in and drop it, not wanting to inflict more unnecessary pain and suffering on her father. But, she wasn't giving them the book. It didn't matter anyway, she'd thought then, as she did now, when they disbanded after the commotion. It wouldn't open people's minds about Loretta. They had all categorized her and shut their minds to her good side long ago. What was the point?

Gingerly running her thumb over the corners of the book, Claudia searched for the entry that Loretta had marked last with the thin gold satin cord attached to the binding. It had seemed like a sign that these last words in the book were marked, so she hadn't bothered with trying to read any of the rest of it. Perhaps it was because leafing through the book seemed like a transgression of sorts, so she'd focused on only what was marked . . . what felt like it was waiting for her. Trying to burn what she'd read into her memory, Claudia focused on the soft linen page before her. And even though she hadn't read the whole contents of her sister's meandering thoughts, what she had read still held her heart in a vice.

She knew her sister's letter would have been perfect, for it summed up the very essence of Loretta Mary Harris. Maybe they would have finally understood Ret . . . then Claudia reminded herself, probably not.

Sighing heavily, she sat down on the bed, paging through the journal to find its center. Claudia shut her eyes again briefly to absorb the quiet. Nate was asleep, she was sure that nobody would call her on the phone. It was a moment when time seemed to stand still. Her apartment was so small that she could hear the hum of the refrigerator and the tick of the kitchen wall clock, just like before. Only the last time, the setting was in her father's house. Correction, Miss Dot's *new* house. But these subtle sounds were still a welcome block to the shouts and table pounding that now rang in her mind, and had numbed her senses six months ago.

Focusing on one sound, then the next, after a while she could pick out the repetitive drip from the kitchen faucet, which blended in with the other comforting rhythms of aloneness. Only after she had sat very still this way for a long time, listening to nothing, did she venture to begin. It was safe now to silently mouth the words in the semi-dark room—just the way she had in that abandoned Jersey kitchen.

Almost transported back, she remembered how everyone had gone upstairs to bed—angry, upset, and leaving her alone with the book in her hand. Thank God. The argument was long over, the dust had settled, and as always, she had been overruled. But they couldn't stop her from quitely reading the words again, and again.

Adjusting her gaze to the broad script on the page, Claudia smiled. As she looked at the title and began, slowly savoring each word, she could only shake her head. Only Ret . . . only Ret.

TIES THAT BIND
Questions to ask The Universe,
or whoever's in control up there!
By: Loretta M. Harris
Date, April 14, 1995, 3:15 A.M.

I should tell you guys up there that my faith is getting shaky. For real this time. Seriously. Nobody down here knows it yet, but I'm losing it. I'm so angry, hurt, scared . . . I don't know what I can tell you that you probably don't already know? It isn't supposed to be like this, is it? Especially when you're trying your best to do what you're supposed to do. This is new for me. You know, being open, vulnerable, compassionate, giving . . . and forgiving. Whatever. Maybe I'm not evolved enough to understand yet, but in the meantime, I could sure use some relief. Don't you guys have any special forces up there, like a SWAT team or something, to go after the bad guys? We need help. Don't you watch the six o'clock news?

I'm trying really, really hard to work with my temper and my revenge trigger finger. Because according to karma, the bumper sticker was right . . . Shit happens— but for a reason. Any how, the way I understand this New Age mess is that you get this group of friends together in your own private little circle of souls. Supposedly, we all made a pact up in heaven a milenia or so ago, to guide each other through the lessons, especially the tough ones. Right? Rather than have anyone else take on the painful role of teacher for such dear friends, we would be the ones to mutually inflict any necessary agnst and drama on each other in order to guide, cajole, motivate, comfort, and love our friends toward their correct paths or missions. . . . So far, so good. Then we'd all eventually leave each other when the time was right and the Big Lessons were learned. Hasta la vista, baby. Then we all come back again in new bodies, playing new roles, to advance to the next level, or to repeat a grade if we missed a cue. That's evolving spiritually. Okay. A buddy system. Teamwork. I can deal with that.

And when we made our eternal commitments, we knew that we would each take on different shapes, sizes, sexes, and colors. But that was supposed to be the musical chairs glory of it all, trying to find each friend's soul amid a sea of humanity. Certainly, nothing so minor as the wrapping of a mere body would stop our instant recognition—for our connection would always be made through the eyes, our window to the soul.

Claudia stopped nervously, and cast her gaze toward the living room. Feeling an eerie sensation of not being alone, she strained to hear Nate's labored breathing. Thank heaven the man snored. At least she could have her privacy without being totally by herself. It was odd. She had never felt this sensation before, or ever feared not having someone in her space while she read Loretta's journal. But when she'd read, *". . . our connection would always be made through the eyes . . . ,"* something made her stop and train her hearing to the silence in the apartment. Almost the same way a dog turns and looks at open, empty space, she felt strangely visited now.

What was it about Nate McGregor that felt so familiar? And his helping her for no apparent reason. . . .

Shaking the weird feeling, Claudia turned her attention back to her sister's elaborate handwriting. Telling herself that this would be the last time she would read it, she allowed her line of vision to pick up where she'd left off . . . all the while hearing the melodic lilt of Loretta's voice as she began again.

. . . Now I know that part has to be true. It's happened to me too many times to blow it off. Not just with men, but with people in general. Like when you meet someone for the first time—they could be man, woman, chick, or child. I either like them immediately or hate them immediately. . . . Okay, I'm still with the theory. Been there. Seen it. Done it. We know by that immediate wash of familiarity that engulfs us—a surge of nothingness that contains everything. Deep, but plausible. To quote my reading . . . "Thus, an etheric, delicate, bond reunites us again." That, I was prepared for. Not too scary.

Claudia chuckled. Yeah, right. "Easy for you to say," she murmured, flipping the page.

So, each time I spotted one of my long-lost friends, I'd almost jump for joy and revel in my knowing. And boy did I have a wild crew! Then we'd come together to love, fight, learn, battle, and become friends again—each time emerging a little wiser for the wear. But what I was never prepared for was the parting. . . . Nothing could have readied me for such pain or emptiness—not even You, God.

Claudia stopped and read the last sentence again. Her sister had made reference to God in the midst of this cosmic stuff that she couldn't fully understand. But that was Loretta—a complex combination of contrasts, dichotomies, and reversals—all and nothing at all. Yet, it gave Claudia pause, because this is what she'd wanted them to see, that her sister did believe, was spiritual and questioning life, right and wrong, and trying to find a way. She needed them to understand that she wasn't just a money hungry, fallen woman who didn't give a thought to her purpose, a divine plan, or other people. That's all she'd wanted them to know.

Claudia sighed and returned to the text, and a sudden warmth settled between her shoulder blades. Looking up quickly, she turned to see what created what felt like residual heat . . . what it would have felt like after someone placed a soft palm on her back. Now she was scaring herself. . . . Nate was still snoring, no one else was in the room, she was just jumpy that's all.

Staving off the creeps, she turned on the light and flopped back on the bed—this time with her back against the headboard, and began reading.

Seriously. It's just that so many of them have left me so suddenly. . . . Yet, I always knew when it was time, and so did they. In the short span of this brief existance I've said goodbye to all of them, one by one. Mom, Dad— after he told me about Dot—even Claud and I mentally

broke stride, though I worry about her, like what she'll
do when she finds out about it all. . . .

Claudia let tears well up in her eyes. She knew Loretta could
never accept Dot, probably because Dot was so rigid and Loretta
was so fiercely independent—which in turn had pushed her
away from their father. She just wished Loretta had trusted her
enough to tell her about what this secret was with Eric. That
didn't have to come between them.

"What couldn't I find out, Loretta?" she whispered almost
unconsciously. "What was it?"

Claudia listened to the silence and closed her eyes to make
the tears of frustration recede. But in the stillness, she didn't
feel like the question posed was even about Eric. Strange, but
it was a knowing that flowed over her senses. It was a distinct
feeling that she couldn't quite put her finger on that felt like
Loretta was describing so much more than her secret problem
with Eric. Turning the possibilities over and over then dropping
the guesswork, she returned her line of vision to the page. . . .

> *. . . Countless lovers and girlfriends have either physi-*
> *cally or mentally passed through my life to make it richer.*
> *So, why is this last parting with a lover-friend so hard?*
> *Perhaps, because I instinctively know that this was my*
> *last connection to the old gang. Maybe the next time we'd*
> *meet could be centuries from now on the other side of*
> *the universe. I'm having trouble with this. Losing every-*
> *body, or having someone lie to me, still pisses me off*
> *and hurts like hell.*

Claudia was forced to stop again, this time by the tears that
blurred her vision. Wiping at them with the back of her hand,
she drew an unsteady breath, trying not to let them splotch the
page and make the ink run.

The deep ache that overcame her almost forced her to return
the journal to her drawer. How could anyone be prepared for

such a parting? Blending in with her sister's words, she became one with the pain that etched itself across the page as she found the courage to read on.

Oh yes, my higher self accepts that this was necessary for growth. Karmic debts have all been paid in full, believe me. I accept that they were taught best by those who loved me the most. But I went to grad school with this one. No mere stranger could have made each lesson so lasting. So, as You say, that was our original agreement, after all. But, dear God in heaven . . . the void that's been left almost makes it impossible to draw a breath without a shudder. Maybe it was in getting ready for this hospital stint that I suddenly realized how much each person—male and female—has enriched my life. I ache for them to be able share the new me that they've helped build, knowing sadly that they can't. Oddly, for them to do so, means that they wouldn't be able to appreciate their work or build their own lives. It's circle logic. Almost like a catch-22. And, at the moment, it doesn't really help the loneliness. You know?

So, okay. We've parted—painfully at times, or quietly drifted away as our orbits changed. And every change was so subtle, yet so compelling, that eventually it couldn't be ignored. Soon, we began to feel out of sync, or in each other's way, almost as if smothered by the very presence of those that we needed so much in our lives before. I'm pretty sure that my new, Eastern, "do good to everyone" rap, ruined at least one major relationship in my life. Hey, you just don't turn a carnivore who's used to hunting big financial game, into a socially acceptable, play by the rules vegetarian, over night. "It DON'T happen"— no matter how scared you are that they'll get hurt. Okay. My mistake. My lesson. So he married somebody else. Done.

Claudia sat stunned with a book in her hands as though she were reading the words for the first time. Perhaps she was, without the veil of grief confusing the meaning or blinding her to intent. "Was that what broke them up? Loretta had gotten religion . . . ?" Claudia almost laughed out loud through the tears. Her sister wouldn't keep doing cutthroat deals with her barracuda business lover, so he got a replacement? Rage replaced the irony . . . there was no justice.

Now she ferociously devoured the remaining words, this time with new eyesight.

That's when you know it's time. Too many foundation issues pull you apart. That's when the ties that bind begin to unravel. Your laughter fades. Your conversations become stilted. You no longer hear or care about what your dear friend, lover, or family member has to say . . . or that your words hurt. I should have seen this one coming. But through all the pain, and oft times the anger; you're supposed to still look for their soul through their tears as well as your own, watch them happily wave you goodbye, then be content in knowing that their mission to help you learn has been completed. That's the high road. The low road is, you just got hurt.

Pulling one clenched fist against her stomach, Claudia fought the urge to cry out. The words on the page replayed so many partings in her own life—the vacancy left after Trevor walked out . . . the lost children . . . the virtual stripping away of all that she was and held dear. How could she have ever imagined that her glamorous, flippant, seemingly secure sister had been so violated by life? Even though she had read the words six months ago, for some reason, not till now did they really, honestly, sink in.

"Oh, Ret . . ." Claudia's words trailed off as she heard Nate turn in his sleep on her sofa. His movement startled her, but helped her composure. Looking down again, she promised to get through the journal entry before he woke up. She even promised to read the rest of it one day, just like her therapist had told her to when she was in rehab.

Well, Lord, if this is true, then you're the only one who really knows how hard it is to say goodbye when it's over. This is, without a doubt, the hardest part of it all—standing on the crest of change and leaping away from the security of relationships that have brought me this far. But I want to get it right this time around. Call me stubborn. You wouldn't be the first. That's why each time I saw goodbye in anyone's eyes, I leapt and tried to never look back. Like Lot's wife, I didn't want to turn into a pathetic pillar of salt and stop growing. But I just couldn't trust myself to even peek back, lest I'd change my mind and stop to beg them all to come with me.

And get this, Lord—my meditation teacher also agrees with your Good Book! Here New Age meets New Testament. She told me that dragging people down my particular path would be wrong. They have to "decide" for themselves, and have complete freedom of choice. I'm told everyone, even my conservative sister—whom I love dearly—has his or her own path to follow, not mine. Wild, huh? Truth comes from the strangest sources. Is that the "free will" concept You talked about?

Can people choose to either go right or left, light or dark? Think long, think wrong—I always say. Make a decision and go for it. We all know what's right or wrong. So why don't they take the high road and stay toward the light? I guess I'm still new to this, and frankly I'm not that well read on the traditional info in the Big Book. But that's why no matter how much it hurt, I've always instinctively been able to take change in stride. That is, up till now. I suppose you could say that I was always able to go with the cosmic flow, and handle my disappointments like a woman—an adult willing to accept the conse-

*quences of my own actions. That seemed fair. You screw
up, you pay karmically. No free rides. Somebody other
than me ought to tell Addison.*

*But unfortunately, "people" back home always mis-
took this philosophy for being cold, and not caring . . .
or being selfish, or worse, accused me of being a user.
Nothing could be farther from the truth. Not one lesson
came free. Trust me! And nobody ever saw the tears I've
cried alone, or knew how badly I was hurt when I got a
cosmic whack. Only You saw that, and even forgave me
up front based on your belief in me. Then I would get
right back up and try harder next time. Really, I did.*

Unable to bear it, Claudia stopped again, allowing an old
rage to rekindle itself. This was the part that she wanted to
read before the entire church. This is what she wanted them to
all hear . . . that her sister was human, bled red blood, cried
real tears, worked hard to get everything that she had, and for
them to finally know how much they had hurt her over the
years.

Why was it so hard for a small community to accept differences? Why did her sister have to be almost shunned for the
crime of being a non-conformist?

Looking at the words, Claudia began whispering them as
though allowing her sister to use her vocal cords to speak for
herself. . . .

*Oh, sure . . . I'd mess up again, eventually, I'm human.
But I'd always try to figure out where I went wrong the
first time, then try not to do that foolish crap again.
Maybe that was my problem? I really had faith, and just
kept getting back up like Rocky. Maybe I should have let
everybody see my heart . . . my weak spot? Then again,
not everybody operates out of that "turn the other
cheek," Zen principle bag. After all, you gotta protect
yourself, don't you? But to just carte blanche hurt people,*

and not think about how they'd feel . . . I never did that. That's just not my style. Okay, well, maybe once or twice with a few lousy lovers—but even that eventually became a lesson—mine and theirs. Hey, I'm digressing from the point. You already know those stories, I just hope it's not true that you were actually invisible and there when it went down. Please! Besides, I've paid dearly for that bogus behavior—I was young and dumb.

This time Claudia laughed. "Weren't we all once, sis."

So, even though the wrongful charges hurt at the time, I followed my gut, knowing that these are probably the same kind of people who nailed Jesus to the cross back in the day. Anyway, regardless of what they said about me, with each parting I always knew I was becoming something different, better, and had always given just as much as I had received.

Nodding in fervent agreement, Claudia's voice trailed off as she continued to silently absorb the words.

But, as I said before, I'm honest enough to admit that I was never prepared for my "guides" to all leave me at once. And though I now stand as a newly renovated being, my echoes carry far into the night—prayers trying to reach those that promised to be there with me when my first group of soulmates were gone. Where are all my dear friends, now that I willingly let them go? Why can't I really talk to my sister these days? How come Mom had to go so soon? I really need them both.

"I don't know, honey. God knows . . . if I had only understood what you were trying to say to me that last time . . . I'm so sorry, Ret."

A sob broke through and eclipsed her whisper. Covering

her mouth with her hand, Claudia closed her eyes until her composure returned. Perhaps she only felt safe reading the journal now, knowing that a living human being was nearby to catch her if she slipped into the void of deep depression again. Maybe that was Nate's role . . . to let her do this one last time so she could be finished with it.

Forcing her gaze back down to the page, she murmured, "Did you send him, Ret? Just so we could have this talk again?" Blinking away the moisture from her eyes, Claudia stared at the words.

Tell me, who will be there to stop the bleeding after life has finally wrenched out my heart? Where are the spiritual workcrews—on the physical plane—to temporarily reinstall a new one . . . to make it beat again, hope again, laugh again, maybe even love again? Where are the ones left to share my deepest secrets, know my unspoken terrors, to understand and care for me? Protect me? Never before have I felt so totally abandonned. When I really thought about it, it was like each person came into my life in stages at critical junctures, layering over and complimenting existing friends to create a dynamic, wonderful, mosaic of living light. Now they're all gone, or out of reach, or don't understand, and in one particular case, don't care.

God, you promised that I'd never be alone, and I gotta tell you, this etheric experience isn't making it. I'm flesh and blood, here and now, and need someone special in my life. Bunk the metaphysical! I'm quitting meditation class when I get out of the hospital, okay?

Because now, for the first time, I have to extend my hand into the darkness without one of them to guide me. I can't even make Claud understand this shit, and we just argue. Truly, must I walk by faith and not by sight? Is that what this is all about? Maybe I'll go back to church, who knows? At least I'll get my sister back. We

*used to be able to really talk. I miss her, especially now
. . . and when she finds out the truth, she's gonna really
need me. But the church stuff is just as hard to understand,
with all of those old parables, and proverbs, and what
not. Right now, I can't understand anything before me.
All I can do is feel.*

*At least for now, God, even if it's just the pain of
change, and my closest circle leaving me, I know I'm
alive . . . and that way, I can still hope. Can't I?*

P.S. Will you at least let me know if I'm getting it right?

Claudia turned the last page of her sister's journal entry
slowly, then quietly closed the small leather book after she
read the final line of the entry twice. How could she have
known how much pain Loretta was in, or how lonely she felt?
Never before had it been made so clear. Guilt continued to tear
through her until it coiled at the bottom of her stomach. Ret
had such a way of masking her pain and hurt. . . .

What made her think about those words now, pull out that
testamony to a life of hurt—especially since she had vowed
to never go there again?

Praying fervently, Claudia whispered into the void before
her, closing her eyes and allowing the tears to silently fall.
"Oh, Ret, I never understood your crazy brand of religion until
now . . . or even knew you could write. Thank God you at least
showed me your tender heart. But how much more of you have
I missed?"

Refusing to sob, Claudia clutched the book to her chest and
swallowed hard. "I promise to meet you on the other side,
sweetheart. I never meant to leave you alone, and don't you
ever leave me again. Just promise."

Chapter 5

Claudia heard Nate stir and looked at the small plastic kitchen clock that hung over the calendar by the table. Two o'clock. He had slept for nearly four hours.

Moving back toward the oven, she tested her cornbread. After reading the journal, she had used the balance of the time to change her bed, oil her feet and scalp with Vaseline, put on a pair of black stretch pants with an oversized mustard-colored cotton shirt, and cook. She had added some earrings, a touch of lip gloss and eye liner, and even a little blush. It was stupid, and she had chided herself when she'd sprayed on a bit of perfume and dusted between her thighs with baby powder. Stupid.

Soon Nate's frame filled the archway, and he yawned sleepily, leaning against the wall and rubbing his eyes at the same time.

"How long was I out?" he asked, stifling another yawn. "Something sure smells good in here."

Claudia smiled and waved her hand toward the stove in the same manner that he had a few hours earlier. "Just wanted to let you know that I wouldn't let all of that good food go to waste. I made cornbread and added in the bacon that we didn't eat for breakfast. The eggs couldn't be salvaged. Sorry. However, we've got macaroni and cheese, greens, baked chicken, jiblet gravy, and iced tea.''

"Get out of here!" he exclaimed, coming closer to the stove to inspect her work. "I swear, girl, I haven't eaten like this in a *long* time. You keep burnin' like that, and I'll keep you in groceries forever," he added laughing, as she slapped his hand away from her greens pot.

"I thought that the Buppies banned this kind of food years ago?" she said with a hand on her hip, and taking a pouty lean backward designed to keep him laughing.

"You and I aren't professionals anymore, so we can kill ourselves with high blood pressure and stroke—don't cha know that, woman?" He laughed, receiving another lick from her wooden spoon as he tried to stick a fork into the cooling macaroni and cheese casserole. "Would you look at the butter oozin' offa that pan," he said with honest admiration. "Uhmp, uhmp, *uhmp.*"

"Well, if I'da known you didn't care about cholesterol levels, I woulda went all the way and fried the chicken." She laughed back, finally offering him a little pinch of corn bread to taste test.

Nate closed his eyes and let them roll under the lids, making her smile deepen. It had been a very long time since anybody appreciated anything she did. The feeling was nice. Dishing him up a large plate and handing it to him, she moved over to the table and sat down.

"You're not going to eat?" he questioned, sounding concerned.

Claudia lowered her gaze and toyed with her flatware. "I'm not sure if I can keep it down, Nate," she said as raw new tears suddenly threatened to spill. "I really feel bad," she added, feeling the burn of humilation creep up her throat, because all that she really wanted was a drink.

"Just start off with the carbohydrates. It'll be rough like this for a few days . . . I'll hang in there with you though, okay. Don't worry, you're not in this alone any longer."

Somehow, his words only made her want to cry all the more. Here she had prince charming sitting at her kitchen table, making every effort to help her, and she was going through withdrawal. She hated herself, and her addiction.

Shaking her head no, Claudia couldn't bring herself to look up at the kind man sitting across from her. "I can't let you do that, you've already done enough."

"I said, I'm here. Now, I'm going to put a little bread and a dab of macaroni and cheese on your plate. Try to get it down, then we'll go from there. Even if you just sip the broth from the greens . . . your body needs nutrition, and is screaming for it. Claudia, you may throw up a few times, and it'll get ugly for a minute before it's finally over. You'll probably curse me out, try to get me to leave, go off and cry, but like I said, I ain't going nowhere. I've been there myself. All right? My life turned upside down four years ago, and for the first year into it, you and I did a lot of the same things it seems."

Nate stood and reached down a small breakfast plate. "Let's start by putting your food on the little ones, that way it's not so intimidating."

She just stared at him as he fixed her a plate and dipped some greens juice into a coffee mug, then sat back down. He was an angel of mercy. Nate ate and chatted amiably, ignoring her dry heaves as she forced down the food. If she hadn't felt so bad, she would have laughed as he scoffed down two plates of food then pushed back in his chair and sighed. Being with him was like balm to her frayed nerves. This man made her feel safe, and yet, he had seen her at her very worst and still accepted her. She wondered why life had cut such a sweet soul such a raw deal? Like most things, it didn't make sense.

"Want to rent a movie?" he said finally, wiping up the last of the gravy with an end of corn bread. "You could probably use the fresh air, and I've got to move or I'm gonna fall asleep in this chair.''

Although it sounded like a good idea, Claudia hesitated for a moment before answering. There were just too many bars to pass on the way to the video store, and she couldn't trust herself. ''I don't have a VCR,'' she said weakly, hoping that that might end the discussion about going out.

''Sure you do!'' he exclaimed and stood up quickly, holding out his hand to her. ''It's built into the bottom of the set. C'mon, let's go get a comedy and a couple of sci-fi's. Or how about a good horror flick, so you can snuggle up next to me on the sofa.''

''No slasher movies, I won't be able to go to sleep.''

Nate gave her a mischievous grin as she stood up and placed her hand in his. *''Aliens II* is my all time favorite, and *The Thing*. We can rent some vintage Richard Pryor to break things up a little.''

She had to laugh, her warden was a mad man. ''Oh, no! I'm not watching that mess so you can laugh at me while I scream my head off.''

Nate was chuckling as he fished through her closet and pulled out her good black wool coat. She looked at him for a moment before putting her arms in the sleeves while he held it. ''Well, okay, maybe *one* horror flick,'' she said smiling, glad that he was going to be with her for the evening.

It was like an odd high school date, and she suddenly felt giddy and nervous around the man that had saved her from selling her coat and her dignity. They had shared so much in such a short time that it was eerie. Never had she felt so completely in tune with another human being. Never had she felt so ironically special.

As they made their way down the steep stairs and out onto the street, Nate immediately took a protective stance, escorting her by the elbow to walk on the inside of the pavement. Men just didn't do that anymore, although she wondered if it had to do with wanting to block her line of vision from the bar next door. Once on the corner of Forty-Fifth, she relaxed a little, she had made it past the first liquor outpost, and refused to look down the street to the adjacent pub on Forty-Sixth that she knew was there beckoning her.

He continued to usher her briskly past the Mosque, and the gaggle of Vietnamese children that played in the street as they neared Chestnut, still talking to her about every current event and world issue imaginable until they were safely inside Plaza Video. It had been hard to keep up with his long strides, yet the cool night air had felt good against her face. But her head was pounding, and her eyes hurt.

Reaching into his leather jacket, he pulled out a pair of dark aviator sunglasses and handed them to her without looking in her direction. "I know" was all he said. "It's too bright in here."

Claudia gratefully accepted the shades, and began to walk down the aisles of movie boxes. The loud overhead televisions that blared coming attractions were making her nauseous, and she was relieved that it took Nate only a few minutes to find the films he wanted so that they could get the hell out of there. She needed fresh air.

Once out on the sidewalk, she held onto his forearm and bent over. "I don't think I'm going to make it," she whispered, swallowing down a heave.

When she tried to stand up, another wave of nausea asailed her and she felt a cold sweat creep over her body.

"Yes you will," he said patiently, reaching into his pocket and handing her two Tums. "Chew on these, and we'll walk slowly this time. I needed to get your blood circulating first. It's going to take a few days for the toxins to get out of your system. Fresh air, good circulation, and solid nutrition is the only way."

He was starting to get on her nerves. Who the hell did this guy think he was? He sounded like a Little League coach, and she glared at him as they began a slow stroll up the street.

"You probably hate me right now, Claud, but that'll pass, too."

She didn't dignify the insightful comment. She didn't want to talk. That only made her head hurt worse.

"Tell me about your family," he said pleasantly, obviously trying to start a stupid conversation. He was *really* getting on her nerves.

"Not much to tell," she snapped back, slowing down from another wave of nausea.

"Then tell me about your sister."

The question made her stop and look at him. He smiled. She could tell that he was pleased with himself, since it was the one thing that could break through her evil spell.

"She was funny, and sassy . . . A real trip," she said, becoming elevated at the good memories she had of Loretta.

By the time they had made it back to the apartment, she had told Nate at least a hundred funny anectdotes about the incomparable Loretta Harris. And they were both laughing.

"Sad thing is, though," she added wistfully, as she opened the door, "the one guy she probably loved, dumped her right before we lost her. The sorry SOB never even came to the funeral, and they had gone together for eight years."

Nate just shook his head as he took off her coat and hung it up. "You can't figure some people," he said furrowing his brow. "A lot of men don't appreciate what they've got till it's gone," he added, his voice sounding distant, as though caught up in his own painful memories.

Breaking his own spell, Nate moved over to the TV and began rustling through the plastic bag containing the movies. "I say we laugh hard first, then scare ourselves silly?"

She smiled, it was a good choice and the perfect medicine. Oddly, the Tums and the walk had settled her stomach a little, and she slipped by him to go into the bathroom to take some Advil.

"Take two," he called behind her, as though reading her mind. "We've got a long night ahead of us."

When she returned, Nate had poured two large glasses of iced tea and was munching on some chips. "More carbos?" he offered with a grin that made her laugh.

"I swear, man! Do you eat like this all the time?" she said giggling and declining his offer, yet surveying his rock solid build that showed no evidence of body fat. How did men do it? If she'd even attempted his food portions the results would have shown the same night!

"Only in good company," he responded casually while getting comfortable, and patting the cushion next to him for her to sit down.

They watched the video, laughed, and Nate added jokes to the already hilarious stand-up routine that was on the set. Amid the fun, a sense of deep peace cloaked her. This was the way things were supposed to be. Fun. Easy. No games and no stress. Friends. She had found a friend, or a friend had found her. It didn't matter which came first, but for the moment, it was nice.

"I haven't had a time like this in years," he said laughing harder. "I swear, the brother is crazy!"

Claudia was wiping her eyes, trying to recover from Pryor's routine, and from Nate's one-liners. "I can't catch my breath." She giggled. "Y'all are both insane."

"We'll it's time for the creep show," he said with a flair, popping up quickly and rummaging through the video bag. *"Aliens II,"* he said decisively with a wink, setting up the new tape and turning off the lights. "I love the Latino woman in this flick. Now, that's a *bad* sister. She takes no prisioners, even at the bitter end."

Claudia just shook her head, watching the man that had just transformed into a big kid beside her. "Lord have mercy," she groaned, as the the movie began. "I hate this stuff."

Snuggling up next to Nate, Claudia tucked her legs under herself and leaned back on his chest. He pulled her in closer, and rested his chin on top of her head, lifting it every now and then to crunch on a barbeque potato chip or to take a sip of iced tea. It was heaven. *Aliens II* or not, she didn't care what excuse they'd used to share this comfortable, companionable, space. Nate felt warm, and big and strong and safe. She knew she could make it with him there to help her.

They both laughed as she screamed at the scary scenes, and every now and then, he insisted on winding it back to review a particulary gruesome one. Men. Did they ever grow up? Finally having made it through the torture of body splitting space creatures, he stood and stretched.

"Bio break," he announced, heading toward the bathroom. "Then, I've got something special for you."

Claudia yawned and stretched where she sat. They had been there for hours, and she hadn't felt as terrible as she'd imagined she should have. The cure all had been Nate. Here she was with a man who had spent the night, cared for her, bought her food, cleaned her dirty drawers, and she didn't even know his last name. Nor did she care. Life was funny.

When Nate returned, he changed the tape. "Got a drama for you. *Presumed Innocent*. Not too mushy, not too scary, and has some suspense in it for me. How about that one to cure the scaries?"

She smiled. "Thank you!" she announced, genuinely glad not to have to sit through another horror flick.

"Then I got a Star Trek flick—not scary, but sci-fi."

"You're a Trekkie, too?" she exclaimed.

"Boldly going where no man has gone before." He chuckled, giving her a sexy wink.

Claudia let the possible double entendre pass. It was a hopeful thought, really. "Then let's watch that instead of the drama."

Nate smiled broadly. "A woman after my own heart. If I'da known, I would have gotten the whole series."

Claudia laughed and shook her head. "One is enough, thank you."

Getting comfortable again, Nate drew her close as they watched the next film. "How do you feel?" he asked tentatively.

"Not great, but not lousy either. Thanks, Nate, you're really making this much better than it could have been," she murmured, giving his arm, which enfolded her, a little squeeze.

Stroking her upper arm, he pecked the top of her head with a kiss. "Just a little time, and you'll be as good as new. Trust me."

She did.

She trusted everything about the man who held her gently and stroked her arm as they watched the movie in companionable silence together. His touch created a warm blanket of protection that radiated through her body and stilled her once-panicked soul. As he continued to rub her arm, she felt a new awareness of him, a stirring that she hadn't felt toward any man in a long time.

Each gentle caress down her arm began to make her stomach muscles tense and release to the rhythm of his strong steady touch. The sensation began to send a wave of yearning warmly up her thighs, and she felt her breath becoming short. It was too soon to feel this way. . . . But his hand stroked the sensitive skin that was so close to the now stinging tip of her breast, which had become hard and ached each time he moved his hand up and down the length of her arm. She could feel his heartbeat against her back, and his even breath sent a current of warm air onto her scalp. It was wanton, but she wanted him.

Trying to garner self-control, Claudia stared at the movie and tried to focus on what was happening on the Starship Enterprise. But what was happening to her body was too immediate to ignore. She felt like she was losing her mind as she sat perfectly still, while Nate kept rubbing her arm, only a fraction away from her breast. It *was* like high school again.

Nuzzling against him a little closer, she was determined to just soak up his warmth and not make a fool of herself. This man was just being nice. Kind. Why would he be interested in some broken-down wreck like her? Trevor never wanted her that way, almost from the very beginning. They had only had sex a couple of times a month, which trailed off to never during the last two years of her marriage—because he was always out with other women and didn't need her for that. Her ex-husband had made it clear that the only reason he'd kept her around was to produce a son, and she'd failed in that endeavor, too. She wasn't one of the tall, thin, light-skinned beauties that he was so fond of. She was short, too dark, and too plump in the behind and hips to be bothered with on a regular basis. But she was a hard worker, and came from a good stable family, so he had married her anyway, for those reasons, she guessed.

Chastising herself, Claudia tried to bring her attention back to the movie. She wasn't even sure what was going on any longer, but watched quietly, pretending to be absorbed and hoping that Nate wouldn't stop his attention to her arm.

He didn't.

His touch had become a slow, lazy stroke, and occasionally his fingertips barely grazed the outer lobe of her heavy aching right breast as they passed it. The ache had cruelly expanded to her lower belly and had worked its way down to where her thighs joined, now creating a moist pool of warmth between her legs. The sensation was nearly unbearable as he kept stroking her arm and making her insides shudder.

Peeping out of the corner of her eye, she glimpsed his hand. It was massive, but very well kept given his occupation. He had big square fingernails that were clean and cut short, and his palm glided smoothly over the fabric of her cotton blouse. Involuntarily, she felt herself turn slightly into his gentle touch, and when his fingertips grazed the hard pebbled tip of her breast, she shut her eyes and drew in a quick breath. What had she just done!

Nate didn't seem to acknowledge her gasp, or move his hand away, or stop the slow excruciating rhythm that was driving her out of her mind. Nor did he ignore her silent request to touch her where she had needed him to for the past hour. He simply let his fingers pass over her nipple and back up her arm then down again, each time sending ribbons of pleasure through her entire body. The other breast almost hurt with the need to be touched. It took everything she had not to cry out, and she slowed her breathing as he finally cupped both of them and caressed her from behind, never saying a word while they pretended to watch the movie.

Soon, he breathed into her hair more deeply, and she shyly allowed her hand to rub his thigh as she nestled back against him. They sat that way for a long time. The throb that pounded between her legs now almost made her gasp each time his palms came over the tips of her breasts. She wanted to feel the full heat of his hands against her skin, wanted him to lift her blouse, to kiss her, to make love to her. It had been too long.

Never in a million years had he expected to be sitting on Claudia Harris's couch, wanting her this much. He hadn't been with anyone since Monica, and that had been nearly five years ago . . . first her delicate mental state after the accident, then his spiral into depression after her funeral . . . then nothing, no desire to go out and chase women in a drinking establishment that was off-limits to him . . . and church wasn't an option he'd wanted to deal with. All together, it had been five years, and now that time factor haunted him, laughed at him, cursed him. . . . He'd been able to shut off those feelings, and had needed to in order to cope. But now he felt those years coalesce into a central fire that consumed his groin.

But it was too soon for them to be doing this! Claudia Harris was a nice woman, a decent woman, a vulnerable woman . . . and he didn't want her to be frightened or feel taken advantage of. That was the last thing she needed. . . . But the slow movement of her hand, just a fraction away from the ache in the length of his groin, threatened his sanity. She was unraveling his intentions quickly, as her petite, soft hand glided over his jeans and down his leg. And her nipples . . . Dear God, the way they felt under his palms. He hadn't felt a woman's body respond to him like that in over ten years. Monica's never did.

His wife had been tall, and gorgeous, and she knew it. His job was to keep his fine socialite in expensive clothes, a nice house, and make her a baby. He thought back on his crème-colored wife, with her cinnamon eyes and long, light brown hair. She'd been sent to the University of Pennsylvania to get an MRS, not an MBA, and he'd initially fallen in love with the package. But in reality, their life together had been surface at best, and trying to make Jason had been the only thing that had kept them bound together. It had been easy to lie to himself then, using the excuse that their fertility problems were at the root of what had been wrong with them. Yet, sitting here now with Claudia, a woman who didn't even know his last name, or expect anything from him but kindness . . . someone willing to offer said same. Someone who actually liked him for who he was, not *what* he was—or where he went to school, or how much money he had. . . . Suddenly, depression crashed in on him. The truth was inescapable.

Removing his hands from her breasts, he kissed the top of Claudia's head. "I don't think I can keep this up much longer and remain a gentleman," he said in a hoarse whisper. "I'm losing my mind."

Claudia looked up at him, but never removed her hand from his leg. Where her palm rested felt like it was burning a hole right though his jeans. "How long's it been for you?" she murmured.

He wasn't prepared for the question, or the intense way that she stared into his eyes. Even with the blue background of deep space flickering on the set in the darkened room, he could see how much she wanted him. "At least five years," he whispered, almost shuddering as she began stroking his thigh again a little higher and closer to the source of his pain.

"Me, too," she said quietly, then brushed his mouth with a kiss.

He returned it tentatively, then deepened it as she opened her mouth to accept his tongue. His heart slammed against his breast bone and he brought his hands to both sides of her face. Their once-gentle kiss became frenzied, and he couldn't trust himself any longer. Breaking away from their embrace, he

gently held her hands as he tried to catch his breath. "Claudia,
I can't take it . . ." Whispering against her hairline in short
spurts he struggled to make her understand. "Listen. We've
got to stop. I don't even have anything on me to protect you,
honey. Okay?"

Claudia's breaths were coming in irregular short rasps as
well. Her arms were pebbled with goose bumps, and the sight
of her arousal tortured him.

"You're right," she whispered heavily. "We have to be
sensible about this."

But somehow, nothing was making sense now. A persistent,
central throb was taking over the common sense in his brain.
He just had to kiss her again. Just once more before they
stopped. But when he reached for her one last time, and she
melted against him, he knew it was all over.

Pulling her onto his lap, Claudia straddled him, and he buried
his head in the soft skin of her neck. She smelled so good. No
expensive perfumes. Just the good, clean, scent of soap and
woman. He could feel his body respond to her every movement
above him, and he lavished his attention on her firm round
bottom as he kissed her deeply and pulled her hips against him
repeatedly. When she threw her head back, he quickly opened
her blouse, and let his hands fuse to her soft hot skin under
them. He couldn't stop, even if he had wanted to.

The sound of the friction created by the fabric caught between
them, deafened her. She didn't care that she still had on her
stretch pants, or that he still had on his jeans. It felt like they
were actually making love, and she couldn't stop. Nate was
causing her body to feel things that had been forgotten for so
long. . . . And he wanted her, really wanted her, which only
stoked her desire. When had any man wanted *her?*

A deep groan escaped from the center of his chest and he
arched up against her hard. Something inside of her immediately
gave way, and she felt her body explode and tremble against
his. Without warning, Nate pulled her to him roughly, then

shuddered twice as he gasped, before finally sinking against her shoulder spent.

After a few moments they both looked at each other sheepishly and grinned.

"Wow" was all that she could manage to say.

"Yeah. Wow," he repeated, taking in deep gulps of air and shaking his head. "I guess it's been a long time for both of us, huh? Maybe too long?" he said still smiling, brushing her mouth with a gentle kiss. Looking at her shyly, then lowering his eyes with embarrassment, he mumbled an awkward apology, "Guess I should go get cleaned up. Never expected that to happen . . . sorry."

Nate's newfound shyness was more endearing than if he had been a suave officinado of love. It was like looking at a smitten high school boy who was afraid to ask you to dance. Touching his face, she smiled before she let him up. "Don't apologize for enjoying yourself a little," she said, feeling young and awkward again herself. "I wanted you, too."

Chapter 6

Nathaniel Winston McGregor had been a man of his word.
He had stayed with her all week, and had performed a veritable
exorcism. Claudia hopped down from the grimy Laundromat
window sill that faced her building across the street and checked
the dryer, adding a few more quarters before returning to her
favorite perch. Lighting a cigarette, she let the smoke curl up
slowly and inhaled. She'd have to give this up, too, she thought,
but one day at a time—as Nate had said.

She refused to look at the bar across the street. Even though
she was hungry, she wouldn't go into the Ethiopian restaurant
next door to the coin-op Laundromat, which also served beer
and wine. Nate had finally trusted her to be on her own for a
few hours, and she wasn't about to blow it. Not after the hell
she'd put that man through.

He had been right about that, too. She had indeed thrown
up—several times, cursed him out—more than once, and even
tried to escape, threatening to call 911 if he didn't get out of
her way. She'd screamed horrible epithets at him, and oddly,

the only one that seemed to get under his skin, was when she'd said she wasn't dealing with no West Indian man.

Claudia smiled. How was she to know? She was referring to Trevor when the argument started! But Nate had stood his ground and held his own against her anti-black-men-from-the-West Indies diatribe. Her smile turned into a chuckle at the thought of the otherwise calm Nate McGregor having a hissy fit.

In the heat of anger she had found out that he was a second-generation, American-born, islander no less! Life was truly bizarre. He had let her rave on and on for hours about every subject imaginable, patiently dealing with her withdrawal hysterics—that is, until she went after his cultural identity. That's where Mr. N. W. McGregor, the second, had drawn a death line in the sand, and she had had enough sense not to cross it. Even withdrawal hadn't made her *that* crazy. She almost giggled again at the memory. Nate had drawn himself up, his back straightening by at least two inches, and he'd let her have it with both barrels. He'd practically gone off, telling her that he came from a long line of people that went back before Columbus even bumped into the islands of St. Kitts and Nevus, and dared her to speak ill of that region of the world. But he'd calmed down quickly, and she'd found out that he wasn't Trevor. Nate wasn't anything like anybody she'd ever known. So much for stereotypes . . .

Claudia let the late September sun warm her face as she sat in the window. She rolled her shoulders and crushed out the half-smoked cigarette and thought of her week with Nate. He had taken her on long walks down Locust Street to the campus, and although she was surly most of the time, they'd both marveled at how that small stretch of real estate could change from night to day if one walked only one block in either direction.

Caught in her own reverie, she gently dismissed a fly that had landed on her forearm. She felt much calmer than she had in a long time . . . more at peace, and didn't even feel it necessary to begrudge an insect a taste of life.

Bemused by the argument going on across the street between her elderly, pesky downstairs neighbor, Mr. Jones, and the Thrift Shop owner, Claudia turned her face to the sun and allowed her thoughts to fuse with the brightness. She had never spent so much special sharing time with any man.

When they went for daily walks they'd always gone down Locust, because it didn't have bars, and as they approached Forty-Second, the properties looked like they had been transported from Manhattan. Large brownstone mansions loomed over hundred-year-old oak trees and cobbled stone pavements. A massive Episcopal seminary held its own against urban encroachment, rimmed by a high-fenced yard where an international mixture of children from the numerous day care centers it housed played in freedom from fear or poverty.

Yet, one block toward Chestnut Street looked like South Vietnam with poor black folks interspered. She had never paid attention to that reality before. With Nate walking beside her, it was as though her awareness opened to the anonymous people slowly filing up and down the street. Most of them dragged aluminum shopping carts full of groceries that had obviously been purchased with food stamps to feed a house full of kids.

In the other direction, one block toward Spruce, was considered University City. That was where Penn students, yuppie white families, cultured blacks, not to mention old gourmet food shops and deli's flourished. Locust Street was the dividing line between the haves and the have-nots. This was the reality that had made Nate McGregor angry enough to sink a fortune into buying up the old neighborhood properties around every campus in the city.

He'd taken her on his building rounds to his apartments located on Forty-Sixth and Spring Garden, then to the ones on Hazel, Cedar, and Baltimore Avenue. He had duplexes everywhere. And she knew that Nate's showing her around was his quiet way of opening himself to her while keeping her under guard from herself.

They'd gone behind Drexel, around to Thirty-Sixth and Hamilton, then all the way up to Temple where he owned a strip of commercial storefronts with apartments above them on Cecil B. Moore Avenue. The man even had real estate near LaSalle College, and out near Villanova. In his laid-back way, Nate had repeatedly shrugged off her awe and said that he had brought at least two buildings every year while he'd practiced law. That's where his money had gone—to provide decent low-income housing to poor people.

It was so strange. She knew he could have charged a small fortune in rents, or made a mint in speculation. But Nate kept all of his properties neat, clean, and available, on barely a pittance from his tenants. Without fanfare, or public recognition, this man had quietly given back to his community. It was obvious that's why his tenants always offered a friendly greeting when he took her along to check the buildings. Bottom line, they respected him.

So did she. In fact, maybe she loved him. She closed her eyes and allowed the Fall sun to create a rose-orange pattern of brightness inside her lids. Nate McGregor had a way of giving without making a person feel obligated or belittled. Claudia thought of all that he'd given to her, all that he'd shown her in one short week. He'd given her nightly baths in peppermint tea steeped water, and had rubbed baby oil over her aching muscles without expecting that she make love to repay him. They'd found special ways to pleasure each other, without going all the way. An immediate shiver swept through her. God, the man was sexy. A slow hand. What was happening to her conservative Ms. Harris mask? At times she'd actually had to talk herself out of begging him to finish what he'd started. Lord knows that she would have gladly given it to him. . . .

Claudia squeezed her lids tighter, creating a kaleidoscope of colors as her body responded to the memory. How long could they keep it going—their chaste but not so chaste relationship?

They'd even laughed together when Nate finally admitted that he'd never purchased a condom—having married before the epidemic of AIDS became public knowledge. Before that, he claimed that his friends had accused him of being ''buck wild,'' as he called it. Never in a million years would she have imagined that she'd want a man to be wild with her. It had been torture to lay with him, enjoy heavy petting, then watch him retreat into the living room. ''Oh . . .'' she whispered, shaking his touch from her mind and trying to pull herself out of the thought. ''Girl, he's got your nose opened, for real.''

Shaking her head, she thought back. Nate McGregor had even held a trash can in front of her face while she threw up, then patiently fed her clear soup again, and brushed her unruly hair. In an instant, the magic was gone. Her thoughts turned in on her and made sharp accusations against her own womanhood. . . . Claudia opened her eyes and looked across the street sadly. No wonder they didn't make love, she thought ruefully, almost shuddering with disgust. Why in the world would a man like that even consider dealing with such a wreck? Pulleeze. And if the shoe had been on the other foot . . . ? She didn't even want to let her mind take such a turn, for she knew what the answer would have been before she met Nate. A staunch, nonnegotiable, hell *no!*

A quick turn of depression suddenly threatened Claudia's composure as she recalled the pain-filled stories that Nate told her about losing his son and his wife. Her emotions felt like they were on a roller coaster. Her life sure seemed to be on one. When he'd taken her by the beautiful old Tudor in Radnor that was once his, she'd swallowed down the pain for this man as they'd watched the new owner's blond children playing on the well-manicured lawn. So much had happened to Nate, yet he still had the patience and caring of a saint. She wondered how people like him held it together, how the human spirit ever endured tragedies of such magnitude without breaking. And yet, he was still open enough to honestly tell her how he'd sold everything of material value after he lost his most precious possession—his family. Most men would have lied. They certainly wouldn't have told a woman that had it not been for their law partner, they might have sold the properties, too.

Casting her gaze across the street to her own building, she was still in awe. For days Nate had tried to get her to understand that it was the giving that had gotten him through. Even though they had bitterly argued religious philosophy at points, there was an odd ring to his concepts. Somehow, those buildings that housed poor people, and gave fledgling entrepreneurs their start, were Nate's only therapy. Now the shoe was indeed on the other foot, and she had gotten to know someone special.

Nobody, not even her family, had taken the time to be gentle to her soul. She wanted to give back something special for him to hold onto, a part of her that went well beyond the physical. Instinctively, she understood that Nate had imparted a rare glimpse inside of himself in order to save her. That peek was enough to let her know that there was still a large hole in his heart. Everything, all of her, felt it. She wondered if it was even possible to bring some peace into this man's life who had done so much for hers.

When the dryer stopped, Claudia moved her laundry basket to the floor in front of it and began folding warm clothes and linens. Standing next to her was an old woman who had staked out the only table in the joint. Obviously warning Claudia not to even think about using the ragged piece of particle board, the elderly lady glared up. Her mouth was set so tight that Claudia had to stifle a smile. Despite her poorly hidden amusement, the woman's expression remained silent, but deadly, as though daring anyone to encroach upon her physical space.

Eyeing Claudia suspiciously, the woman finally spoke in a surly voice. "Hate comin' in here. Wastes a whole damned day, just sittin' around, waitin' on clothes," she said curtly, adjusting her lopsided gray wig and wiping her sweaty brow with her sleeve.

Claudia nodded. "Know whatcha mean. Takes forever."

The old woman stopped folding clothes, and leaned against the table. "Hear tell that cha back around these parts, and Nate

McGregor's taken a liking to ya. Good one, that Nate. Girl, treat that boy nice, he's been through an awful lot.''

Although stunned by the intrusion, Claudia nodded her head yes. That's as much as she was willing to give the old busybody standing next to her. She had come too far to let anyone, or anything, threaten her peace. Millie Thompson, from the third floor, Miss Eye Witness News herself, had probably spilled the beans on Nate's week-long stay. Or it could have been miserable old Mr. Jones, from down on the first level, who'd spread the word. His routine was to either go to church or to pester the proprietors along Forty-Fifth Street all day long with his complaints about the traffic, noise levels, trash . . . color of the sky, the weather. . . . Come to think of it, he was probably the culprit, since he'd hit his ceiling a couple of times with a broom handle when she'd been crying, or when she and Nate had laughed too loud. If Millie had told on her, it was for the sake of pure gossip alone, not to complain—since everybody knew the Thompson kids created the noisiest apartment out of the three in the building. Whatever. She hated when people pried into her personal life! Peace was escaping her. It was too hot in that small place for this mess. Not today.

The old woman smoothed the front of her wrinkled shift and shook out a worn blue towel with a pop, clearly becoming peeved by Claudia's noncommunicative mood. She didn't care. She wasn't about to let a total stranger get into her business— she hated it enough when so-called friends and family tried to do that.

"Well, like I said," the matron finally huffed indignantly, pulling out several sheets from the dryer next to her big hip, "Nate's a good one. Sho hope ya 'ppreciate whatcha got.''

Claudia let out a long breath. She had to remember that she was talking to a senior citizen, and the only way to deal was to give the woman a one-liner or two, then get out of there.

"I know," Claudia said looking at the elderly lady, and meaning it. "There's nobody as nice, and he deserves a little happiness. I frankly don't know how he's made it this far.''

A silent understanding passed between the two women, and the older woman's eyes softened. ''God don't put no more on ya, than you kin handle.''

Claudia stiffened at the remark. It was too pat, too much like the old platitudes that had made her lose her mind in the first place. ''God?'' she said sarcastically. ''There's no excuse for what He did to me, or Nate McGregor. Why do people always excuse the inexcusable?'' she added with impatience, quickly returning to her task.

The old woman didn't move, and seemed to be considering her words before she spoke. ''I'm eighty-three years old, and I've lived long enough to know that God ain't the one who brings misery and heartache. But He's the only one to help ya through it.''

Claudia didn't respond immediately. She wasn't in the mood to debate this particular subject. Not now. Actually, the truth was, she'd never planned to discuss this mess ever again in life. But the old woman was still glaring at her, and if the woman wanted a fight, this time she wasn't going to back down.

''I suppose you've got it all figured out, huh? With your pious, nosy ways, and righteous self! And if folks don't practice your particular brand of religion, or live the way you think they should, then they're outcasts, right—and deserve whatever thunderbolt hits them? Is that it?'' she nearly yelled, feeling defensive, and allowing herself to get whipped up into a tizzy over the long-standing internal argument that she'd never addressed out loud before.

''Well, you don't know the half of it, lady. So mind your business,'' she snapped, pressing on angrily, and trying to steady her voice while shaking her mother's face out of her mind. Moms Harris would have *turned over* to hear her daughter speak to an older person like that, Claudia thought, still fuming. But she'd had enough of people telling her what to do, or think.

The woman shook her head and clucked her tongue, folding her arms over an ample bosom. ''Used to be like you once. Ol' folks couldn't tell me nothin'. Found out da hard way dat it don't matter much whacha call Him, so long as you *do* call Him, when ya need Him.''

Claudia turned away from the woman and kept folding her laundry.

"Can I tell you a story?" the old woman began again calmly, appearing unperturbed.

Claudia didn't answer, but soon the woman's steady gaze bore into her back, forcing her to turn around impatiently. "So, tell your story, ma'am. Everybody's got one.''

The woman returned a snaggle-toothed grin that Claudia hadn't expected. ''You's right. Everybody's got a story, indeed. Like, about twenty-five years ago, 'bout seventy-one or seventy-two or so, I was ridin' on the number forty-two bus. You know, the one that goes 'round pass the hospital?''

Claudia drew a deep breath and let it out noisily. ''Yeah, I know the one. So what's your point?''

"Well," the woman went on undaunted, "we was all tired and iratable like—I used to do day's work, and my feet was swoll up real bad. Didn't nobody wanna hear nothin' from nobody. Jus' like you acting now . . . We was all squeezed up like sardines in a can. Wasn't no air. Was hot as the blazes in there. Just wanted to get home.''

Claudia started folding again. This woman was going to make her break her vow to Nate. She'd cross the street and go to the bar for sure.

"Well, any ol' way . . . This bum comes on the bus, droppin' his change, stinking and mumblin' to hisself—crazy like. Didn't see a lot a street folks in them days, so ya know all da white folks goin' back to the fancy houses 'round Penn drew up an squinched away from 'im. Only made people mo mad an evil. Well, dat bum was crazy, but he wasn't stupid. He seen the way folk looked at him like he was dirt, and he pulled out a bottle and started talkin' real loud. Finally, an old immigrint white lady says for him to shut up, he's disturbin' da peace. Everybody, said, 'Yeah . . . shut up ya bum, or get off.' Den dat man straightened his back, an put away his bottle.

Wiped the tears from his eyes, an tol' 'em all he was somebody once. Said he used to sing opera with Paul Robeson—did ya know Robeson lived in Philly? His sister's house it up 'round Fiftieth an something in West Philly.''

Claudia had stopped folding her laundry and was looking at the woman intently. She wasn't sure of where the story was headed, but it had the familiar ring of a parable to it. "Yes, I know about Robeson.''

"Well, it was the firs' time I heard tell 'bout his roots. Any ol' how, everybody kep' yellin' to that man to shut up—said he was a lyin' drunk. 'Specially that old immigrint woman. Said he wouldn't know opera iffin he tripped ov'r it. Then the man tol' some more. Said he spoke five languages—Russian, Romanian, Czech, some more I cain't recall. And everybody laughed, until he cussed that ol' immigrint out in her own mother tongue. Well, Jesus, that ol' lady started cryin'—said she ain't heard her language spoke like that in years since da war. They started talkin', an babblin', an cryin'—all in dis here language,'' the woman said emphatically, slapping her meaty hand on the table.

"Chile, ya shoulda seen it!'' she exclaimed. "Folks, black an white was standin' wit dey mouths open. Bus driver could hardly drive for peepin' in the rear view mirror. Den, outta no where, that dirty ol' man busts out in song. Couldn't hear no mo' whiskey in his voice. Sounded like a church angel. Sang in perfec' pitch. I should know, I sings on my choir and can carry a note myself. But he had a *trained* voice, like, uh . . . a Marian Anderson voice. From dat day forth, I never judged a book by its cover. Everytime I think I done heard it all—I hears some mo'.''

While the story had a fantastic quality to it, Claudia still wasn't convinced that it had any relevance beyond an old lady trying to get into her business. To quickly end the discourse that was sure to be a waste of time, she decided to return a polite closing remark to the woman, hoping that would be enough to satisfy the bible matron.

Siphoning her reserves of old-fashioned home training, especially the one ingrained in her to respect her elders, Claudia pasted on a smile and took a deep breath for patience.

"Well, like I said, we've all got a story, and our *own* beliefs. Hope you have a good day," she added, pulling the last of her clothes from the large industrial dryer barrel. She'd fold them at home, it wasn't worth it to hang around and deal with this mess.

"Lost two sons in Vietnam, my grandson, Juney, to Desert Storm, a husband to stroke some fifteen years ago, and I'm raisin' my grand babies on a fixed income by myself. Drugs done took their mother, and her mind. Like I said, He don't put no more on ya, than you kin bear," the woman said triumphantly, obviously ignoring the queue to end the conversation.

Claudia stopped and looked at the woman hard. "And is that supposed to be an example of His so-called divine justice?" she snapped sarcastically. "How can you still believe that He's in your corner, when He let horrible things happen to you?" Claudia was incredulous. She'd had enough. Why couldn't some folks take a hint and leave you alone? All she wanted to do was to wash her damned clothes and dry them in peace!

"Uhmm, Uhmm. Shame you ain't lived long enough to understand His ways," the old lady said, shaking her head and folding a small child's undershirt. "When evil comes knockin' at cha door, God'll sometimes let cha answer it. But, He always sends His army in 'fore it's too late."

"Oh, pulleeze," Claudia sighed, angrily shaking the wrinkles out of a blouse.

"He ain't never promised nobody an easy row to hoe. But what He did say, was that He wouldn't abandon ya in yo final hour a need."

Claudia gave the elderly woman a sideways glance and rolled her eyes, shaking her head. There was no arguing with old people! Their logic was designed to make you crazy—that's probably why they lived so long, just so they could work on your nerves.

Steadfast, the woman continued, taking out a rumpled tissue from her sleeve and dabbing her brow. "For example, did ya ever go hungry when ya didn't have no job? Did ya always have a roof ov'r ya head?" she pressed on relentlessly. "When yo hour was the darkness, did a person ya didn' know hep ya? An did things kinda work out, even when ya wasn't tryin'?"

The comment made Claudia go still. Someone *had* come to her aide, out of the blue, just when she couldn't take it anymore. Nate McGregor.

The old woman gave a pleased little grunt, and her smile broadened with victory. "My ol' granmaw used to tell us about hard times in her day. An them days was much worse den we'll ever know. Said dat even in pitch darkness, a tiny match kin throw enough light to see by. Dats what He does, honey. Throws a little light, so's you kin find yo own way."

Claudia considered her words for what felt like a long time. The old woman nodded, and waited for a response, humming softly and pointing up to the ceiling with a crooked, gnarled, finger. It was a stalemate. She hated this stuff.

"What about the homeless, and people dying of diseases where there's no cure . . . Or wars, and babies dying of starvation? And how about people of different religions, like Muslims or Jews or whoever—or even those with lifestyles different than most ministers sanction? Does God answer them?" Claudia tossed back firmly. Maybe it was a draw, but she'd go down fighting.

The elderly woman looked Claudia dead in the eyes and frowned. "We's *all* His children. He don' judge no book by it's cover, girl. Don' cha know that? He done *wrote* the book on every life. Do a mother ever stop loving, or refuse to go to her baby's rescue—jus' cause dat chile don't call her Mommy? She hear it cryin', an dats all she need to know 'bout her youngun. You ain't makin' no sense, an as a educated woman, you outta know better," the woman said with disgust. "I swear! I cain't stand folks who go 'round making judgments on other folk. That ain't nobody's bizness but God's," she pronounced.

Claudia almost smiled at the irony. Here this woman thought that she was the narrow-minded, judgmental one, and had missed the point entirely. Perhaps they were kindred spirits of sorts.

''Now, 'bout them other thangs in dis worl' of heartbreak and sorrow . . . well, dat ain't God's hand in it. Cain't blame Him for what He didn't do. Dat's the evilness of man. But on the better side, man's goodness shines through when a person drops a blanket off to a cold urchin' layin' on the street, or a soldier gives his life to save a chile, or a stranger pulls somebody out of a smashed up car, or a policeman takes a bullet tryin' to save somebody . . . You kin hear dat on da news every day. Or when a man, like Nate McGregor, lets us live somewhere almost free, an keeps up da buildin' for us po folk—when he coulda charged the sky. Now, dats when God's army is at work. An His folks move in quiet an mysterious ways. Dey good works ain't always advatized. But, trus' me when I tell ya, I've lived long enough to see thangs balance out. One thang fer sure, the world is very round.''

''But if God is so powerful, then why does He let these tragic things happen in the first place?'' Claudia wasn't combative or angry any longer when she'd asked the question. She truly wanted an answer, and this old woman seemed to possess an undefinable wisdom that offered both hope and strength. Moms had been right, elderly people deserved respect, if for no other reason than the purple heart of courage it took to keep on living after life had beaten them down. Claudia waited patiently as the woman adjusted her dental plate and thought about how to reply.

''Ain't got no easy answer to that fer ya, baby. Maybe I'll only figure it out when I'm gone on to glory. Could be the devil's way of fellin' God's soldiers—somethin' to make 'em lose faith an give up. That's the only way evil kin beat cha, when ya start doin' evil yo'self cause ya think it don't pay to be nice no mo'. Seen it plenty times.'' She shrugged. ''Ain't for me to say. Jus' knows what an ol' woman knows, is all.

God don't always come when ya ready fer Him, but He's always on time. Done saved me at the eleventh hour, fifty-ninth minute, plenty 'nough to witness that truth to ya today."

Claudia stood frozen by the old woman's conviction. "But, with all that's happened to you, and how you ended up, aren't you even angry?" she whispered.

"Been mad enough to go out of my natchel mind," the woman said quietly, as she began folding the last of her load. "Done cried me a river of tears, too, 'specially when I lost my boys. But, even though I was mad wit Him, God didn't git mad wit me. No, sir. He sent messenger's in to help me push on, sured me up with people I didn't even know, and gave me enough strength to keep raisin' them children . . ." She sighed, tearing up, and looking at Claudia thoughtfully. "Lissen to His angels, chile, deys the ones we love dats gone on to glory. Sometime, He calls 'em early, cause He needs 'em so bad on His side. Sometime, He'll leave 'em here to fight direc'ly. But, dey hear ya too, doll. Don' cha ever stop calling on the ones you love. Dey kin feel yo tears, and hear yo wails . . . jus' like He can."

"I'm sorry," Claudia said, touching the old lady's arm. "I know it must have been terrible for you."

The old woman patted her hand, and wiped the moisture from her hazy bluish-brown eyes and smiled. "See, yo heart still has some God lef' in it, or ya wouldn't a cared a damn about an ol', tired, woman dat cha don't even know. This is what the devil is tryin' to do, honey. Make people so miserable they can't give a kind word, or a smile, or a helpin' hand to a neighbor. And jus' when you think ol' Slew Foot's won, somethin' like this happens to let cha know that God is still around."

Heaving the last of her clothes into her cart, the old woman sighed heavily. "Gots work to do. Cain't stand around all day, dispensin' advice."

Claudia was at a loss for words and only nodded.

The old woman patted her cheek as she moved to leave and

Claudia held the door open for her. "Don't cha go losin' yo faith now, baby," she warned in a serious voice. "Sometimes, that's all ya got lef' in this world to stand between you and the dark side of thangs. Keep yo candle of faith burnin' bright."

She watched the old woman draw herself up with dignity, and hoist her piles of clothes in the rusty metal shopping cart with two wheels on it down the short flight of steps to the pavement. Claudia studied the matron's haggard, dark, lined face and her labored arthritic gait. This person, who she didn't even know, had freely shared her story, a testamony, one where she'd borne up under a life of hardship and tears. And yet, she still believed in the fundamental goodness of man—and of her God. It was compelling to see this woman of eighty-three years haul a mule's burden of children's laundry down the street, stopping occasionally to catch her breath and to rub her hip.

If Claudia had ever wanted a drink, that spectacle stopped the urge more than Nate's quiet ministration's ever did, more than any preacher's sermon ever had, or a counselor's educated, sterile, advice ever could. What she'd just witnessed, was the universal truth of an indominable human spirit, and the power of steadfast belief—by whatever name anybody called it.

Chapter 7

Nate slammed the telephone receiver against its cradle and punched his desk. Fury ricocheted through him like nine-milimeter gunshots. *"Sonofabitch!"*

For a moment, he stood trembling, as his rage seeped from every pore. He absolutely hated Eric Addison, and the way he'd relentlessly tried every angle to encroach upon his Cecil B. Moore Avenue properties for the last six months. There had to be a reason the SOB wanted that particular strip of commercial real estate so badly now. He could tell by Eric's not-too-thinly veiled threat that something had escalated beyond the bastard's previous weak claims of wanting them purely for market speculation. He'd never sell to that bloodsucker. Never! It was a matter of principle.

Nate crossed the study of his Spruce Street brownstone and stalked into the bedroom. Flinging open his clothes closet, he reached into the back section and pulled out his best navy blues. He eyed the garments dispassionately, then flung his choice onto the bed with irritation. It had been four years since he'd suited up and gone to war—but this, gentlemen, was war!

he declared to himself, as he searched for a starched white monogrammed shirt and silk tie. He would be in command, in control, and take no prisoners. *The counselor* was back.

Twenty minutes later, Nate emerged from the bedroom—clean shaven, with trimmed hair, and in battle gear. Adjusting his tie in the long foyer mirror, he gave his corporate armor the once-over-lightly as though preparing for a military inspection. Albeit, the suit was a little loose—he had subsisted on cans of tuna fish, pork & beans, cheese steaks and only an occasional balanced meal at The American Diner—and his shirt was a bit yellowed—having stayed in the same plastic cleaners bag for so long. It would have to do. Cologne could perhaps take the dusty smell out of everything. Fortunately, Laggerfeld had an indefinite shelf life, if kept tightly sealed. His good Boyd's suit was not a problem, it was a classic that never lost its style. Nor were his black wing tips—standard Florsheim's lasted forever. But the tie . . . well, who gave a damn if nobody wore reps any more. This wasn't a fashion show, it was war.

Crossing the street and heading down Forty-Sixth and Spruce, he impatiently watched the traffic for any signs of a cab. As he approached the corner of Forty-Fifth, he thought of Claudia. He'd been gone for hours. It was nearly three o'clock, but there was no time to stop or call. He had to get to City Hall before four. Finally, as he made his way down the steep hill to Forty-Third, he saw a taxi and hailed it—but it was off duty and whirred by him. Damn! He should have never sold the BMW! What was he thinking when he told Ed to sell everything? Thank God his partner had resisted his wishes and had only sold the Tudor and shipped the more painfully sentimental relics to his extended family in New York.

There was no cab to be found until he reached Thirty-Eighth, and it was already three ten in the afternoon. Crushing a twenty into the driver's hand, Nate made the man understand that time was of the essence. When they finally hit the traffic circle around City Hall courtyard, he hopped out of the vehicle that was mired in traffic, and flanked the four lanes of semiparked cars until he reached the pavement to safety. Three thirty.

Half running, half walking, Nate snaked his way through the building labyrinth until he found the prothonotary's office. He had good friends on the inside there, people who would possibly remember him from his old days on the legal chicken circuit. But once inside, his heart sank. Not even Lucille was there to greet him.

Finally getting a young woman's attention, he inquired in a low voice, "Is Lucille Jackson still in this office?"

The young woman with large gold hoop earrings and too much clerage adjusted her half blond, half brunette, slick finger-waved hair with a long sparkled orange talon. "Nope, she retired two years ago when the city was going through all that union mess. But, can I help you?" she smiled a little too eagerly.

Nate shook his head, and tried to steady his voice. "What about Angel Ramirez?"

The clerk just rolled her eyes, and pointed out the door with annoyance. "He's over in the Mayor's Office of Minority Affairs now. I got work to do, and this ain't the information department, *okay?*"

Nate mumbled a quick thank you and headed out the door to try to find Ramirez. They had been buddies for a long time, and he could count on his friend to give him the lowdown on why his strip had recently become such hot property. In that outrageous telephone conversation with Addison, it had been clearly inferred that his other buildings might receive undue Licensing and Inspection scrutiny if he didn't cooperate. And if they wanted to squeeze him, no establishment could withstand a fine-tooth comb, microscopic evaluation from L&I. Especially older section eights. It was true that anybody's buildings could be shut down for the most minor violation, and everybody knew it. That's why everybody went along with the program, and paid the cost to be the boss.

Scaling a flight of stairs, Nate thought about how Addison Development had gobbled up every choice minority city and state construction contract, PennDot bid, building sheriff sale, and 203(k) vacancy. His nemesis always seemed to get in on every Planning Commission Task Force—garnering the inside track on whatever was going down at HUD or the Redevelopment Authority before it happened. Addison had created a veritable dynasty within the last eight years. So, if they were after his measly one-block commercial strip, then something big was obviously in the planning stages that hadn't hit the Redevelopment Authority general grapevine yet. But if Addison wanted to participate in regentrification, he could buy his own land and do it. Nate McGregor was not selling!

Tentatively opening the door, Nate looked around to see if he could spot his friend. When he finally got the attention of one of the secretaries, he tried to steady the impatience in his voice. "Is Mr. Angel Ramirez available?"

"You got an appointment?" the woman said curtly in a bored voice.

"Just tell him Nate McGregor is here," he returned in an authoritative tone. "He'll know what it's about."

The woman took her time after letting out a long disgusted breath. It was obvious that she didn't want to deal with any intrusion that might upset her schedule so close to quitting time. But he glared at her steadily to let her know that he would not be moved. He didn't have time for that today. His entire life's work was at stake.

Nate could see Ramirez approaching him quickly with a smile, and he rushed past the surly woman who stood in the aisle to clasp his friend by the upper arms.

"Man, I'm so glad to see you," Nate said in an excited voice. "Sorry to barge in on you like this, but I need to talk to you about something important."

"Compadre! Long time no see. I've always got time for you, man. C'mon back to my office so we can catch up," Ramirez said, smiling, then turned to his secretary. "Miriam, hold all calls."

When they entered the sumptuous office, Nate surveyed the

new environment with appreciation. ''Looks like a lot of things have changed around here.''

''It's good to see you back, counselor,'' his friend said with a wide grin. ''Yeah, things change, and you're a sight for sore eyes.''

Nate studied the man before him, and for a fleeting moment, wondered if it he still had the right to ask a favor after so long.

Ramirez interrupted his thoughts, and began speaking in a quiet voice. ''Yo, man, we've all been real worried about you. You sort of dropped off the face of the earth, and we didn't want to upset you or nothing . . . I mean, after everything you've been through. We would just ask Ed from time to time how you were, and he'd just say that you were making it. What can I do for you, man? If I can help, just let me know, and it's done.''

Nate looked at his friend of long years. ''Addison is leaning on me to sell my strip up on Cecil B. Moore, and I know it's not just because he likes the area. That barracuda doesn't make a move unless it's an extremely profitable one.''

''Yeah, like his recent marriage to DiGiovanni's daughter,'' Ramirez said just above a whisper, clearly nervous about where the conversation was headed.

''Wait, a black man married the daughter of a South-Philly-by-way-of-South-Jersey Italian boss? I know I've been out of contact for a while, but some things just don't happen.''

''It's complicated, man. Dangerous, but brilliant, on DiGiovanni's part. She was his third daughter, and he sacrificed her for business.''

''I don't want to involve you in anything hot, man,'' Nate said reassuringly. ''I just want to know what I'm dealing with.''

Ramirez nodded. ''Look, we go way back, right? So, if I can help, *de nada*—no problem.''

''I've been out of the loop for a while, and haven't been keeping up on the local politics,'' Nate added, feeling strangely disassociated and out of sync.

''Well, let me catch you up in short order,'' Ramirez said

in a low confidential tone. "Addison has increased his holdings fourfold with that marriage. And the marriage was to more than just DiGiovanni's daughter. He's been able to get the backing necessary to effectively bid on the larger minority contracting jobs that the rest of the struggling small minority businesses can't get insured or bonded for. Now, DiGiovanni's got a sure win for any state, federal, or city job that requires minority content. One hand washes the other, man. You know the deal."

"But what's that got to do with Cecil B. Moore Avenue?"

"This may be purely conjecture on my part, Nate, but it's small potatoes in comparison to DiGiovanni's usual moves. If Addison is that crazy, the stupid SOB probably cut this little deal on his own, and has no intentions of sharing the profits from his scam with his father-in-law."

"What scam?"

Ramirez shook his head. "The bastard's beating poor people out of their money."

Nate raised one eye brow and leaned in closer.

"He's set up a nonprofit agency, supposedly to give poor, small, minority businesses their first storefronts. He's sending over a bogus appraiser to say that each building is worth fifty to eighty thousand dollars."

"What!" Nate exclaimed, almost standing up. "Those storefronts need at least sixty thousand dollars worth of work each to come up to commercial code. That's why I haven't rented them yet. The base value can't be more than ten grand."

Ramirez let out a deep breath. "I'm handcuffed on this. It's an ugly business that a lot of people way up are involved in. What they are probably planning to do is give out these inflated mortgages through the nonprofit for eighty thousand. Then they'll send their guys from Licenses and Inspection over to code them, giving the new owners ninety days to fix the impossible."

Nate straightened in his chair. "And since we know that no small entrepreneur has that kind of cash flow, the building will be padlocked, and the owners will be unable to make the mortgage payments, thus foreclosing the property back to Addison's *helpful* nonprofit who gave them their start since the nonprofit is doing the loans. What a sweet scam."

"But wait, there's more," Ramirez interjected. "Then, those properties would have an appraised market value of eighty thousand a piece. Not bad for a days work on an eleven-store strip. So, when Temple University wants to buy up that block to make way for the new stadium and parking facilities expansion and their own clean storefronts—ones that won't turn away spectators who might otherwise have to pass through the badlands, that block will carry a price tag of eight hundred and eighty thousand dollars. And Temple will pay it, especially after the amount of money they've sunk into the stadium project. That's a profit margin of seven hundred and seventy thousand dollars. The only part I haven't been able to figure out is how Addison could legally move the profits from that venture to his personal accounts. But it's still one hell of a return on investment for a six-month period—since none of those poor people will be able to hold out much longer than that."

Nate stood and looked at his friend. "Over my dead body," he said evenly.

"Maybe, amigo, if you don't watch your step."

Chapter 8

Something was definitely wrong. Nate had left her a little past noon, and now it was getting dark. He hadn't even called. Claudia drew her legs beneath her and lit another cigarette. She didn't bother to turn on the lights in the apartment, and simply let the early rose-orange haze of the autumn evening filter into the room.

She had been here before. Yet, strangely, something about the upbeat way Nate had left her to go on building rounds today just didn't fit with his sudden AWOL. True, she'd only really known him for a week. The two years of living in his building, and seeing him occaisionally, didn't count. Not now. Especially not now. The cold light of day reality was, she *didn't* know him. Nor had he made love to her. Maybe he had completed his so-called savior mission and was done with her. . . . Maybe that was his modus operandi, to save fallen, broken sparrows, then when they were healed, he left in the dead of night. Just her luck to be a part of his hero complex—or some other kind of neurosis. Claudia shook her head in disgust and let it fall back on the cushion. Nate was too good to be true and she should have seen it coming.

Well, at least he hadn't used her physically. Nate would always stop just short of that, for some reason. Jesus. Maybe he was gay? She gasped quickly as her hand flew over her mouth, but she immediately banished the thought. ''Don't even go there Claudia Harris. Don't even go there,'' she chided herself in a low murmur and shook off a shiver. The man didn't seem to have any problem getting aroused, he just didn't finish what he started. Maybe he just didn't want it to go any farther than a friendship? Possible. Hopeful. Depressing.

Claudia's mind hurled into other dark possibilities, and she steeled herself against the disappointment that came with them. She must have been crazy to expect that any commitment would be made to her. Not this soon anyway, if ever. But it was as though Nate had walked out of her apartment as one person, and she felt sure that someone different would return.

What if the kind, sensitive, honest man she'd known briefly had really been perpetrating fraud? Or what if he had a woman whom he could only keep at bay for a week? That was plausible. Or, maybe worse, what if she was right in her first assumptions that Nate McGregor was on some kind of hero trip—only dealing with injured sparrows? What happened when his little birds could fly again? Did he go after another damsel in distress? And like Superman, could he only leap tall buildings with a single bound to save somebody, then land them gently on the curb before flying away to his next mission? Was making love *all the way* some sort of kriptonite for him? She wanted to laugh and cry at the same time.

Here she was, all dressed up with no where to go on a Friday night. And he'd promised her that tonight would be special. It was the first time in a long time that she even felt like her old self, or had any expectations for an evening. Then poof, just like that, the man in her life disappears. Claudia inhaled deeply and allowed her mind to wander. Stop it, Claud. You have no right, the rational side of her brain protested. This man had done the world for her, and now it was time to stand on her own two feet. She'd been lucky. He had treated her nice, didn't take advantage of her, and was more than a help. Consider his passing through as a blessing, she thought sullenly. That's all.

As soon as the last part of the statement crossed her mind, Claudia froze. She had said the words mentally in a minute, yet traceable thought. It was more like a quiet prayer than a conversation with herself. Almost something akin to a prayer of thanks directed toward the one being that she hadn't been on speaking terms with for a long time. She allowed a moment to pass, then crushed out her cigarette and let out a deep, tired sigh.

"I've been so angry with you, Lord," her voice quavered with repressed emotion. "I tried so hard to follow the rules, and do the right thing. But you never protected me from any of the terrible things that happened, and I just can't understand what I've done so wrong."

Claudia could feel the familiar knot building in the base of her stomach, and she listened intently to the traffic noises of the city. Nights in the city had a distinctly different sound from those of her semi-rural South Jersey past. Fire engines and police cars seemed to blare louder and more frequently. You could hear footsteps better, and the music from the bar next door pulsed nonstop. There were more adult voices, and less children's playful outbursts to be heard as pedestrians made their way up and down the block. You could hear metal grates going down to protect store fronts from the perils of night, and car motors seemed to start more loudly when called on to carry their owners safely home. It was so different from Jersey, where the early evening gave you crickets and an occasional night bird's song.

Yet, the din also had an oddly soothing quality. Claudia let the background noise filter past her mind, and focused her thoughts on the old woman that she'd talked to in the Laundromat. "Is that it?" she whispered into the semi-dark room. Did

He deliver messages through others—strange bits of scattered information like a giant jigsaw puzzle?

The room seemed so quiet that she could almost hear the beat of her own heart.

"If it was only for a moment, then thank you for saving me. Thank you for sending Nate."

There, she had done it. Made her peace of sorts. But there was still so much left unanswered. So much that still hurt so badly. "You said to lay it on the altar . . . Well, I tried that. And, it didn't work."

Claudia felt the cellophane that encased the half-smoked pack of cigarettes. "Sorry, I need one. I know you're not supposed to have a conversation with God with a cigarette hanging out of your mouth, but at this point, I feel like I'm already in hell."

She inhaled deeply, a thick coating of smoke residue making her tongue feel like dirty cotton. She ignored the sensation. It was a safer option at the moment than a drink. She tried to swallow down the tears, but gave up, allowing large hot splotches to drop from the end of her chin onto her silk skirt.

"Okay, Lord, I hope your complaint department is taking notes." Claudia closed her eyes and let her head rest back on the overstuffed recliner. Unconsciously, her free hand traveled across her lower belly, and she stroked it gingerly as she issued up her heart to the silence in the room.

"All I ever wanted was to have a family and someone to love me and grow old with. A lot of money never mattered, neither did the fast lane. Why would something so basic and good be so hard to come by?"

There was no answer except her own breathing.

"I didn't expect an answer to that one," she said sadly, taking another drag.

As true darkness settled in and the street lights came on slowly, she thought back on her marriage. How many nights had she waited up for Trevor in that same chair, only to watch him sashay in boldly with a look of sheer contempt on his face.

He'd always acted like it was his right to do as he pleased, and
had said so enough times that even now it sickened her with
anger.

"Okay, maybe it was for the best that I didn't have two kids
for him. I'll give you that. Even Loretta told me as much,"
she said weakly, really accepting the logic of not having borne
Trevor's children for the first time. What would she have done
if she had two kids to support in her condition now? Working
in the school system, she'd witnessed firsthand the results that
messed-up parents had on their children. She had dealt with
emotionally damaged youth every day. Just watching it, and
feeling so helpless, had begun to drag her down. The problem
was so severe, so devastating, and so complex. . . . Even if
she'd divorced after she'd had children, the thought of having
to fight with a trifling man through family court—or being tied
to him for life by the lives they had created. . . . She would've
gone crazy long before the rest of the tragedies hit. Perhaps
both she and those children had been spared. All right. One
for God. But that still left three or four issues on her side of
the argument.

As Claudia took another long drag, she realized that maybe
there were two points on God's side of the scoreboard instead
of just one. "I was tired of working in a big corporation," she
admitted quietly. "Yeah, okay, the layoff was good mentally,
but bad financially, so I started teaching. Wasn't that giving
back? Wasn't that good?"

She sat very still, then answered her own question in her
mind. The teaching had been a good thing to do, but her heart
broke daily as she saw what was going wrong with her students.
Their lives had been crippled before they'd had a chance to
begin. Claudia thought back honestly to the way she almost
wept her way home on the bus daily, wishing she had her own
children—knowing that she would have been a good mother.
It was all so confusing and totally unfair.

Sure, she wanted to work with children that needed help.
But not within the confines of *the system*. What was going on

in there seemed designed to hinder any true growth for the
young people she encountered. Before that job, she had tried
her own business and failed. Why was she going down this
mental spiral again? It was history. What was done was done.

But when she left the insurance company, she'd known at
gut level that she had to work for herself somehow. Yet on the
pittance they gave her for a severance package, how the hell
could she have ever begun to afford her own school? That was
what she had really wanted from the beginning. Her own school.
A place to help disadvantaged kids find their potential. Not
some crazy little mail-order business. Maybe that's why the
thing never worked. It wasn't her true love, but like a job, it
was a living. Claudia's mind reeled on the subject, and she
concluded that it was futile to keep thinking about it. That topic
was dead and didn't even make her angry anymore. So maybe
He had delivered her out of some painful and unhealthy job
situations, but then to cast her on SSI? Forget it, she told herself.
It was a draw on that point.

"But what about Moms? She was still relatively young."

Claudia let a long ash from the end of her Benson &Hedges
fall into the tin ashtray that balanced on the arm of the chair.
On that point she had Him, and she still hadn't gotten to the
issue of Loretta. In her mind's eye she could see the vivacious
woman who had always loved her. "Mom," she whispered
hoarsely. "I miss you so much."

Pain gripped Claudia's chest, but no anger came with it this
time. Just a dull ache. She blew out a slow stream of smoke
and sighed, but no tears fell. As she turned her head toward
the window, Claudia looked at the vacant Laundromat across
the street and thought again of the old woman who stood there
describing how she'd lost her husband, sons, and grandson.

Then it became so clear. So frighteningly clear. How would
her mother ever have dealt with burying Loretta—her child,
her first baby? Claudia closed her eyes and felt her throat
tighten. She knew firsthand that it was always worse on the
ones left behind. Her father had someone now to fill the void.

But her mother would have changed, and her soul would have died from the slow mental torture of losing a grown child. At least her mother had gone quickly. Quickly enough to still believe that her children were fine, that they'd someday give her grandchildren, and still firm in her belief that they would live a good life. Perhaps there had been some mercy in the way He took her.

"If she had to go, thank you for sparing her this ugliness."

Claudia's voice had become almost a whimper, and she let go of the sob that had been trying to fight its way out for nearly an hour. "I can thank you for freeing me from Trevor, I can thank you for sparing my children, I can thank you for getting me out of a toxic career path, and I sincerely thank you for Nate . . . But I'll never understand why you took my sister."

Crushing out the cigarette, she let the tears fall without wiping them away. There was no sense to the end of a young, vital life. Sitting there in the dark room, she could come to terms with the rest of it, even come to terms with trying to rebuild her own life again. Nate had given her hope, and restored her faith that there were good people in the world—even if he was gone now, too. But she knew that there would always be an indescribable hollow in her heart when she thought of Loretta's death. Until that was answered, until that part made sense, she and God could only be on civil terms at best.

Claudia allowed the tension to drain from her body. She wasn't angry or worried about Nate's whereabouts anymore— just tired. It was a strange fatigue. Something almost close to peace. Maybe, finally, surrender.

Nate hurried down JFK Boulevard, and stood outside on the corner for a moment to get his bearings. He had just missed Ed, his old partner, and had wanted to try to catch up with him at one of the local happy hour spots where he was sure Ed would be. Although it was risky and against his own recovery process, he had to find him. But where were the current watering holes these days? Doug Hedgeman's on Thirteenth and Spider Kelly's on Mole Street were gone—having been torn down to make way for the new Justice Center. The Second Office, home away from home for the barristers, used to be on Thirteenth and Race, but was demolished to make way for the new Convention Center. He'd have to catch up to Ed at home later.

With the old taverns gone, that meant that none of the old bartender's were around to drop him tidbits of information. The realization that he wasn't connected hit him like a ton of bricks. He was an outsider now. Suddenly it felt like he had been transported to a new city in a different time zone. He began to panic, like someone disoriented by a stroke who had lost their way. He had to go to somewhere familiar, find someone familiar, anywhere that he wouldn't feel like a displaced ghost. It was a feeling of complete vertigo.

At five thirty, the only person that he might be able to track down immediately was Isabella, Ramirez's cousin in Camden. They'd flirted and been friends for years, and she had always kept her finger on the pulse of the underground network. In fact, she was probably more of a source for the goings-on in City Hall than her cousin. It was a well-known equation that, if you wanted to know anything about anybody, ask their secretary. And Isabella had not only cocktail waitressed at The Second Office for years and knew all the players, she and a couple of her girlfriends had also temped by day for several firms in the area. But how the hell was he going to get over to Jersey? He'd left his van parked in West Philly and didn't want to chance bumping into Claudia until he settled his business. He'd call her later, and could only hope that she'd be okay until then.

Changing directions, he hurried down to the rent-a-car office. As he hopped into the mid-sized sedan, he fought with his brain to recall the exact address over on east 28th Street. Did Isabella's block come in on Lincoln, or was she on the numbered street? Exasperated, Nate just decided to cruise around until he found it.

When he finally spotted the tiny row house, he sighed a breath of relief. But his temporary enthusiasm was halted by a barrage of reality checks. What if she was working a night shift, hostessing somewhere? Or what if she had a date, or a husband by now, who wouldn't understand an innocent pop-call? For that matter, what if they'd moved? He was handling this all wrong, and bumbling everywhere. What the hell was the matter with him? He used to be so on-point, so sure. . . .

Nate pushed the issues out of his mind and walked up the short flight of concrete steps and rang the bell. He could immediately hear a clamor of women's voices inside, speaking in an agitated flurry of Spanish. When Mrs. Gonzales opened the door and smiled, all of his previous fears dissipated.

"Oh, Señor McGregor, you are a sight for sore eyes!" she exclaimed, reaching up to give him a meaty hug. "Come in, come in. My prayers have been with you for so long," she urged, taking him by the hand and half dragging him over the doorsill.

It felt so good to be somewhere that hadn't changed in half a decade. "Señora, I think of you all often. It's wonderful to see you, too," he said, genuinely glad to bask in the older woman's warmth. Returning her hug, he added, "And I hope your family's been well?"

"Sí. Everyone is very fine. You *must* stay and have something to eat. I have just come in from work, and Isabella doesn't have class tonight, so she should be in soon. Please tell me that you'll stay?"

It was a Latino verson of Southern hospitality, with a touch of motherly matchmaking added. Nate smiled. "Of course, but only if it's no bother?" It was a rhetorical comment, since Mrs. Gonzales had inquired about the state of his childless marriage for years. And now that he was a widower . . .

Her smile broadened and she clicked her tongue in mock annoyance. "Trouble? For a nice, handsome, attorney friend of my nephew to wait for Isabella?" she said with a dismissing wave of her hand. "But, you will have to wait in the parlor with my mother until I can get something ready. Okay?"

The short woman hurried past him. Within seconds, a heated barrage ensued between Mrs. Gonzales and the older woman who sat in an overstuffed wingback chair with her arms folded in unmistakable defiance. Although they didn't speak to each other in English, it wasn't hard to tell that he had been the cause of the commotion.

Nervously moving toward the sofa, Nate looked at the stern expressions that passed between the two women. "If I've come at a bad time," he hesitated, "I can come back later when—"

"No, no, don't be silly. My mother will behave herself and watch TV," Mrs. Gonzales said hurriedly, cutting him off and flashing a warning glare at the older woman in the chair.

"Now, Mama, *por favor,* you will not scare him with your crazy talk. He is a guest in this house, and we do not make guests feel unwelcomed." Then as though nothing out of the ordinary had happened, Mrs. Gonzales turned to him and smiled reassuringly. "It is all right. She is just getting on in years and cannot leave the old ways behind. Would you like some tea or coffee?"

Nate respectfully declined the offer and watched the senior Mrs. Gonzales from the corner of his eye while pretending to look at the news program. The younger of the two had disappeared into the kitchen, and he sat in silence with a woman who appeared to be in her late eighties. She never uttered a word until they could hear the rustle of pots and pans in the kitchen.

"I know what you are thinking," the elderly lady began in a low voice. "That I do not want you to see my granddaughter, Isabella, because you are Negro."

Nate had to smile, because that's just what appeared to be the trouble. What else could've been wrong? Hell, the older generation in his family had acted the same way when he decided not to marry a girl from the West Indies. Even though

Monica was African-American, they'd acted like he had brought home an alien, and put her through a virtual FBI security clearance screening before they relented. Her lineage, her pedigree, her intentions . . . they'd truly embarrassed him the first time he'd brought her home. Nate had to smile as the shoe was tied to the other foot—his.

Deferring to age, he offered the old woman a graceful way out. Anything to avoid the possibility of another embarrasing altercation between Mrs. Gonzales one and two.

Taking a deep breath, Nate steadied the mirth in his voice. "No. I understand that I am not Catholic, and—"

"Ach!" she huffed and waved a feeble hand. "God is God."

Nate only nodded. For whatever the reason, the old lady didn't like him, so he'd leave well enough alone. Besides, he just wanted to talk to his old *platonic* friend—not get married. But to get that message across, he'd need more than the ability to speak fluent Spanish, which he couldn't. He'd need a neon sign.

"I know that my Isabella is not for you, is why," she finally said with a tone of impatience. "I have tried to tell my daughter, Maria, this so many times. But she does not listen to me, or what the spirits have to say."

Nate returned a blank look and just nodded. He knew better than to even address the subject. When his grandmother and Aunt Flo used to start that hoodoo mess, he would get out of Dodge. Fast. That stuff from the old country was beyond comprehension, and there was no way to logically debate with people once they got on the subject.

Apparently not getting enough of a response from him, the senior citizen pressed on with her conviction. "I know Maria wants for a husband with a good title for Isabella, and I told her there is one waiting for the girl. But it is not you. She doesn't understand that the saints guide the way they want to—not they way you decide. Comprendo?"

Nate nodded his head yes. "I agree. We should all leave well enough alone." There, that should close the issue, he thought, offering her a pleasant smile before returning his attention to the nightly news.

She answered his peaceful gesture with a snort of dissatisfaction. "You have good manners to humor an old woman. I can see why Maria wishes it was you. But I can tell you do not believe in what I say."

He was busted. The woman sitting across from him was definitely old, but she was obviously not senile.

"Ma'am, I haven't lived long enough to be as wise as you."

"And very good with the words, too, Mr. Attorney. You flatter this old woman, but do not answer my question."

She was as tough as his grandmother. Nate chuckled. "I'm sorry."

"No, it is not your fault. You have a warm and handsome smile. But you are still a baby, a puppy. When you are ninety-two, then you will understand."

"I hope so," he said honestly. "People don't live that long these days."

"But you have so many angels looking over you. This is what I must talk about now."

He hated this quasi-religion superstitious hocus pocus, and could tell that he was about to embark upon a "Twilight Zone" conversation. Old people.

As though the elderly woman had read his mind, she broke into a wide toothless grin. "I see. So, you need some evidence, eh?"

"No, Ma'am, I just—"

"You have a woman in your life now, who has touched your heart deeply."

Nate became still for a moment, but then the rational side of his brain dissected the comment and he relaxed. What healthy, average male didn't have a female companion? A good try. Out of courtesy, he nodded in the affirmative to confirm her guess.

"You knew this girl for a long time, a few years, but recently, you have become close."

Again he stilled, and the old woman smiled knowingly.

"She has had some problems, and you have helped her. But soon she will help you. This is a good girl. Clean and decent. Which is why you have not touched her the way a man touches a woman, yet—even though you want to. All in time."

Nate felt his face flush and he coughed as he tried to think of a respectable way to reply. He was literally stunned by the accuracy of her charge, and nobody knew about Claudia. Nobody.

Nodding her head slowly with triumph, the woman began again. "Now, you believe me?"

"I don't know what I believe," he stammered.

"Well, it is a start."

They both sat in silence for a moment, then she spoke again in a very low voice. "You and this girl are in great peril from dark forces. Please be very careful, Señor. I will light a candle and pray for you. You have already lost a great deal. That was the will of God. But this can be avoided if you listen to the spirits who guide you. Watch for the signs."

Nate was paralyzed by the comment and fixed a steady gaze on the woman before him but did not speak.

"There are two women in your life that must come to help you. One is the small brown girl who is here. The other was very close to her . . . She is taller, lighter, not *blanca*, but more like crème in coffee. Colored. She is in the spirit realm. She died an untimely death, and she guards the one you love. There is something that she must tell you, her soul does not rest. Do not fear, she will help protect you, but—"

"Mama! I thought we agreed to not discuss this craziness with our guest. Ever."

The junior Mrs. Gonzales was standing in the doorway with one hand on her hip and seemed to be extremely perturbed. The older of the two only shook her head with obvious disgust.

"Maria, I am trying to save this boy's life, and you are interfering with my work!"

From there, the conversation switched to Spanish again, and

a heated debate ensued. Nate tried to inject a mild defense for the grandmother, while treading delicately within the boundary of politeness in an attempt to assure the younger Mrs. Gonzales that he had not been offended. It was hopeless. Were it not for the sound of a key in the door, he wouldn't have known what to do next.

All three participants in half English, half Spanish chaos stopped when Isabella entered the room.

"What is going on in here?" Isabella exclaimed, before squealing with delight and rushing over to give him a hug. "Nate McGregor? Tell me I'm dreaming! How are you?"

Relieved to have such a timely distraction, he held Isabella out from him a ways then returned her hug. "I'm just fine, and you look fantastic. So what's this I hear about you being back in school?"

"Let me take you for a bite to eat and I'll tell you all about it."

The two older women looked horrified.

"I have just prepared dinner, and you don't ask a gentleman out. Isabella!" Mrs. Gonzales chided sternly.

"Mama, please. He didn't come here to sit and listen to all of this confusion."

Nate braced himself for another outburst, which came again in Spanish. But to his relief, Isabella began ushering him out the door as she continued to make her point. Turning to the two older women he shrugged quickly. "It was nice meeting you again." Before he could say anything else, Isabella's firm tug, however, helped end his goodbye.

"Come back again when my daughter will allow you to have dinner. *Cuando volvera usted?*" he heard her mother call behind him.

"*No se olvide!*" her grandmother called out strongly. "Don't forget, all right!"

Once out on the sidewalk Isabella turned to him and grinned. "See, next time you'll call ahead first. With those two, I imagine you've had quite a visit."

Nate shook his head and laughed. "Oh, God! You don't know the half of it. They remind me of my aunties."

She gave his arm an affectionate squeeze. "C'mon, I'll drive. You can leave your car here. We'd better go before Mama comes out on the steps."

They drove for a short while, laughing as Isabella caught him up on the latest who's-sleeping-with-who gossip until they reached the diner on route 130. Once settled into the booth, Isabella became more serious and her gaze was tender.

"We were all so worried about you, Nate. Angel and the gang would ask Ed how you were from time to time . . . It must have been terrible."

He looked at the beautiful young woman before him, her rich dark hair catching the light as she tossed it behind her ear nervously. "I'm much better now. Really. But, how are you?"

She smiled and looked down at her silverware. "I'm seeing someone. He's really nice."

A rush of relief washed through him. He had always secretly wondered what would have happened between them were he not married, and when that eventuality became a reality, he couldn't deal with any woman. The last person he would have wanted to hurt or burden with his four-year bout with alcohol and depression was this wonderful creature sitting before him. He was divided, if not slightly conflicted, about Isabella being spoken for by someone new.

"He sounds special. So I'm nosey, as your big brother, how did you two meet?"

She returned another shy smile. "At the hospital. I work there now in personnel. I'm not temping or waitressing anymore. I'm going to Camden County Community College, and then I'll try to transfer to Rutgers to become a nurse. That's what I always wanted to do."

"Well, he's a lucky man to have captured your heart," he said with honest admiration. "So, tell me about him." Feeling a tug of competitiveness, he just had to ask.

She stopped for a moment as the waitress came to take their

orders, and then spoke in a low, confidential tone. "Promise not to tell Angel?"

The secrecy bothered him a little, but he nodded his consent. "Is there something wrong with him that you don't want your cousin to know?"

Isabella looked back at him for a moment then laughed. "Oh, no. He's wonderful. He's a doctor! Can you believe it? But if Mama and Grandma found out, they'd scare him away. And . . . He's not Latino, or Catholic. They'd die if I brought a gringo home. That's the problem. I just want to be engaged before I tell anybody about him. Especially after what happened before I met Steve."

He knew he was prying, but he'd always found this twenty-eight-year-old woman extremely attractive. Although their relationship had been strictly platonic, she did stir something in him every time he saw her.

"What happened before that was so bad? Do I have to get together a posse with Ramirez and break some guy's knee-caps?" he said, half joking.

"No, God will get that jerk."

"So tell me."

"It's ancient history, but about a year ago I was temping over at Addison Development and met the suave Mr. Addison himself."

Nate felt his grip tighten on his water glass. "And."

Isabella hung her head and looked down at her napkin. "I was only there for a day or two, but he got my number and would meet me for dinner or a drink. One thing lead to another, and I really fell for this guy."

"He's a snake. You don't need to get anywhere near him." Nate was almost nauseous from the thought of Eric Addison putting his hands on her.

"You don't have to tell me. I was so stupid, and found out the hard way."

Her eyes had an additional shine from the tears that he knew she held back. It confirmed his suspicion. She'd slept with him.

"He told me I was the only one, and made me think we were a couple. You know. So I told Mama ... Stupid."

"Don't do that to yourself, honey. He's just a low-life who preys on people."

"Well, I went to his office, and he wasn't in. So I was going to leave a note for him, just a cute little I-love-you note. But his partner was there—some tall, gorgeous, black chick ... Well, we wound up having sort of an argument. I found out that he was seeing her, too, which explained why I only got to temp for a couple of days while she was on vacation. I could die everytime I think about it."

Nate was speechless. He could see the hurt registered on her face. Maybe he would still break Addison's kneecaps, or at least his jaw.

"Do you know that he had the nerve to call me about six months ago and ask me to temp while he went on his honeymoon? I told him that he and his partner would have to find another fool. Then he said that he wasn't marrying his partner, and she was no longer at the firm or in his life—but he'd love to see me when he got back. It may sound crazy, but I even felt bad for his lady partner. She was probably just as upset as I was, and she had to work there every day. So I just told him to drop dead."

"Is that why you left Philly to work in Jersey?"

"No, not really. I just felt like I wanted to be respected and stop working these dead-end jobs where I could be pushed around. You know? So, I finally had to tell Mama what happened. She was so mad ... I made her promise not to tell Grandma, cause she probably would have burned a candle on him. But you know my mother. Sooner or later she told, and Grandma swears the man is the devil himself! It took a long time for them to let it be, and I just asked her to help me get a good job. Unfortunately, Mama couldn't get me into Cooper Medical Center, where she works. But her friend, Mrs. Alvarez, got me a permanant secretary job at Rancocas Valley. It's a commute, but I get full tuition remission if I work days, and I can go to school at night."

"Good for you. Isabella, I've always admired you, and knew that you deserved good things to happen for you."

"I met Steve there in the cafeteria. Can you believe it? He's an intern, and has to make all the rounds on all wards. A lot of times I would see him in Pediatrics, too, because I would hang out there to try to learn from the nurses. So one day we had coffee, and he asked me what I wanted to do. I told him, and he encouraged me to go back to school."

When their meal came, Nate was glad for the interruption. He didn't even want to discuss why he had stopped by to see Isabella now. She had obviously gone on with her life, and it was a positive change for her. To reintroduce her to anything associated with that slime-ball, Addison, seemed inappropriate.

"I've been talking about myself all this time," Isabella said while munching on a fry. "Enough about me, how about you?"

He tried to skillfully deflect the probe into his rather uneventful existance, but he could tell from the look on Isabella's face that the attempt would be futile. "Okay," he finally said, giving in to her smile. "I've met someone really nice, too."

Isabella nearly startled him when she reached over quickly and took both of his hands. "Oh, thank God! Do you know that I've had the biggest crush on you since forever?"

He laughed to disguise how flattered he was by her admission, but for the life of him, he could not understand female logic. Rather than ask for an explanation, he returned the compliment with true admiration. "Really? Well, not as big as the crush I've always had on you."

She let her gaze slide away from his, her complexion becoming rosey from the blush that crept over her cheeks. "I thought that you might have come for more than a friendship bite to eat . . . and now with Steve, it would have been so hard to choose."

Nate had to chuckle. He understood the dilemma well . . . and she had definitely assuaged his ego.

"That sounded so—"

He held up his hand to stop her awkward apology. "It sounded just perfect. Everytime I see you, Isabella, I get a slight case of the butterflies. I didn't want you to take this wrong either, and was glad when you told me you had somebody. Truthfully, if you didn't, well . . . Let's just say it might have been hard to do the right thing."

They both sat for a while in silence, enjoying their meal and each other's company. Finally, unable to contain himself, Nate allowed his mind to wander back to the thing that haunted him earlier. Eric Addison.

"You know, Isa, Eric is an equal opportunity exploiter. He's been after some of my properties, and is probably going to get some of his inside flunkies at L&I to code violate me soon."

She covered her mouth with her hand and gasped. "No!"

"Nobody is able to withstand a fine-tooth comb, especially with the older buildings. Something's always wrong with them. The key is, does the landlord jump right on it and fix it when there is a problem? That's how you tell who's trying to make an honest effort, versus who's trying to be a slumlord."

"Why that no good, low-life—"

"I know, I know," Nate interjected calmly. "I wasn't going to say anything, especially after I heard that you had been in a relationship with Addison, but it was gnawing at me. I know that you used to know a lot of people in town . . . And I've been so out of it lately . . ."

"What do you need, Nate? I can find out what this bastard is up to. You know I will, too."

"I know, Isa. But I don't want to do anything that could get you in trouble with this guy. He's dangerous."

"Well, I know some pretty dangerous guys, too. I don't deal with them, but my cousins . . . You know what I'm talking about?"

"Yeah, well, I'm trying to find out who his inside man is. The person who will either code me or go around checking the buildings. See, the way I figure it is, I can have my tenants look out for any strange people hanging around and asking questions. That way, I'll know before it goes down, and can fix the problem before they code me. But I've got so many buildings around the city, that I don't want to call all my tenants and start some mass hysteria or anything. Besides, it's only me and two other guys doing the maintenance, since for the most part, everything is in fairly good condition. But I can't be sure that on the day they come, they won't find some minor crap to jump on. It's harrassment. Pure and simple. And I've just gotta protect whatever's being singled out."

Isabella frowned as she folded her hands under her chin. "You know, there was this sort of sleezy guy that came in twice when I was working there. Then, when I'd be out for a drink with Addision, a few times he got up from our table to go over to the bar and talk to him. Once, I remember, he handed the guy an envelope, but Eric was pissed that the guy came to our table to get it."

"What did this guy look like?"

"Just your average Joe. Brown hair, brown eyes, about five nine, kinda thin."

"Nationality?"

"He was a white guy, but not Italian."

"What makes you say that?"

"When I say brown, I mean sandy, not dark brown hair or eyes. And Eric called him by a last name that didn't sound Italian. Something like Jenks? Maybe Jenkins?"

"I'll keep my eyes peeled. Thanks, Isa."

"Wait a minute. You know, Nate, come to think of it, I thought I saw him in the hospital for about a week, wearing a maintenance uniform—like around the time I started six months ago. But then, I never saw him again after that, or the guy who looked like him anyway."

Nate turned his spoon over and over again and let his mind sort out the pattern of information that Isabella had given him. It was sketchy at best, but it was worth a shot.

"I don't want you to get into any kind of trouble on the job, but do you ever run across personnel files when you're in the office there?''

Isabella hesitated, and he rushed in and censored himself. ''Look, forget it. It's not that important. I know what the guy looks like and that's enough. Do you want some dessert?''

She didn't answer immediately, but then shook her head no. ''This job is really important for me, you know, Nate?''

''I'm sorry. Seriously. Forget it. Let's order some coffee, okay?''

''No, but, if it's not the guy, then it's not the guy. But what if Addision had sent that slime around to check up on me or something? That's scary.''

Nate hadn't considered that, and it was unnerving. ''I'm telling you, the guy is sick. He might have been pissed that you dumped him and meant no. Eric Addison has an ego the size of Canada, so maybe once he saw you, and called for a last ditch effort, he gave up.''

''Eric did call me the week I saw that guy hanging around the hospital. Like I said, about six months ago, though. I haven't heard from him since, so it's probably nothing. However, I don't like it.''

''Neither do I.''

''Well, one thing's for sure, I'd love to see him get his.''

''Darling, you'd have to get in a very long line.''

When their places were cleared, he ordered coffee and a piece of lemon meringue pie for each of them, despite Isabella's half-hearted protest. He could see her mind still grappling with the information, and he was truly sorry that he'd ruined her once-sunny disposition.

''Tell you what, Nate,'' she said, following the comment with a sip of coffee. ''I'll go back in the files and look up all the temporary and part-time maintenance workers whose last names begin with Jen. I'll only go back six months.''

''Uh-uh, I said forget it and I mean it. I shouldn't have even gotten into this.''

"Hey, you aren't the only one that has a grudge against Eric. Besides, if he has some jerk stalking me, I wanna know.''

"How are you going to go through all of those files without getting caught?"

"Counselor, I study in my office at night. With Mama and Grandma at home, can you blame me?''

They both laughed.

"Anyway, I use the computer, with my boss's permission, all the time to do my assignments. And I'll have Steve there, who works weird hours, to drive me home if it gets too late. If I can narrow it down on the system, then I can look in the file cabinet for the guy's picture. Everybody has to have a badge to work on any floor. In his file, I can get name, rank, serial number—but most importantly, his social security number.''

"If I have a number, Isa, *and* a picture, I can find out anything—from where he works to if he has a criminal record. If the bastard's got a record, I can get him picked up for jaywalking near my buildings.''

"And if you get rid of him, Nate, through honest means, of course,'' she said smiling, "then I can sleep at night.''

She had an open and shut case. They'd both benefit, thwart Addison, and it was obvious that Isabella was clearly up for a little feminine revenge. Hell hath no fury . . .

"But only, I repeat, only, if you can do it without something crazy going down on your job. You've come too far.''

"And we go back, you and I, real far, too, Nate. This guy shouldn't be allowed to just walk on everybody.''

"You're a hard case, Gonzales. What am I going to do with you?''

"Meet me for lunch in the cafeteria in a couple of days so I can give you your info.''

Chapter 9

Claudia stood at the closet doorway and rummaged in the darkness. Pulling her only good purse off of one of the back hooks on the closet wall, she yanked at the coat that she had previously wanted to sell, freeing it from a hanger and sliding it on. Claudia grimaced as the wool texture enveloped her. Darned coat just reminded her of the funeral. . . .

But that didn't matter now, she had to go next door. She told herself that she could do it. She could simply go into the bar next door and buy some cigarettes. Why should she have to walk all the way down to the Seven-Eleven when there was a machine that carried her brand right next door? Besides, at ten o'clock at night, that was a dangerous proposition— especially since she was all dressed up and looked like she had money on her. What a joke. When her shin collided with the edge of the coffee table, she muttered a curse, and continued to pat around with her hand until she felt the cold metal of her keys.

Minutes later she pulled her lapels up with annoyance, and sheilded herself from the chill in the air. Or was it an internal chill that ran down her spine? she wondered, as she looked at the front door of the Watusi Pub. Taking a deep breath, Claudia steadied herself and fixed her gaze on the cigarette machine while opening the door. She'd get in and out. That's it. Simple.

Without looking down, she felt her bag for the familiar placement of the clasp. It wasn't there. Inspecting the unfamiliar expensive leather more closely, she almost gasped as she brought it up near her face with both hands. This wasn't her bag at all. It was Loretta's.

For an instant she couldn't breathe, and she stood blocking the narrow aisle as people bumped and pushed her about, making their way to and from the center bar. Her mind scrambled for an answer, then it hit her. This was the bag that her sister had carried to the hospital the day she died. When they gave her Loretta's personal effects, Claudia remembered being in a daze. The nurses had put Loretta's clothing in a plastic bag, but she was already in possession of her sister's purse, and had held onto it while Loretta went in for surgery. She could remember Loretta's upbeat admonishments. . . . "Girl, this bag cost me three hundred dollars! I've got my gold Amex in there, my Rolex, credit cards, and driver's license. Don't you go puttin' it on the floor or somethin'—that's bad luck. And I'll have your hide if I get *victed*. You can't trust these people who work in here . . ."

Fresh tears welled in Claudia's eyes, and the distinctive designer logo on the front of the purse became blurry. She hadn't set that bag down for a minute while Loretta was in surgery. She had hung onto it like a frightened child clutching a rag doll, and had never let go of it the entire time she waited for her father and Miss Dot to get to the hospital. Nor had she let go of it while she drove home that night. Claudia could remember vividly how she had ignored the business papers, numbly rifling through them until she found something personal—something that would make her know that Loretta was still there. Another chill ran through her as she recalled how she had sat with the wallet in her lap for a long time, looking at the pictures that held so many memories until the hurt was too much to bear. Almost in a trance, she remembered how she had calmly hung it on the back hook in her coat closet, thinking at the time, Loretta would be needing it when she came home from the hospital—her sister could not be dead.

"Yo, Claudia. Where you been at, stranger?"

Claudia looked up slowly toward the direction of the voice, her eyes needing a moment to focus, and her brain requiring much longer to string together the words until they made sense.

"Uhmph, Uhmph, *Uhmph!* Baby, you look good for being gone a whole week. Done found yourself another watering hole uptown, or what?"

Claudia stared at the bartender, but didn't move.

"The usual? A little shot of Stoli, straight-up?"

Claudia shook her head no, and began backing toward the door, but a new flow of patrons bustled her in more closely to the bar.

"Not tonight, Jamal," she said weakly.

"Oh, waitin' on your new Sugar Daddy to get here to hook you up? Well, I know where you live, girl. You okay wit me. Just run a tab till he gets here."

"I don't have a Sugar Daddy—"

"Yeah, and I ain't pourin' licka. Look at ch'you, *baby.* You sho' look good *tonight!* Got'cha hair all fried, dyed, and laid to the side. Silk dress on, high heels, makeup. Brick house action, if you ask me."

Claudia couldn't move.

"Since you one of my regulars, and so fine tonight, this one is on me," he said while pouring, and set a brimming glass on the edge of the bar.

"Yo, man. That's discrimination," a patron called from behind her.

Jamal laughed and filled a beer order. "Hey, I'm a discriminatin' gentleman when in the company of a fine woman."

The three men in front of her laughed and one got up. "Hey,

suga, c'mon up here and keep us company. If your man don't show up, we got somethin' for ya.''

"I just need change for the cigarette machine," she said, finally finding her voice. "I don't drink anymore."

"Oh, pulleeze!" she heard a woman mutter from the seat to her left. "Can *I* get some service in here or what?"

"Chill out, Ester," Jamal said with a brilliant smile. "A man can only get to 'em one at a time."

She had to get out of there. She'd just walk the block and a half to the store. As Claudia turned and headed toward the door, she heard a familiar voice over the din. "Get the lady a ginger ale."

Again, her brain was not assimilating this new information fast enough. She turned toward the direction of the voice, forcing her eyes to focus through the haze of smoke and dim blue and red lights that engulfed her. It was Nate.

Unable to move, she watched him as Jamal took back the shot glass of vodka and replaced it with a clean tall glass of bubbling substance. She didn't advance toward the familiar face that stared at her without smiling. Instead, she turned and bolted out of the establishment, ignoring the jeers and commotion behind her. She needed air.

Claudia stood on the curb for a moment to still herself. She needed to run, needed to cry, needed distance. Anything. Turning toward the Wingz joint, she began to run, ignoring the footsteps behind her and the voice that repeatedly called her name.

Her arm jerked and she spun around to face Nate, then she snatched away from him as she walked briskly toward her objective. To hell with him.

"Claudia, look, let me explain."

"Explain what?" she said, her chest heaving from the exertion and a sudden burst of anger. "Explain that you promised to come back in a couple of hours and we'd go out? Or explain why you were sitting in a bar!"

Nate moved in front of her and held both of her upper arms.

"Look, I had business to take care of, all right? And since when do I have to report in to you like I'm in boot camp or something?"

She was stunned by his response, and she blinked twice. "You're right," she said as evenly as possible. "You don't."

Claudia began walking again, and refused to look at the man who paced beside her. She felt so foolish. Here she had laid claim on him after only a week, and was acting like she was his wife. It was pathetic. What was wrong with her?

Nate didn't come inside the store as she purchased her cigarettes, but when she opened the door to leave, he was still there. She brushed by him without a word, but the fact that he was all dressed up in a suit had not escaped her.

As they more slowly made their way back up the street, she glanced at Nate from the corner of her eye. He looked so different, so in charge, and so thoroughly handsome. She had been right. He had left her apartment as one person, only to return as someone else. It was obvious that this was the way he used to look all the time when he was a hotshot attorney. Claudia's logic ran unchecked. Why would someone like him ever want, or stay with, someone like her? It had been brief, it had been nice, but it was clearly over.

"I'm sorry, Claud," he mumbled as she neared the steps of her apartment.

"Like you said, you don't owe me any explanation," she mumbled back quietly, still looking down. "I'm sorry, too."

"I should have called, but I've had so much on my mind lately." Touching her arm, he stopped her advance up the steps.

"Have you eaten?" she asked remotely.

"Yeah, but why don't you come by my place so we can talk?"

"That's okay," she mumbled again, fishing for her keys.

"No. It's not. I need to talk to you."

Nate's expression held an intensity that demanded an answer. Feeling herself sway to his request, Claudia nodded. "Aren't you going to come in?"

"I don't live here," he said plainly, reaching for her hand.

"I thought you lived in the basement apartment? All of your mail comes here, and I've always seen you going in and out of the side door that leads down there."

"It's sort of crazy, but nobody knows where I live," he chuckled, ushering her toward Spruce Street.

Claudia stopped and raised one eye brow, growing suspicious.

"You in some kind of trouble?" Her mind raced forward. Maybe drug money had helped fund all of his property purchases? Maybe his whole story about being an attorney was a lie? What was she getting herself into?

Nate laughed and shook his head as she stood looking at him, not willing to budge until she got a plausible explanation.

"No. Nothing illegal. It's just that when everything crashed in on me, I did start living in the basement of that building. It's the closest one to my house—which felt too big to stay in all by myself at the time. I needed to regroup, so I made it my office and a place to lay my head. But as soon as my tenants found out that that's where I lived, I got no peace."

They started walking again.

"Claudia, people would call me at two in the morning for heating problems, plumbing problems, you name it. Finally, I got sick of not having a little haven of my own, so I moved around the corner into the house . . . and fixed it up a little just so I'd have somewhere to go. I still keep my mail at the building, park my van across from the bar with an extra house key behind the license plate, and my phone is listed in the yellow and white pages at the apartment address. When I'm gone, I just call forward the phone to my real spot. Or, if I don't want to deal with the damned thing ringing off the hook, I just let the answering machine in the basement on Forty-Fifth pick up. That way I can get some sleep, watch a movie or the game. I only wear a beeper during bad weather or during the day anymore. Folks were killing me. Satisfied?"

Finally, she smiled. She *was* satisfied, and the dread that had imposed itself on her for hours began to slowly lift. Turning onto Spruce, she finally voiced her second concern. "Nate, why were you in a bar? I know it's not my business, but . . ."

"Like I told you earlier, it was business. There were some people in there that I needed to talk to. If you'd stayed long enough, you would have noticed that I was drinking a club soda with a twist of lime," he said grinning.

Claudia studied him from the corner of her eye. "Did you see me when I first walked in?"

"Yup."

"Then, why'd you let those men hassle me?"

"Wanted to see what you'd do," he said, shrugging and still smiling. "You passed the test."

"The test!" Now she was angry. Seriously pissed off. Who in the hell was this guy to judge her like that? Games. She hated games.

Nate stopped her with a gentle tug on her arm. "You're gonna walk a hole right into this pavement, woman. Look, I didn't go into the bar to *test* you, okay. I had to catch up with the folks around here that know what's going on. Somebody is screwing with my buildings. When I saw you come in, I was frankly stunned. Then, I'll confess, I wanted to see if you were going to break your promise to me. If you had . . . Well, it would have put a serious strain on our relationship."

Relationship? Did he say they were in a relationship? All she could do was stare at the man.

"Don't you believe me?"

She didn't move, or dare breathe. Her heart was beating too fast.

Nate bent down and brushed her mouth with a light kiss. "See, no alcohol. Better?"

She stood stock still. This man *was* honest. He wasn't going anywhere. And he had claimed her. All she could do was nod.

"All right, Miss Harris, can we go now so I can get out of these duds and into some jeans and a T-shirt?" Then he hesitated a moment. "You look really nice tonight."

Nate's expression became contrite as a sudden flash of understanding reflected in his eyes.

"I really messed up, didn't I? Oh, man. I'm sorry. You're all dressed up because we were supposed to go out, and I'm talking about breaking down my gear to sit at home and flop on the couch. If you still want to go out, we can . . ."

"It's okay," she said, not masking the disappointment in her voice. "Some other time."

Nate looked down at the ground as he spoke. "You know, I'm so used to rolling on my own, and having no social agenda . . . I mean, going out . . . It's just that I really don't have myself in tune to that anymore."

She reached for his hand and their gazes met. "I know what you mean," she said honestly. "It'll be nice just having some company." Claudia offered him a weak smile as they made their way in silence up Spruce Street.

As they neared the corner of Forty-Sixth, she hesitated and looked at the large delapidated mansion that graced the corner. Nate let out a low chuckle, and stopped to look at her.

"No, that's not mine. It's a monstrosity that would take at least a quarter million in repairs just to fix it up."

Claudia was absolutely outdone. "A monstrosity? Are you blind, man? Can't you see the potential of this building?" Brushing past Nate she ran up the double-wide concrete steps. "Look at it, Nate. Really look at it. This thing must have eight to ten bedrooms . . . And the architecture . . ."

Nate watched absolute passion engulf Claudia's face. In the brief time that they'd spent together, he had never heard such fervor in her voice. She was pressing her nose against the glass of the porch window and cupping her hands around her eyes, to see what, he couldn't imagine. The entire building was dark, and only the lights from the street behind the abandoned house lit the inside. With a great deal of trepidation, he walked up the stairs to join her on the wide, open porch, half hoping that they wouldn't fall through the dry-rotted wood. He never imagined that Claudia was the materialistic type. But when it

came to houses, weren't all women? Perhaps, like always, he
was a bad judge of character when it came to women. He began
to regret ever telling her that he was fairly well-off financially.

"Just look at these white columns. This place looks like
Tara in *Gone with the Wind*," she said, sweeping her arms
about and smiling broadly.

She had a nice smile. Correction, a beautiful smile. But he
wasn't about to sink a fortune into restoring *Tara* in West
Philadelphia.

"Oh, Nate, and the inside," she said in almost a swoon.
"It has eighteen-foot ceilings. *Eighteen foot!* With a crystal
chandelier in the center ballroom . . . Oh, and the foyer . . . It's
marble. *Marble.* Look, look over here," she insisted, pulling
his sleeve and forcing his face closer to the dirty glass than he
wanted, "Look at that walk-in fireplace. Who in their right
mind could just abandon a place like this?"

"Somebody who didn't want to heat this damn place in the
winter," he said dryly, trying to ward off her enthusiasm. "Or
spend a mint in asbestos and lead paint removal."

"No vision," she said indignantly. "I'd heard that there's
even a theater in the basement. Can you stand it?"

"No."

"What's with you?" she finally snapped, losing her buoy-
ancy and turning around to face him.

"Look," he said, ready to walk her back to her apartment,
"I may have some property, but I'm not Daddy Warbucks,
and—"

"What!" she cut him off, cocking her head to the side. "Do
you think I am asking *you* to buy this?"

Nate cringed inwardly. He didn't know what to think, but
the look of outright shock in her expression told him he'd
definitely blundered somewhere.

Claudia didn't even wait for him to answer. She'd just sucked
her teeth and walked down the steps, heading back in the
direction of her own apartment. All hell was breaking loose

and he didn't know why. It had been like this all day. Maybe he should've just stayed home and skipped forward till tomorrow.

"Hey, Claud, wait a minute!" he called, jumping down the steps two at a time to catch up with the firey female who was again stomping down the street. For a little person, she sure could walk heavy when she was mad. Damn.

Spinning on him, she caught him off guard and they almost collided. "Of all the arrogant, egotistical, male macho innuendo I have ever heard in my life! What do you think I'd do, Nate McGregor? Sit at home and play bridge like a high-society matron, and fill up eight bedrooms with babies? Or, no—maybe I'd just have dinner parties and entertain the elite of Philadelphia in my West Philadelphia mansion that my *man* brought for me. Pulleeze!"

Nate just stared at her. Black women had a way of throwing their neck into gear with one hand on their hip, at the same time the other hand waved to the rhythm of their argument, when they were really fed up. It was poetry in motion. And despite all of his upbringing and experience that told him to never laugh when one was torqued this tight, he couldn't help himself. Claudia Harris was on a roll.

Finally putting up his hand as he let a chuckle escape, he gave in. "Sistah, my sistah," he drawled for emphasis, "you win. I'm sorry."

She drew a deep breath, obviously winded from fussing, which made him smile harder.

"Nate, that place is perfect for a school. Okay? That's all I was saying, is all."

"A school?"

"Yes. A damned school. Someplace that is right in the heart of the city, where our inner-city kids could have a chance to thrive. That's it. A decent place where they could learn the three R's, and about their history, and culture, and maybe the arts, and maybe how to run legit businesses. Something that isn't taught in the sixty-student corrals they call classrooms, or in buildings that look like maximum security prisons. Okay."

He was taken aback by the new dimension of Claudia Harris that had been revealed to him right out on the corner in the street. Now he really felt foolish. He'd had it all wrong. Shame washed over him, and he reached for her hands, knowing how shallow his assessment of her had been.

"Baby, I'm sorry. I didn't know that's what you saw when you were peeking through that window . . . I just—"

"Just thought I was spending your money for you and going on a shopping spree."

Hurt replaced the anger in her eyes, and her shoulders slumped with an exhale of breath. What had he done? She was not Monica.

"Let's walk and talk," was all he could say now, and she grudgingly moved beside him without saying a word.

During their half-block walk toward his house there was an awful silence. It was a draw, and something fragile had cracked open a void between them. Timing, his timing stank. And again, he was playing it all wrong with everyone, oddly out of sync with his environment and the people in it.

She could not believe Nate thought so little of her as they crossed the threshold of his home. Suddenly, Claudia wanted to go home, too. Not to her apartment, but to her *home*. She wanted to go up to her old bedroom and find her high school penant and memorabilia still there, along with her old teddy bears that boyfriends had won for her at Great Adventure. She wanted the same curtains to be there, not the new mini blinds that Miss Doris had installed when the room was redecorated. She also wanted her mother to be there, standing in the arch of the kitchen doorway, with her red and white stripped apron hugging her long waist, holding a big wooden spoon in her hand. Claudia needed those arms to fold around her now, and those time-roughened hands to smooth back her hair. There was nothing like the feeling of being pulled into her mother's embrace, where just the beating of that other soul's heart could still her own.

She took in her surroundings slowly, cautiously, trying to

get a bead on this person that she really didn't know—and who, obviously, didn't know her. His house was so different from what she expected, and she surveyed the quiet, conservative tappings of the mysterious man who ushered her through the vestibule of the turn-of-the-century brownstone.

When he helped her out of her coat, she let her gaze rove over the imposing mahogany furniture that graced the living room. It looked like something out of an old Victorian movie—everything from the highly polished antique wood moldings, the parquet wood floors, burgundy and crème brocade sofa, and dark green leather wing chair by the spotless fireplace that stood on a plush oriental rug next to a Tiffany floor lamp. The second door leading from the vestibule was a heavy imposing oak that held what had to be the original stained, leaded, beveled glass in it.

"I've got some iced tea in the fridge, or some soda?"

Claudia shook her head and declined the offer.

"C'mon back to the kitchen with me. I'll put on some tea."

As she followed Nate past the dining room she stopped in awe. There was an immaculately polished table that could easily seat twelve, shined so magnificently that looked like it was made of glass. Without thinking, she ran her fingers over the edge of it. The moss colored brocade chairs that matched were elaborately carved with high backs, and standing in a corner all by itself, was an ornate, eight-foot china cabinet, filled with delicate crystal on every shelf. She hadn't even noticed that Nate had stopped beside her until he flicked on the light. When it came on, the light danced from the glasses and the table surfaces with splendor.

"This is breathtaking," she said in a genuine amazement.

"I sold everything from my home with Monica, but I could never part with my grandmother's stuff."

Claudia allowed her gaze to rove over the old silver oval frames that held yellowed restored photos on the wall. She walked over to them on impulse, and touched the gilded edges carefully.

"That's my great-uncle, Sinclair. He came to this country first, then brought over my grandfather."

Nate stepped beside her, but she didn't need to look at him to see the pride, it had been registered in his voice.

"That's my Auntie Alma and Auntie Bertice. They were my grandmother's younger sisters. Nemom worked as a domestic, and Pop worked as a skilled carpenter. Every year during the depression, he got to keep a piece of his own work in lieu of pay, if it didn't sell. It took him ten years to give this to my grandmother." Nate turned and motioned for her attention toward the china cabinet. "He and Uncle Sinclair built that by hand, and the china, like the stuff in the living room, and some of my bedroom pieces, came from the estate of the old woman that my grandmother worked for. In those days, people who went into service worked at one place for a lifetime. When their employers died, sometimes things would come their way."

She looked at the longevity that surrounded her in the room, and again at the pictures on the wall, then back to Nate. "They must have struggled all their lives. How in the world did they manage to keep the faith?"

"I don't even begin to know, Claudia," he said shaking his head. "My grandmother was given a full set of silver with the service included. The old white woman said her children were ungrateful, and that my grandmother had been more to her than they had. The way Nemom told it, the woman said that since she'd spent her life polishing that silver, my grandmother should have it. To hell with the kids," he said smiling. "Pop's story, however, is the one that keeps me going."

Claudia looked at him questioningly. "Could it be any harder than what you just told me? Kids, a depression, a life of humble servitude . . . I can't even imagine."

Nate looked at the pictures as he spoke, shaking his head, his voice full of respect. "Pop left the islands at seventeen. He was trying to hook up with Sinclair, but, due to World War One, all immigration had been banned. So, he and a buddy, Melvin, stowed away on a ship that they thought was headed for the States. Only problem was, it was bound for Cuba, and they wound up in an internment camp, cutting sugarcane for pennies. The way I understand it, Cuba was worse than the wild, wild West in those days. Folks even went to church with a machete strapped on. Supposedly, Melvin died from malaria, and Pop escaped the plantations and made it to the city by foot. There's where he got a message to Sinclair who sent money to bring him to the States.''

She was speechless, and just allowed her fingers to graze another tintype.

''That's Melvin McGregor, my uncle, standing with my dad.''

''I thought he died?''

''Pop's buddy Melvin did die in Cuba, so as a tribute, Pop vowed that his first son would be named after his friend. Therefore, contrary to tradition, my grandfather's first son was named after his friend. His second son, my father, was named after his grandfather—which broke tradition again. Then came me, the second iteration, so I'm a second instead of being a third— because of the way my father wanted to pay tribute instead of taking direct credit for making his babies. We never made it to a third,'' he said wistfully. ''Wouldn't have been anyway, since Monica's family insisted that the boy be named after her father.''

''You know,'' she murmured quietly, trying to staunch the pain from the wound that she knew could never fully heal, ''most people from the States can't go back past their grandparents. I think it's really a blessing, and a source of strength to know your history—to know first-hand account of the struggles. It sort of makes your own pale in comparison, and I think that's what's wrong with the kids today. They have no idea of what people went through, or the sacrifice and discipline required to get this far. I wish I had something like this to hang onto.''

He reached out and touched her jawline, studying her face carefully as he spoke. ''Claud, that's why I was so angry when you said all that stuff about my people jumping off of banana boats, and such. They carried themselves with such dignity, and without formal education, were so well read ... When I got into school, a big Ivy League institution where kids came from households that my grandmother and aunts probably cleaned house for, I considered it blasphemy to get less than an A.''

She covered his hand with her own. "Nate, I am so sorry. I had no idea."

He smiled and gave her a little peck. "It wasn't your fault. You were coming down, and I wish you could have seen how I behaved week one."

Shame forced her to look away from him. "Is this your mother?" Claudia let her fingers trace the edge of the silver oval frame that held a proud looking matron with beautiful eyes, standing next to a dapper young Nathaniel Winston McGregor, senior.

"Yes. That was Mom."

Nate turned and walked toward the doorway that led to the kitchen. Instinctively, she knew that their tour of the past was over and understood the sensation that had made him end it. As she crossed the threshold, it was like walking into another era in a different house. Everything was modern. There was a black Krups coffee/espresso/cappaccino maker set on a black and white marble counter, a jet microwave hung over a separate built-in wall oven and broiler, and a small, twelve-inch Sony TV balanced on the edge of the glass and chrome breakfast table.

Newspapers were on every chair surface. Old *Newsweek*, *Business Week*, and *Black Enterprise* magazines were disguarded on the floor by a chair. An old coffee cup rested beside a stack of bills and a calculator, and a jar of nuts and bolts stood beside it. Immediately, she felt better. There was something comforting in the disarray. Somehow she just needed to know that Nate McGregor wasn't perfect.

"Sorry about the mess," he said scooping up an arm-load

of newspapers so she could sit down. "Wasn't expecting company," he added sheepishly, looking around with confusion for where he might throw them.

"Well, you saw *my* place, so don't even worry about it," she said, stifling a giggle as he opened an almost empty refrigerator. "Guess this is sort of like your real office, huh?"

"Yeah, this is where I hide out. Truthfully," he said closing the refrigerator and opening the cabinets to look for coffee cups, "I only use the bedroom, kitchen, the bathroom, and sometimes I go into my music room. No reason to dirty up the whole house just for one person."

"But, Nate," she protested, "why would you buy a three-story house with a basement, if you only use four rooms?" Claudia was incredulous.

"I didn't. My crazy partner, Ed, handled my investments while I was away, and shipped all of my stuff here. I had no idea about this place, and wouldn't have bought it, but he insisted that I had to live like a human being at some point. I think he was hopeful that I'd join him in practice again one day . . . So, I turned one of the six bedrooms into a music room upstairs. One I use, the other is where I store my file cabinet, and papers, and stuff I generally don't want to look at. The basement is just an additional storage area—overflow from the apartments. I thought about knocking out the front wall once, and turning it into a garage. But it would take too much trouble to tear up the landscaping. Plus, I'm sure the neighbors would have a fit if I broke the front line of the lawns. So, I made the third floor into its own two bedroom apartment."

He fiddled about casually and continued as he placed two mismatched cups in front of her.

"I've got a nice Penn grad student from Thailand up there. He's quiet, pays his rent on time, has his own separate entrance from the side yard, doesn't party, and doesn't bother me."

Claudia just shook her head. Dealing with Nate was like peeling back layer after layer of onion skin. Just when she thought she had him pegged, she learned more about this enigma of a man.

"Well, at least you allow yourself some music. And I thought *I* was bad."

Both of them laughed as Nate handed her several boxes of herbal teas to make a selection. "Name your poison," he said, filling up the kettle and turning on the gas burner in the center butcher block island range. "Want to see my moldy oldies?"

She laughed again, feeling the familiar ease between them return. "Absolutely," she said, choosing mint, and handing the boxes back to him. "Now, don't try to tell me you didn't party in your day."

Nate opened an obscure door that she hadn't noticed and grinned. "Party? Me? *Girl*, I defined the word! C'mon, I'll show you."

She almost had to take the narrow winding back staircase two steps at a time to keep up with him. It was obvious that Nate was used to scaling these daily, and she wondered if he even used the massive front stairway that lead to his museum living room. It was all she could do to keep her high heels from scratching the immaculate wood floors of the long hallway, and she followed behind him virtually on tip toes. Giggling with the thought of being banished from Nate's basketball court floors, she was relieved when they entered the bedroom-turned-music room and her feet sunk into deep-pile beige carpet.

He didn't seem to be paying any attention to her as he went right over to an elaborate stereo system that took up four levels of the built-in wood bookcases. The room was cozy and lived in, with a big, neutral, overstuffed sofa, a tan leather recliner, small oval antique coffee table, and a well-used fireplace.

"I see why you live in here," she exclaimed, moving over to the fireplace as he rummaged for albums.

"This is the inner sanctum. The Bat cave," he said triumphantly, turning on an old LTD ballard. "And this, my dear, was the seventies. Not a CD in the joint."

"Jeffrey Osborne! On the Wings of Love? Oh stop, you're killing me!"

"But wait, I've got Chaka Khan, Luther, Heatwave, The Emotions, Sister Sledge, EWF, as in, Earth, Wind, and Fire—and let us not forget, The Ohio Players, The Isley Brothers, The Commodores with Lionel Ritchie, not to mention, Stevie, the eighth wonder of the universe! But wait a minute, wait a minute," he said, sounding like a D.J. and rummaging some more. "Where are my old divas? Minnie Ripperton, Denise—my girl, Denise, Denise, *my Black Butterfly,* Phoebe Snow, Miss Thang, Miss Roberta *Flack,* Gladys, Re Re—the unmitigated queen of soul, and oh, my yes, *Phyllis* Hyman—Good, God! My Amazon diva of all divas, where are you . . . ?"

She was nearly doubled over with a sudden case of the giggles just watching him, and she kicked off her high heels without a second thought. The rug felt so good under her feet as she swayed and sang off key with the music. It was, indeed, the best hiding place in the world.

He looked at her and chuckled, and she couldn't tell which one of them was having more fun. Nate's boyish expression was one of sheer ecstasy, and she laughed with him as they time traveled back to the decade before the fall, letting out short squeals of recognition as he hunted and pecked through his treasures.

Following his line of vision to an album collection that took up the balance of the floor-to-ceiling bookcase on one side of the room, she had to smile as she looked at the impressive, leather bound law books that took up the other wall. Nate McGregor was definitely two people. A crazy, schizophrenic, complex individual, just like herself.

Humming and bopping to the beat, he walked over to the fireplace and threw on a couple of stray logs. Lighting it with the end of a half burnt newspaper, he called over the music, "Pick out something good, girl. We are here to party! I'll be back in a flash."

The fire caught slowly and she stood in front of the wall of albums, marveling as she sorted through them. From the corner of her eye, she watched him dash through the adjoining bathroom door and into the next room over. She could hear him bumping around and muttering to himself, as he searched for something to put on. By the time he returned, donning a pair of gray sweatpants and a T-shirt, she had settled on Stevie Wonder.

"You've got to play this, Nate. It's perfect."

Grabbing the album from her, he nodded with agreement and put on *I Wish*. As the Bass notes kicked in and the up-tempo music started, Nate popped his fingers and began pecking his neck, singing so loud and so off-key that she almost couldn't keep the beat, overcome again with laughter.

When the song ended, they had sung their lungs out, and were still laughing and winded as a slow ballard came on. "Can I stand a chance?" he said, using an old pick up line.

Still laughing, she stepped into his arms as they slow dragged around the room.

"All we need now is a blue light, and a basement."

"Ain't that the truth," she murmured, snuggling into his shoulder.

Maybe she was home.

Chapter 10

Their kiss began with a slow smolder, tentatively testing for acceptance, needing reassurance along the way. The music had stopped, yet she still felt transported to a time that she thought had been lost forever. She felt so secure in this moment, so safe from her world of worries . . .

"Oh, no!" Nate broke away from their embrace and headed out of the door, yelling over his shoulder. "Gonna burn down the house. The water's still on."

Dazed, she stood in the middle of the floor, and wrapped her arms around her waist. "Need any help?"

"No," he called up from the back stairs. "But that was a close one."

She began to wonder if Nate was referring more to their embrace than the kettle on the stove. Both were obviously past the boiling point, and he was definitely going to turn off the burner. Reluctantly, she flopped down on the sofa and waited for him to return. What was wrong between them? She was scared, too, but he seemed totally panicked. Reflexively, her mind wandered to the photos downstairs in the dining room.

Oddly, she hadn't recalled seeing one of his son or his wife. Even without their pictures hung, maybe there were just too many ghosts—too many issues to contend with before they became more than friends.

"Sorry 'bout that," he said cheerfully, bringing in two steaming mugs slowly and edging them onto the table. "Be careful, though. They're really hot."

After putting on another album, Nate sat down next to her. "You look blue. What's wrong?"

"I'm okay. This is really nice."

Nate glanced at her, but didn't look convinced. After an awkward moment of consideration, he popped up again, and left the room, yelling down the hall. "Forgot the napkins."

He was clearly becoming a basket case. She'd try to calm him down, if he sat still long enough.

When he got back, he plopped down next to her and handed her a napkin, an unopened sleeve of Oreo cookies, and a half eaten bag of Chip's Ahoys. "If we're gonna go back to the old days, we might as well go all the way."

She smiled and leaned over to kiss him, but he just gave her a peck and hopped up again and rushed over to the albums. "Want to hear some Roberta Flack? Or how about some Phyllis? Or—"

"Nate," she said, cutting him off gently. "Come sit down, and just relax for a minute."

After setting up the stereo with Grover Washington, he hesitantly took a seat next to her and immediately reached for his hot tea. She didn't say a word, but just smiled and opened the chocolate chip cookies and handed him one. Then she waited patiently as he downed it, chasing it with a swig of too-hot tea that burned his mouth in the process.

"Man! This is really hot," he blurted out as soon as he could swallow while reaching for another cookie. "Want one?"

She shook her head no. "You're nervous aren't you?"

Nate choked on the unswallowed crumbs from his mouthful

of cookie, and she had to slap his back before he could collect himself enough to speak.

"Me? Nervous? About what?" he wheezed, taking another sip of hot tea.

Fearing a possible catastrophe, Claudia gingerly pryed his cup away from him and sat it down on the coffee table. Touching his cheek gently, she tried to soothe his shattered nerves.

"Nate, I'm scared, too. All week long, we've been coming very close to this, but then all of a sudden we get cold feet and stop. And that's all right. We don't have to rush. There's no pressure here. I guess I'm sort of at fault, because I enjoy being around you so much . . . It's so different . . . If you don't think of me that way, I'd still want to be friends."

He looked down at his bare feet and let out a long breath. "You're out of your mind if you think that I don't think of you that way. And, no, I guess I don't want to be just friends . . ."

His confession seemed to actually cause him physical pain as he twisted the bag of cookies shut with a little too much force. She could see him glance at her from the corner of his eye, and she knew that silence would be the best course of action now. She was used to male rejection; at least on that level, Trevor had trained her well. But she didn't want to make this an issue and risk losing a wonderful friend. So she waited for him to respond or not respond. Either way, she just liked his company.

Finally, Nate drew a deep breath. "Like we talked about that first time it got heated between us, it's been over four years—almost five, and I have no idea of what'll happen or if it can happen, you know what I mean?" he stammered. "Plus, I always had a drink first. I just don't want to see that disappointing look on your face, if . . . I'm a lot older than you. Forty-one, and you can't be more than in your early thirties . . ."

She let her hand stroke the nape of his neck to stop his words. He seemed to be so torn, and in such turmoil, that she was at a loss for how to make it right. Again, another layer had been peeled back.

Choosing her words carefully, she tried to reassure him. "There is no way to disappoint someone when you're giving your heart. This won't be the olympics, and I'm not judging you. It's been as long for me, too."

"But you're a woman," he interrupted with a shy smile. "It does make a difference."

Claudia shook her head, refusing to allow him to let his fears take root. "I had someone tell me to my face—*my husband,* no less—that I didn't turn him on. But, you know what?" she added, forcing him to look at her. "What your words didn't say, your actions did. And each time you gave my tired, achy, evil, angry body a bath, then rubbed me down with baby oil, you made love to me with your gentle touch. None of us are perfect, Nate. Yet, you have a way of making me feel special and pretty again."

"You are pretty, Claudia," he whispered, staring at her for what felt like a long time.

"And we can take it one day at a time, okay?"

"Okay," he said in a low voice, brushing her mouth with a kiss.

The sensation of his breath against her lips made her stomach muscles tighten with anticipation. She returned his kiss tenderly, and soon she could taste the sweetness of the chocolate in his mouth as their tongues met. With ever bolder moves, he deepened each kiss, until she could feel the tension in his arm that now held her close enough to share his heartbeat. She wasn't sure of whether or not she was trembling harder than he was while they sat kissing, touching each other gently, questioning whether to continue. Yet, beneath the surface of their hesitant caresses and soft kisses, there was an undercurrent of repressed passion that begged for permission to escape.

Finally, Nate just looked at her intensely, and stood up, extending his hand. She placed hers in his and followed him into the bedroom, now herself becoming the one who was terrified. He must have seen the panic in her expression, because he took her face between his palms and placed tiny kisses on her nose, her eyelids, and her cheeks, until he covered every surface.

"You're beautiful, inside and out, Claudia Harris. Your husband was a fool."

Unbuttoning the front of her silk shirtdress slowly, he never lost eye contact with her until he lowered his head to place a kiss behind each fastening that he opened. As he slid down the length of her to kneel, she couldn't watch as her skin caught fire. Forced to close her eyes to the wondrous sensation of his touch, she was almost unaware of the silk garment as it fell away. His breath was now molten against her stomach, and his hands had become steady as he removed her half slip and stockings. As though reading his mind, she stepped out of the loose clothing at her feet, and he quickly pushed them aside, burning her thigh with his cheek. When he covered her belly with deep, warm kisses, and caressed her bottom with his palms, she felt herself sway as an involuntary moan escaped her lips.

With her eyes still closed, she felt him gently pushing her backward until her legs touched the high bed. Being with Nate felt so natural, as though they had been together before. . . . The awkwardness had vanished, and without hesitation she followed his silent request to sit on the edge of it while he removed her bra and panties.

Being with him was like falling from a high cliff without fear. In trust she let go, allowing herself to rest on her elbows while her head hung back with her eyes still closed. The wait for him to touch her was torturous. He was so close, yet felt so far away from her arms. She could hear him rustling about only inches from her, removing his clothes, all the while landing kisses on her legs as he took off his T-shirt and sweatpants. Unable to stand it any longer, she raised her head and opened her eyes, staring into his briefly before he brought his body up to blanket hers.

The initial skin on skin contact singed her, forcing her to

close her eyes again as she arched against him. This time, he took her mouth hungrily, and she returned his ardent kiss with unrestrained desire. The inferno that had been beneath the surface broke through their wall of isolation, consuming them both in a flash fire as he moved against her.

When he left her mouth, he began a trail of torment down the center of her body. She could only cry out as he buried his face between her thighs, taking her past the edge of shame. Tears crept from behind her tightly shut lids as his mouth drew her passion to the fore. Nothing mattered while he continued to decimate her inhibitions. Although she dug into the comforter with clenched fists as a wave of anguishing pleasure swept through her, Nate held her firmly under her bottom. His message was clear, he was determined to drive her insane.

Without warning, a convulsion ripped through her, and she heaved and crashed into the explosive sensation again as a second wave of ecstasy quickly followed it. When she felt Nate's warmth cover her this time, he was breathing hard and his entire body was now like granite.

"I'll just be a moment, baby," he managed between deep gulps of air, hesitating for a second as though grappling with the rational side of his brain.

She watched in agony, waiting for his touch again as he crossed the wide expanse of bed to reach the night stand. Just looking at him sent a current through her. She could see his upper arms trembling while he sat on the edge with his back to her. When he took another audible breath, she felt it. They had been connected in those brief few moments. . . .

She studied his strong back and the deep valley his spine created between the muscles that flanked it. Each time he took a breath, she watched the way his shoulders expanded and contracted over his deep chocolate skin. Watching the way the muscles in his massive upper arms rippled as he worked with the unseen package his hands now held made them seem all the more like they were designed to hold her.

Anticipation swept through her body, and she tried to steady her own breathing when she heard the sound of the foil tearing. For just an instant, she allowed herself to dream. What if they could be like this forever, not needing condoms, not needing to protect themselves, perhaps even making babies . . . ?

Nate's return to her was swift, and again he covered her with his body, trembling from restraint and letting a deep exhale escape through his nose. "I don't want to hurt you, baby. You're so delicate, and you haven't for so long . . ."

Finishing his sentence with a kiss, she smoothed his strong shoulders with her hands and held onto his upper arms. Looking at him squarely, she whispered, "I want you, and I won't break. Let go, Nate, and allow yourself to feel."

Their gazes locked in a moment of silent understanding. His answer was immediate, and he took her mouth harshly—the way she knew he needed to take her body. Yet, as they fused together as one, he opened her gently, moving against her in a slow joining until she had accepted all of him. With an agonized gasp, he stopped momentarily and shuddered, drawing a deep breath as he filled her completely. The sound of his voice and the shudder that ran through him, also ran through her. It was as if the sensation had become an electrical current that now bound and charged two touching wires without a ground.

"Let it go, baby," she moaned against his cheek as she arched up against him and held him tighter.

It seemed to be the permission he needed. She understood that Nate had to feel her acceptance of him through her open responses, not just hear the words. His grip immediately tightened around her shoulders, and each withdrawal and return that he made became a punishing rhythm of pleasure. Her body now responded on its own, matching his pace, causing her to wrap her legs around his waist as she hung onto his shoulders for dear life. When his breathing became ragged and harsh against her temple, she could feel herself give way to another convulsion of pleasure. Giving in and letting go, he threw his head back, shuddered hard, and groaned her name.

They lay together for what felt like a long while. Nate held her tightly, and he moaned deep within his chest each time he let out a breath. She felt paralyzed and sated, basking in the warmth that radiated between them, never wanting to let him go. Paradise. Pure and simple.

Finally, he tried to raise himself, but gave up when the muscles in his upper arms trembled beneath his own weight. "Oh, God . . . , woman," he murmured hoarsely. "Oh, dear, God."

When he could lift himself, he kissed her and looked at her intensely. Watching him watch her, there was no way for her to wipe the satisfied, lazy, smile from her face.

"Where have you been all my life?" she whispered, brushing his mouth with a kiss.

"Too damn busy, and too damned crazy to pay attention to gold in my own back yard, I suppose."

Nate heaved himself up with effort and left her, heading toward the bathroom. "Would you like something to drink?" he called over his shoulder, not waiting for her answer.

After a few minutes, she could hear him walk down and rummage around in the kitchen. Claudia turned over and sighed, pulling the thick pillows of the old fashioned rice bed under her chin. She felt like she had died and gone to heaven, and hadn't even realized that she'd slipped off to sleep until Nate appeared at her side with a glass of soda.

"You better take a sip of this," he said with a sly wink, running the cold glass down the center of her back, causing her to giggle. "My transmission has been out of commission for a long time, but it's warmed up now."

She sat up in the bed, and took the glass from him, running her fingers through her tossled hair. "I think I may have stripped a gear," she said smiling and taking a leisurely sip.

He chuckled and kissed her wet lips, picking a cube of ice from her glass and rolling it around in his mouth. There was no hesitancy about his demeanor this time as he reached for her breast and gently caressed the tip of it, sending new ribbons of pleasure through her.

"I love the way your body responds," he murmured, replacing his touch with a deep, cold kiss that ignited her again. "I'm not sure if I can get enough of you, lady," he whispered, taking away her glass and setting it on the nightstand.

She kissed the top of his head and cradled it against her breasts while his hands roved over her body as though they were made of velvet. "I'm all yours," she whispered back. "I'm not going anywhere."

"Neither am I, baby," he murmured against her neck, pushing her back gently, and blanketing her again. "I promise."

Chapter 11

Claudia turned her cheek to a new place on the pillows and allowed her skin to absorb the warm rays of the sun. She didn't open her eyes as her senses began to come alive with the steady rise and fall of Nate's chest at her back. Trying to preserve the little bit of heaven she had just found, she snuggled into him and prayed that none of last night had been a dream.

Somehow, they had managed to create an oasis, a protected place far away from the blaring fire engines, police sirens, and urban noise that had besieged the night. This morning, she refused to ask how long it would last. Yet, when she felt Nate's grip tighten around her waist, it was clear that he'd remembered his promise, even in his sleep.

"So, I wasn't dreaming?" she heard him whisper in a deep voice that reverberated through her back.

It felt good. Almost too good to be true.

"Uhm, uhm," she murmured in response, tangling her legs with his and enjoying the lazy comfort between them.

"I haven't wakened up with anybody in a long time, Claud. I almost don't know how to act."

His words poured over her soul, and his breath sent a warm current along her scalp.

"I know what you mean. Wasn't sure if it would ever be like this again," she said softly, filling with emotion as she laced her fingers through his. "Can't we stay here forever?"

She could feel him slowly chuckle before she heard it.

"Wouldn't mind a bit, baby. I could stand this. How 'bout you?"

"Yeah? I could get used to this," she whispered with her eyes still closed, sensing his body begin to awaken.

"Yeah. Most definitely."

Nate's response had taken on a deliberately sexy tone, and his once easy grip had become a slow, mind-unraveling stroke down her side.

"How do you do this to me?" Claudia shuddered, tensing against the new sensations that his hand created.

"Was about to ask you the same question," he murmured, kissing her shoulder. "Can't seem to get enough of you."

Joining to her in one easy motion, a low groan escaped him before he stopped. "Oh, baby, I hate to have to get up . . ."

"Do you have to?" Her words had formed on their own, just as her body had responded of its own free will. The thought of breaking the warm seal between them was unbearable.

Moving against her again, his breathing had become ragged. "Don't know if I can this time . . . you feel so good without anything between us . . ."

She answered him without speaking, encouraging him to stay inside of her, begging him silently to be a part of her forever. How could she think with the smooth hardness of his skin colliding against her warmth . . . every ridge and pulsing vein that she hadn't been able to feel inside of her the night before . . . every texture that bonded them . . . his breaths now fusing with deep moans that vibrated through her and tore at her mind . . . the way his arm clasped her to his torso until she thought she might break. . . . Her heart and body resisted her mind until they won, making her face what she had tried so hard to deny. She had fallen in love with him. His words were now formed with his motions, which matched her own . . . as though he'd read both her mind and her heart, answering her prayer.

When Nate shuddered hard and convulsed into her depths, she almost whimpered with pleasure. It all felt so right, so natural. . . . They had become one.

They were both breathing deeply as he kissed the curve of her neck. "You hungry?" he finally murmured, while they lay together still joined, soaking in each other's satisfied warmth.

It was her turn to chuckle. "Do you ever stop thinking about food?"

"Gotta fuel this engine, baby. Last thing I remember is some cookies." He laughed easily, leaning in to kiss her shoulder. "Can't keep runnin' all night and all day on E."

"If somethin' to eat'll keep you runnin' like this, I'll feed you all the time, hon. Don't you worry 'bout that."

He laughed again, rolling her over to face him. "This could get to be a habit, you know?"

"Yeah . . ." she said in a slow drawl. "Oh, yeah."

Nate brushed her lips as he got up. "How about if I install a refrigerator up here? I could take out the armoire and set it in the corner," he chuckled on his way to the bathroom. "Who needs clothes, since we'll never leave this room?"

Claudia pulled the blankets back up and laughed. "What? And no stove, too? How'm I gonna make sausage, and grits, and eggs, and coffee, and—"

"Oh, girl, stop! You are *definitely* gonna make me lock the door and throw away the key," he called over his shoulder. "Might even install bars on the windows up here to keep you from escaping."

Claudia could hear him laughing from the other side of the door, as she sank into the pillows with another satisfied groan. The man was going to kill her. Absolutely, positively put her in an early grave. But did she care? Whatta way to go.

When Nate returned, he stopped at the edge of the bed and smiled at her.

"Oh, no," she said giggling, while hopping off her side of the bed and hustling out of the room. "I'm brushing my teeth, taking a shower, and peeing first."

"If I wasn't so hungry, we might have to negotiate," he yelled as she shut the door. "But, there is the rest of the day left, you know."

The early fall breeze stung her face as they made their way down to the diner. The leaves were just starting to turn with the first hint of orange and yellow, and the heavy scent of burning wood still hung in the morning air. Along the short stretch of homes they passed, she imagined the people's lives behind the doors. Fireplaces ... families ... tree-lined, quiet streets. Nate had truly found an oasis in the middle of the war zone. Maybe that's what her father and mother had tried to find when they'd moved to Jersey years ago.

As they neared the end of the block, she stopped again briefly to look at the old abandoned mansion that graced the corner.

"Guess it doesn't look so bad in the daylight," he said smiling at her. "But it would still cost a fortune to renovate."

"Yeah, I know," she answered wistfully, not really looking at him. "One day, Nate, I'm going to find a way to turn this into what it should be. You watch and see."

His smile seemed to soften as he reached for her face. "Somehow, lady, I know you can do anything you put your mind to. Remember, I saw you raise the dead."

Suddenly shy, she looked down, covering his hand with her own. "Let's go get you some breakfast before we find ourselves turned around and back at your house."

"Good idea," he murmured, but still not moving.

The way he looked at her ... though not a man of many words, Nate McGregor's eyes could speak volumes. And when he did say something, each phrase was always weighted with a deeper meaning that made one feel a sense of peace.

"I want to go home, Nate," she said quietly, allowing herself to fuse with his stare. "I need to. It's been a long time."

"Know what you mean, baby," he said in nearly a whisper, taking her hand and turning toward the house.

She had to smile.

"No, I meant Jersey. I need to mend the fence there."

Appearing a little startled, then disappointed, Nate stopped and looked at her. "Oh, sure . . . I mean . . . I just thought—"

"That, too," she said, cutting him off gently, and giving him a reassuring kiss. "But it's been so long since I've seen my family. Being with you made me think of them."

"Is that good or bad?"

He seemed so disappointed that she had to stifle another smile. Taking his hand, she squeezed it as they began walking in the direction of the diner again. "Real good, Nate. It's good. I love them a lot, and I've had this wall up ever since Moms and Ret were gone. But now . . . I don't feel angry any more. It's like a stone has been lifted from my heart. Does that make sense?"

"That's just how you make me feel, Claud. Yeah. That's real good."

They walked together without speaking until they rounded the next corner, enjoying just the presence of one another.

"Dear, God in heaven! What happened?"

Nate dropped her hand and ran down the street in the direction of her apartment. In heels, she couldn't keep up with him, but she could see where he was headed. For a moment, all she could do was watch in horror as Nate hurdled a yellow police barricade. Stunned by the scene, she looked on as he stood in the middle of Forty-Fifth Street shaking his head. When she could finally propel herself forward again to catch up to him, it felt like it took forever for her mind to register what she saw.

It was all gone. The entire corner. The bar had been gutted. The building that used to house her apartment was a shell, and smoke still rose from the charred remains. The sidewalk was littered with half-melted dolls, children's toys, warped refrigerators, and smoking clothes. . . . It looked like a scene out of Beirut.

Claudia wanted to vomit, and she stood back from the site, almost afraid that she might stumble upon a body in the pile of ashen wreckage. Tears blurred her vision, and she felt her whole body recoil as Nate cursed and kicked discarded pots and pans away from the heap.

"That's where all the sirens were headed last night, Claud! Can you believe it! I left my answering service turned on in the building and my calls forwarded here. No wonder the phone never rang last night," he yelled, kicking at the pile again. "The damned machine was probably on fire. I've gotta call Ed. He's probably having a heart attack."

Claudia covered her face, and her sobs drowned out Nate's words. "I knew it was too good to be true," she wailed, turning away, unable to face the wreckage. "I have to go home, Nate. Please. Take me home."

The hysteria of her own voice chilled her. The immediate violation tore at her insides and began to push her dangerously close to a place she'd vowed to never visit again. Nate's embrace was the only thing that seemed real, and as he led her to his van, she couldn't remove her hands from her face or stop the tears.

His words seemed far away as he spoke and started the motor. Her mind could only make out portions of what he was saying.

"Tell me how to get there, honey. I need directions. It'll be okay . . ."

Shaking her head, she vaguely recited the way home to him by rote. It was as though someone else was answering his questions. She wasn't here any longer. She had gone.

* * *

The sound of too much quiet brought her hazy thoughts into focus as she uncurled from the fetal position that had trapped her in the bed. It was dark, nighttime . . . a strange night with no sirens, no loud bar laughs, no car horns, no sound of Nate sleeping protectively at her back—just crickets and an occasional dog barking in the distance.

How long had she been here? Claudia's gaze traveled around what used to be her room. Had there been no renovations, even in the dark she would have found comfort in the familiar shadows and shapes that always seemed to take on their own life—like they sometimes did when she was a child. Yet, even now those shapes seemed to move . . . ever so slightly . . . not enough to really cause an adult to panic, but enough to make the heart beat fast and to make her squint to be sure they hadn't. But at the moment, being an adult didn't help any more than her crying did as a child. One shape in particular, near the closet, seemed to catch the silvery light of the moon, to move then go still, then reform itself into a different shape just on the outer edges of the door.

Old clothes, Claudia told herself repeatedly, trying to summon the courage to go downstairs where she was sure her father and Dot would be. Just old clothes—under her black coat probably, or maybe her dress . . . thrown over something else. She stilled herself and took deep steadying breaths. All she had to do was to put her feet over the edge of the bed and lean over to click on the nightstand light. She didn't even have to keep her eyes open.

Timid at first, she swung one foot then the other over the edge of the bed, finally finding the additional courage she needed to reach out her hand until it connected with the lamp. Victorious, she allowed her fingers to slowly follow the curves of the cool porcelain base, tracing it with the gentle touch of a lover until she found the switch and clicked it on.

Perspiration had encroached upon her shoulder blades and a thin trickle of moisture now crept down the center of her back. With her gaze focused on the closet door, she sat mouth agape. No clothes hung over the edge of the frame the way she and Loretta used to toss and fling them there when they were teenagers. They'd always done that—just out of habit, then Moms would get angry and they'd be in trouble for it, too. No coat covered these invisible items that she'd imagined to be responsible for the tall flowing shape near that door . . . no silk dress added to their dimensions.

Claudia shot her gaze around the room and her line of vision was transfixed by the neat spread of clothes left on the chair. Her silk dress and stockings shared the chair as though a valet had laid them there. Her shoes were paired together evenly on the floor next to the chair, and her coat wasn't even in the room. Dot's work. It had been Dot who'd undressed her. That's right . . . it was all coming back. Nate had brought her there and Dot had helped her get into bed.

Looking back and forth between the half ajar closet door and the overstuffed bedroom chair, Claudia wrapped her arms around herself and shivered. She would not scream. She would grab her old robe off of the back of the bedroom door where Dot had been kind enough to hang it, then she would make a calm entrance downstairs into the living room.

A new fear suddenly enveloped her, eclipsing any thoughts of a phantom intruder by her closet. She'd obviously slept for hours, trying to forget the pain and shock of finding her apartment in ruins—which meant that the last little bit of anything she'd held dear in the world had gone up in smoke . . . along with all of Nate's work, all of the food he'd bought to restock and restart her life. She had no where to live, hadn't even kept up renters insurance . . . and dear God, Loretta's journal, the one she kept neatly in her dresser drawer!

Bitter sobs crashed through the still of the room as she blindly reached for the robe and ran down the steps. Her father and Miss Dot met her at the bottom. They were already standing and half in motion as if they were on their way up when they'd heard her cries.

Warm arms encircled her and led her to the sofa. "Hush,

baby . . . I know, honey." They unsuccessfully tried to calm her.

"Everything's gone," she wailed into the jumble of arms that surrounded her. "Ret's journal, pictures . . . Moms's throw that she made herself . . . the things money can never replace."

The words had stopped but the rocking hadn't. After a while, the tears subsided and they brought tissues. Her throat hurt and felt like it had sealed shut. It didn't matter anyway, there was nothing more to say.

"We was real worried about you, baby. Glad your friend was good enough to bring you all the way here. Seems like a nice young man. He was real concerned when he left . . . said he'd be checking on you."

Claudia could only nod to the sound of her father's voice. Her eyes stung too much to open them, and her breath was too heavy to use for speech. An anvil blocked the space between her lungs and her breastbone, the place where her heart used to be.

"The worst was Ret's journal," she finally whispered, "that was all I had left from her."

She could feel Miss Dot's arm slip from around her shoulders and a breeze rushed in when she broke their tight seal to stand.

"Don't worry about things now, honey. Sometimes you have to let things go. As long as you have your health and strength, that's blessing enough. I'm going to put on some tea so you can relax."

Her father's warmth replaced the warmth that Dot's vacancy had temporarily removed. Claudia allowed her head to find refuge in his shoulder, still strong for all his years. "Daddy, do you think that once someone has had a problem that they'll always have problems?"

She could feel him shift her to a closer position and he began rubbing her arm.

"Don't know exactly. Trouble seems to be a part of life. Maybe Moms and Ret are the lucky ones? Sometimes I wonder 'bout that."

She searched for a way to make him understand what she didn't want to admit herself. Perhaps it was unfair to put him in the position of validating fears that they could never really discuss, but right now, she needed his reassurance, so she pressed on.

"I'm not talking about trouble, like the fire, or losing a job. I mean personal troubles."

There was an ever so slight shift of his body, a stiffening yet not a pulling away.

"Baby, Dot could probably answer that better than me . . . just like Moms was always better at talking to you girls. What does a man know? Trouble is trouble, can happen once or every day of your life. Sometimes it can haunt you even in your sleep. Dot would know better about how women take these things. Y'all are more sensitive, that's how God made it and probably why y'all pray more. Ask Dot."

Claudia's soul found a new low as it slowly sank from the disappointment. She had wanted to talk . . . deeply, just for once.

"Ask Dot what?" The small perky woman chimed in as she returned from the kitchen appearing just a little too chipper for the occasion.

But that was Dot's way. She seemed to thrive on helping the distressed, so Claudia was sure that Dot was in her glory now. She had someone to labor over and attend to. Her stay here was going to be hell.

Setting down a china cup of tea on a tray, she took up a position next to Claudia as her father almost bolted to a stand to make room for her.

"Woman things," her father said tentatively. "The girl has some questions, since Ret's journal burned and all . . . woman things that no man can answer. Talk to her, Dot, she needs some motherin'. I'm going down to the lodge to give y'all some room to air it all out."

Claudia stared at him dispassionately. How many times had this scene played itself out. First with Ret, then with her, neither of them getting what they truly wanted or needed—his opinion, his voice . . . his wisdom. She thought of Nate.

"C'mere, chile. Dot knows how hard these last few years have been on you, baby."

Claudia allowed the older woman to pull her against her breasts without resistance, but also without feeling. She knew in her heart as Dot stroked her head that this attention was more medicine for Dot than it was for herself. But it didn't hurt either of them to exchange needs in this way. What was the harm? If it made Dot feel useful, then fine. If it kept her from having to dredge through the gore of her life, then fine. Just like always, it would always be fine. She just wondered if that same, fine, neat way of sweeping things under the rug for years had led to everything piling up so high that it leapt out and frightened her, and everybody else for that matter, that day in the church?

"Dot, tea's getting cold," she murmured after a long while. Her lower back was starting to hurt from the unnatural way she had to twist into Dot's embrace.

"Oh, baby, I'm sorry. Was just enjoying a rare chance to hold you in my arms. Want me to reheat it for you?"

"No, that's okay," Claudia whispered. "You've already done too much. Thanks," she said taking the cup from the saucer and bringing the lukewarm substance to her mouth. She hated to rob Dot of the tiny oasis of mothering that she'd found, but her back was cramping and she really needed to stand to work it out. However, that physical distancing would have been too hurtful a gesture, so she opted for long stretches to retrieve the tea saucer from the tray.

"No trouble at all. Here let me reach that for you."

Dot hadn't given her a breath of space and the effect was smothering.

"I'm not an invalid," Claudia said quietly, trying her best not to hurt Dot's feelings.

Dot's expression sagged. "I know, baby. But you've been through a lot. I just want to help, is all."

There was no way to win this unseen struggle. Dot was on a mission of mercy, her father was pledged to serve and protect, but not to talk. Claudia sighed from deep within her soul. Why did love have to be so complex?

Dot eyed her steadily as she finally stood, stretched, and sat back down a foot away. The action created more than a twelve-inch canyon on the sofa, it created a barrier.

"I want to ask you something, Dot ... something very serious."

Claudia was caught off guard by the tears that glistened in Dot's eyes.

"I knew the day would come when you would."

Puzzled, Claudia chalked it up to the new space between them on the sofa.

"I wonder what trouble follows you, of the personal kind. I mean, I wasn't able to carry my babies, you know ... then, what happened in the church, then something I saw in my room that made me wonder if the mental trouble had come back—"

Dot held up her hand as tears coursed down her face. "Certain kinds of trouble is passed in the genes. I told your father. I told him to tell you so you'd be careful, but he never did."

They both looked at each other for a long time. They had both been engaged in the same conversation but nothing was connecting. It was like two people dancing to the same song, but their rhythms were out of sync—by just a step. What was happening could even be likened to two travelers going down the same road but each turning off at a different point toward a different objective. Claudia could feel it, but couldn't exactly put her finger on it. She had been trying to head the discussion toward the nervous breakdown, and had been wondering whether or not the trauma of finding her apartment in ashes had effected her vision or judgment enough to see things in her old bedroom—now the guest room. What road was Dot on? That took over the steering in her mind, and she decided to see where Dot was headed.

"You mean Moms had trouble carrying children? Or had a nervous breakdown? Is that why there was a big gap between me and Ret?"

They both looked at each other, and now it was Dot's turn to go for more space. The older woman smoothed the front of her apron and stood up, taking Claudia's tea cup from her hands in the process.

"After Ret was born, there were some problems. You came much later. Your mother was able to handle it all in time."

Claudia watched Dot's back and stood slowly. The answer she received was like a cryptogram, a parable . . . layers deep.

When she reached the doorway of the kitchen, she leaned on the molding and watched Dot take an extraordinarily long time to fix a cup of micowaved tea. Dot neatly unfolded and refolded the big box of Lipton bags, perfectly positioning her carefully chosen bag in the center of the cup, then shortened the string by looping the tag through the handle. Claudia watched on with a hawk's concentration as Dot extended the time it takes to refill a tiny cup with water, open a microwave, and carefully place a cup in the center. Dot almost seemed to read the directions twice as she timidly pressed two minutes on the timer, hit start, then watched the now lit turntable go round and round. When Dot slowly reached for the sugar bowl, Claudia's frayed nerves couldn't take it anymore.

"Dot, this has got to stop. What is so bad about telling me about Moms's condition. Maybe if I had known . . ."

"You might have lost your childhood and innocence," Dot picked up where she'd trailed off. "Just don't blame your father too much for not telling you sooner. You were the one that he was closest to, and the one that he doted on. It's never been a secret that you were his favorite, and to have you think bad of him . . . well, maybe it would kill him."

Dot had turned around to look her square in the face. It was almost a challenging expression that said, "Don't try me, child, I know what I'm talking about," without any words to that effect being exchanged.

"I don't blame him for not telling me," Claudia said with exasperation, taking the tea out of the microwave before it was ready. "I just saw something strange in my room—the guest room, I mean, and I wanted to be sure that I wasn't relapsing, mentally."

Dot sat down heavily at the kitchen table and let her head drop into her hands. Her round shoulders seemed to lower by two inches as obvious relief swept through her.

"Is that all, honey? Lord have mercy." Dot had dragged out the sentence like someone who'd just set down a ton of bricks. "What did you see?"

Claudia stared at her, the apparition no longer seemed important. It was as though the strange occurrence had led her into something deeper and more important than the thing that had initially frightened her. This time Claudia hedged.

"I was lying in bed and it was dark . . . I saw a silvery shadow near the closet and at first I thought I'd hung my old clothes over the door like me and Ret would do as kids. But for some reason they seemed to be moving ever so slightly, so I got scared and turned on the light. That's when I got really scared—because my clothes were in a neat pile on the chair, not on the door. So, what was on the door?"

Dot's eyes were wide and she reached out her hands toward Claudia who responded by filling them with her own.

"Let's start with some prayer, The Lord's Prayer, then pray to merciful God for the forgiveness of our sins, that the dead may rest in peace. Amen."

Although Claudia had chimed in with an amen or two of her own, and Dot prayed on fervently for five minutes, she watched this church-going woman's tormented, tear-streaked face through a bizarre veil of detachment. Something beyond even the possibility of a ghost had sent Dot into a tizzy. The woman was hyperventilating so bad, and calling on her Jesus so hard, that Claudia was sure that there was another layer to be removed from this onion.

When Dot had said her final amen, Claudia walked over to

her side of the table and kissed her cheek, wiped her face, and went to the sink to fetch and wet a paper towel for her eyes and nose. Breathing heavily, Dot accepted the cold compress and blotted her entire face.

"Lord forgive us both, child. You had a right to know."

Claudia just stared at her. There was compassion in her gaze this time when she peered at Dot. "Dot, say it plain so I can get this into my head and understand it all. Help me understand. Please."

"Oh, baby, didn't your sister's book spell it out plain enough? How can I explain what wasn't right then and ain't right now?"

Claudia sat very still. "The journal," she whispered, more as a question than a response. But it was gone now, destroyed before she'd even read it all ... then it dawned on her, this was why it had caused such a ruckus when she'd wanted to read it before the congregation. Something was in there that went way beyond Loretta's metaphysical belief system. It was never about that.

"You shouldn't have found out that way," Dot said with resignation and beginning to tear again. "But, it's all water under the bridge, though."

"I want to hear your side," Claudia said as evenly as she could to draw Dot out. "Like they say, there's always three sides to a story ... your side, Ret's side, and the truth."

It was all she could do to steady her heartbeat, to keep her insides from leaping out of the center of her chest while she watched Dot try to grapple with where to begin.

"Like I said, Loretta was first because of the problems ... then there were more problems."

Dot's delivery was slow and painfully specific. "Your dad and I knew each other, first. That was back in the North Carolina days. We were going to get married ... after high school ... but in youth, we had crossed the line before we were really old enough. Do you understand?"

Dot's eyes slid away from Claudia's in shame, and Claudia knew exactly what she meant by *crossed the line*. It was another parable, polite phraseology to describe what *Newsweek* would plaster across its cover page today. Claudia inhaled deeply and her heart wrenched at Dot's pain. Why should she have had to carry around such a burden for all these years? Why was the joy of discovery so cloaked with negativity that it would make a sixty-five-year-old woman hang her head? If she hadn't been so incredulous, she would have been angry.

"Oh, Dot ... you two loved each other, right?" Claudia extended her hands across the table and clasped the older woman's in her own.

"I was a good girl, Claudia," she nearly choked back, "and yes, we loved each other very much. But that wasn't enough in those days. I didn't know that I was in trouble until I started getting the pains ... then the gush of blood came. I was in school."

All Claudia could do was squeeze Dot's hands tighter. Dot's gaze was far away and she seemed so much older now. It was as though the journey through time had taken a present-day toll on her. Dabbing at the corners of her eyes with the crumpled paper towel, Dot drew another breath and let it out slowly through her mouth.

"My mama thought my cycle had come on, like my teacher did. But when the pains wouldn't go away, and the clumps got bigger ... then it came out all in one whole piece ..."

Claudia almost stopped her, and she shut her own eyes as the too-recent memory of her own miscarriages bore into her skull. "You were just a baby," she whispered.

"I was only fifteen, your father was only seventeen. They wouldn't even let him find out how I was. They chased him away. But after a whole summer of waiting for me to come back to school in the fall, he got a chance to talk to me on the way home from school. By then, my father had stopped penning me up like a barnyard animal, and I guess that day my mama was too tired of the fighting and shouting and crying to keep vigil. So, I told your father everything and we both cried together for a long time, just him hugging me and me hugging him. Then he said he wasn't lettin' me go back home . . . said he'd find a county somewhere that we could go get married without my parents' permission. We ran away. That's when the big trouble started.''

Dot pulled her hands away and stood on shaky legs. All Claudia could do was watch her. The older woman moved slowly to the box of tea bags and began the excruciating process all over again. But this time she talked as she worked, as though making the tea was a therapeutic distraction to the horror of her story.

''Like I said, honey, we loved each other. Was only gone a few days before they caught us, with no money and no car and what-not. But don't need that much time when you that young and that much in love . . . all you need is the crickets for music and the gentle breeze and the stars in the sky . . . don't seem like money or time or tomorrow even matters. But then you find out that it does. Tomorrow can come with a vengeance. Threatened to lock your father up, but I wasn't across state lines yet, and he wasn't eighteen, praise the Lord. So, they just separated us again. This time I got sent to live with my aunt in North Philadelphia till I graduated. Nobody told him when I was leaving or where I was going. His parents snatched the mail first, since they didn't want no more trouble. My parents had made it clear that they felt I would be marrying down since I had come from a long line of school teachers and he had come from a long line of tobacco pickers. Thought I'd go out of my mind, I loved him so . . . When the bleeding started again, I did. I was alone this time in my aunt's bathroom.''

Swallowing hard, a familiarity branded it's meaning into Claudia's soul. She stared at Dot and Dot stared back at her. Mustering courage, Claudia broke the deadlock.

''You had two miscarriages and a breakdown . . . we have a lot in common.''

Dot smiled sadly. ''Yup. Deed we do, chile. Like they used to say down South, mayhaps we do.''

"They should have let you all just get married." Claudia's voice quavered with an insight that was too strange to sort out.

Almost reading her mind, Dot filled in the blanks. "Darlin', it would have saved a whole lot of heartbreak. Sometimes the well-meaning interference of people gets in the way of God's true intentions. I tried to tell them that, but I couldn't stop crying long enough to get the words out. Didn't take you to a psychiatrist in those days; took you to a minister. Minister made me cry all the more, and feel wretched and dirty. When I stopped crying, I also stopped talking for almost a year. Then one day I saw a young couple walking down the street holding hands, and I went in the house and tried to find a vein to open up in my arm. When my aunt found me I was almost gone . . . by the time I got out of the hospital, she didn't want any more to do with raising my mother's sick child—so she sent me home."

Dot moved the wide bangle from her wrist and turned it over for Claudia to inspect. It was as though Dot wanted to give her tangible evidence of her story, to make it real and permanent in Claudia's mind. With all the tenderness she could force into her fingertips, Claudia grazed the light scars at Dot's wrists that she had never seen before.

Satisfied that she'd made her point, Dot folded her hands in front of her with the ragged wet paper towel between her palms. "I defied my parents and ran to look for him. He was my husband to be, we had made a vow . . . but the big war had just broke and he had been sent to Jersey, Fort Dix. Odd, we had passed each other like two ships in the night. Do you know what that feels like, Claudia? To be so close to a dream then have it snatched away?"

Claudia nodded, her thoughts flickering to Nate then back to the incredible tale of passion and youth that sprang from the most unlikely source sitting before her.

"Yeah, well . . ." Dot sighed heavily in a tired voice. "For a moment, it gave me something to live for. Hope. Sometimes that's all you've got. So, I went back to church, tried to seal up my split with God. Made a lot of promises—some of which I didn't keep.''

"Wait a minute, *you* fell out with God?"

Dot chuckled, ''Chile, are you kidding me? Humph. Wasn't on no speaking terms after what I'd been through. Was too mad. Lost my babies, my husband to be . . . got just that close, then found out that he might be killed in a war overseas some where. But then, it was the fact that he was overseas that made me start praying—for somebody else other than myself. That was the first step back. Caring about more than me.''

"I can understand that,'' Claudia said quietly. ''Like when you don't care about yourself, but care enough about somebody else to put your riff with faith aside.'' She let a lopsided grin overtake her face. ''You sort of say, 'Now God, I'm angry at you, but that's between me and you. But if you care anything about anything I've ever begged you for, please, please, please don't let this person I love get hurt. Used to pray like that for my sister all the time.'' After a moment her voice became quiet again, ''I think I made Nate pray like that for me.''

Two sets of eyes and minds became one as they sat facing each other and telling the unvarnished truth.

"Exactly my point, baby. Then you start trying to cut deals with the Lord. Mine was a tough one. 'If you just let him come back in one piece, I'll finish school, go back to church, and follow your way.' '' Dot laughed as new tears ran down her cheeks freely. ''The bargain saved my sanity, got me through school, and your father came home alive, but he'd married a girl from Jersey before he'd left.''

Claudia's hand flew over her mouth and a stabbing pain of empathy cut her voice to a whisper. ''Oh, Dot . . .''

"I heard it from his cousin . . . wasn't much left to do by then but try to teach school children and go to church. The Lord had won, at least your father was alive.''

"But you weren't.''

"No, I wasn't, baby. Probably why I never married. Didn't want nobody but him.''

''That was a horrible deal . . . Dot, it wasn't fair . . . I know he didn't know . . .''

''Nope, never told him. Didn't want to bust up his situation, or go against my vow. Just left it alone. So, honey, be careful of what you pray for, you just might get it.''

Amazement slowed her breathing to a crawl. ''That's why I've had so much trouble with this faith thing. Seems like too much is so unfair. Where's the calvary when you need them?''

Dot just shrugged and stood, this time taking the two cups away from the table to place them in the sink. ''They come, when they get ready.''

The answer didn't sit well with Claudia. Seeming to hear Claudia's silent question, Dot talked from her position at the sink without turning around.

''Sometimes things happen for a reason . . . like my having to return up North to take care of my aunt who was dying five years after the war was over. I was the only unmarried one left, my mother was sick herself but had my eldest sister to care for her since her family still lived with my parents. Or, like me getting a job at a Philadelphia school. Then like me seeing your father again for the first time in a church that my girlfriend took me to in Lawnside . . . but he was with his wife and new baby. Then God gave me enough sense to go back home after my aunt died two weeks later. Things happen for a reason.''

''What did you do?'' Claudia's mouth was agape. ''All of that unfinished business . . .''

''Said hi, and tried not to cry. There was nothing else to do. I wasn't the run-around kind, and neither was your father. But, he took it as bad as I did. You could see it in his face. He was stricken.''

''Did he ever try to look you up?'' Claudia was cautious, but the nagging question was burning a hole in her brain.

''Eight years later when my father died. His mother and my father died a month apart and he was still there helping his family sort out their affairs. Was a lot of Harris kin, and with his father gone and his mother passing, there was a lot of squabbling . . . or, at least that's what he told your mother . . . and that's when some more trouble started.''

It was Claudia's turn to stand and gather distance around herself. She could feel something pending about the way Dot's story wound and weaved around her heart, and the smoky sadness that haunted Dot's eyes looked too reminiscent of her own. ''I think I need a cigarette. I know you don't allow it in your house, Dot, but can we go on the porch? Just let me get my bag . . . by the way, where is my bag?''

''Yeah, let's sit a spell on the porch, honey. Go get your cancer, your bag is hanging in the closet in your room. Think the night air could do us both some good.''

Without thinking about the recent terror that her room had imposed, Claudia raced through the small house, bound up the stairs and reached into the closet toward the hooks. Then she stopped. Odd that the pull-chain light was on inside, and she wondered whether her father had turned it on to allay her fears. Quickly finding her purse she yanked it off the hook and fled the room. Something was definitely wrong. Her father had never gone back upstairs, and they had never discussed what spooked her . . . so how would he have known to turn on the closet light? Besides, he was such a stickler about not burning unnecessary electric. She'd been sitting there with Dot the whole time.

''Dot, Dot, did you turn on the closet light?'' she huffed as she flopped beside Dot on the porch swing. Tiny gnats were swirling just beyond the protective screening, creating a circle dance under the flood light. Claudia rustled through her purse without looking at it, all the while her vision focused on Dot.

Dot sighed and smiled, looking out at the blue-black sky. ''No here's the real dilemma of signs. Don't know which ones to look for, or who sent them. Can't tell if y'all want me to finish what we started, or not. Just don't know.''

Her question hung in the air and danced like the gnats, just like Claudia's unanswered question.

"No, baby. You ain't crazy, and your father wouldn't leave electric burning like that."

"What are you saying?" Claudia could barely hold the cigarette as she tried to light it.

"I'm saying that the truth will always out, and who ever decided to scare you into my arms and into my kitchen wanted us to talk. Same with the fire. It was time for you to come home."

Claudia was dragging so hard that it sent her into a coughing fit. "Who ever? Don't you mean *what ever,* Dot?"

"No. I said what I mean. Who. Ever. There are several angels to choose from . . . anybody with a good heart that's gone on to glory is an angel . . . your sister, your mother, my mother, any of your grandparents really, maybe your brother and sister—"

"My brother and sister?"

Dot didn't take her gaze away from the night sky. "First one my mama said was a boy, second one I saw myself, it was a girl. Only one that lived was you."

The cigarette had burned down to Claudia's fingers and she dropped it without crushing the ember out. Dot placidly reached down and returned it to the ash tray, rubbing her foot against the spot on the indoor-outdoor carpet where it had fallen.

"I saw him in North Carolina, during that whole month he was down there. My father was dying and had called for him to make his peace, suppose the old man didn't want to go on to glory without righting a long-ago wrong. He'd just lost his mother, I was losing my father . . . and his marriage was not what he'd expected . . . there were problems. He'll have to tell you about that. I can only speak to what I know and have seen through my own eyes. But, when two people still have unfinished business, unfinished love, sometimes they pick the wrong time to finish it. Sad times and death's door tend to make people remember how much time has passed and how little time is left."

The stars in the sky became blurry and the moon seemed to swallow them whole. "How did Moms come to raise me?"

Dot never flinched, just closed her eyes slowly. "For nine months your father traveled back and forth from Jersey to North Carolina to take care of me. They were in separate bedrooms, and it didn't look like any more children were coming. He said he had a teenage cousin in trouble . . . that he found out when all the funeral mess broke loose, and asked your mother to step in. She was a decent soul, and did . . . without asking too many questions. She thought it might save their marriage, and it did. I gave them signed papers and he left for Philly with you in his arms. You were my third that I lost, and I took it like the punishment I felt I deserved. Hadn't seen him in thirty-three years, although he sent every picture, every report card, every moment of your life to me by mail. That's why you're his special child, and why he married me so soon after your mother died. We all got some of what we wanted . . . she got to save her marriage, he got to love our child, I got to have him a little while as my husband. Like I said, all in His time."

"Ret knew . . ." she whispered too dazed to react.

"Yes," Dot said in a weary tone, nodding her head slowly, "couldn't accept it when your mother died. She was cleaning out your mother's closets after the funeral and found the papers that had my name on them. By then she had met me and knew I was hardly a teenage cousin. Come to think of it, that's probably who's been in your closet tonight."

Claudia wrapped her arms around herself and stood, moving toward the screen and the light. She was numb.

"Don't be afraid of your sister, honey. Maybe she's got something else to tell you. Like you said, there's her side, my side, and the truth. Truth is the only thing that can rest a soul. So, listen to her, thank her, and just pray that she finds peace."

Chapter 12

The sound of footsteps on the front porch startled her, and she trained her vision toward the entrance to the kitchen as her ears registered the sound of a key in the front door. Although these were normal sounds, all of her senses were keenly alert. Claudia could actually feel the hair on the back of her neck bristling. It was impossible to turn her attention back to the mound of credit cards, papers, and personal effects that she'd dumped on the table from Loretta's purse.

"Thought you and Dot'd be sleep by now."

Claudia studied her father's weathered expression. He seemed much older to her, and not quite as invincible as she'd once perceived him. A few hours away and he'd returned like a time traveler who had been beaten by the unforgiving ravages of memory.

"Nah, couldn't sleep . . . but you look tired," she finally said, returning her gaze to the pile of objects on the table.

She noticed how he hadn't looked her in the eyes since he'd walked into the room. He had addressed the refrigerator, not her directly. Nor had he chosen to sit down. Usually, he would

have crossed the floor, given her a big smile and a kiss that
always went with his generous hug. Tonight only the space
between them wrapped around her.

"You want some tea?" she said delicately, trying to find a
way to let him know that they had to talk.

"Naw, it's pretty late," he said in a weary tone, still speaking
to the refrigerator, "and it probably won't mix well with the
beers . . . You ought to get some rest yourself."

Claudia shook her head no. She had been far too jittery to
venture going back into the bedroom to sleep. When Dot turned
in, she'd just lied to Dot, telling her that she'd be up soon. But
how in the world was she supposed to sleep with a possible
ghost in her room, not to mention everything else that had
happened? Besides, she had slept for the better part of the day.
Her whole routine was reversed now . . . just like her life.

Obviously searching for a way to close the dead-end discussion, her father glanced at the table. "Don't need to worry
about all them papers and bills now. You can just give them
to me and I'll give them to her attorney just like I did after
she passed."

Feeling territorial about the last shred of connection she had
to her sister, Claudia began scooping the contents of Loretta's
purse back into various compartments in the bag.

"What attorney? I didn't know she had an attorney?"

Her father sighed heavily and leaned against the refrigerator,
this time addressing his shoes as he spoke.

"Sometimes people have a lot going on that other people
don't know about. Your sister was no exception. Me and Dot'll
take care of it."

She allowed the underlying meaning of the comment to pass,
wishing with all her heart that there could be a way to bridge
the gulf that had opened between them. But she wasn't about
to give him the last shred of her sister without resistance. Loretta
was gone, the journal was gone, her apartment and everything
she owned was gone, and due to her hysterics, Nate was probably gone . . . and less than an hour ago, part of her identity had

just unraveled on the back porch. She was not letting go of anything else without a fight.

"Who is her attorney?"

"I dunno, doesn't matter much now does it, baby girl? Just some man who came around after the funeral, said he was the executor of Loretta's estate. Given the accident at the hospital, he wanted to be sure that the hospital wasn't trying to wriggle out of any insurance claim we might be due. So, he asked me and Dot to collect all of Ret's papers here, and any notes or files she had in her condo, and to give them to him. Figured it was all right since they worked for the same place. Was partners or somethin'. Me and Dot was so tore up . . . plus people had gone in and robbed the poor girl's place while we was all at the funeral . . . and then you was *away* and everything, so we did. Was just easier that way. We'll take care of it."

Her father's comment sent a jolt of defiance through her. Her back had become a tight column and she could feel her heartbeat down her spine.

"Did he show you any proof of who he was? Was there a notary's seal, or Ret's signature on anything?"

This time her father looked at her directly, but his voice failed to form at his slightly parted lips. His gaze slid away gradually, returning to the laces of his shoes.

"I ain't no businessman, Claud . . . just a father who's lost a daughter."

"Oh, Daddy!" she exclaimed, winding her hands more tightly around the leather shoulder strap of the bag. "He could have been from the hospital, or from anywhere! You just handed over all of Ret's paperwork, her business files, everything without knowing who you were giving them to?" She was incredulous and had to sit back in the chair like a person who'd taken a belly blow.

"He left his address so we could bring everything to him. Works downtown where Ret used to work, that's why we thought it was all right." Her father's voice was defensive but soft. "You don't know what me and Dot's been through with all of this. We don't care about no money, Claudia, or who might steal a little piece of change. The hospital was found out to be clean; it was Ret who drank gin before she went under the knife. Can't blame them for that, can you?''

Claudia sat very, very still. Too many portions of what he'd said pried loose emotions from her depths. Her mind felt like it was under siege, and she'd have to use that organ to keep herself from screaming. Instead, she found the lowest tone her voice could register to make him understand. "Ret never drank gin. Her poison was vodka. Absolut. That's all she would touch. Something's wrong."

The elderly man's dark face went ashen. Almost weaving as he made his way to the table to sit down, his eyes begged for mercy. Her father's voice was less than a whisper when he spoke. "You never said anything about that to us before . . . like when all the questions came up . . . we all heard the autopsy report, but you never said a word. Are you sure, baby?''

Claudia took the charge stoically. "I was in shock, Daddy. I wasn't a drinker then, and it never sank in before. Now I'm a recovering alcoholic, and yes, I know what I'm talking about. It makes a difference.''

Her father shook his head. "Don't talk about yourself like that, baby. You ain't no alky. You had problems, is all. But I don't think the hospital or the insurance company would try to go out of their way to kill somebody . . . the insurance company paid off her bills and her condo. What more was we supposed to do?''

"Mistakes and malpractice happens everyday. You watch the news.''

"Rare. Don't happen round here too much. People would raise such a fuss, would be all over which is the bad hospitals and which is the good ones. Then the state would shut them down anyway. Sure, there's a few bad doctors, I'll give you that. But Ret always had to have the best. Don't seem like she would go to no jackleg for nothin'. That girl was well off; didn't have to.''

Steadfast, she would not allow her father to retreat into denial and sweep this under the rug. She pulled out the heavy artillery and went for his heart so that she could connect with his mind.

"Daddy, you know why I'm down here tonight?"

"Suppose because you and Dot talked . . . that's why you holdin' onta Ret's bag so hard. Ain't nothin' in it that's gonna take away the hurt, honey. Let me and Dot handle it, okay?"

She watched him kneed the salt and pepper shakers between his strong weather-beaten fingers like worry beads.

"Yeah, we talked. And because a light went on in my room by itself."

This time he stared at her. "What'chu talkin' about, girl?"

She paused, listened, and considered. He was afraid. She could tell. It was as simple as the way the Southern accent that he had tried to unsuccessfully disguise for years, had deepened and retreated to the place he called home. His cadence was a rhythm that drew her into lockstep, fusing with her mostly Northeast speech patterns, and stretching their genetic memory link like a taunt rubber band between regions. It was a voice that she had to echo once she heard it; a second language that she'd known all her life. It crept out at odd times, education no barrier to the rhythm. Sometimes when she was relaxed, it slipped up her throat to caress her lips. But most often, it would come when she was tired or angry or scared. She was all of those things now. He probably was, too.

"I ain't crazy," she finally exhaled with a sigh. "You didn't turn on the light in my closet before you left, did ya?"

"You know I don' waste no unnecessary 'lectric. Y'all waz downstairs anyway."

"And Dot said she didn't, plus she was sittin' with me. When I left the room it was off, but it was on after we started talking about the *trouble*. Saw it when I went upstairs to get my smokes. She ain't restin', Daddy. Like I said, something's wrong."

Her father pushed back from the table and stood with renewed energy and began pacing the floor like a cat that needed to go out.

"Look, baby girl. The past is the past, and Ret got a lot to be angry about. Cain't change a lick of it, though the good Lord knows I woulda."

Claudia remained still, wondering for a moment which part of his life he would have changed. She felt hot tears stinging her eyes way back in the sockets, but she refused to allow the tears to fall this time. In this moment, she needed to be strong— not for herself, but for her father.

"Daddy, you can't change love. Not now, or yesterday's. Listen to me ... I love you. Period. You're still my father. I can't imagine what you all went through, including Moms. I'm not blaming you. Enough of that went around for a lifetime, I'm sure. How can I blame you when you worked at Campbell's Soup for practically thirty years by day until they shut the plant, and at the hospital at night mopping floors so we all wouldn't want for anything? How can I hate a man who kissed my forehead every night—thinking I was asleep, but who knew I was secretly waiting up for him to come home from work ... the same man who pulled me into his lap on his only day off and read me the Sunday Funnies. Or the man who stood and clapped and yelled, 'that's *my* baby girl!' at every little stupid dance recital, honor roll assembly, or graduation. Or the man that walked me down the aisle like a king giving away his princess bride ... ? You were always there for me, Daddy ... that should stand for something. Shouldn't it repay your debt by now? You been paying for more than thirty years! You can't stop talking to me ... now. If anything, that's what I blamed you for. That's what hurt."

"I thought you already knew ... like Ret knew and blamed me," his voice trailed off in a garbled sob. "Could take it from her, but not from my baby girl ... not my Claudie."

She went to him and held him, not allowing the space to continue between them. "Daddy," her voice soothed as she stroked the tension from his back and held him in an embrace.

"How can I blame that man for being young and in love and having his heart torn out by the root by people who didn't know better? How can I blame you for loving us all enough, especially Moms and Ret, to put your passions, your dreams, your heart on the back burner for thirty-some years, just to do what you thought was the right thing? And Lord knows what Dot gave up . . . that poor woman . . . that poor girl . . ."

A sob caught her father's intended response, and he turned his face away toward the cabinets, leaned on them and gave way to the tide that he needed to wash himself clean. Panic swept through her. She had never seen her father really cry. Not like this. Silent tears at her mother's funeral, at Ret's, but not deep, down home gasps of breath and pain. As she quickly came to his other side, he turned away from her again, shame washed with anguish reflected in his eyes as he tried to avoid her attempt to hug him.

She had seen this in Nate; the furtive look of a man trapped by emotions too deep and too damning to ever allow to surface. When she reached for her father again, he nearly collapsed into her arms and she staggered to hold him.

"Don't deserve no daughter like you," he said breathing heavily through the quakes of sobs. "Didn't think God would hear such a prayer. He took my two grandbabies like he took my other children . . . and thought he took Loretta by the drink out of punishment for all that'd happened. Then he gave you my problems with the drink . . . couldn't watch it no more, Claud . . . Even if it seemed like justice."

She raised her father's contorted face in her hands and a calm came over her from an unknown well within. Her voice was a breath of a whisper, forcing him to open his eyes and strain to hear her.

"No, Daddy. That ain't God way . . . to break your soul and make your spirit cry out for mercy. No. My God is a kind, loving, forgiving God who gave his only begotten Son for man's sins . . . God would never strike down innocent children . . ."

She swallowed hard and pulled from every source of inspiration that she'd ever heard. Her father was in her arms, begging her to explain a world of heartbreak and pain. He needed her, and his pain seeped into the marrow of her bones. Her daddy needed her, just like he'd always been there when she was a little girl. She closed her eyes as she spoke, allowing the woman from the Laundromat to walk with her down the long road of possible explanations in her mind. But, as she visualized the old woman, with courage sealed into every line of her face, she *felt* the words. Knew them by heart . . . by understanding . . . by faith. It was not an intellectual explanation that came, but an acknowledgment of something much greater. It was a knowing . . . that a force unseen and greater than herself had sent an angel to her in the Laundromat that day . . . a warrior angel who could walk with her when she didn't know the way alone.

Her voice became strong, forceful, solid. "Daddy, believe me, He would never take a good-hearted man and separate him from a good-hearted woman, both who were just babies themselves when it happened. Don't beat yourself anymore about this, Daddy. Let it rest."

He searched her face with his gaze, his eyes darting to every part of it as though he was seeing her for the first time. It was as though he was trying to absorb the words that they both knew he wanted so desperately to believe—words that she hadn't spoken in over six months . . . but they rang so true, so central to their thread of existence. . . .

"I tried to. That's why I gave them everything without a question, baby girl," he whispered, covering her hands at the sides of his face with his own. "Don't you understand that's why I just gave the man the papers? We didn't have the energy to dig through this thing, to try to squabble over money. We wanted to let the dead stay buried . . . Now you tellin' me that my first livin' baby's spirit done come back here angry enough to haunt the rest of me and Dot's life." He closed his eyes and new tears silently tracked down his cheeks. "If it's gotta be this way, then I pray that God take me now. Would rather just go now, cause I cain't take no mo.''

She kissed her father's forehead and squeezed the tips of his fingers where they had slipped under her own. ''She's not angry at you, Daddy . . . or Dot. That's what she was trying to say in the part of the journal I read . . . that's why she was trying to get some spirituality in her life, so she could cope with her feelings.''

''Then why did she come back tonight?'' His voice was pained and his eyes held a vacant question within them that she couldn't immediately answer.

''Because I'm here,'' she whispered after a long pause. ''She came to my room—not yours or Dot's. Daddy, it's a feeling, but it's something to do with the papers you gave away . . . some unfinished financial business connected with her old job. She had come to me in a state, and started talking about it 'round about a week before she went into the hospital. But we got sidetracked . . .''

The question mark in his eyes deepened and his tone became more normalized with every breath he took. ''You think somebody tried to kill my baby? What'chu sayin', Claud?''

Claudia hesitated, not knowing what to say. How did one describe a feeling, or a hunch that had only developed within minutes of her father's confession about the papers? What did she have to go on, really? What was she even talking about? Why was she throwing out conjecture on something so fragile and so close cutting to her father's heart?

Her hands fell away from his face slowly and she leaned on them against the stove. ''I can't say . . . only that if Ret wanted to haunt you, she would have come to you the night she died, not just when I came back here. Maybe I wasn't strong enough right after it happened, and she knew that and waited. And, I know that she never drank gin, so either the coroner's autopsy report was wrong, or the clerk who typed it up made a mistake. Or, somehow, gin found it's way into her anesthesia—because she wouldn't have drunk it if they gave it to her, especially knowing that she was going into surgery. Loretta was wild, but she wasn't crazy, Daddy. Besides, I drove her to the hospital, remember, and she was clear as a bell. So, if it did happen at all, it would have had to have happened after they took her back and prepped her.''

Without asking for permission, Claudia went to the table, grabbed her cigarettes and lit one. Pacing to the sink to use it as an auxiliary ashtray where she stood, Claudia turned her back to her father and spoke to the stars while looking out of the window. ''. . . Then you say that some man connected with her old firm comes around and wants all of her papers, but when you and Dot get to her apartment, somebody has already been in there. What was reported stolen?''

''Nothing,'' her father said quietly. ''The place was just riffled through. We thought some kids looking for quick cash might have gone in there . . . but the TV and VCR were still there . . . her jewelry, too . . .''

''Think about it, Daddy,'' she said after a long drag. ''Kids would have taken a lot out of Ret's place. Then my place burns, and I know the owner well. That building was up to code.''

''Couldn't have been the same people, now you really reaching for the clouds, girl. Grief will make your mind conjure up a lot of things,'' her father said quickly, the panic resonant in his voice. '' 'Sides, it was all on the six o'clock news. Said there wasn't no smoke detectors and it started in the basement . . . old rags and turpentine and junk was down there too close to a space heater that the super probably left on. Lookin' for the owner now since an old man died in the blaze—couldn't get out of the windows because of the bars. Died with the keys in his hand. Terrible shame.''

Claudia's hand flew over her mouth. ''Mr. Jones . . . oh, no.'' Her voice trembled and threatened to break. ''Trapped by the bars . . . ?''

''That's why they lookin' for the owner now. Was kids in the building, too, but everybody else got out all right. Lady upstairs on the third floor was lucky to be up and awake with

her youngest baby at no-o'clock in the morning. She smelled
smoke, but fire hadn't reached her floor yet. Wound up throwing
kids down to the man who ran the bar next door. Firemen got
to her with a ladder. Glad you was out to a party with your
gentleman friend . . . Can you imagine?'' he said shaking his
head in disgust mixed with relief. ''Uhmph, uhmph, uhmph,
don't make sense what some'll do for money. Hope they find
him and do what they thinking about. Said they gonna try to
take that slumlord down for manslaughter due to negligence—
count of the old man's life, I think they said.''

''Manslaughter?'' Claudia spun around to face her father.
''Impossible.''

''Claudia, baby,'' he said calmly, trying unsuccessfully to
soothe her. ''It was on the news. I ain't makin' that up.''

''They're wrong,'' she nearly screamed, stopping her father
in his tracks when he tried to move toward her to comfort her.
''There *were* smoke detectors! I saw him install them myself,
and I was with him all week long! He didn't have *junk* in the
basement, or a space heater on. It was immaculate down there
. . . Just papers, and bills, a little furniture and a small refrigerator . . . but organized. No. No. Something is wrong, Daddy.
That's why Loretta is here. Don't you see?''

The old man paused and looked at her real hard. ''If what
you sayin' is true, then you better call the authorities and set
this to right. Don't make sense for an honest man to go to jail.
They stopped by here today anyway, wantin' to talk to you about
it. But me and Dot fended 'em off till tomorrow morning—on
account of you seemed to relapse into depression. Even that
attorney who took Ret's papers came by this afternoon while
you was sleep . . . said he heard through his legal connections
that there'd been trouble and wanted to be sure the family was
all right—all that we had just been through . . . and since Loretta
used to work with them, so—''

''He never even came to the funeral, or sent a spray, after
being her lover and business partner for eight years, Daddy!

Get it through your mind, these are no friends of the bereaved Harris family! That black, son-of-a—''

''Girl, you wrong as rain, wasn't no black man that came down here. You confusing everything and everybody you's in so much pain.''

She was breathing hard and turning in circles in the middle of the floor, hoping that a direction would come. Refraining from the urge to shake her father, she wrapped her arms around herself instead. ''Daddy, was the man from Addison Development?''

Her father walked over to a small shelf above the kitchen table and fished around the loose papers and nicknacks that it housed. ''I cain't remember . . . let me call for Dot. Or, I can wait till morning, we ain't gettin' no where on sheer speculation tonight.''

''Wake her up,'' she said through urgent breaths. ''Tell her she's gotta find the man's name from where you left the papers.''

Her father's stance suddenly became rigid. ''Why? Why tonight? We all tired, and been through a lot. Cooler heads may prevail in the morning, and Dot don't need to be upset. Probably should go check on her now—'specially if she been listening to us hollerin' and cryin'. Poor woman might think it was on account of her. She's sensitive that way.''

They had distanced again and Claudia's nerves swayed and snapped under the weight of the heavy void.

''You don't need to protect Dot, I told her how I feel . . . did it so she could get a decent night's sleep. But, this ain't about her or no trouble from no thirty years ago. Look, you may be in danger, I may be in danger, and a decent man who I love may be in danger. Now go wake her up!''

''Now hold on.'' Her father had formed a barrier with his body blocking the doorway between the kitchen and the dining room. ''I ain't waking Dot up on hystronics. We ain't got no facts.''

''What did the nice white man from Loretta's job say, word

for word?'' she gave in momentarily, sarcasm singeing her voice. She was almost too weak to think.

Her father drew a breath and seemed to ignore her tone. ''Said that he'd heard about the fire, and wanted to know if you were able to salvage any of your belongings . . . and left five hundred dollars for you, *in cash,* as a personal donation because me and Dot said all you got out wit was the clothes on your back. He said he was sorry, and that if you needed anything, that you could call him. Like I told you, Dot wrote down the number.''

''What did he look like?''

Her father sighed. ''Plain, nothin' to speak of . . . medium build, brownish hair. A white man. Why?''

''That's *not* who Loretta worked for. She worked for a black man, a big real estate magnet named Eric Addison, who was also her lover. She and her lover fell out over some white woman he married, but she wasn't going to let go of some big business thing in Philly that we never finished the conversation about. They had probably searched through the things you gave them, and when they didn't find what they wanted, they turned to me, her sister—the only other person she'd be likely to trust. Do you hear me, Daddy? But I was away . . . first at the hospital, then as a damned-near recluse for the short time I was back. They probably thought I didn't have anything in my possession because I had never come sniffing around trying to get money from them. And if they were watching me, God knows they knew I needed it . . . But why now?''

Her father's eyes, once glassy from tears, were now glassy with fear. ''Claudia, you scarin' me, baby. You think Ret got herself mixed up with some drug people, or something?''

''I don't know, Daddy.''

''But if they started the fire . . . like you said about Ret haunting me and Dot, if they were after you, baby girl, they didn't have to wait six months to do that. They coulda kicked down your raggedy apartment door anytime . . . or, like you speculatin', could have got you in the hospital.''

"Yeah . . . or, they could have waited to see where, or if, what they wanted surfaced without drawing attention to themselves."

"Then, like you said, what changed in the wind to make them all of a sudden wake up and decide to burn you out and kill an old man in the process?"

Claudia leaned on the refrigerator for support, tilted her head back, and closed her eyes. She needed time to think, but couldn't allow that luxury with Nate in trouble and authorities coming in the morning.

"Nate!" she whispered, in a conspiratorial tone. "Daddy, didn't you say that it started in the basement?"

"Yeah, but what's—"

"I started seeing the man who lived in the basement last week, that's how I know that there weren't any rags, or a space heater . . . they probably thought I gave what they wanted to him, so they torched the whole building to get to both of us."

This time he stared at her without resistance. "Dear God in heaven . . . I better go wake Dot."

Chapter 13

Nate sat in horror as he tried to comprehend what had happened to his friend. Ed's fragile jawline was distorted and cast a blue-purple haze beneath his once honey-colored skin. His lower lip looked as though it had been filled, and dark stitches strained across the swollen bulb of it. One eye was completely shut and blackened, and a deep gash fractured it's way across the thinning center of his silky hair. The bridge of his nose was hidden beneath thick white tape, and Ed's breathing was labored as he tried to find a comfortable way to position the bulk of his forearm cast.

"Like I told Stephanie," Ed said softly, barely moving his jaw as he spoke, "they forced their way into my office late last night, wanted to know where you were staying, and wanted me to hand over your titles—they thought I still had power of attorney over the properties." After considerable effort to shift himself in his recliner, Ed coughed and tried to begin again. "We're leaving for a while. I've got Stephanie and the kids, you know, Nate. I didn't think Addison would go this far."

Nate was nearly speechless, and the broiling rage within him was held in check only out of concern for his friend's life.

"Ed," Nate began slowly, "did you go to the police yet?"

Ed tried to shake his head no, but it was obvious that the beating now tortured every muscle of his slight frame. "They said that they'd go after the kids if I did . . . I was just glad to be alive."

"But, you had to say something when you went to the hospital. Didn't they have questions?"

Tears had summoned their way to Ed's eyes and he blinked them back and looked down. His voice quavered with a mixture of rage, fear, and shame.

"Stephanie was hysterical—and I told her, as well as the hospital authorities, that I had been mugged in Center City. That's why I didn't answer the phones, my pager, or cell-phone all day. I was in the hospital. When I got home, I heard your message and saw what happened to your building on the news."

As one lonely tear broke over the ridge of his lower eyelash, Ed looked up to the ceiling to fight off the deluge that now filled his eyes. Nate watched it slowly cascade down Ed's cheek, feeling an anger so deep within his soul that he almost had to pray to restrain it. Paternal instinct made him want to leap from his chair, which faced Ed's, and hug him the way a man hugs a child, fully, yet gently. This was the person who had saved his life, the one who'd kept his head during times of crisis. Now that same person sat before him shattered, frightened . . . the sight of such devastation made him want to wretch. The walls within Ed's expansive Villanova study seemed to close around him. He felt small, tiny, helpless . . . like a speck of cosmic dust raging against a tornado.

"I'm so sorry, man." Nate's voice shook with an explosive blend of toxic emotions. Nothing else would come from his mouth as he battled his mind for something, anything, to say. But there were no words that could right this wrong; only actions.

"Thought I'd go down to my mom's house in Virginia for

a while. The kids could use a break, they're spooked, too . . . seeing their father this way. The hardest part was facing my wife and kids like this.'' Ed swallowed hard. ''Now, they don't think I can protect them, and truthfully, I don't know that I can. A part of our world has changed. Steph wants me to close the practice and take a job as a professor at Morehouse. She even called her father, who is on the board, to push it through. Steph said Villanova isn't far enough away from the viral infection of city life for her.''

Ed let out another long breath. ''Used to be a time when I would stand my ground and fight because we were fighting civil rights issues, human rights issues, for justice. Even dreamed of being the next Thurgood Marshall one day.'' His laugh was pained and cynical. ''But I feel so violated, Nate . . . If the Klan had gone after me, then I would have raised the issue to media heights and would have led the charge against injustice. But this . . .''

''Look man, you don't have to explain. You take Stephanie and the kids away for a while and let me run the firm until you've had a chance to feel better and decide.''

It was the only option that Nate could think of immediately. This was the only way he could ever begin to repay his dear friend.

An eerie quiet settled between them and Ed looked at him with an odd mixture of understanding and resistance.

''Funny,'' Ed said with a sad smile, ''remember I said that to you a few years back? Now I know how you felt.''

Nate hadn't considered it, and he leaned back in his chair to absorb the turn of events.

''Yeah,'' he said after a while . ''I felt stripped, broken, like I wanted to pack it all in. But you were a good enough friend not to let me. And, Ed, you never rubbed my nose in it, or let anybody know how bad off my head was.''

Compassion filled Ed's eyes as he lowered them before he spoke. ''Nate, man, you and I go way back. You don't have to think about that. It never happened.''

More silence encased them as they sat in separate chairs, each wondering how much more strain their deep bond of friendship could take. Nate had to protect his friend, his partner, who was like a brother. Yet, he also needed Ed's help to stay out of jail and to testify to the beating and any of the other information that could be amassed against Addison. But their friendship came first.

"It did happen, Ed, and what happened to you was just as real. You regroup, get your head together for however long that takes—but I'm not about to let you go down, or have them run us out of business."

Ed seemed tentative. "Nate . . . they put a gun to my head while two other guys kicked the living shit out of me. This isn't a paper chase anymore, where attorneys duke it out in court. It's gone far beyond that."

Fire burned within Nate's skull, making the dim light of the study almost too bright for his eyes. "Was Addison with them?"

Hesitating before he spoke, Ed cast his line of vision toward the window. "No. He never does his own dirty work. He sends in the soft touch first, then the thugs. An old man is dead . . . maybe even a woman, because of them."

Nate's senses trained on Ed's words like a hunting dog. "No. The woman is fine. I drove her home after the blaze."

"You couldn't have, Nate. She's been dead for six months."

Something congealed in his gut. A new survivalist instinct that he'd never needed around Ed made him wary. Something primal told him there was a critical detail that he needed to pursue. He'd picked up a foul scent.

"Yeah, perhaps I'm way off base," Nate said, forcing his body to appear to relax. "I guess I need to focus on the old man's death. That broke my heart when I heard it."

Cautious now, Ed shifted to a direct gaze, holding Nate's eyes with his own.

"I'm glad you were finally out *gettin' some,*" he laughed a little too awkwardly, "otherwise you might have gone up in the blaze."

Nate allowed a false chuckle. "Just some chick I met in the supermarket. I've been out of circulation so long, I picked up some dame by buying her groceries. Man, she had four screaming kids, so I took her by my real spot. I'm glad they didn't know about that haven."

He watched Ed's face with an expert's vision; an eye trained to detect a lie. He hated games. . . . It was worse with those he loved.

Ed's shoulders relaxed. "Good for you, man. Wow. I thought they'd found you over at Forty-Fifth Street, at first."

He'd been correct. They'd beaten everything out of Ed, but not his haven. Yet, he had to be sure with a cross-examination.

Tension made an involuntary muscle in Nate's face jump under his cheek. "You told them that's where they could find me? *Only at Forty-Fifth?*"

"I had to give them something . . . I just prayed that would be enough, and that you'd be home—your real home."

Watching the guilt wash over Ed, it was confirmed. The brownstone was safe for the moment. But he needed more information before Ed bolted from the city.

"Good move . . . with a little Divine Intervention," he said evenly, trying to assuage Ed's guilt. "It's okay, man. You had to give them something."

His friend stood on wobbly legs and walked over to a file cabinet. It seemed as though he was using his last ounce of strength to pull open a drawer with one hand. Nate watched him intently but didn't breathe, much less move. Something was still wrong.

"I told them that I had turned power back over to you late last year, which I did." Ed retrieved a large brown envelope and walked slowly back to the chair. "I'm ready to turn it all over to you, the business, that is. I've already made my decision, Nate. You don't have to hold a spot for me, and I can't represent you."

He sat down heavily and flung the brown envelope into Nate's lap. Nate looked down with disinterest and let it rest on his thighs.

"You really want to give me the business, just sign it over? Why not take a silent position like you offered to me . . . or just go on sabbatical? I can run it while you're gone."

Ed stared toward the door that led from the study into the living room. "I can't." His voice had become a whisper. "This is the only way."

The envelope called Nate, but the distant way Ed looked at the door told him something beyond the fear of physical reprisal entered into the equation. Again, it was a feeling that hit his gut like a stone.

"Who was the soft touch, and how did she die?"

He watched Ed's gaze slide to the envelop and his friend's voice sounded hollow, ghost-like as he whispered the truth.

"She came to me about eight month's ago . . . and told me that she and another woman wanted to start a nonprofit housing project that would give micro-entrepreneurs a store front with living space above it. She told me that she needed an attorney to file the 501 (c) 3 paperwork, and to help her develop proposals for foundations and investors."

"And, she was beautiful." Nate allowed his head to drop back and he'd closed his eyes as he said the words. He could hear Ed swallow.

"Very beautiful . . . and kind-hearted . . ."

"And easy to talk to . . ." Nate sighed.

Acid curdled in his stomach. He wanted to punch and hug his dear friend at the same time. Ed didn't respond.

"Aw, man . . . don't tell me . . ." Nate's voice was nearly a plea.

"Steph, and I . . . for years . . . I mean . . . things haven't been . . ."

Nate held up his hand and squeezed his eyes shut harder, stopping the string of unfinished phrases Ed offered. They spoke volumes.

"Did you invest in her nonprofit as a funder, and if so, what did you put up as collateral?"

"The Cecil B. Moores."

"Damn!"

Nate shot out of his chair and paced the floor. "Jesus, man. For some tail?"

"Keep your voice down," Ed urged. "Steph . . . Look, as terrible as it is, it's not as bad for you as you think. She's the only one who got hurt in this, lost everything she'd put up . . . could've been killed behind it, who knows? Or, it could have been a freak accident . . . just like the old man was an accident, okay. Now, I have to get out or I'll bring disaster to the firm . . . maybe even go up for murder."

"Murder?"

Confusion tore at Nate's insides as he found his way back to the chair. Clawing at his hair he dropped into the seat, slumped, and let his head hang between his knees. "Start at the beginning, counselor."

"I needed somebody to talk to," Ed said in a far away voice. "Things had been so sterile for so long . . . Steph and I had become practically roommates . . . As long as her social agenda wasn't disturbed, and the money kept flowing, well . . ." Ed hesitated and glanced at the door, then returned his gaze to the window. "But *she* was electric. Alive . . . She was also a decent human being. She had a down-home side too, Nate . . . a quiet side that was tender that nobody but me ever saw. She was gorgeous, smart, and funny, and had a mind like a steel trap."

Nate groaned. "You fell in love with that trap, man, didn't you?"

Nate finally looked up at his friend who was now staring toward the large bay window again. It was as though the window had become a portal to another time and another dimension for Ed, offering him a vision from the past that he'd lost forever. Nate understood Ed's temptation, and grieved for his loss, for he had walked ten miles in the same shoes. If Monica had lived, perhaps he would have been just as vulnerable to a black widow. He let out a sigh of frustration.

"I've never met a woman like her, who possessed all of those qualities in one package. And, Nate, man, she had a heart, or she wouldn't have risked herself the way she did to try to save the firm."

Nate offered no response as he looked at his friend growing old under the strain. It was a transformation that seemed to take place right before his eyes.

"What happened, Ed?" he said as gently as possible. "I need the details, as painful as they are."

Tears coursed down Ed's face silently and he made no effort to wipe them away as he continued to stare out of the window. "After I set up her business, and backed it by the initial collateral required to attract funding investors, her partner raised some seven-hundred thousand in cash. We'd become lovers by then, and I wanted to leave Steph . . . but the kids . . . I couldn't . . . She even understood that, man. Do you hear me? She understood that."

Nate didn't have time to encourage Ed's fantasy, so he cut to the chase. "How did she die? Why would you be implicated if she did?"

"In the hospital . . . it was probably for the best. Clean, quick. Originally we all thought that they gave her the wrong dosage of anesthesia, but then they found alcohol in her system, so she actually killed herself. Maybe she took a shot that morning to steady her nerves, who knows? Because we didn't drink or eat after midnight. Her sister drove her to the hospital, because we could never spend the whole night together, but I was with her the night before it happened, and there were questions. I also came to the hospital just before they prepped her . . . to give her a quick kiss, and let her know that I'd be there for her when she got out. They'd seen me at the hospital, even though her family didn't know who I was. We were discrete. But, she never came home."

The story brought a coil of fire down Nate's back. "What was her name?"

"Loretta Harris," Ed whispered, starting to tear again.

Nate refused to let the gasp push past his lips. Repressing the urge made his ears ring. Claudia.

"Who was her partner?"

"Maria DiGiovanni."

This time his stomach lurched in earnest. Her last name was like a death camp.

"How is our firm implicated in anything?"

Ed paused. "Open the envelop."

He kept his eyes on Ed's face as his hands gently slipped the contents from the envelop into his lap. The texture changed from the rough manila exterior to the glossy finish of what felt like several eight by ten photos. When he looked down, he closed his eyes briefly and drew a breath. Steadying himself, he scanned the other legal contents and slipped the papers back into the envelope, then looked up at his partner.

"They took pictures of us, Nate. Even of me at the hospital."

"I saw."

"But she helped us."

"How?"

"She told me what was going to go down . . . that she, too, had been used . . . that Addison had married her partner and they were forcing her off the project. So, she signed her half back over to me, then I signed it back to you . . . remember late last year when I suddenly gave up my power of attorney over your properties? That's why. I couldn't trust myself to hold up under the pressure when they asked for my half back. I would have given it to them in a heartbeat."

"So, that's why they kicked your ass."

"Yes, because she died without telling them that I didn't have power of attorney to buy and sell or invest for you anymore, or that she had given over her investments to me. She had an original notarized set, I had one, and you have one. Triplicate. At first they didn't believe me . . . they dropped the photos on me a week earlier. Then when I kept the same story, they paid me a visit. I showed them a set of the originals, which they took—you're only holding copies of the papers in your hands. Like I said, Nate, she saved us. She turned everything back and didn't even want a dime. She cried in my arms like a baby and said that she was sorry to have dragged me into something like this. She had a good heart, Nate. She wasn't a pirana. I immediately saw the consequences and put everything in your name, and told her that's how it would be okay . . .''

"Yeah, and that just put a bounty on my head. Are you crazy?" Nate's nerves frayed and popped as he stood again. The numb expression on Ed's face made Nate want to turn and hit him. "Man, follow the paper trail here! Use your big head now, instead of the little one you were using for that chick. They kicked the shit out of you so that you'd give them your portion, and DiGiovanni would have it all, which means her new husband, Addison, *has it all*. But, there was a wrinkle . . . a complication, let's say. You no longer have the properties, and no longer have power of attorney to get them back. So, they tell you to find me and get it back from me, any way you can. So, they leave, caucus, and decide that a quicker way for them to wrap this up neatly is, they can kill me—like in a four A.M. slumlord blaze when I'm supposed to be asleep! And, since they probably have my will, too—since you had to give it up, I'm sure, they also know that everything I own goes back to you—so that you can run the firm in the advent of my untimely demise. Remember, when I wrote that will, when I *thought* I had problems and was suicidal?'' Nate laughed and threw his head back. He felt a sudden rush of hysteria pulse in his veins. "So, you knowing that, bail out of the firm, and again, give me back all of my shit. What are friends for?"

Ed's eyes were wide and his gaze darted from object to object in the room. "I don't know what to do, Nate. I didn't think of it that way. I knew you hadn't been involved in any scandals. They didn't have anything on you, and you were stronger than me . . . had more heart, even when you were all messed up. Until she died, and they threatened to kill me, I didn't know what they were capable of . . . What are we going to do?''

Nate continued to pace. He needed motion to bring the blood back to his brain. "First, you need to go somewhere safe to preserve your marriage, your dignity, and your reputation—like Virginia. I can't guarantee your life. The only way to possibly save it, is for me to openly become their bait. I need to surface so that they know the big dog is back on the block. That way, they'll be diverted back to me instead of you, Steph, or the kids. They need to know that the fight is one-on-one, so that no more innocent people get hurt."

They stared at each other for a long time.

"I'm so sorry, man," Ed said thickly with emotion.

Nate walked over and hugged him gingerly, aware of his wounds.

"Don't mention it, man. It never happened."

Dot had been efficient as always, staving off visitors, amassing a pile of clothing donations from the church, and collecting the barrage of phone calls of concern from all of her friends. Not one call had been from Nate, and the visitors and calls that had come in were from people whom she'd expected had abandoned her a long time ago. Maybe she had been wrong? she thought as the realization crept into her mind. Maybe she had been too angry at the world to give their words or offers of assistance any credence before. She'd judged *them* the way she'd felt they'd always judged her sister—lumped everything and everybody together in a big pot of foul soup.

Claudia stood at the bottom of the living room staircase leaning on Dot and the banister for support. For a moment she felt like a child, and wished her father was there on the other side of her instead of the banister. She'd told him to get some rest; he had to be as bone weary as she was now. But he'd claimed that he had to go to the church for one more box. Why now, when she was too tired from staying up all last night until the pink-gold dawn splashed the sky, did she have to face this? How could she go through an interrogation at eight thirty in the morning? She still had her robe on!

Claudia kneaded the tiny slips from the message pad in her hands like dough, rolling them, unfolding them, and reordering them as she intently watched the two detectives before her.

"My name is Detective Wilson, and this is Detective McKinney," the first one said evenly. "Your mother said that your family has experienced a great loss recently, and this fire was overwhelming. Let us first offer our condolences, and we're sorry to have to put you through the painful details at a time like this, but we need answers so that we can deal with the person who allowed this to happen."

Claudia nodded her assent as Dot stood by her side, still wary of the salt and pepper team that the authorities had sent.

"Do you have any identification?" Claudia asked as a reflex. She trusted no one at this point.

The two men exchanged a glance and produced identification for her to review. Satisfied that it was legitimate, Claudia moved to the sofa and sat down heavily without offering them a seat.

Again, they glanced at each other, and this time they addressed Dot when they asked whether or not it was all right to sit across from Claudia. Receiving Dot's permission, they sat down.

Each muscle in her body was drawn piano wire tight, and as she watched the black detective lean forward from the ottoman, and the white detective shift into a laid-back position in the recliner. She knew they were going to work her good-cop, bad-cop style. She was ready.

"Mrs. Harris," the first officer said in an authoritative tone directed toward Dot, "we would just like a few minutes with your daughter alone."

Dot looked from Claudia, to the agents and back again, appearing unmoved by the sudden shift in the man's approach.

"It's all right, Dot," Claudia finally conceded. "Why don't

you make us some tea?'' Searching Dot's face and measuring the anxiety, she added, ''It'll be all right. I'm okay now.''

The older woman's shoulders seemed to relax and she let out a breath as she moved toward the kitchen. Turning back once before she left the room, Dot's eyes narrowed and conveyed a serious warning before she spoke. ''Now don't you go upsetting my child. She's been through enough.'' She lingered long enough to coax a nod of compliance from them, then her heavy-hipped frame was gone. It was like watching a mother bear growl low in her throat before allowing an intruder to leave her den with his life. It was comforting to know just how much Dot was in her corner.

Claudia kept her eyes focused on the tiny slips of paper in her hands. Where was Nate? She needed not only his moral support, but his legal advice now. If they'd only been able to talk before the officers came, she would have known what stance to take . . . how much to reveal, how much to hide, how to protect him. . . .

''Seems like a lot of people have been concerned about you,'' the suit named Wilson said while eyeing her handful of messages.

Instinct took over the fatigue, and she immediately decided that it would be far better to appear like a distraught victim, than anything else. This way, they would trust her and waste time on whatever trail she sent them on. It could at least be a diversion until she talked to Nate.

''Yeah,'' she said in a weary tone, ''it's a shame that tragedy has to strike before you can know who your real friends are.'' Leaning forward she stretched out her hand and gave the rumpled pile to the suit seated on the ottoman. ''My girlfriends have been calling since they heard about the fire on the news.'' It was a credibility move, designed to imply that she had nothing to hide.

Wilson reviewed the pile briefly and handed the notes to McKinney for inspection.

''I know this has been a terrible loss,'' McKinney said in a too-compassionate voice that came across as patronizing. "Did the owner try to contact you, or to help you and the other tenants in any way?"

Her insides constricted but her exterior remained sad and placid looking. She could do this, good cop or bad.

"No," she said, still looking at her empty hands. "Just this man named Mr. Jenkins, who I don't know. He's in the pile of messages . . . but he only left a pager number."

From her peripheral vision, Claudia watched the two exchange a look of concern.

"Did Mr. Jenkins work for your landlord?" Wilson said, accepting the stack of messages from McKinney and handing them back to her—all but the message from Mr. Jenkins.

They were trying to trap her. How would she know who worked for her landlord unless she had contact with him on a regular basis—contact that went beyond mailing in a monthly rental payment? Claudia retreated farther into her passive victim role and redirected the trap.

"I don't know," she said slowly, as though trying to recall anything about McGregor Realty. "I'd just drop my payments by the office on Fortieth Street on the first of the month, and the lady that worked there would take it and give me a receipt. I never saw a Mr. Jenkins when I went in there. In fact, all I know is that he's white. I've never seen him. My parents dealt with him."

"Well, then why is this Mr. Jenkins, that you don't know, trying to contact you?"

If her nerves weren't so shattered, she would have almost smiled. The diversion away from Nate had momentarily worked and she could feel the bait tempting them to bite. Shrugging, she let out a sigh of exasperation. "He's the man that left me five hundred dollars. For what, I don't know?"

Both detectives were now leaning forward in their seats. Claudia stood and retrieved the envelop from the sideboard in the dining room and handed it to them before she sat down.

Again both men reviewed the envelop, but this time McKinney put it in his breast pocket. "That's a lot of money to leave somebody you don't know." His voice had become tight and authoritative, no longer with a calm, good-cop sound. "Tell me what you know about this Mr. Jenkins."

Claudia looked at both men squarely in the face. "He came around after my sister died, and bilked my parents out of all of her important papers . . . bills, anything she had in her business files. The same day as the funeral, my sister's condo was robbed, but nothing was reported stolen. It just looked like somebody had ransacked the place looking for something. Then, my parents get a call from this man who claimed to work with my sister's firm, Addison Development, and he meets them and takes everything that they could find. They were in so much grief, and are elderly . . . they didn't know any better. Then, all of a sudden, my apartment goes up in flames. I wish *you* would do *your* job and tell me who the hell this Mr. Jenkins is."

Appearing to brush off the insult, Wilson slowly removed a small pad and a pen from his suit breast pocket and began to jot down notes. "Was your sister in any kind of trouble?"

Claudia let out a sigh, glad that they were sufficiently baited and hooked. Realizing that this was the only way to reopen her sister's case, and at the same time divert their attention away from her relationship with Nate, she very carefully dropped tidbits in the murky waters as she reeled them in.

"Yeah, I guess she was in trouble, since they killed her."

Wilson stopped writing and he held her in an intense gaze. "How did your sister die? Who killed her?"

"Can't say exactly."

It was McKinney's turn now, and she watched the slightly heavy, balding man pull himself to the edge of the recliner and place his hands on his knees. "Can't say, or won't say?"

"Can't," Claudia said firmly, never losing eye contact.

''Did they threaten you?'' Wilson asked without looking at his partner.

''They burned me out, then left five hundred dollars. I'm no fool. I can take a hint.''

McKinney stood and walked over to the couch and sat down, invading the distance that had been her private fortress. ''Listen to me, young lady, this sequence of events sounds extremely dangerous. If you know who has been terrorizing your family, then you need to make us aware of the perpetrator. Because, as I'm sure you know, they won't just go away quietly if they think you have anything on them.''

Although she hated the way the man had called her, ''young lady,'' she also knew that part of what he said was right. Only, how could she get them to go after a case that had been settled and closed on sheer speculation? Her mind screamed for a solution, and all it came up with was a blank. So she waited. She needed time to think.

But apparently her silence was too much for the suit named Wilson to tolerate. He stood and leaned on the wall between the kitchen and the dining room, fidgeting with the click button on his pen.

''Let's start again,'' Wilson said quietly, using his voice to coax her out. ''You said they killed your sister, and we want to know how she died?''

Claudia never flinched. ''Loretta went in for routine surgery because they saw a shadow on her lung X-ray. She was a smoker, and cancer runs in our family. So, she went in for a biopsy, and was supposed to come home the same day. But, there was a so-called problem with her anesthesia, and she died on the table.''

Again the officer stopped writing, but this time they exchanged a deflated glance of disappointment. When she saw it, she immediately panicked, because her fish were slipping off their hooks.

''What makes you think that your sister was in enough trouble that someone would have to have bribed an MD—a person who would have had to risk his entire medical career, to slip your sister the wrong anesthesia? Malpractice and accidents happen everyday. I think—''

''So does murder,'' she said through her teeth without measuring her tone. ''Don't you read the paper?''

Rage unleashed itself from her intestines, and she folded her hands carefully in her lap to regain composure. They were at a delicate juncture, and any perceived hysteria on her part now could make them question her sanity. Before they'd even begun, it had occurred to her that her short hospital stay would come into question eventually anyway, especially if the whole thing went to court. Therefore, she focused on her objective, knowing that it was better to keep in character than to break now and cause a scene.

''I'm sorry,'' she said when they didn't respond. ''We've all been so upset.''

''No apology necessary, ma'am,'' Wilson said, now taking on the good-cop role. ''We're just trying to help and get to the bottom of this. Help us help you, Miss Harris. Why do you think the hospital is involved?''

She knew she had to be careful now. Just like her father had shown her, she had spooked the fish and it would be a while before they came back to the same spot in the pond to pick at the bait she'd left. It was time to get quiet and let the water go still.

''I don't think the hospital did it, necessarily.'' Her tone was wistful and as passive as she could make it.

''But you said she died in the hospital?'' McKinney said, sniffing closer to the bait.

''Yes, the coroner's report said that my sister had a high blood alcohol count that mixed wrong with the anesthesia . . . therefore the insurance investigators said that hospital wasn't liable for what the patient had not disclosed in advance upon admission. Our family had no claim, except accidental death. So, my parents never pursued it. But two things stand out in my mind as peculiar. One, my sister did drink, but not gin like the report said they'd found. Only vodka, Absolut, and she was very particular with her vices—just like she only smoked Benson & Hedges—menthols. Never a deviation. And two, they do blood work *before* they take you under. Just before. That's why it takes so long for surgery prep—stuff goes down to the lab and comes back, right? So, if there was any alcohol in her system, why wouldn't it have shown up then? So, with all of these other issues that seem to have coincidentally followed, like our unknown Mr. Jenkins wanting all of her papers and stuff, I can only draw two conclusions; either the hospital is liable because there was an error in the pre-op lab reports, or somebody not associated with the hospital got in there and did something to her anesthesia before they gave it to her.''

Wilson had started writing again, and McKinney's eyes never left her face. They seemed to believe her, or at the very least, she could tell that her comment sounded circumstantial enough to give them pause.

After a moment of hesitation, the second suit adjusted himself to lean in closer toward her. ''This man, Jenkins,'' McKinney questioned without blinking, ''said he was with your sister's firm? What do they do?''

''I think they're real estate developers.'' Claudia had let her gaze scan both faces when she'd answered.

''Big, like McGregor's,'' Wilson chimed in scribbling furiously.

The phone rang and her blood froze in her veins. Her eyes darted nervously toward the kitchen entrance, and the detectives trained their line of vision on her. When she heard Dot's amiable, ''Don't worry about her none, baby . . .'' trail off, Claudia relaxed. Just another friend inquiring about her situation. It wasn't Jenkins or Nate. The officers seemed to read her body language and relax again, too, but this time their expressions were unreadable as Wilson spoke.

''This man may not be connected to Addison Developers,

but could have known where your sister worked and used that as a cover. Whatever you do, contact us immediately if anything else happens, Jenkins calls again, your former landlord, Nate McGregor, tries to contact you, or if anyone calls you from her former place of employ. Mr. Jenkins could very well be working for McGregor.''

Sensing a wrong turn of events, new panic rippled through her system with a shot of adrenaline propelling it through her once frozen veins. She kept her voice calm . . . maybe too calm.

''Okay, I will. Just seems so strange, you know? They kept the buildings up so well, and all. I even had one of the smoke detectors in the hallway near my door, and if I fried fish, it would go off. So, I know for a fact that the batteries were good. Then, for them to say on the news that there weren't any smoke detectors found in the building at all . . . when I had to pass right by it that night before I left to go out and party . . .'' Claudia allowed her voice to trail off as she shook her head for emphasis. ''Then that fight my sister had with Addison the week before she died . . . That's why I'm just not sure, but it seems very strange to me.''

She held her breath as the two exchanged a meaningful glance and Wilson took to his pad again.

''You say there were smoke detectors in your building? Working ones?'' Wilson asked looking up from his pad.

''Yes. Always.''

''What fight?'' McKinney asked, double-teaming her. ''How long ago did you say?''

''A week before she died, my sister told me that Addison, who was also her business partner and lover, had married another woman. But it was in what she didn't say, and how she was talking about them being tied together in business no matter what . . .'' Claudia stopped and issued a quick prayer. The detectives seemed hooked, she just hoped she wouldn't snap the line again this time. ''I had told her to get another job, and she said that she had him, quote, 'by the short hairs,' if you'll excuse me, and would get even. She'd basically said that they were tied together in a way deeper than marriage, and she'd leave the firm over her dead body—in so many words. And, that's what happened.''

Real tears had formed in her eyes and spilled down her cheeks. This part of what she said was no act. Appearing satisfied, McKinney stood giving her back her distance.

''You've been most helpful, Miss Harris,'' he said, offering a nod to Wilson. ''Please take care of yourself and remember what we said.''

''Contact us if any of these people try to get in touch with you,''Wilson added. ''It seems like your sister was tied up with a bad bunch, and we have some work to do to untangle this ball of yarn.''

Returning from her guard post in the kitchen, Dot entered the room without any tea, and without making any apologies for eavesdropping.

''I'm glad you all are finished with all of this questioning business, and I *told you* not to upset my baby.'' Dot's eyes held a fearless quality that Claudia had never seen in her before. Dot glared at the intruders as she plunked down on the couch next to her, wrapping a protective arm around Claudia. ''I think it's high time for you all to leave.''

Obviously used to hostile exchanges with overprotective family members, the two men walked toward the door without any change in their strides or demeanor.

''Thank you for your time,'' the one named McKinney intoned like a robot.

''We'll contact you if we have any more questions,'' the other said as he pulled the door shut behind them.

Dot let out a loud ''Humph,'' and pulled her arm around Claudia's shoulders in tighter. ''Look, honey,'' she said fishing out a crumpled piece of paper from her apron pocket with the other hand, ''that nice young colored boy, Nate, they're trying to blame everything on called while you were in here with the police. Didn't want to add no more fuel to the fire. Forgive the reference, baby. Just upsets me so.''

She stared at Dot and gave her a hug. ''Thanks, Mom,'' she said in a low whisper, feeling Dot's arms tighten around her. ''Besides you and Dad, he's all I've got left now.''

Chapter 14

"Let us get this straight, McGregor. You claim that you hit all the bars in the area last night then went home to crash. Therefore, between two A.M. and four A.M. you were supposedly in bed asleep when the blaze occurred—but nobody can substantiate your whereabouts, right?"

"Correct."

Nate shifted uneasily in the hard metal chair facing a somber black man that he approximated to be near his own age, while the voice of the white man who stood pacing continued to riddle his senses from behind. It had been hours.

"That's not good, McGregor. You don't have an alibi. I thought all attorneys had an alibi. What took you so long to come in here, when there's been an APB out on you for almost forty-eight hours?"

"I didn't hear about the all-points-bulletin until late that night—the same evening as the blaze—when I saw the news. We've been over this a hundred times ... I turned myself in willingly because I am here to cooperate. My day went like this: after I woke up, around ten A.M., I was hungry and planned to go to The American Diner on Forty-Second for some breakfast before I began my rounds. At approximately eleven thirty A.M., I left the house and walked by my first property, located on Forty-Fifth, on the way to the diner. That's when I saw my building and—''

''We've been over that crap before, counselor. That was yesterday! Why did it take you a whole night, a morning, and an afternoon to turn yourself into the authorities for questioning when you knew we had a warrant out for you since the day before? Tell us something we haven't heard.''

Each time the man seated before him spoke, his voice was filled with the recognizable disdain that is only reserved for one's own kind. It was a sick hatred, mixed with jealousy and a rage that knew no limits, usually hurled against those crabs that had made it out of the barrel. Nate knew what the black detective before him thought before he'd opened his mouth; that he was educated, privileged, had money, had the nerve to abuse the system in some way on top of everything else, and therefore didn't deserve any more breaks than he'd already amassed in his lousy life. It was written all over the brother's face.

''Look, man,'' Nate began, jarring the black man's senses with a term that they could both identify with, ''I saw my building burned to the ground and headed straight for my partner's house. But, he wasn't home. Dig? So I went around trying to find out what happened myself, and getting in touch with my insurance carrier, and another attorney who could represent us in case there was additional liability. That took all of yesterday, and that's basic business sense. I didn't know that an old man had died in the blaze until I saw the news.''

Detective Wilson pushed back in his chair and by now McKinney was sitting precariously on the edge of the worn oblong table that separated them.

''That was yesterday. What about today?''

''I had business to conduct. Needed to find out who burned down my building.'' There was no apology in Nate's voice.

"No, counselor, that's police business. Now you're a private eye or something? Well, if you're such a good detective, where's your partner now?" Wilson asked flatly, not giving an inch.

"Probably in Virginia."

McKinney leaned into him and squinted, scratching the bald spot on his head. "Hold it. I thought you said he wasn't home. So, how do you know that he's in Virginia?"

"It's a long story," Nate said stretching his achy limbs under the table.

"Don't play with us, *man*. We got time, you don't," Wilson shot back, looking as though he would come across the table to slug him.

"I'm not saying that I'm not going to answer you, *man*," Nate seethed. "But the whole story is complex and involves a lot of conjecture at this point."

"Are you trying to call us stupid, or something? What, we can't handle complex information? I oughtta kick your arrogant . . . !"

Wilson had come across the table and grabbed a handful of Nate's shirt, ripping a portion of it as Nate pulled back to avoid a blow. McKinney had joined the fray separating the two would-be combatants, and his face was now red and sweaty from the sudden exertion.

"Hey, hey, come on now. We won't get anywhere like this. Let's just stick to what happened in this long explanation. Cool off, Wilson, and let the man talk."

"I hate his kind, Mac. I really hate them! What they do to our neighborhoods, all for a buck. This bastard would probably sell his mama on the corner if she could still turn a dollar."

Nate was breathing hard now. To hell with propriety. "The only mother I'd sell is yours."

This time McKinney could barely referee the match as the two lunged at each other again, catching him in the middle. He had to pull his partner off of Nate by wrapping his arms around his waist and body slamming him against the interrogation room wall.

"Are you crazy, Wil? He's a freakin' attorney for Christ's sake." By now McKinney was huffing out each word and sweating profusely as he held his grip on his partner. "The department's got enough problems to contend with already, we don't need to make him into a martyr."

Wilson brushed off his suit and walked to the farthest corner in the tiny room. Folding his arms across his chest, he leaned against a windowsill, glaring at both men who occupied the opposite side of the room. Nate sat down heavily and pushed his chair back from the table, inspecting his suit and shirt for damage, then looked up in disgust to meet Wilson's glare. McKinney's gaze shot nervously between the two, who were locked in a stare-down challenge. It had become a pissing contest.

"McGregor, how do you know your partner went to Virginia, and when did you find this out?" McKinney said slowly without breaking eye contact, obviously trying to redirect the discussion to the relevant issues at hand.

Nate slowly composed himself with great effort. He hated the look in Wilson's eyes; the look of judgment without justice, without evidence.

"The first time I went by his house, nobody was home. I went about my other errands all day trying to get in touch with the other people I mentioned, calling Ed every half hour for six hours. I didn't get him until early evening, but by then, I knew something was wrong. That's when I went past his house for the last attempt and found him packed."

"What was wrong?" McKinney had asked the question while staring at Wilson.

"I found out that my partner had been beaten to shit. Busted lip, skull fracture, broken nose, broken arm, and scared to death. That's why he packed his wife and kids up and went to Virginia."

McKinney rubbed his chin and began pacing again, this time

in front of Nate before he sat down in Wilson's abandoned chair across from him. "Do you have any idea who would have wanted to take your partner out, or why?"

"That's the conjecture part," Nate admitted cautiously, still looking at Wilson as he spoke. "I think my partner, inadvertently, made some investments in an organization that was silently backed by Addison Development. Ed Washington had no idea about this when he sank his money and my Cecil B. Moore properties into what he thought was a safe bet. Then, I believe, Addison sent some of his henchmen over to get my partner to sign over his portion of the investments, effectively giving away the Cecil B. Moores. That's why he got beat nearly to death."

As he waited for the cops' slow-coming response, he could only hope that the information he just gave them would be enough to cover Ed's involvement without some misguided accusations being levied against his foolish, but innocent best friend.

"You know, that's the second time I've heard this guy's name today." McKinney's voice was quiet as he looked at his partner.

"Where did you hear it the first time?"

"We're the ones asking questions here," Wilson shot from across the room.

Nate sat back in his chair. Were they on to Claudia? A thin trickle of sweat rolled down his back. Couldn't be. He'd been extremely careful not to contact her so that she wouldn't be implicated, and his brief call earlier in the day was just to check to see if she was all right. He hadn't even left a number, and had turned off his answering machine at the house so she couldn't leave a message. He just hoped that she wasn't frantic enough to call the real estate office to leave a message there.

"What do you know about a Loretta Harris?" Wilson grilled, walking toward the table and picking up a brown manila envelope from the shelf on the way. "A little birdie dropped these and the negatives in my mailbox this morning."

Nate thought he would vomit as the envelop slid toward him. Claudia. They had gotten to her and she had given them this? Why?

Pushing the photos away toward Wilson, Nate's shoulders slumped. "I've seen them."

"Your partner sure's got himself in a jam," McKinney said eyeing the exterior of the envelop and placing it in the center of the table. "But, for the moment, he's out of state, and these papers have your name all over them. This kind of thing could put a strain on a partnership and a marriage. Enough of a strain that somebody could get killed—by a partner, or for a partner. Maybe like an old man and the girl in the picture."

He could only stare down at his feet. Obviously his attempts to cover Ed hadn't worked, and just as Ed thought, he would be smeared by perception, not reality. But why wouldn't Claudia have told him about this? Did she think he was involved with the murder of her sister? He could only assume that she'd found them at home tucked away in her sister's room somewhere, panicked, then called the police.

"Loretta Harris was the front for the nonprofit that my partner invested in unwittingly. She later died under mysterious circumstances in a hospital in Jersey."

"So, we've heard," Wilson said sounding unimpressed. "But I have a problem with the fact that everywhere you go, or any time your name pops up, there seems to be a body lying around afterward. Plus, you have this unaccounted-for time that nobody can substantiate. See, that bothers me. You'd better get an alibi quick, *man*. Dig up a girlfriend, or partner, or tenant, somebody who can say where you were, or you won't see any free time again in this century. *Dig?*"

Nate felt his heart stop. He didn't even breathe.

"For example," McKinney said stoically, "we know that you rented a car and went to Jersey the same night of the fire, and didn't return it until twenty-four hours later."

Perspiration was starting to bead on Nate's forehead, and both detectives were now standing as they began their pacing routine around him, circling him like buzzards waiting for the last twitch before moving in. The effect was dizzying.

"You can't pinpoint where you were this afternoon, and now we've got another dead girl, found in a hospital dumpster. Pretty thing too with—"

"What!" Nate shot of his chair like someone had burned him. Tears constricted his throat and the flurry of questions he needed answered caught below his Adam's apple. "When?" he croaked turning toward the wall and leaning on it with both elbows. "Just tell me when."

"You'd better sit down, McGregor, and start giving us some hard answers. None of this conjecture bullcrap about Addison, either." Wilson was on him first and obviously enjoying every minute of his torture. "All we know for a fact is that you and your partner invested with this chick that used to work for Addison. That's the only connection to Addison, at this point. I think what happened is, when you found out your boy was doing her behind your back, and had signed over your properties and was going to cut you out, *you* kicked his ass—but not before paying somebody to tamper with that woman's anesthesia, someone who worked at the hospital, had access, and knew what they were doing."

"Isabella . . ." Nate whispered, too dumbfounded for caution. He had to call her, had to tell her that it was too dangerous to even think about investigating anything at the hospital now.

"Oh, so now we have a name and a nursing student. Somebody with access and knowhow. Your lady does your partner's lady for a little extra cut in the deal . . . Now we just might be getting somewhere," McKinney said with a smile, leading him back to the chair and pushing him down in it hard. "Then a little domestic dispute happens today, around percentages, and things get out of hand . . . and the poor girl couldn't take a punch like a man. Sit down, you slimeball, and talk to us straight."

Wilson gloated as he continued to beat him with words. "And that's who you paid a visit to in Jersey, before the fire went down. The fire was just a ruse, or maybe a way to raise some insurance quick cash to get your properties back, or to destroy evidence hidden in the basement of that building ... haven't worked that out. The old man was just in the way, and that was probably the only accident in this whole sick, money-grubbing scheme of yours."

He was too stricken with grief to care what they thought at this point. All he had absorbed was the fact that Claudia was dead. "How and when did the girl die?" This was all his mind could process.

"Late this afternoon," McKinney said, losing some of his smugness.

It was as though Nate's stricken condition unraveled an edge of the tightly knit case that Wilson was trying to sew up. Nate's eyes searched McKinney's face and a gut knowing passed between them. He could tell that McKinney knew something was wrong.

Opening the envelope carefully, McKinney drew out a note that was attached by a huge paper clip to pictures, strips of negatives, and a bulk of papers. Shaking a key out onto the table without touching it, he reached into his breast pocket and pulled out a pair of Ben Franklin reading glasses.

"She addressed it to you, and says here that she found the information you asked her about the other day. The man's name is Jenkins, and she left his social security number. Said she still had an old key, and had gone in last night on a hunch that there might be something on him in the files that you could use ... that is, after hearing about the fire on the news." McKinney went on paraphrasing, not caring that the pain squeezed the air out of his lungs. "Says here that she thought you could destroy the negatives and use the social security number to protect yourself. What were you going to do, make it look like Jenkins never worked for you by killing him, too? Must have loved you a lot, only to have you turn on her. Since there was no sign of struggle at the door, we can only ascertain that she let the person in and knew the person who beat her to death in her own apartment before dumping her body. Read it and weep, buddy.''

Nate didn't touch the note or read it when McKinney slid it across the table. He just stared out the window. The facts caused his mind to fracture. Which girl were they talking about, Claudia or Isabella? Confusion tore at his brain and grief deadened his ear drums. He hadn't been able to clearly understand a thing once they'd said another Jersey girl had died.

Growing impatient, Wilson took a seat on the edge of the table. ''Her mother and grandmother gave this to us this afternoon, after we IDed her and went to the house. Philly and Jersey officials are involved because she died in her Philly apartment, but was dumped across the river. Damned thing was sitting out on her old bedroom dresser at her mom's house in Camden with your name scrawled across the front of it.''

''Isabella, dead?''

''As a door nail.'' Wilson answered his question without emotion. ''Beaten so bad that they won't be able to open the casket at her funeral.''

While there was a sense of relief that it wasn't Claudia, the fact that it was Isabella only made him recede deeper into the darkness within himself. He had sent her to her death, not knowing that Loretta had been killed, his partner would be beaten, and an old man would die in a blaze. If he'd only known, no way in God's name would he have involved Isabella. And she went farther than he'd ever intended . . . What, beyond feminine revenge had prompted her to go so far as to return to Addison's lair—with a key no less? He was so weak with grief and guilt that he could barely sit upright in the chair. He needed a drink. A stiff one with no chaser.

''We have enough to go on now to book you on three counts of homicide alone, not to mention a laundry list of other offenses.'' Wilson was triumphant as he walked toward the door and motioned through the glass for two officers to enter. ''Read him his rights and take his sorry ass downstairs to lockup, gentlemen.''

Two blue uniforms flanked Nate and began a monotone litany that he knew by heart. He wasn't even paying attention when they grabbed him under his elbows and hoisted him to his feet. Cold steel immediately bound his hands, but momentarily unleashed the paralysis that had bound his mind. His eyes locked with McKinney's. "I'll give you this one thread to go by, McKinney. Isabella lived with her parents—that wasn't her apartment. That was probably one of several of Addison's bachelor pads, and the one he'd given to Isabella when they were lovers. He's got access to high-end property as a developer. But ever since he married DiGiovanni's daughter, he probably has to be even more discrete."

All four men stopped moving Nate toward the door, and the officers dropped their hands from his shoulders.

"He married Maria DiGiovanni?" Wilson was incredulous.

"Look at the papers, man. Originals are in there, right? Showing first Loretta Harris in partnership with Maria DiGiovanni, then my partner and Harris and DiGiovanni. He probably stashed everything from Loretta's old pad in Isabella's old spot until he could decide how to dispose of it, then Isa found the motherload."

McKinney looked at the papers and ran his hand over the raised seals. "They look like originals . . . Yeah, Wil, it's like the man said."

"Loretta Harris probably had one of his apartments, too, at one point, in addition to her condo. Even though they're rented in the women's names, follow the paper trail—ask yourself, who owns the buildings?"

"Take off the cuffs," Wilson said in a low voice. "Now."

Nate's heart raced ahead of his mind as the puzzle started to fit and the breath of near freedom filled his lungs.

"The key in that envelope doesn't fit anything I own, or probably any file in Addison's office. Check it out."

McKinney sat down. "Jesus, a DiGiovanni?"

"The devil's daughter," Nate breathed heavily. "How did you find the apartment?"

"Reports came into the Round House that neighbors heard a domestic dispute ... a woman screaming," Wilson said, leaning against the wall as if for support. "We didn't connect it at first—happens every three minutes, a woman gets beat by her husband or lover. But when the girl was found in Jersey and there wasn't any blood at the scene ... given how badly she was mangled, we pushed it through forensics and matched the blood types. Then we went to the family's house."

Taking in big gulps of air to stave off the dry heaves, Nate found himself bending over and retching, although nothing came up from his two day fast.

"He probably didn't have time to go by there to see what she'd left what she'd stolen. He usually doesn't do his own dirty work. He sends somebody else in ... somebody untraceable. Run the social security number, and I'll bet that it's either phoney or the man's name isn't Jenkins. You need to put a car on both the Gonzales family and the Harris family. They may be in danger as perceived loose ends."

Nate watched both officers as they surveyed the envelop and cast an inside glance to each other.

"You're not planning any out of town trips or vacations abroad are you, McGregor?" Wilson's voice had become less attack oriented, if not a little bit concerned.

Nate shook his head no.

"Let him go," McKinney said quietly. "Even if he runs from us, he can't run from DiGiovanni. He's probably a dead man walking now, anyway."

Chapter 15

This time he was not invited in when the door was opened to the tiny Camden row house. Angel Ramirez peered at him through the screen and he could see a host of family and mourners lining the house interior like packed sardines.

"We ain't got nothin' to talk about, man. I thought we was like family. How could you?"

Nate eyes connected with his friend's before they lowered. The ravages of fatigue had obviously taken its toll, as did the constant renewal of tears. But he was not about to relent. He loved Isabella like a sister, and Angel like a brother. He and the Gonzales-Ramirez family went way back—too far back. He would not lose them to Addison's lies, or the police department's confusion.

"Your grandmother had a vision about this. We need to walk and talk . . . like brothers."

Ramirez hesitated as a younger male cousin suddenly flanked his side.

"We ought to do him right here on the steps. Got no business coming by the house after what he did to Isa, man."

Every muscle in the teen's body was poised to strike without warning. Nate could see youth, rage, and pain pump through his veins, and for a moment he wondered if the kid was packing. His handsome face was drawn tight with a glare, and the muscle in his jaw twitched rhythmically as they waited for Ramirez's verdict. Nate didn't move. It was like watching a cobra.

Appearing to consider the option first, Ramirez finally put his hand on the teenager's shoulder. "If you upset my mother, your mother, and our grandmother—"

"They're already upset! Ain't no justice but street justice, man. Cops don't care. He's out on the street already."

"If you upset the women and old men, I will kill you myself." Ramirez continued in a dangerously low tone. "Comprendo?" He waited a beat before repeating himself. "I said, comprendo?" Only when the young man shrugged off his hold and nodded defiantly did Ramirez open the latch to the screen to come out.

But Nate still stood a step lower than the teen who glared down at him through the screen door. The position was unsettling and he stepped back and down to the sidewalk to let Ramirez pass to join him.

The kid had not let Nate out of his sight, and in almost a whisper he said to Ramirez's back. "Yeah, cuz, it can wait till after the funeral."

Ramirez whirled around catching them both by surprise with an uncharacteristic, sudden fury. "No. Mama told him about the visions . . . and she let him in the house before, so this isn't the man that did her. Go inside."

More tentative now, Ramirez's young cousin seemed to recoil at the mention of the vision. "Mama told *him* about it . . . ?"

"Go inside, like I told you. There is more to this than your young, foolish ass knows. Don't get involved. This ain't about gang-banging."

The teenager disappeared from the door immediately and Ramirez again turned his back to the house and began a slow stride up the block. Nate fell in step and said nothing for a while as people came up to Ramirez, hugged him, cried on him, looked from Ramirez to Nate strangely, then made their way toward the family house.

Finally as they passed the corner stores and came to an abandoned field, Ramirez let out a deep sigh.

''Give me a cigarette, man.''

Nate reached into his pocket and pulled one out and lit it for his friend, then lit one for himself.

''That little promenade around the neighborhood just bought you some life insurance.''

''I didn't kill her . . .'' Nate's voice trailed off to a near murmur.

''Not directly.'' Ramirez focused on the cigarette and didn't look up as he spoke. ''But you sent her to her death by having her poke around in things that should have been left alone.''

There was no way to answer to the truth with anything but the truth. ''I never meant for it to happen like this. I didn't know how dangerous it was . . . only a week had only gone by since we spoke in the diner . . . I couldn't get to her before it went down. I never knew . . .''

For the first time since they'd begun walking, Ramirez looked up. ''It was that gringo she was seeing at the hospital, wasn't it? It was his fancy apartment that he beat her in, then drove her to her job and left her like a dog in the alley . . .'' Ramirez's voice cracked and broke, and he covered his face with his hands. ''She was just a baby, man. My beautiful Isa . . .''

Nate moved in with caution and hugged his friend hard when he felt the resistance go out.

''No. This time you got it wrong. Your Mama was right. It was a black man. Addison.''

Ramirez looked up through bloodshot eyes and the question they held haunted them like a nightmare. ''Why?''

''She used to deal with him, man.''

Grief turned to sudden rage as Ramirez lowered his shoulder

and charged at Nate. The impact made them both hit the ground, with Ramirez on top choking the life out of him.

"Dirty, filthy liar! Not my Isa! Never. Say you lie to me," he raged through sobs, but his grip was loosening as he sputtered. "Say it is a lie. Please, man."

Carefully prying his friend's hands away from his throat, Nate rolled over and coughed. Sitting up with effort, he slung an arm over Ramirez's shoulder and pulled him in as his friend let the hurt pour out.

When the sobs subsided, Nate let go of his hold and stood, extending a hand to help Ramirez to his feet. "I never lied to you, man. This hurts so bad, I wish I had a lie good enough to make it better."

Nate brushed the red-clay dirt and tufts of grass from his friend's suit, then his own. "We can't go back up the street like this. Let's sit down out here for a while and share a few smokes. I'll tell you what I know."

She thought she would go out of her mind. It had been over twelve hours since the police had visited the house and Nate had called. He hadn't left a number, only said to stay at the house and he would contact her again. But the question was, when? She had been so nervous that she might miss his call that, she'd even pulled the phone into the bathroom when she had to go or when she took her bath. It was maddening.

Still too afraid to rest in her own room, she had taken a blanket out on the back porch. The fresh fall air and the changing leaves were a balm to her nervous system. A gentle breeze occasionally slipped between the delicate folds of her white cotton-lace gown and matching robe. She loved the texture of the cotton mixed with the air, the way it billowed the long bottom and belled out the sleeves. She almost felt celestial, like she could fly. . . .

But as it grew dark, and the temperature dropped, she could feel Mother Nature gently coaxing her to go inside. Claudia moved her hand against the contents within her sister's bag that now doubled for a pillow. Her quests all day had been easy, simple, not a complex layering of tasks to add to her stress. If things could only stay that way. . . . She sighed and continued her blind, feeling search for the last remnants within her crumpled pack of cigarettes. With only one cigarette left, she had been nursing the pack slowly all day, since her father and Dot had refused to buy her any more.

As she lit it slowly, the red embers glowed bright against the cloak of darkness that surrounded her. The semidarkness was like another blanket. It was peaceful, despite the chilly night air, and she watched the few bugs left in the season dance under the flood light at the other corner of the porch. Inhaling slowly, she savored her last cigarette. This would be her last one, just like Nate had shown her how to let it go after the last drink. . . .

"You know, Ret," she said in a whisper, enjoying the quiet that settled on the house after her father and Dot had gone to bed, "this mess will kill you. I'm quitting for good."

Filling her lungs with another deep inhale, Claudia let the smoke slowly filter out through her nose. It was going to be hard. How was she going to rebuild her life? What if Nate wasn't a part of it, or worse, was wrongly imprisoned? She was doubtful that the police would ever get to the bottom of it, especially since everything seemed so iffy at best.

Claudia hit the a long ash against the side of the aluminum ash tray, but the entire lit portion broke off and fell down between the cushions. "Damn," she muttered, hopping up quickly and throwing the blanket to the ground and toppling the open purse contents on the porch floor. Still fishing in the out-door furniture cushions, she tried to find the lit end before it burned a whole in Dot's new upholstery.

"Still making a mess, I see."

The resonant male voice made her spin around so quickly that she almost lost her balance. It took her mind several seconds to process the outline that leaned against the screen door even though her eyes had already adjusted to the semidarkness.

"Nate," she whispered urgently, and ran to unlock the screen. "You nearly scared me to death. Where have you been? Why'd you come through the back yard?"

He looked around then came into the enclosure. "Can you douse the light? It's better if my whereabouts remain unknown at this point."

Although she was glad to see him, his comment made her hesitate and grow nervous. But she honored his request by flicking off the flood light, ending the moth's dance.

"Sit down . . . wait a minute, let me check. I dropped a hot ash." After fluffing the pillows, she removed the throw from the floor and tossed it into an adjacent chair. "Spilled everything in my purse," she said fussing at herself as she picked up the contents and dropped them on the table, "Or, I should say Ret's bag. I was never the type to carry such an exp—"

Nate's warm hands on her shoulders stopped her flurry of words and she became motionless as he pulled her into an embrace.

"You're afraid of me now, aren't you, Claud?"

There was no escaping his truth and she only nodded and returned his hug awkwardly. "There's a lot going on right now . . . I don't know what you're mixed up in, Nate, but it seems serious. I tried my best to lead the authorities off of your trail by telling them everything I knew about my sister's death, and the man named Jenkins, who took all of her papers from my parents. I never told them that I knew you, but I didn't lie either . . . well, not exactly. I just played dumb and over-whelmed, which wasn't hard."

He raised her chin with his finger so that her eyes met his. In the moonlight she could see the pain in them, which caused her to tighten her hold on the man who felt so far away now.

"Don't ever think of yourself as dumb again, baby. No. Your mind works just fine, so do your instincts. You have every right to be wary . . . and I'm glad you told the police that Jenkins had been by your parents house asking for papers that your sister used to own. There's so much I have to tell you, most of which may make you want to run away from me forever.''

Brushing her mouth with a kiss, he pulled her into him so hard that she could barely breathe.

''Earlier today I thought you were dead,'' he said in a harsh emotion-filled whisper. ''I just needed to hold you in my arms again.''

His warmth replaced the blanket and shielded her from the air, creating a seal of protection that could not be seen with the naked eye. It was a feeling, a down deep knowing that permeated her soul.

''I was so worried, then when I didn't hear from you . . . I didn't know what to think.''

This time his kiss was more urgent, like a flash fire that catches in the underbrush. She returned it with like force, then slowly eased away to let it smolder without feeding it. She needed answers.

''Let's sit down,'' she said gently, taking him by the hand to join her on the swing couch. ''So much has happened in the last few days, that I almost don't know where to begin.'' Claudia hesitated, not sure of whether or not she should even tell him about the apparition. It didn't seem relevant, so she started with the visit from the police and filled in the blanks regarding her theory that someone had tampered with her sister's anesthesia.

Nate was stunned. ''You know what's funny,'' he said looking at her squarely, ''you and I never discussed this theory, and yet we both gave the police the same story. We also came up with the same name, Jenkins. So, no, Claudia. You aren't crazy.''

As his story unfolded she sat on the edge of the swing wide-eyed. Tears formed but didn't fall as he began to describe the relationship between Ret and his partner.

''She couldn't go through with it, Nate, because she had found a source of inner strength . . . Some call it truth, some call it religion. All I know is, Ret was never the kind to hurt innocent people. She'd bilk a corporation in a minute, or do an insurance company. Her philosophy was that they were thieves anyway, and didn't care about their employees. But for her to do an honest man . . . one who loved her as much as I'm sure your partner did—I know she couldn't go through with it. And that principle cost her her life.''

Nodding in agreement, Nate just looked down for a moment before he spoke. ''Today a young girl, a dear friend, was murdered because she was trying to find out information that could stop Addison. I went to the family's house, and the people are so broken up . . . Claudia, I don't know how I can live with this.''

She reached over and drew him into her arms. ''Nate,'' she whispered, ''you didn't kill her, nor would you have asked her to help you if you knew how dangerous these people were. Let it go.''

He clung to her for what felt like a long time. Each moment that passed felt as though his body was drinking in her love and trust as sustenance. And the more his skin drank, the more flowed from her heart, yielding at will to the hope of tomorrow he needed now.

''I can't protect you, baby.'' Nate's voice was thick with emotion. ''They have an unmarked car from the police parked down the street, and even I got in here without them spotting me. I have to find a way to shut Addison down completely.''

Claudia sat back horrified. ''You aren't talking about killing a man, are you? Tell me you haven't gone off the deep end?''

''I wish I had the heart to do something like that, but it would haunt me. No. Taking a person's life in calculated cold blood isn't something I could stomach.''

Slightly relieved, she adjusted herself again in his arms. ''Do you believe in divine intervention?'' She could feel Nate shrug as her cheek rested against the warmth of his chest.

''I wouldn't rule it out at this point, Claud. An old lady's vision stopped an entire family from starting a vendetta against me.''

She sat back again and looked at him cautiously. ''Tell me about the vision.''

Nate drew a breath and let it out slowly. ''She was the girl's grandmother. The night of the fire I had been in Jersey earlier to meet with Isa to tell her about my hunch. I found out that, like your sister, Addison had used her. But before we met, I had to wait for her at her mom's house . . . in the parlor with her grandmother. She told me all about the beautiful brown girl who loved me, and who would help me. She said I was in a lot of trouble. But, Claud, none of this had gone down yet. And nobody knew about you. Nobody. They still don't . . . and I want to keep it that way until this cools down. Then, she said that a light-skinned woman on the other side, a spirit who was tall and beautiful, would help you help me. It was weird, so I never thought about it until Ramirez said it again today, and you just asked.''

''Ret,'' she whispered, elongating her sister's name as the story connected with an unknown source within her. ''That's why she can't rest.''

''I don't doubt that she would, given all of this.''

''No. No. You don't understand.'' Claudia reached for her bag and then threw it on the chair, having forgotten that she was all out of cigarettes and had promised the cosmos that she would stop smoking.

''Want one,'' he offered, lighting one for himself.

''No. I promised Ret I'd stop.''

Nate stared at her, but she wasn't offended.

''We all thought that Ret had turned on the light in my closet because she wanted to finish unfinished business between me, Dot, and Daddy. Then, as me and Daddy talked into the wee hours of the night, it became clear that something was wrong with the way she died. And I knew—you know how you can feel things in your gut but can't explain it . . . ? Well, I knew that her appearance wasn't about old family business, it was about the more pressing issues of the present.''

Nate inhaled and looked at her, allowing the smoke to ride away in the direction of the wind. ''You think your sister appeared and turned on the light in your room?''

''I know it sounds crazy, but—''

''No, it doesn't,'' he countered, standing and walking toward the screen. He looked off into the distance, then up at the stars. ''No. It doesn't. I've often felt a presence of protection . . . even as a child. I used to think it was my grandmother . . . then more recently, that it could be my mother. Many times in my life when things could have gone a certain way—a wrong way, I felt saved, just in the nick of time. Nemom used to call them guardian angels . . . the ancestors who come back to watch over you.''

She joined his side and looped her arm around his waist as her head nestled against his shoulder. ''She's trying to guide us, Nate. Trying to right the terrible wrongs. But, I don't know what we can do, or how to know what messages she's trying to send us.''

He kissed the top of her head, then the bridge of her nose. ''The police have one set of originals. Those came from Loretta's files, but Isa intercepted them before she was killed and her mother and grandmother got the package to the police. Divine Guidance. Sure, they may be able to clear my name, and Ed's name . . . however, Addison is slippery, like an eel. He'll let his henchmen take the fall and will come out like a martyred black professional. Then, he'll be hunting us down for eternity. I can't live like that, Claud, and won't let you live like that. No. I don't think the police will be as effective as DiGiovanni. But we'll need every ounce of luck we can get on our side to pull off this long shot.''

Again, her body tensed as Nate crushed out his cigarette. ''What do you mean?''

''My partner had the other set, which they nearly beat him to death to get. He had a copy stashed, but a xerox copy isn't admissible as evidence, and DiGiovanni wouldn't go for it—because it could have been tampered with. The copy that was filed with the state, I'm sure has been destroyed, since Addison has a number of favors outstanding in the street. He could easily call in a marker, or threaten someone, or bribe them to get that paperwork to disappear. But, there has to be one more original floating around somewhere, and that's what I need to prove to DiGiovanni that Addison was using his daughter to devise a scheme that he didn't even know about. If there was a way to get to the top man, and show him indisputable evidence, then Addison would fall under Sicilian law . . . he wouldn't bother us again. That, I guarantee you.''

Claudia slackened her hold around Nate's waist and moved to the swing and plunked down. ''Sounds too dangerous, Nate. Call me naive, but you just don't walk up to a mob boss and drape a long story on him, or tell him that a ghost sent you. First of all, how do you even find such a person? Second of all, how do we know that he doesn't know his daughter is connected to this business scheme? Maybe he even set it up himself?''

Nate shook his head as he walked over to the swing and sat down next to her. ''First of all, I know for a fact that DiGiovanni believes in the spirit world. He has to. He's Sicilian.''

Claudia smiled. ''That's a vast generalization, too big of a stereotype to hang your life on, Nate. But, what if we could find out who does his readings . . . like, if he goes to a psychic?''

This time Nate laughed. ''Not an option, and far too dangerous.''

''Okay,'' she said sitting back and folding her arms in good humor, ''what would you propose? How are you going to find him?''

''You don't find him, you let him find you.''

All of the mirth had gone out of her voice. ''I don't like it, Nate. I thought you were just joking around. I don't need to find you in cement shoes at the bottom of the Delaware River either. Like I asked before, how do you know that he didn't set this up himself, anyway?''

Nate stretched his arms and legs out in front of him. ''I don't like the sound of it either, Claud. It was a crazy idea. Guess I'm just reaching for straws. I just thought that based on the way people are from the old country, having seen a lot of this kind of thing from every nationality during my law practice, that DiGiovanni would have never directly linked *his daughter* with anything that would leave bodies around. There's an old code, 'Never involve the women or children in a man's business dealings.' It's only the new Syndicate that has violated that code of ethics, or that old code of honor amongst thieves. Usually the older generation takes the risk, then, Kennedy style, they put the kids up in clean, well-funded businesses. Especially the daughters. Just like anybody else, they want their kids to have a piece of the American dream without any of the past around to haunt them.''

She considered his words carefully. There was a ring of truth to what he said . . . but, still, it was too crazy, and her man was betting his life.

''I'll take my chances with the police,'' she finally said. ''No more digging around for evidence, no more talk of mobsters. Can't we just give the authorities anything we have and try to live like normal people from here on out?''

Nate caressed her cheek with the back of his hand, and lowered his mouth to hers, filling it with long awaited warmth.

''Yes, baby,'' he breathed against her lips. ''Nothing is worth risking what we have.''

They sat that way for a long time, tasting each other's mouths . . . gently probing, gently reassuring.

''Do you know that I could have gone to jail today for triple life without ever being able to do this again? Or, worse, you could have been the one they found, and I'd never be able to tell you how much I love you?''

''Life is too precious to waste it . . . and time is too uncertain, isn't it?''

His kiss deepened and she could feel him tense as he lowered her down on the swing. Soon he became her blanket again, and his warmth drenched her skin. "Where's your father and Dot?" Nate's voice had grown husky with want and he never waited for her answer. Instead he brushed her lips and made his tongue dance with hers, responding to her movements instead of the possibility of being discovered.

With each tender nip down her neck, he asked her to tell him what he wanted to hear. She heard his insistent request that required no words to understand. She needed him, too. She needed the pleasure to block out the fear . . . needed his warmth to make her feel safe . . . needed his physical joining to make tomorrow seem possible. And as the underbrush caught fire again within her, he answered those needs like an inferno, searing all of her to him and bonding them.

"They've been asleep for hours," she breathed, urging him to continue when he hesitated and looked around.

Nate sat up. "I could have sworn I heard something."

Too caught up in the wondrous feeling he'd enfolded around her she pulled him to her. "Nothing but crickets, and stars . . . and us."

But Nate seemed distracted and he kept staring off in the distance near the corner of the porch. "It was silvery, like a light or something that . . . I don't know?"

Claudia sat up and stared at the same corner. A haze that was not quite discernable seemed to hover around the flood light switch. In an instant, it clicked on.

"Did you see that?" he said quietly, almost holding his breath as he spoke. "She's here. I felt it."

"Let's go in the house," Claudia whispered, not letting go of his arm. "I'm scared."

"No. Don't be. She's—"

"I want to go in. Please."

Claudia only stood when Nate stood first, and she tried to press her body into his side for protection as she grabbed the blanket from the chair. Sweeping it around her shoulders to block the sudden stinging cold, a loud clatter made her nearly jump out of her skin.

"You just knocked your purse over," he said with a smile. "C'mon, let's get you inside before you hurt yourself."

But as Nate bent to pick up the fallen handbag, he stopped short. "How long have you been carrying this around with you."

"What? What's wrong?" She let go a breath of relief when he pointed to the table. "It's just stuff from my sister's handbag ... she gave it to me to hold when she went in the hospital, and I just hung onto it for sentimental reasons. Maybe I should have given it away to the church? Now can we go?"

"Claudia, what are these papers?"

"I don't know. Let's go inside. I've got the creeps out here. Please, Nate. I'm in no mood to play detective when I think we just saw a ghost!"

Nate seemed to ignore her as he collected the papers and tucked them under his arm. When they got to the shed entrance, she slapped on the light with her head half under the blanket and a vice grip digging into his upper arm. She was thankful that she had at least left the stove light on, and she pushed Nate ahead of her so he could turn on the big, over-head fan light. Once the kitchen was fully illuminated, she relaxed—a little.

"See!" she said in a harsh whisper, her eyes darting around the room. "It's just like it happened the other night—only that time I didn't see the light go on by itself."

Nate didn't seem to be listening to her. His focus was totally absorbed by the papers he held in his hands. When he finally looked up, Claudia stopped breathing.

"Baby, she just gave us the third set."

Chapter 16

Claudia drew the blanket up to her neck and yawned as the sun warmed her face. Nate had cuddled with her on the porch swing until daybreak, allaying her fears, allowing her to pour out her heart and tell him about Dot and Dad. The sharing fed a mutual hunger, as he told her things he'd never told a soul . . . some funny anecdotes from his childhood, some sad things, the intricacies of his failed marriage . . . She needed the cleansing of truth with no secrets. Somehow making him understand who she was, and how she came to be, and coming to know the same about him, provided an unbreakable connection that went far beyond the physical connection that had been forestalled. They had made love with words instead of their bodies that night . . . just like it had been in the beginning. They were friends first.

She pressed her palm to the spot next to her face that Nate had vacated, wondering when they would be free to love each other, to laugh together, and to share time openly again. She felt robbed by the situation, for something precious was now cloaked in stealth and could only be shared in snippets of stolen moments. Even Loretta had taken their precious peace, and she was beginning to resent the ghostly intrusion. All she wanted was for her life to return to normal, untarnished by legal problems, vendettas, or restless spirits.

Suddenly, her normal routine worries about paying bills, finding a job, and setting up a new apartment seemed minuscule in comparison to what loomed over her now. Claudia pulled herself up and turned her face toward the sun, allowing the golden rays to shower her. She had to make a decision. Either she would continue to be a victim, or she would go about taking some control over the events in her life.

"No more," she said quietly, opening her eyes to the back-yards that dotted the landscape. "Today is another day. Time is too precious to waste."

When she entered the kitchen, Dot and Dad had not come downstairs yet. She glanced at the wall clock and grabbed a mug from the cabinet for tea. It was only 6:30 A.M. In another half hour, Dot would probably be down first, humming around her and trying to baby her to death.

Claudia smiled as she set the microwave timer on two minutes. She had come to have a new appreciation for Dot's hovering, and understood it all too well. Dot had missed years of mothering and caring for her child, all she wanted to do now was to make up for lost time. But that was just the unfortunate thing, one cannot make up for lost time by doing everything one would have done.

Claudia focused on the lit interior of the oven and watched the mug turn around and around in the same spot. You have to do something different, she thought, it's not a linear process, or you'll just keep going in circles. All of the variables change as time progresses. What she needed from Dot now was not what Dot could have given her as a child. But what Dot wanted to give now, was what she'd missed giving over the years. They would have to strike a new balance, one where they both gave and received different things that would give them equal joy.

Pulling the hot water out of the microwave, Claudia began rummaging for a tea bag and some honey. She took a long time, just like Dot had. The completion of the task was not the objective of making tea, it was a way to think through a problem, to develop a solution while one busied the hands with something routine. Then drinking the tea was not about sustenance, it was something to do while one mulled over a problem, watching the steam rise and take different shapes, just like one's ideas.

She was going to contact Loretta's metaphysical instructor. That was something different. That was something active, not passive. If her sister wanted to guide her, then there had to be a mediator, a translator, a way for her to get the information without being afraid all the time. Because fear was robbing her, and had robbed her of too much already.

Claudia took a deep sip of the hot substance before her, then reached into the purse that hung on the kitchen chair and pulled out her sisters wallet. She'd remembered seeing the card with a center city address. The place was around South Street somewhere . . . The Third Eye . . . or was it Birds of Paradise? Yes, she would find out and go there today.

Triumphant, Claudia stood in the small South Street shop and looked around at the books and trinkets on display. A calming aroma of frankincense filled the air and the nature music gave one the feeling of being in a tropical rain forest. The whole establishment surrounded one with a sense of tranquility. Indeed, it was paradise, and she felt like she could lift her body to the music and take flight.

Today she was calm. Today, for the first time in years, she felt in control. She had accomplished more today than she had in a very long time. She had been able to successfully make Dot understand why she needed to go out—alone—without hurting Dot's feelings. As a compromise, she had dispatched Dot to sort through the clothing donations to separate out the good things from the not-so-good, so that she could begin rebuilding her wardrobe. Happy to have some way to help and to be involved, Dot had eagerly begun in her organized way.

Her father had been given her newly typed and updated resume, and was going to go to the church to run off several copies so that she could begin a job search in earnest. Why hadn't she done this before? When she called her friends, they were all supportive. When she called her former employers, they all said that they'd give her outstanding recommendations, and that her need to take time off was human and to be expected. Why had she feared reaching out, feared letting people know that she needed their assistance? As the day had progressed, she'd found out that much of her isolation was based on what she'd *supposed* people thought—not based on what they really did think of her.

Then she had called several apartment complexes, just to get an estimate, so that she could set a goal and give her parents a timetable for how long she would stay. This was a compromise, instead of the indefinite idea of staying until forever. No. Even though she could understand their desire to want to protect her from the world indefinitely, she had decided to only stay until she could get a job and save up for the rent and normal expenses—and had thanked them for their love and support that she no longer took for granted. They didn't have to do this, and she had even thanked God that she still had parents. Nate didn't.

The beautiful figurines and stones caught her attention in the shop. One day, when she got back on her feet, she would come back and decorate her new space with the intriguing international relics. Change. A healing change of environment and mind-set was needed. She had even called the few creditors that she had left and told them about the fire, then made suitable payment arrangements. This would allow her to rebuild her credit, to be able to afford to make her space into something that brought her joy. It was action. It was adult. It was responsible. She would never give her power away again. And although

Nate would have probably helped her, she was determined to rebuild her life on her own. It was therapeutic.

"Hi. I am Celeste. Welcome to Birds of Paradise, may I help you?"

Claudia looked up from the counter and smiled at the older woman who had pleasantly addressed her. She wore a rich, deep-purple African bouba with heavy embroidery, and her hair was twisted with neat nubian locks that shown with an exquisite silver that marked her age. The woman's face practically glowed ... she was radiant, and had it not been for the glistening silver in her hair, Claudia would have pegged her to be about forty.

"I'm Loretta Harris's sister," she said, awe and respect lacing her voice, "I called earlier."

The woman smiled and motioned to another younger woman in the back of the store. When she moved her arm in a grand sweeping motion, her wrists sparkled and chimed from the heavy sterling bangles that adorned them. In that peaceful, nature-filled environment, she looked like the original mother of all of humanity. Her eyes were so kind, so gentle ... her voice so exotic and soothing. Yes, she had to be the one that reigned over the harvests, breathed life into babies, ended droughts, and could see past, present, and future. . . . Claudia was not afraid.

"Come, child," she said as the younger woman came to the front to help the few other browsing customers, "I have been waiting for you for a long time."

Claudia followed the woman, allowing her accent to wash over her and the sweet trail of her scented body oil to penetrate her senses. The air caught in her large garment and it billowed as she walked, making her exit into the back of the shop look like a regal procession.

Once she had pulled a bamboo screen between them and the shop, the woman lit a small pot of water on a two burner stove, and began going around the small space lighting candles and pots of incense. Claudia scanned this new dense terrain that was filled with a wondrous profusion of green plants, cut flowers in tall vases, candles, little marble carved Buddahs, Japanese rice paper tapestries, African wood masks, a Native American medicine wheel, Caribbean sun-splashed watercolors, and stained glass windows from a church.

"Please, sit. Relax. It is important to have a peaceful environment to attract good vibrations."

"I love this," Claudia said with genuine awe. "I can see why my sister would leave the hectic pace to come here once a week. This is therapy for the soul."

The older woman took a seat on a hand-carved Ashanti stool, and again waved her magnificent arm of bangles toward a shorter stool for Claudia to sit down. A low, coffee-table-height, intricately carved teak-wood table separated them. Claudia ran her fingers over the edges, and looked up and smiled.

"You like beautiful things, but haven't allowed yourself the space to enjoy them. You deserve them, Claudia. We all do."

Claudia laughed. "I can't afford to live like this ... or to ever fill my apartment with these treasures from around the world. But yes, I do appreciate them."

Celeste clicked her tongue and took the hot pot off the stove. Without asking Claudia, she began pouring two small cups of a greenish looking tea. "You can do anything you want. But, you have to believe that you deserve it, and then visualize a positive outcome. Like, having babies."

Midair, Claudia stopped the cup from reaching her mouth. "Did my sister tell you about that, too?"

Again, Celeste clucked her tongue and smiled deeply. "No. It is written all over your face. You did well to stop poisoning your body with alcohol and nicotine. It won't be long."

Ignoring her shock, Celeste set the pot on a woven mat and took a sip of her own tea. Then she began arranging a series of stones in her hand, waving them over a tiny smoking pot of incense. Each pass through the smoke, she shut her eyes and her lips moved to a silent prayer. Claudia sipped her tea and watched intently as the older woman performed the ritual she couldn't understand.

"My, my, my . . . what are we going to do with you, Loretta?" she said smiling as she looked at the stones. "You cannot go around flicking on lights and scaring your family. It is undignified."

A sudden chill went down Claudia's back, and she could feel the old fears returning. She had never told this woman about the lights.

"Let go of it," Celeste said without looking up. "Tension is negative energy and very difficult to work with, or to work around. I tried to tell your sister this on so many occasions. She had a strong will, you know . . . I tried to tell her that the willow bends with the storm and is thus saved, while the oak stands against it and snaps. This is what happened. She stood against a storm of dark energy, instead of bending and using light to illuminate it."

Too intrigued to be totally afraid, Claudia's gaze darted from the stones on the table that Celeste had thrown to her gentle, wise eyes. "But does that mean you have to just let evil people do whatever they want to you?"

Now Celeste chuckled. "No. No. You sound so much like our Loretta. Understand," she said, moving the stones around to different positions, "that all forces are made up of energy, and The Universe will try to keep a balance. So, when there is too much dark, one must shine a great deal of light. And," she added sighing, "when there's abundant light, dark will try to eclipse it."

"What should I do now? Loretta is still not at rest, and some very evil people are trying to hurt the people I love. How do I protect myself . . . and them?"

"With lots of light," Celeste said offhandedly. "If anyone asks you a question, tell them the truth. The total truth. Negative energy can only hide in dark places . . . secret places. And, stay in constant contact with the higher sources through meditation or prayer. You'd be surprised at the results. Then turn it over to those greater and wiser than yourself to handle.''

''You're saying to just pray on it?'' Claudia was incredulous, and Celeste's satisfied smile told her that the older woman had heard the remark before.

''Definitely. You see, child, the reason one must do nothing sometimes is so that The Universe can do everything. It will sort itself out, in its own time. But often, we as impatient children rush in and do something to cause a ripple. Then the powers that be have to not only correct the original problem, but they have to go in and straighten out the mess we've made. Then, we get impatient again, and do something else, which only compounds the problem further. We are oblivious to the fact that The Universe is trying hard to correct itself in the most benign way possible . . . which takes time. Then, after we have tampered and tampered and tampered with the process, we are amazed that The Universe has to take a dramatic stance, like creating a storm or a flood or an earthquake to straighten things out again. Sometimes we just need to be still, to listen, to act by not acting.''

Confusion made her hold her tongue as she watched the older woman work with the stones. Each portion of what Celeste said needed to be translated, because she didn't have a frame of reference for the new vocabulary and concepts.

''Do you know why I have objects from everywhere in the world?'' Celeste grinned as she took a deep sip of tea.

''I guess because you like beautiful things, and with a shop you can afford to travel and collect them?'' Claudia shrugged and finished the warm contents in her cup.

''True. On the surface. But the deeper truth is, they are all the same things—spiritually.''

Claudia returned her eager smile with a blank stare. She didn't get it.

''All of the peoples believe in something greater than themselves, believe that nature is the link between humanity and the heavens, that the earth can provide medicines to heal every malady known, they all believe in ancestors and light. The truth is, there are vast differences between all of these cultures—on the surface, but culling away man's cosmetic viewpoint, there is no difference at all. This is what I mean by tell the truth. Not at the top layer, but from the foundation up.''

Celeste smiled at Claudia with warmth. ''Why are you looking for an apartment now? The truth.''

Nothing surprised her about the female shaman who sat before her, so the fact that she had never told Celeste that she was looking for a place didn't come as a shock. This woman seemed to have an intuitive sense that could summon her deepest desires. ''I guess,'' Claudia said after a long pause to find the right answer, ''because I need my own space.''

''A surface truth,'' Celeste said hastily, getting up to rummage around the small space. ''Everyone needs their own space and a place to live once they reach maturity.''

''I don't know what you're looking for?'' Claudia was truly baffled.

''This is not a test, but it is about simplicity,'' the older woman remarked as she returned to her chair with a small purple crystalline rock. ''What happened that would make you have to find another apartment?''

''My apartment was burned down by those terrible people at Addison Development.''

''Yes . . . Illuminating darkness with light. Truth.''

They looked at each other for a long time, and the older woman seemed pleased as she placed the small rock inside Claudia's palm.

''So, child, when you call around to look for a new apartment, tell the people the truth.''

''I can't do that, I don't have any evidence that—''

''Close your eyes. What does your gut tell you? What does your heart tell you?''

Claudia settled down and closed her eyes. After a while she whispered, ''I know it's true, Miss Celeste.''

Two warm hands enveloped her own and the exotic sound

of the shaman's voice filled her spirit. "Are these the same people who killed your sister?"

"Yes," she whispered, feeling tears beginning to form under her lids.

"And do you know why?"

"Because she threatened to expose them, and threatened to tell the man's new wife that she had been used. Now a young girl and an old man have been killed, too, and an innocent man has had to take flight and leave the city. An innocent man who was with me ... making love to me the night of the fire is being set up ..."

Two big tears rolled down Claudia's cheeks and she opened her eyes to meet Celeste's satisfied gaze.

"Very, very good," she whispered, wiping Claudia's tears with the tips of her fingers. "Today, you have come a long way ... You have a good man," she hesitated, "but he is impatient, and has forced The Universe into motion again. Hopefully, you will be able to correct it in time."

"Nate ... Oh, God, no."

Celeste retrieved her hands again and held her in a steady, calming gaze. "Be still, my child. Continue on your own path. Finish with the apartment search today, and remember to tell the truth. Call employers, too ... call everyone. One of those calls will respond with light. Let go of it now, you can worry later, if you must. But for now, close your eyes and tell me what you see? Let your mind float."

She was almost too distracted to float, but somehow the combination of Celeste's voice and the thick aroma of the incense made it easier to drift.

"I see people laughing and talking in a small space."

"What kind of people?"

"Women, mostly. They aren't dressed ... some are, some aren't."

"What are they talking about?"

Claudia hesitated. "I can't tell what they're saying, the space seems small ... they're in rows and talking happily ... But I hear a man's voice. I can't make that out either . . . It's muffled, sounds like it's inside a can.''

"Is the voice familiar?"

"No, I don't know this man's voice."

"Follow his voice, find the space that his voice comes from."

"It's dark. Pitch black."

"Then go outside of where his voice emanates from. Concentrate."

"All I can see is a number. Twelve. That's it. A small number twelve."

Celeste gave her hands another satisfied squeeze. "Open your eyes child, you are starting to see. Remember what I told you about truth, complete your path *today*—it's still early in the afternoon . . . and remember what you saw. This may help to readjust things."

Without being told, Claudia could sense that their meeting had come to an end. Vast disappointment weighted her, for it seemed that the whole exercise—while pleasant—was totally pointless. Other than taking a visit to a place that her sister once frequented, and getting a glimpse into another dimension of Loretta's personality, what was the point?

She had come there looking for a psychic. Maybe even someone who could do a seance and contact her sister to get some definitive answers. She had prepared herself to be amazed, and frightened. But she was never prepared to sit in an open sunny room with a friendly lady, having tea and looking at stones while they discussed general philosophy and the woman's love for art. This was not why she had come there.

As she follow Miss Celeste out to the front of the store, she thanked her and handed her the purple stone which she had inadvertently kept clutched in her hands.

"No, child," the older woman smiled. "This is an amethyst crystal to open your third eye and give you more clarity. It was your sister's, therefore, you should have it."

Awed, Claudia thanked the woman again and left the shop, rolling the stone around and around in her palm. She had come for one thing, only to be given something else. . . . At least she had another one of Loretta's treasures.

She had spent the entire second half of the day on the phone calling places in Philly and Jersey, telling the truth, as shaman Celeste had put it. But it still didn't get her one decent apartment at a price she could afford, especially in Philly, or a job lead that she could do anything with. In fact, it seemed to only make people get nosey and start going down entirely pointless paths of questioning, which in turn, slowed down the whole process.

Claudia stood and stretched. She wished she had thought to buy a pack of cigarettes before Dot and Dad had taken the car to the market. Both of them had seemed so pleased with her efforts though, she hated to disappoint them by relapsing. This was nothing but a case of boredom, she told herself. The wait for Nate's call wore on her, as did the "nothing to do in the house" syndrome. She had been through all of the donations that Dot had arranged while she was gone. She even typed ten cover letters and addressed the envelopes, and her father had taken them to drop in the box when he and Dot left for the market. Dot's house was always immaculate, so there was no housework to keep her busy, and as per Dot's normal efficiency, dinner was already cooling on the top of the stove with a scratch cake along side it for dessert. She had returned all of her friend's calls and had written out thank you notes to everyone who had sent a donation. Maybe she could catch a quick nap?

When in doubt, go to sleep, she thought, pacing out to the back porch and plopping herself on the swing. She knew that sooner or later she would have to come to terms with sleeping in the house. But, that would be a challenge for another day . . . sometime before hard winter set in.

Her thoughts drifted peacefully as her body gave in to the pull of honest fatigue. She had accomplished a lot in one day, and had to admit that she was truly proud of herself for trying.

And although her attempts were fruitless, she had tried. That was the important difference. She had tried today.

Judging from the way the sun cast a deep red inside her eye lids instead of a brilliant yellow, she could feel evening descending. It was comforting to feel in tune with her environment, even if the pace was a little slower than she would have expected. And, in truth, the visit to the shop was new, different, and peaceful, although a little strange. But she reasoned that newness was always a bit odd. Yet, Celeste had said to pray, a recommendation that her grandmother would have approved of . . . now that was strange. Two people from totally different worlds and perspectives giving the same advice . . . just like the old woman in the Laundromat. Claudia smiled with her eyes closed, and began drifting.

She could hear women talking, laughing, and gabbing with water splashing in the background. Showers, she thought lazily, and turned over. Women's showers. Peripherally, she could hear a car pull up. . . . "Good," she murmured, Dot and Dad would be home. If she could only force herself up from the swing. The warm spot she made had become so comfortable. . . . She should get the key and open the door for them. Their hands would be full, and she would tell Dot to go and sit down while she helped Daddy unload. In just a minute, she would get the key . . . she went down the row . . . twelve . . . she stopped at twelve and opened the door . . . a man's voice yelled.

Claudia sat up abruptly as her dream slowly dissipated and reality came to the fore. Then she heard it again, a doorbell, loud knocking, a man's voice calling her name. Gathering up the blanket, she ran to the front door and put the key that was always hidden behind the curtains into the lock and turned it.

"Are you Miss Harris, the late Loretta Harris's sister?"

"Yes," she stammered, squinting her eyes and trying to get them to focus in the bright lights.

"We're from Action News. Can we come in and talk to you?"

The lights and the noise were disorienting. She had just

sprinted to the door from a dead sleep, and her vision and hearing weren't connecting to her thought processes yet.

"We know this has to be upsetting," the man pressed on. "But we hear that you have a story to tell that may shed some light on the recent blaze that took the life of an elderly man. A story that may also save a very prominent attorney in Philadelphia. Can we talk to you?"

The lights still blinded her as she opened the door wider and nodded. Something about light. Celeste had said that darkness has to be illuminated. To tell the truth . . . they would come to her. . . .

She made her way to the sofa and asked the three men to sit down. One sat before her in the same chair that the detectives had occupied. The one holding the camera knelt before her on the rug. The other remained standing and holding a bright light.

"Thank you," the seated man said, extending his arms with a microphone in his hand. "As I said, I know this must be difficult, but today we got calls from several realtors in the area who said that you told them that Addison Development had burned down your building. Is that true?"

"Yes," she said evenly, a new calm gripping her. "They also killed my sister."

The man who held the microphone had a hungry look in his eyes. "Can you tell us why you believe this to be true?"

A new confidence swept through her. This was the lights they'd seen together in the shop. She would use it to illuminate the darkness. She would fight their lies with truth and get the authorities to move, to take action. Perhaps The Universe was correcting itself.

"My sister worked for Addison Development, and Eric Addison was attempting to defraud small business people out of their store fronts on Cecil B. Moore Avenue—but first, he had to get poor attorney McGregor to sign those properties over. So he set up this bogus nonprofit with my sister and Maria DiGiovanni. Then he married Maria and killed my sister."

The reporter was almost trembling. "Eric Addison, of Addison Development, married Maria DiGiovanni?"

"Yes. To give DiGiovanni access to minority contracts going down in Philadelphia, and in turn, Addison would get a bigger share of all construction jobs. The money would stay in the family under different names. But I don't think her father knows about this other side deal."

"What makes you say that?" The reporter was incredulous.

"Because, he's a father and I'm sure he loves his daughter . . . and no parent wants to see their child implicated in anything this sordid. Gaining an advantage on state and federal contracts is just a manipulation of paper through a clean business. What Addison dragged her into has cost three people their lives, and nearly a fourth."

"Three people? Who, Miss? Can you give us some names?"

"Yes. A young woman named Isabella Gonzales was found in a dumpster behind the same hospital that my sister mysteriously died in. She had given a big envelope to her parents, and they gave it to the police. In the package were business papers to substantiate my claim. She also gave them a man's social security number who had been lurking around the hospital posing as a maintenance man during the same time my sister's anesthesia was tampered with . . . and this same Mr. Jenkins was the one who came to my parent's house asking for all of my sister's business effects. He said he worked for my sister's firm, Addison Development, and was her attorney of record. But, he's not an attorney."

The reporter sat back in the recliner for a moment as though winded, but Claudia had found steam and was on a roll. She was talking so fast, telling them about Ed Washington being beaten up, how the police had this information already but were stalling on it . . . then it hit her, like a flash out of the blue.

"Tell them that the key goes to locker number twelve."

The reporter blinked twice. "What key?"

"There's a man's voice in the locker . . . I don't know where it is, but you will get the rest of the story in locker number twelve. Give this to the police, and don't broadcast that part, because they'll get there first.''

All three men looked at each other then back at Claudia.

''From the Gonzales girl . . . She was young, beautiful, and kind. She left the police a key, Nate told me. It doesn't go to a file, or a door, it goes to a locker where women are.''

''Nate. Nate McGregor?''

''Yes.''

''You know him?''

''I love him.''

''Wait a minute,'' the reporter said leaning forward anxiously. ''Do you know where he is now?''

''I wish I did,'' she admitted sadly. ''But he and I were together the night my apartment burned. That's why neither one of us got hurt. That's the truth, and I'll take a lie detector test to prove it. Nate McGregor was in my arms, not in a basement lighting matches that night. He's a decent man being framed.''

''Jeese E. Christmas . . .'' the reporter said standing and running his hands through his hair. ''We're talking state and federal contract fixing, connections to one of the largest crime families, connections to one of the largest African American developers, a triple murder, a hospital's negligence with security measures, an attorney on a flight from justice, paid hit men and extortionists . . . This is one hell of a story! Can I use your phone? I think we may need to do a special report instead of an insert, fellahs.''

By the time Dot and her father drove up, their driveway was so loaded by vans and cars that they had to park halfway down the street. The interior of the house was buzzing with reporters from every branch of the media. Newspapers, television stations, talk radio stations, you name it, they were there. People filed in and out of the kitchen and paced as they waited to use the phone. Lights were everywhere, creating a subterranean heat that could only be escaped on the porch. Claudia peeped out of the window as neighbors held vigil on their front lawns, awed by the sudden excitement that had taken over the always quiet Harris house.

When she caught a glimpse of her parent's faces before a hoard of cameras and news people swallowed them, she was suddenly afraid. What had she done? And based on what premise, information from her dead sister's psychic? Hadn't Nate told her to stay low key, that he didn't want her implicated? The sheer panic that was etched on Dot's face was enough to make her recoil in shame.

Somehow her father had been able to cut a path through the throng to usher Dot into the house. But as soon as he stepped into his own living room, they were barraged again. He made a beeline for the stairs and helped Dot slip to safety, then he stood at the top of the steps and issued his command over the hubbub which had died down when he began to speak.

"You all have five minutes to leave my house and to return my family's privacy."

"But, Mister Harris," someone yelled from the middle of the room, "your daughter invited us in."

"Yeah," another voice called out, "you all have a story that's worth telling."

Her father stared at her and she cringed. His eyes held anger and a level of contempt that had never been cast in her direction. "This is *my* house, not my daughter's. I am telling you to leave now, or I'll call the police and have you bodily removed for trespassing. My wife is tired, and I'm tired. And I've got food melting in the trunk of my car."

"But, sir," a voice called out, "can't you just give us one comment?"

Her father turned without a word and walked up the steps and slammed the door. A disgruntled murmur made its way through the crowd and lights and cameras shut down as people began to slowly file out of the house. As fast as the storm had been whipped up, it was over, and Claudia knew they'd be onto the next story. They had gotten what they came for, a show. A media spectacle that hungered after the dirt and grime in people's lives. The first camera crew had already gone before the late comers arrived. All she could hope for now was that they'd heed her advice and tell the police about locker number twelve, instead of the general public. But, then, that was even speculation.

Heading toward the car to retrieve the food that her parents left, she wondered, how could this be light?

He sat in the back of the small but elegant catering shop and stared at the black and white television with disinterest. Acute hunger had driven him to the Moveable Feast, and his warm friendship with the proprietor made him know that it was safe to go in and relax for a while. Joan always made fried chicken dinners, buttermilk biscuits, and melt-in-your-mouth macaroni and cheese with fresh collards on the side for her weekend regulars. Just knowing that he could stop near home, without going home, gave him a feeling of comfort. Her Forty-Fifth and Spruce Street shop was a haven, and only a block away. He needed the proximity under safe cover to sort out his next move.

"You're awfully quiet tonight," she said with a warm pretty smile. "I thought my cast-iron fried chicken would perk you up a little bit?"

He looked at the tall lithe woman whose steel gray eyes matched the stunning salt and pepper silver in her short afro. She had always made him feel special by giving him a spot in the private section of the back to take his meals. Perhaps it was a break in her routine, and the company while she worked that had made her extend the initial offer that had become a habit. Tonight he basked in the extra attention she gave him, and the casual conversation that helped his food digest better. His brain hurt.

"Joan, you know your platters are the best around. It's not

the food tonight, hon. Got a lot on my mind ever since the building around the corner went up in smoke.''

"Know what you mean," she said quietly, but still moving between large pots and an industrial oven. "Life. Can never figure out what's going to happen."

They looked up in unison as the news came on. Riveted to the screen by the headline, Joan covered her mouth with horror. Nate sat transfixed, a forkful of macaroni and cheese held suspended midair between his mouth and the plate. What had Claudia done?

"Nate, this is getting too deep for me, hon. I can't have the mob coming in here looking for you, babe . . . as much as I love you. Too many bodies are hitting the ground. You understand, don't you?"

"I hear you, Joan. The last thing I'd want to do is have trouble follow me over here. Just wrap up my plate and I'm gone. No offense taken, this is real."

Joan hurriedly wrapped his plate and pushed him out the door like he was a robber, then flipped the sign over to read CLOSED, and hit the lights. She had every right to be afraid. Hell, he was now, too. It had been enough to have the authorities on him, but between his evidence, and his buddy from law school, Joe Collins, he had regained some semblance of peace . . . felt some remote sense of control. As long as it was a legal battle. But now Claudia had flushed the tiger out of the bushes, and both DiGiovanni and Addison would have to respond. With force.

Where was he going to go, especially at this hour of night? He hadn't really been able to sleep for days, and the half of the healthy platter that he had eaten felt like it was drugging him. Earlier, before the news, he had considered going back to Claudia's in Jersey. He'd even been foolish enough to think that he might be able to catch her alone again on the back porch, and that maybe this time, a ghost—or whatever it was— wouldn't interrupt what had been started.

He needed to move, and home seemed like the only resort.

Claudia's was off limits, a hotel would be a death trap if he
was followed since his van would be a beacon, his partner was
out of town and no doubt had the alarm on, his buildings were
probably staked out and had too many dark basements where
anything could go down. . . . Joan had put him out, the Gonzales
family was in mourning, and Jamal's bar was a pile of rubble.
New York, maybe? Maybe he could grab an overnight bag and
blend into the vastness of the city? There he could laugh and
drink rum punch and fall into dialect and stay with family that
he hadn't seen in years . . . yeah, he needed a drink. Or, he
could walk ten more paces and just lay his tired body down
for a few hours. The last choice called to him like a temptress.
Sleep. Darkness . . . peace. . . .

Pain!

Nate felt his legs go out from under him as his skull spilt.
Street lights whirled then touched the sky and concrete collided
with his shoulder and jaw. All the air left his body at once as
another blow blunted his remaining senses.

Darkness.

Chapter 17

"First of all, I don't have to speak to you without a warrant or my attorney present." Eric Addison leaned back in his plush burgundy leather chair and ran his manicured hands over the brass studs along the sides. "But, because I have nothing to hide, I have agreed to briefly entertain you in my home tonight, gentlemen. When I am ready to end this conversation, I will. Understood?"

The two detectives didn't respond but kept their voices monotone, even. There was a greater objective at stake.

"What was your relationship to one, Loretta Harris?" Wilson asked, trying to keep his cool.

Addison smiled. "She was a former employee."

"Did the relationship become intimate?" McKinney pressed. They had been going in circles for the last forty-five minutes.

"At one point, then I met my lovely wife, Maria, and it was over."

"Did you know Isabella Gonzales?"

Addison grew visibly irritated, and he stood and walked over to the expansive bar that housed top-shelf liquors by the fireplace in the den. "Look, gentlemen, I am forty-three years old and haven't been a boy scout with the women. There are a lot of eligible, beautiful women in this city that I have known either through business affiliations, or personally, or both. Make your point." He let the Courvoisier warm in the glass as he rolled the large brandy snifter between his palms, then he took a generous sip of the dark golden-brown substance and returned to his chair.

"The point is, Mr. Addison, that both of these women have died and there have been allegations that you might be involved in those deaths."

"So I've heard on the news," he said evenly, allowing his smile to broaden, "and if I thought the little bitch who came up with that story had any assets, I'd have my attorney submit a vicious slander suit as soon as the courts opened in the morning. But, at this point, it isn't worth chasing down a poor vagrant who has a history of mental problems, now is it? On the other hand, a nice healthy law suit against the city and the police department for harassment and unfounded allegations might be worth my while."

"We're only doing our job," McKinney said defensively, "and we have the right to question anybody who might have a motive. Your liaisons give us a motive."

"So you do. But have you considered the fact that this woman openly admitted to being McGregor's lover? That's also motive enough to cover for him and to give him an alibi."

Both detectives looked at each other but didn't respond.

"Did she tell you that when you asked her directly? Did you even question her?"

"We questioned her," Wilson said sullenly.

"But she didn't tell you that, did she? She went to the media instead, no doubt after McGregor told her how to angle it."

"She's prepared to take a lie detector test," McKinney retorted, now the one obviously trying to keep his cool.

"Spare me, detective," Addison said, taking another swig. "You and I both know that lie detector tests are not admissible as evidence in court, and that someone who suffers from extreme psychosis can beat a test. It's been proven. So that was just more media hype designed by McGregor. He's as guilty as sin, and he's trying to get his case tried in the media instead of in a court of law where it won't hold up.''

Again the detectives exchanged a glance.

"Listen, the Harris girl's sister and I did have an affair, but when I found out that she was trying to run a scam, I dumped her. She had weaseled her way into befriending Maria DiGiovanni, and worked her magic on Maria, too. That's why her name appears on what she thought would be a nice, nonprofit, charitable cause. Maria is already rich, and through her family, has every possible business connection imaginable. Why would she stoop to a scam? Loretta was a poor-girl wanna-be, and her sister is, too. Think about it.''

Wilson stood and McKinney pulled himself up slowly from his chair.

"You look tired, boys. Why don't you go home and get yourselves a good night's sleep.''

"I have only one question,'' Wilson said, rage clearly blazing in his eyes, "where is this Mr. Jenkins?''

Addison hesitated only a beat before he took another sip. "I think before you waste your time looking for a phantom hit man, one who probably works for McGregor anyway, you might consider another few questions. Number one, McGregor and Harris were together—supposedly screwing their brains out the night the fire took place. At the very least, we know that they were together, and they're also coincidentally the only two people who didn't go up in smoke. Number two, McGregor had a close relationship with Isabella Gonzales, he had taken her to dinner shortly before she died. Maybe both women found out he was two-timing them and an altercation broke out? Or, since Ms. Harris is heir to her sister's half of the deal, McGregor went with the money and Ms. Harris helped dispose of the body. As for a third point, Loretta Harris was no angel, her hands were dirty, too. Everybody who knew her could vouch that she was a party-hearty kind of girl. Alcohol in her system before surgery doesn't surprise me in the least. Loretta was self-destructive, that's why she could never be my wife.''

McKinney followed Wilson across the threshold of the three-acre Marlton estate. He could tell that his partner was sick with rage, but they were at another dead-end. Three bodies had shown up, and now the media was involved and the pressure was on to close it out with a hard suspect. As much as his gut went against it, they had to haul McGregor in.

''You thinking what I'm thinking?'' McKinney said to his partner.

Wilson stared out the car window and the muscle in his jaw pulsed. ''The guy is smooth. *Too smooth. . . .*''

''You think he did it?''

''Can't prove it. Addison's shit is air tight. But something about this isn't right. What's your gut hunch?''

''It stinks.''

''McGregor's gonna take the rap for this unless we get a break in the case.''

''The department is calling for blood. You have to decide if it'll be yours or McGregor's. We're running out of time.''

Wilson ran his hands through his hair and let the window down. ''They don't pay us enough for this bullshit, Mac.''

''Shame that Harris girl went to the press. All she did was get the politicians involved and herself implicated as a possible lover-accomplice with a history of mental problems. Man. Seemed like a nice family, too.''

''Yeah. Let's go pick the brother up. Might save his life, or buy him a few days any way.''

A throbbing anvil had replaced what used to be his head. Every muscle in his body ached from the cramped position that he'd been forced into during an indefinite ride somewhere. As he'd gone in and out of consciousness, he thought he heard traffic, laughter. . . . For all he knew he was dead already, and was just experiencing his welcome to hell.

Cold water shocked his system into full alertness.

"Get the son-of-a-bitch out of the trunk and put him in the limo. Keep the blindfold on him until he gets in."

He couldn't get a bead on the voices that muttered and cursed and shoved at his sore body. But he didn't need anyone to tell him that his life hung in a very delicate balance.

He fell headfirst onto a soft leather seat that broke his forward motion. With his wrists still connected together with a plastic wire, he tried to summon the strength to pull himself upright, and was jerked hard by what felt like several pair of hands until he was positioned properly.

"Cut the wire and take off the blindfold," a deep authoritative voice commanded. "He's no threat. Give the man a shot of whiskey and let him talk."

Suddenly the blindfold was yanked from his face, and his body was roughly pushed forward as someone pulled at and cut the cords that dug into his wrists. It took a moment for his eyes to adjust to the dim light within the limo interior. He held his breath and said a brief silent prayer as he stared at Mario DiGiovanni.

"The Puerto Ricans tell me that you have been looking for me," DiGiovanni smiled, pouring a drink and handing it to Nate. "Then the news reports make it necessary to have a conversation."

"I don't drink alcohol anymore," he said in the calmest tone he could manage.

Two men who sat beside him looked at DiGiovanni, then at Nate. When DiGiovanni laughed, they relaxed.

"An honest man. Well, it's been a long time. Get the man a Coke."

Glaring at him, the guard reached into the small refrigerator and pulled out a can and popped the tab. Nate accepted the soda from the guard who flanked his left and took a sip when DiGiovanni nodded.

"Now. Let's begin at the beginning. Why are you looking for me, and why is your lady-friend spreading vicious rumors about my daughter?"

"Sir," Nate began in his most polite tone, "I think she may have married a man that was using her."

"I see," DiGiovanni said, swallowing a bit of his drink then setting the glass down on the small table that separated them. "So, now you are interested in my family's welfare. How nice. Comforting."

In his peripheral vision, one of the guards smiled, the other didn't. Nate kept his gaze focused directly on DiGiovanni.

"My partner got beat up pretty bad," he said pausing for effect, "and I don't think that came from you."

"Who is your partner?"

"Ed Washington."

DiGiovanni looked from one guard to the next and shrugged. "People get mugged in the city every day. That's why I live in the suburbs. It's safer. So what does this have to do with Maria?"

Growing bold, Nate pressed on. "Addison used to deal with my lady's sister. Loretta Harris. During the same time he was dating Maria. He was also dealing with Isabella Gonzales, during the time when he was asking for Maria's hand in marriage."

DiGiovanni frowned and rubbed his chin. "You know this for a fact, or is this gossip?"

"I know it's a fact because he had two of his apartments in different sections of Center City leased in these women's names. But I would bet that they never paid rent."

He watched the old man consider his words.

"So. My new son-in-law is a whore. Okay. As long as he does his business discretely, and doesn't bring shame to my daughter. He's a man. That's not against the law. This is what you came to tell me?"

"No," Nate said, growing nervous. "He put your daughter's name on a corporation with one of his lovers, Loretta Harris.

His goal was to get a third investor, my partner, to underwrite the mortgage scam with my properties on Cecil B. Moore in Philly. Your daughter put up several hundred thousand dollars of her own cash to attract Ed and to make it look legit—but I know that she couldn't have known what was really going on. Then Loretta shows up dead with only my partner and your daughter, now Addison's wife, holding the papers. After my partner got beat to a pulp, Addison realized that he'd signed everything back over to me. Loretta Harris had gone to my partner and warned him. All of it was supposed to go back to Maria, therefore go back to Addison's control.''

"Talk to me straight," DiGiovanni said, his calm exterior giving way to fangs. "Why? Why all this trouble for a little nonprofit company? It's small potatoes, not even a million dollars."

"Because what he wants sits on prime speculating land near the new Temple stadium, for one. And for two, Addison is a greedy bastard. And for three, the thrill of doing it behind your back and making a profit without giving you a cut. On paper, it would just look like his wife, your daughter who you'd never monitor, made some good investments. But guess what, he's all ready to siphon those profits off for a deal he's got working in the Caribbean, under Fairways Resorts. That part wasn't in the news.''

"You'd better have some hard evidence."

Nate looked at the two guards that flanked him and back to DiGiovanni. "Can I go into my jacket pocket?"

They all nodded.

Nate produced the originals that had fallen out of Claudia's bag earlier. "There were three originals of the deal with your daughter's name and Loretta's name on them. They beat Ed up and took his. Isabella lost her life by getting Loretta's copy, probably when she went back to her apartment where it was stashed. How she got in there, I don't know. The police have those. Whatever was once filed by the state is probably long gone. Look at the docs and the dates. The next set contains the addition of Ed Washington's name. The last set I had never seen before, so I called a West Indian buddy of mine in New York and we ran it through underground channels. They're for the Fairways deal. That's why bodies are dropping all over the place. The total deal is twenty-three mil, and the expected revenues from the resort can't even be calculated. He has to put up good faith money of a couple of mil himself by the end of next month, and was planning on doing so through your daughter to get a few wealthy Arabs and Africans to build the resort. He couldn't dredge her accounts directly, or you'd find out—so everything had to run through the nonprofit first to get lost in the laundry. Simply stated, he cut you out, man, and used your own daughter to do it.''

DiGiovanni held the papers, then reached into his pocket for reading glasses. After an interminable time, he looked up at Nate.

"I gave that bastard too much for this to be true. These are very serious charges . . . Where did you get the papers?''

Again, Nate hesitated and swallowed hard, setting the Coke down gently on the top of the refrigerator unit.

"Do you believe in ghosts?''

DiGiovanni sat back and considered him with a penetrating gaze. "Don't play with me.''

"I am dead serious. Do you believe in ghosts?''

"Where did you get the papers?''

It was Nate's turn to consider DiGiovanni. Instinctively he knew he had struck a chord. It was in the way that his captor refused to deny his belief.

"My lady, the dead woman's sister, went home after the fire. She was shaken. All she had was the clothes on her back from when she'd spent the night at my house. She also had her sister's pocketbook, the one her sister had given her to hold in the hospital. When her sister died, she never went through it. All the poor kid could do was clutch it to her stomach and wail. But, the other night, we were sitting on the porch at night and a silvery mist came through the yard.''

Nate paused for emphasis as he watched the two guards watch DiGiovanni instead of him. There was a shift, he could feel it as DiGiovanni seemed to become less menacing.

"A silvery cloud . . . or mist? But, how did the papers come about?"

Nate shook his head and took his time to edit the story for full effect. "We were sitting there in the dark, because I didn't want the police to know I was there. All of a sudden the damned light clicked on by itself, and my lady jumped up and knocked over the bag. She said she thought it was her sister, since the way Loretta died, and since she used to go to a psychic regularly . . . Once everything settled down, the papers were showing out of the top of that purse. My lady had been carrying them around, not knowing what they were, for six months."

The old man rubbed his chin and sat back. Then he laughed, and the guards only smiled.

"Pretty incredible story, young man. Well, too bad I'm not the superstitious type. But, I am concerned about these papers and the fact that dead bodies are falling all around my daughter. You say the police don't know about the Fairways deal?"

"No. My girlfriend doesn't even know. After seeing the ghost of her dead sister, she was too upset. She just told me to take them and get them out of the house."

"Wise. You shouldn't leave the goods of the dead lying around where there is unrest. Tell you what," the old man said, downing the drink that he'd set aside and pouring another, "tonight, I have decided to let you live. If you turn out to be an honest man, then I owe you. If you turn out to be a liar . . . then I owe you. Either way, we shall meet again. Let us keep this transaction between us men. Capice?"

It was nearly 2 A.M. before he climbed out of the trunk. He was only glad that they'd let him get in and out on his own recognizance instead of slugging him in the head again. He didn't even mind the long walk down Delaware Avenue to where he could cross the foot-bridge and hail a cab. Hell, he was simply happy to be alive. He just wondered which trigger had pushed DiGiovanni to pick him up? The conversation with Ramirez or Claudia's media hype. Both seemed like a life insurance policy at this point. He was too highly visible to hit for the moment, and too many people had a vested interest in pinning their dirt on him.

But as he paid the cab and it pulled away, two men got out of an unmarked sedan and headed in his direction. When they held up badges and yelled for him not to move, Nate just closed his eyes.

"Let's go inside, McGregor. We need to talk."

He briefly glanced from McKinney to Wilson as he slowly made his way up the steps and opened his front door. In a weird sort of way, the presence of the police did make him feel more secure, albeit he was sure that the outcome would be his ultimate incarceration. But the prospect of prison seemed better than the trunk, or a possible gunshot to the back of his head under the Delaware Avenue I-95 extension.

When he had secured the door and turned on a side lamp, both officers looked around, surveying his environment quickly before they sat down.

"Nice spot," McKinney said with genuine admiration. "You're one lucky son-of-a-bitch. Must have a guardian angel."

Nate ignored the comment as he flopped in a chair across from the sofa. His head was splitting and the soreness in his body, along with the lack of sleep, didn't do much for his disposition. "I don't feel lucky."

Wilson leaned forward and smiled. "Kicked your ass pretty good, huh?"

Nate just closed his eyes and let his head sink back against the pillows.

"The lady in that shop up the street said she was worried and had watched you out of her back window. Said she saw two big white guys hit you and throw you in the trunk of a car with Jersey tags. So, we staked out your house hoping that you'd come back in one piece, cause we needed to talk to you.''

Nate groaned. ''So I guess I finally have a good alibi, huh, Wilson?''

''Yeah,'' McKinney laughed. ''Half-eaten plate of food is still in the bushes. So we know you were at the shop eating when everything went down.''

For the first time since they had started talking, Nate opened his eyes. ''What went down?''

''Can't find the Harris girl,'' Wilson said soberly. ''We went by her spot around nine P.M., she had some kind of altercation with her family and had gone for a walk. They called us worried sick when she didn't come back within the hour. So, we immediately came your way—but then we got this call into the station about you being abducted. Wondered if she showed up where ever they took you?''

''No,'' Nate stammered, fear halting his speech. ''If they hurt her . . .''

''I know, I know, man,'' Wilson said compassionately. ''She seems like a nice young woman, and I don't say that about most. We'll try to find her.''

''We paid a visit to Addison tonight as well. His story is airtight, but it stinks. We're betting on you, McGregor. Christ only knows why. But we don't think you did it.'' McKinney was staring at him in earnest now. ''Problem is, if this thing goes down the way it's set up, sooner or later we're going to have to bring you in and book you. Right now, our records show that you were abducted, and we plan to use that for about twenty-four to forty-eight hours to buy some time. Understand. We never saw you.''

''But you've got to help us,'' Wilson said, standing now and pacing toward the fireplace. ''Your girlfriend gave a hot tip to the news anchor who had enough sense to tell us instead of broadcasting it.''

''What did she say? I thought we had discussed everything?''

Nate was still numb from the likelihood that the DiGiovanni henchmen had taken Claudia as insurance while they investigated his story. If he could prove his theory, there would only be a slim possibility that they'd let her live.

"She said that the key we got in Isabella Gonzales's package didn't go to any apartment or file cabinet. We figured that we'd draw a blank with that anyway, because with all the attention on this, Addison would surely have time to change the locks." McKinney stood and joined his partner near the mantle. "None of the keys we found in the dead girl's handbag went to the apartment anyway, so just as we suspected, Addison created another dead-end. She told the reporter that it went to a locker, a place with women in showers. So, we could only figure that it was some kind of health club or gym. That's what we need to ask you about, since you were a good friend of Gonzales, and her family is so distraught they can't seem to take any kind of questioning right now."

"Think hard," Wilson said in a low tone, "it's all we got left to go on. And we don't even know if anything will come of it. It's a long shot. A *real* long shot."

"Marlton," Nate said sitting up straight. "She used to go to this place in Marlton, New Jersey. Off of route seventy-three."

"I know where you're talking about," Wilson said nodding and heading toward the door.

McKinney followed and Nate got up, escorted them to the door and turned the lock.

"That's the same area Addison lives in ... figures, since they used to deal with each other." McKinney rubbed his chin and glanced around one last time. "Hopefully they haven't cleaned out her gym stuff yet. I'll call the boys in Jersey and tell them to get the owner to open up."

She had made herself as small as possible in the bottom of Nate's massive walk-in closet. The sound of multiple male voices squeezed the air from her lungs and she breathed in tiny sips through her mouth. She had to get away from her parent's house once she'd realized that she had put them in danger. DiGiovanni could have come in there and wiped out the entire family. Or, Addison could send his hit man Jenkins by there to burn her parents' house to the ground. Even though they'd worry, she knew they'd call the police. And once it was reported that she'd fled, whoever was after her and Nate would hunt her down instead of the innocent elderly couple that she loved. Her father had been right. Her actions were foolish and endangered the whole family.

Heavy footsteps approached the stairs and mounted them. Claudia squeezed her eyes shut so tightly that speckles of light formed under the lids. What if it wasn't Nate? She hadn't recognized any of the voices. What if it was the DiGiovanni clan, just sending in an advance team to search then destroy the house? Or, what if it was Jenkins and his crew, sent out to throw kerosene around and to burn down this property with her trapped in it? Each new possibility was more horrible than the one before it. When she heard a man enter the room, she nearly passed out, but the amount of adrenaline pumping through her system kept her alert and nauseous.

The door slid back, and she screamed. The man yelled and a lamp came hurling in her direction which she reflexively blocked with her forearm.

"Claudia?"

Nate pulled her to her feet but her eyes were still shut tight as she cringed toward the closet wall. He moved toward her so fast that her mind hadn't caught up with her vision.

"It's me, baby. It's all right," he said in a soothing voice, trying to coax her out.

As soon as her brain could assemble the fragmented pieces, she found his chest and sobbed. "I was so scared, Nate. I had to run away so they wouldn't go after Dot and Daddy. I made such a mess," she wailed, shaking hard and almost vomiting from the held-back fear. "A psychic told me to tell the truth in the light . . . it was the stupidest thing I have ever done!"

Nate pressed her to him hard and stroked her hair and back as though he were trying to absorb every ounce of her fear into his own body. "Baby, I thought they had taken you. Oh, God, I was so worried . . ." His voice was shaky as he dug his face into her hair. "Your media hype may have saved my life tonight," he whispered. "Now we're both too visible to just kill outright. Whoever is after us will have to plan in advance, and work around the media."

His words and warmth soothed her. As his hands passed her shoulder blades and made their way up her neck she could feel her heartbeat slowing to his gentle rhythm. In the midst of this swirling storm, he provided the eye of the tornado, a place where calm reigned if only for a moment.

When she reached her hand up, he winced. Drawing it back carefully, she looked at the tips of her fingers and saw blood. "What happened?" she asked in a very quiet voice, holding him back so that she could look in his eyes. "Baby, you look so tired."

His shoulders slumped and he moved away from her to sit on the side of the bed. "I met with DiGiovanni tonight. The blow to the head came with the limo service."

She stared at him. "Dear God . . ."

In reflex she hastened to the bathroom and wet a towel, bringing it to him to apply to the growing knot at the back of his skull. But each time she tried to apply the compress, Nate would wince and pull away.

"You have to have somebody look at this," she said gently. "C'mon, we've got to at least clean it up."

"I'm so tired, baby," he whispered, slowly going horizontal on the bed. "I just have to lie down for a few hours."

"But you can't go to sleep with a concussion . . . you could slip into a coma, or something."

Nate's eyes were closed and he was immobile, stretched diagonally on the bed.

"A coma would be the most humane thing to happen to me," he croaked, his voice sounding farther and farther away. "Just let me die in my sleep."

The smell of coffee brewing assailed his senses, but he could not open his eyes. Even though the mini-blinds were closed, the least little bit of light felt like a knife was gouging out his eyes and digging its way to the back of his brain. The smell of breakfast food made him want to retch, and he turned over slowly in the tangled sheets. He could hear light footsteps coming, but couldn't manage to sit up. It had been a long time since he felt this bad. His worst hangover hadn't done this to him.

"Good morning," the soft female voice said as he felt a tiny depression of weight at the foot of the bed. "You've been asleep for seven hours and I just wanted to be sure you were conscious."

Nate groaned and tried to pull himself up. He could feel two smooth hands under his arm pits hoisting him to a sitting position. The change in altitude made the stabbing pain in his head worsen, and he immediately brought his hands up to either side of it and pressed hard.

"Open your mouth and take four of these."

He didn't bother to question what it was that she slid into his dry mouth. He just followed her instructions and took a sip of the warm substance that he couldn't taste when she brought it to his lips. The combined sludge of tablets and what he assumed was coffee went down hard and burned at the bottom of his belly.

"I'm gonna be sick," he said, turning over the side of the bed. But when nothing came up, he sank back down against the pillows.

"We've got to get you to a doctor. You've got to get a head X-ray . . . this could be serious, like a fractured skull."

He waved her away with his hand. "Nah, they're professional

hit men. They know how to make it hurt but keep you alive until they're really ready to do you.'' He tried to chuckle, but the shaking sensation only made the pain worse.

"That's not funny, Nate.''

"No. It's not. But I don't have time to go to the emergency room and wait around for four to five hours.''

He could hear her sigh. "Then you have to eat something, and get a base in your stomach. You've been running on E for days now.''

His head hurt too much to argue, even an argument designed for his own good. All he could muster was a weak "Okay" as a compromise. Then he fought gravity again and propped up on one elbow while she brought small portions of soft eggs and toast to his mouth. When had anybody but his mother done this for him? he wondered, as Claudia continued to shovel nourishment into his body. Damn it had been a lifetime since anybody really took care of him.

"Feeling better?'' Her question was followed by a light kiss on his forehead as she removed the tray from the nightstand.

He did feel a little improved, and the coffee had helped him wake up. "Yeah, baby . . . you're just what the doctor ordered. But it may be a few days until I get to a hundred percent. I could get used to this, you know?''

Her smile warmed him and he eased back to a prone position. Yeah, this was all right, even with the headache. His baby was alive. He was alive. The police were on his side. . . . Claudia's footsteps got farther and farther away. . . . He could get used to this.

Chapter 18

It felt good to feel needed again.

Claudia threw her head back and opened her arms wide in the middle of the kitchen. "Thank You," she murmured out loud, and laughed. It had been so long since she had helped anyone . . . Before Loretta's death, she helped everyone . . . no request ever went unanswered; she was there for everyone—giving till it hurt. And when she broke, she stopped giving completely.

Yet, it wasn't until she held a fork to Nate's parched lips that she came to understand the need for balance—the wonderful gift one received back from the giving of oneself freely without any expectations or strings attached. Before the giving felt like work, sacrifice, and many times it was given without what Moms used to call Grace. Now, she knew that she had a right to say no when she felt overextended, because in truth, giving freely should make her feel as light and as fulfilled as she felt now.

As she cleaned and busied herself around the kitchen, stacking dishes and clearing off enough space to have a late lunch with Nate at the table, she came to understand Dot's fastidious-ness even more. It wasn't about cleaning, it was about doing for her father. And in return, he ran errands all the time for Dot—because it wasn't about the errand, it was about doing for Dot at the drop of a hat.

The smell of old garbage stopped her in her tracks, and she routed around for a trash bag. Tickled that Nate would really be surprised when he finally got up, she hauled a load to the back door and relined his can with a fresh bag. She couldn't believe that she had reached this age to find this out. Moms did for everyone in the neighborhood and the church, but not with the sheer joy that should have gone into the giving. She stopped and separated a twist tie from the group. Perhaps because Moms felt so robbed, or so martyred by the whole thing that had gone on between Dot and Dad . . . her mind wandered.

Wasn't that how she felt in her own marriage? Martyred. Yes. She did things that were expected, not because she wanted to, but because they were expected . . . and thus, there was little joy in doing anything. Her heart ached for Moms, and for a moment she wished that she could heat up some tea, sit down at the table, and just talk to her about what she felt. There was no conflict, though, she loved both women equally, yet in very different ways.

The stench of the rotting food made her stomach turn. The last thing Nate needed to do was to come downstairs and try to eat with that putrid odor. Hurriedly, she tied up the bag and flung open the back door. It was gorgeous outside, and the breeze that passed her swept through the kitchen and created a natural air-freshener. She was nearly giddy as she bustled down the steps to put the garbage in the side yard. Maybe she'd try her hand at a scratch cake, depending on what she could scrounge up. There were some eggs . . . flour . . . a couple of sticks of butter. . . .

"Don't move."

Cold steel stung her cheek and she froze. The bag of garbage toppled to the bottom of the steps and broke open.

"A mutual friend of ours wants to have a conversation with you. Walk quietly and you won't get your head blown off."

Her vocal chords were paralyzed. The man at her side dug his fingers into her arm, but she was already numb. She followed him without struggle, aware of the hard metal object that now stabbed into her kidneys. When she saw his vehicle, she tried to look in her peripheral vision for the kind of unmarked police car that usually sat at the corner of her house in Jersey. Nothing. She wondered if McKinney and Wilson were at her parents' . . . too far away to help her now.

He shoved her into the dark blue Lincoln Towne Car from the drivers' side, holding the gun on her low so that any passers-by wouldn't immediately notice it. Here, in broad daylight, she was being abducted, and a few people walked by—totally unaware of what was going on. The urge to scream was out-weighed by her fear. She was almost glad that Nate was upstairs asleep, because had he known, he might have taken the bullet designed for her.

She studied the dirty hands and the rough face of the medium-build, Caucasian male in his early forties. Every facet of who he was, what he smelled like, what his voice sounded like, what he looked like, she burned into her memory in case she lived. When the driver pulled the car away from the curb, he jumped a light, then barreled down Chestnut Street toward Center City. She had to remember where he took her. As they made a hard turn onto Thirtieth, for a moment she thought he might try to get her out of the city, but then they made another hard merge onto I-676 and she knew the waterfront was the probable destination.

Resting the gun on his lap and grabbing the car phone, he issued a warning glare in Claudia's direction. Renewed terror pulsed through her veins. They were moving too fast for her to bail out. Traffic was whizzing by on either side. And she knew she'd lose in a struggle over the gun. He was closer to it.

"Yo, Jenks," he said with a satisfied grin. "Got her."

After a moment of receiving instructions he repeated the last phrase. "Same building basement? Okay. Done. Then bring her up to you, in Loretta's old apartment. Penthouse. Yeah."

Hearing her sister's name made her want to pass out. Sweat created a circle of moisture on her shirt just above her breasts, and she swayed with every dip and swerve of the car motion. But she watched the driver carefully. Something was wrong. It was as though he was racing against time; the question was, why, especially when they had all the time in the world to kill her?

"No. He wasn't there, like I told you. DiGiovanni got him last night . . . The babe in the food shop down the street had called the cops, I picked it up on the police scanner and beat them there. She thought I was Five-O, so she started telling me all about how Nate McGregor got hit in the head by two Italian looking dudes and forced into a car trunk with Jersey tags . . . Yeah, those aren't our guys . . . Right. I went back to Addison's and he told me that the chick wasn't at her parents . . . after a couple of hours of watching the old folks' house, I figured the only place she could be was hiding at McGregor's. Yeah . . . like I said . . . It was beautiful."

He laughed, not looking at her, "Jenks, she opened the freakin' door and walked right into me! Ha! Can you believe it? Hell no. The place is one of them turn of the century solid brick deals . . . yeah, yeah . . . like a damned fortress. Woulda taken forever to get inside."

Her captor's demeanor was shifting. He listened and pressed the phone closer to his ear as they turned off the expressway and headed for the Society Hill high-rise that her sister once occupied.

"Look, if they had let him go, then I'd be concerned. But I'm telling you, only the chick was home. After staking out her parents', I sat in front of the house all night . . . from four

A.M. Yeah, the cops must know he's dead, because they didn't even waste the manpower by leaving a car in front of the house. Yeah ... like I said, they knew he was a goner, probably once they talked to the store lady. Okay. Five minutes.''

It felt like they were being swallowed alive as the car bumped over the lip of the garage entrance and they descended into darkness. The driver pulled off into a remote site and didn't speak to her, just dragged her out by the arm so hard it felt as though it might pop from the socket. It was all she could do to keep up with his pace, then he abruptly stopped, and tapped on a black door. She could hear the tumbler turn and her heartbeat throb an answer in her eyes.

The room was completely black, and she was thrust forward by a hard shove. Her thighs collided with a desk, and she quickly jutted her hands out in front of her to break her fall.

''So, we have to go to these extremes to get our property back.''

Claudia listened hard to the smooth male voice that spoke. It seemed vaguely familiar.

He hated waiting for Addison to play his little mind games with his women before he did 'em. Jenkins paced the abandoned apartment and wiped the sweat from his face. It was always simpler to just take them out at a distance with a silencer. Or, twice for surety in the back of the head. But with Addison, he liked to toy with them first, like a big cat torturing a mouse. It wasn't professional. When he worked for DiGiovanni, it was always a clean, professional hit. No women, no children, no old folks. Just business.

The apartment was stifling. He couldn't open the window, or turn on the fans ... like Addison wanted it, it had to look like she had come back into her sister's old apartment and got whacked. That would leave a lot of potential suspects ... DiGiovanni, McGregor if he was still alive, or Ed Washington. If Addison didn't have the info about how he and Gino stole from DiGiovanni in a safe deposit somewhere, he would have bailed out of this job a long time ago. Starting with the chick in the hospital. He'd tried to tell him that it was much too complex . . . too risky. They should have just done her. Then the damned Puerto Rican chick. He had to pull Addison off of her and finish the job. Blood and guts was too risky . . . too much could show up in an autopsy. But that was Addison's style. Living on the edge. The bastard got a rise out of it.

Jenkins continued to pace, waiting for his last kill to be brought up to him on the maintenance elevator from the garage level. "C'mon, what's taking so long," he muttered. He needed a cigarette in the worst way. What the hell, he'd smoke it and flush it. Even if the cops smelled smoke, they knew the Harris chick smoked. . . .

By this point, his eyes had adjusted to the semidarkness, even though every mini-blind in the joint was shut. Pulling out his last butt, he struck one of two matches left in the matchbook. It went out.

"What the hey?"

Jenkins looked around nervously. There wasn't any breeze in the room. No air circulated whatsoever. . . . He struck the last match and before he could lower the tip of his cigarette to it, it went out.

"Cheap-assed, gas station matches," he muttered angrily, carefully collecting the two blackened matches and shoving them in his pocket as he headed toward the kitchen. Flipping a burner dial on with the cigarette dangling from his mouth, he cursed and banged on the stove when it failed to light, not bothering to replace the knob that dropped to the floor from his tirade.

"I'm stuck in a hole waiting to kill some chick and can't even get a light. Tell me, where's the justice?"

Nate stretched and yawned. A thumping noise down the hall roused him slightly, and he called out to Claudia without opening his eyes. When she didn't respond, he forced his body to gradually come back to life. What was all that banging? If she was going to clean up, she could have just a little mercy on his soul. . . .

He swung his legs over the side of the bed, and slipped on his sneakers, breaking the backs down as he pressed his full weight on them. His head was still in too fragile a condition for him to attempt bending over. He still had his pants on and a T-shirt. The thought of Claudia trying to undress him and lug him under the covers made him smile. He must have been too heavy for her to move . . . but, after something else to eat, he could rectify that. . . .

Maybe not. Nate held onto the wall in the hallway. He still didn't quite have his sea legs yet. The blows felt much worse this morning than they had the night before. Starting again slowly, he suddenly saw the source of the banging. It was the door to the back staircase thumping as a draft caught it. "Claud . . ." he called out, stopping in the bathroom to relieve his bladder. "Gotta close them windows, girl. You're gonna freeze us out tonight."

Still she didn't answer.

Growing concerned, he hastened the process of washing his hands and face and slipped his feet firmly into his shoes. The backstairs door continued to thump as he slowly descended, listening intently for sounds of movement. At the bottom he just stared.

The back door was wide open, the kitchen was spotless, a stray cat was in the overturned garbage that was strewn down his back steps. He was wild.

Turning several times in the same spot at first, he finally willed direction to his legs. The backyard. No sign. The dining room. No sign. His gaze cut across the living room and he bound up the stairs yelling her name as her searched from room to room. No sign. The cordless phone went into his sweater sleeve and out again as he dialed and dressed at the same time.

"McKinney or Wilson. No. I can't leave a message. Tell

them a friend called and Addison's got her. It wasn't DiGiovanni. He doesn't do women and children.''

"Your sister was a real pistol . . . seems to run in the family. Where's my paperwork?''

Claudia clutched her hands together and began to say the Lord's Prayer in her mind.

"We've been in here for ten minutes and all you can do is breathe—or hold your breath. This is no fun. If Loretta were here, she'd be trying to scratch my eyes out, or something far more delicious.''

Claudia didn't speak to the voice that murmured in the darkness. It was so smooth . . . so lethal . . . so like the voice in her dream. In her dream. Yes. She had to play a hunch and bring light to the darkness. Tell the truth.

"She is here.''

The voice laughed. "My dear, I'm asking you nicely. Where's my paperwork.''

"With DiGiovanni.''

She felt lightning strike across her face and her head snap back. Claudia laughed. He was afraid of DiGiovanni and Nate had given him what was in Loretta's purse.

"So, you do have some fire in you? That will make it interesting.''

"Do you believe in ghosts?'' she said rubbing her face. "It's not being smart, it's about the papers.''

There was silence and she stiffened her body in expectation of a blow that didn't come.

"Talk to me,'' the voice said as it began to move around the room.

Craning her neck to the shuffling sounds, she began slowly. "My sister never told me what was going on, but she gave me her purse to hold when she was in the hospital. I never opened it until a week ago when all of this madness began.''

"Interesting. So you held onto her purse, and . . .''

"And when you burned down the building, I had it on me. That's the only reason it didn't go up in smoke. That's why I wanted to know, do you believe in ghosts?"

The voice laughed a rich, deep, sexy tone that was so close to her face she could feel its breath. "Where is it now?"

"With DiGiovanni. Nate's home asleep. They dropped him off around three after they took it from him . . . I was hiding in the closet upstairs since one. He always kept a spare key under the side yard mat for his tenant."

This time she wasn't ready for the lightning that struck her, or the closed fist that came with it. The impact toppled her against some furniture and she could feel a body behind her hoisting her up to her feet to possibly take another blow. Cowering under her forearms, she shielded her face . . . and then she saw it . . . but she was nearly seeing stars from the punch. It was so dark, but the silvery mist. . . .

"She's here," she whispered, in a voice so confident that the room went still. "See it, isn't she beautiful?"

"This bitch is crazy," the voice that sounded like the driver said. "She gave it to McGregor, who handed it over to DiGiovanni. There's no more we can do, boss."

"Shut up, I have to think!" The smooth voice had lost all of its controlled smugness and it circled the small room like a trapped demon. "Do you see it . . . maybe the buildings got a gas leak, or something?"

"I see it, but I think we need to clean this up first and let Jenkins do his job. Then we can deal with that later."

"But it's odorless, its colorless, but I can definitely see something . . ."

"It's her," she said triumphantly.

"That doesn't save you though."

Claudia got very still. "Yes she will. She brings light to dark places."

Both voices laughed and stopped suddenly as the light switch went on by itself.

* * *

Forty-five minutes with that Harris woman, and not a cigarette or a drink of booze in the place. . . . Jenkins walked near the front of the apartment to avoid the gaseous odor coming from the range. It didn't matter, they'd do her quick by strangulation, no need to pop her. The girl was probably dead already, anyway. Addison had beaten Isabella to death in fifteen minutes. He hated messy jobs.

Jenkins rubbed his eyes. They were watering from the fumes, and he was glad that all of the tenants had been moved to two floors lower earlier in the year under the guise of renovations so they could do what had to be done without interference from the cops. That had been the problem with the Gonzales job. Addison did her right in her apartment, the one down on four where there were neighbors.

Another five minutes . . . he decided, then he was going downstairs. His vision was getting blurry and he was seeing silvery blobs of light moving in and out of the rooms. He moved toward the door and stopped as a cool breeze went past him. Where was the damned draft coming from?

He followed the cool sensation toward the kitchen and stood in the middle of it. Transfixed, he watched a silvery indefinite shape hover near the stove, then dissipate to reform near the light . . . then it clicked on.

The entire building rocked, hurling Claudia against the door and Addison and the car driver against the far wall beneath a fallen pipe. Her body had knocked the door ajar and, dazed, she tried to scramble to her feet as all the lights suddenly went out. Thick billows of black smoke caught in her lungs as she ran blindly in the direction of the garage opening. Gunshots and sirens and falling glass collided with her ears. Screams and people running on the sidewalk called out a direction of safety to her. Traffic sounds, cars screeching . . . She ran blindly and blended into the crowd behind the fast-forming barricade of humanity. When she saw the first uniformed suit, she held onto it.

"Addison blew up the building. He's trying to kill me!"

"Ramirez, listen to me. I have to get a message to DiGiovanni."

His friend was silent and the static from the pay phone crackled with ambivalence.

"Addison took Claudia! Do you hear me, man?"

"It's all over the news. It's too late, my dear friend . . . I am so sorry." Ramirez's voice was gentle.

"No! It can't be."

"The high-rise went up due to a strange gas leak in the Penthouse apartment that her sister used to occupy . . . It's an eight-alarmer and they still don't know if they have all the residents out. Nobody can get within ten blocks of it, even with a helicopter, the smoke is so bad . . . You have to let it go, man . . . just like I had to let Isa go."

"No. That's where you're wrong," Nate's voice cracked and broke. "You're wrong, man. If he killed her, I'm gonna do him. Personally. This is to the bone."

"Look, when you lost your wife, we lost you for four years . . . But to kill a man, counselor, you gonna do life. Because this is in anger, and you'll leave a trail."

Nate ignored his friend and pressed on. His heart was gone, his ears were hearing platitudes, his mind absorbed none of it.

"Ramirez, I know that you know how to get to him. You work in minority contracts, DiGiovanni gets the first tip on contracts. We go too far back to bullshit each other. Politics makes for strange bedfellows, and I'm not judging. Just find him. I'll stand in the middle of Broad Street if necessary. Hell, I even called the cops. Because there's another piece of this that has to be dealt with. Me, you, McKinney and Wilson, and DiGiovanni can strike a deal with whatever they find. Locker number twelve. Tell him that. They can pick me up at the diner.''

''I want you to listen to this, Mario,'' McKinney said switching on the tape recorder as they all sat in silence. A large black leather case rested on a marble coffee table between them, filled to capacity with micro cassettes.

Wilson looked at his partner, then to Nate. ''This is one sick bastard. Can we put him away with it?''

All eyes focused on Nate. He knew that they wanted his legal take on it before it went to the DA. ''If you can show that he taped these conversations himself, all these conversations that Addison kept—like a recorded personal diary, are admissible. But, if he was taped unwittingly . . . or these were police tapes that didn't go through proper channels . . .''

''What should be the issue?'' Ramirez yelled, standing. ''You got these from my dead niece's locker, under normal police investigation of a homicide . . . and they're labeled in *his* own handwriting. This is what he tried to beat out of Isa, the location of the tapes and his missing document that showed the resort deal . . . that's far more damaging than the nonprofit scam. It tells everything . . . names, amounts of money agreed upon, and implied hits! He told Jenkins to abduct Isa, to bring her to him!''

McKinney stood and walked over to Ramirez and patted his back to calm him, helping him to return to a large velvet chair.

''Yes, it could be argued that he actually made the tapes from his answering machine, given his handwriting appears on the labels.'' Nate's gaze flowed across the sumptuous DiGiovanni living room that was filled with rare antiques. The large bay window drew his attention, and he stared out into the night.

DiGiovanni's voice was mellow when he spoke, not authoritative and menacing. ''I once said that I would owe you if you were right. I am a man of honor, a man of my word. That's why I have friends in many strange places . . . What can I do to repay you?''

''Nothing. Thank you.''

''Please. This has been an ugly affair. I have heard a man blaspheme my daughter, use her like she was a toy . . . my word and kindness has been forsaken by a man who would put up a resort without telling me . . . Ramirez has lost a niece . . . and sadly you have lost a friend and a lover. Surely, there must be something?''

''You know,'' Nate said slowly, ''all she ever wanted was a school . . . I was going to surprise her with the mansion on Forty-Sixth and Spruce, and incorporate a nonprofit . . . do all the paperwork, get her started . . .''

DiGiovanni smiled broadly. ''I am familiar with that property . . . A palace . . . eight months, maybe nine . . . it has lead paint, asbestos, but my men can do this. No problem. No cost to my friend to have her name on such a fine monument.''

Nate could only shake his head no. ''You see, she would have brought life to that place. It was hers . . . I couldn't see it without her . . . You had to know her.''

All of the men in the small circle looked down at the floor. DiGiovanni's expression clouded over and he cast his gaze out the window. ''This is why we never involve the women. It is tragic enough when you lose a son. I have lost one, and my dear wife, God rest her soul, was never the same. If I had lost my Maria . . . No, my good friend. I understand. It is just our way to repay a debt of such magnitude . . . I thought there might be something . . . but for an honest man, there is very little but what's important.''

Nate looked at the old man and smiled sadly, not ashamed of the tears that filled his eyes. ''Unless you can raise the dead, there is nothing.''

Wilson let out a deep breath. ''We'll hunt the bastard down, McGregor. That's the least we can do. He could have an accident in a real bad part of the penal system. His smooth ass wouldn't last a night in—''

"No." DiGiovanni said harshly. "He falls under Sicilian law now. He has injured my family, and many old and new friends. There was a time when we kept this amongst the men— he has brought this to my daughter, even. The new breed know of no such code. Lessons must be learned the old way."

"Look," McKinney interjected nervously, "we can't endorse any actions like that . . . I mean, as police officers."

"You don't have to. What happens, happens. That is why it won't be discussed in front of the counselor, or the politician, or you. You are friends, and what you know could hurt you. Go about your routine. Bring the case, and clear all the names. Leave what is Sicilian to a Sicilian. Your hands stay clean. You have done me a great service, and I am in debt to you more than you can know."

DiGiovanni walked over to the bar and pulled out four long-stemmed cordial glasses, a tumbler glass and a can of soda. Pouring a round of Sambuca in each cordial and lighting it, he slowly proceeded back to the coffee table. Once each of the four cordials had been removed from his thick hands, he then went back and retrieved the Coke and the short tumbler, handing both to Nate.

"I must tell my sad friend a little truth . . ." DiGiovanni waited patiently until Nate looked up again. "I knew you did not lie to me the night we first met . . . because you asked me a question that only an honest man would ask."

All eyes focused on the old man who stood in the middle of the circle with a glass raised.

"My friend asked me, did I believe in ghosts? And I could not answer, because I was afraid. A man in my position has many ghosts. So, I thought about this, and what these people meant to you . . . Isabella, Loretta, now Claudia . . . and you came to me for your ghosts, unafraid. You took a very big risk, for your ghosts . . . and for your partner who deserted you. You are a man of honor, and would die for your principles. I respect this . . . Therefore, I say *salute!* We must avenge the dead in accordance with our occupations, and let the dead rest in peace."

In unison, all seated picked up their glasses and downed the contents.

"*Salute!*"

Chapter 19

The blue uniform held her too long, asked too many questions
. . . wanted to follow protocol and help her join the other distraught survivors in the vans and ambulances behind the barriers.
His goal was crowd control, not information gathering. His grip
was so strong as he ushered her in the wrong direction . . .

Pandemonium broke out in the streets, and they could barely
hear each other. He took her meaning figuratively instead of
literally. She could not get him to understand that she wasn't
a tenant. She wasn't talking about Addison's building management practices, but that he was actually going to kill her!

Over her shoulder she could see Addison and the other man—
searching, pushing through, gaining on her. She held the blue
suit by both arms and looked him dead in the face.

"Listen to me, call detectives McKinney and Wilson. Tell
them I'm alive and trying to stay that way."

Then she was gone.

Running and bumping through the throng she headed south—
away from the fire, away from the killers . . . she needed a
haven. Never looking back she just ran until the muscles in

her legs trembled and sent stabs of pain through her, only to be matched by the knife that cut her lungs. But she couldn't stop. Not when they were so close, could jump out from anywhere and just level their guns and shoot her.

That's when she saw it. A haven. Heaven. Paradise. BIRDS OF PARADISE. Less than fifty feet ahead of her.

Claudia tumbled in the door wide-eyed, shocking patrons and the young woman at the register. "Celeste. Please," she wheezed and gagged.

The young woman moved fast, throwing the bolt on the door and screaming for Celeste. She was the first person to help her, the first to act without requiring an explanation. Claudia held onto the edge of the counter and dragged huge gulps of air into her lungs.

The older woman pushed a panic button under the register, and cleared her shop quickly. She told her patrons that the young hysterical woman near the register had been attacked, and apologized that her store was now closed for the day. Tears of gratitude ran down Claudia's cheeks. Her whole body shook with sobs as Celeste quickly moved her beyond the small tea area to the back of the shop, through a steel door that she bolted behind them, and up to the second level. For the first time since she had been taken from Nate's, she felt some semblance of protection.

Celeste brought cold cloths and made her lie down on the fouton. The young woman, Celeste's daughter, Nicole, brought her lukewarm peppermint tea and a phone.

"I saw it already, chile," Celeste said quietly, bringing the tea to Claudia's lips. "I was meditating . . . you had been on my mind so heavy these days after the news reports, and then I saw this very bright light. But it was not a good light. It was red, and angry, and went dark with smoke. Then I heard the blast, and heard the fire engines. I knew."

"She saved my life," Claudia whispered, her voice cracking with the overload of emotions that raced through her. "She came . . . they even saw her, but didn't know what it was. Then, just as always, she turned on the lights and the place exploded. They think it was a gas main, but it wasn't. They put a gun to my head, Celeste. Kidnapped me from Nate's house. They were going to kill me when *my sister blew up the building by turning on the lights!''*

Her voice had escalated and she was rocking as she spoke, but Celeste patted her hair back and picked up the cordless phone.

"Who are the detectives?"

"Wilson and McKinney," Claudia whispered.

Nicole looked on wide-eyed and draped an arm around Claudia from the other side.

Celeste was very specific in her message, she was not about to open the door to any other police officers but the ones Wilson and McKinney. She spent nearly ten minutes repeating the events in the receiver while Claudia whispered her explanation. She was too stricken to handle an interrogation. She wanted to go home.

"Call your parents. Now," Celeste ordered, folding her arms over her ample bosom. "They must be worried sick. Tell them where you are, and that traffic is so horrible with the fire, that it may take a while for the police or anybody else to come get you. Then I will talk to them."

When she heard Dot's voice, she really wailed. It was as though Dot's tears merged with hers over the phone. Her father didn't try to hide his worry, and when Celeste got on, her soothing lilt seemed to cascade reassurance through them all.

"I have to call Nate," she finally said, beginning to curl up in a little ball on the fouton.

"No, my dear," Celeste whispered and kissed her forehead. "If his house has been broken into, we don't know if that would put you both in danger. Wait for the police. That is better."

Nicole brought a handmade Indian blanket and draped it over Claudia, and lit a white candle as she turned off the overhead light. Both women filed out of the room, and Nicole turned back, asking, ''Mom, you hit the panic button a while ago, a squad car should have been here by now, even with the big fire, right?''

Claudia sat up. Celeste stopped. Nicole held onto her mother's arm.

''The panic button goes through the first floor business phone box. Pick up the phone again Claudia.''

Tears splashed the fouton. ''No dial tone.''

''Sucker is on the second level—back fire escapes. He knows where this is because your sister brought him here . . . Used to talk to him about it all the time.'' Celeste went into a large chest that sat by the fouton, flinging aside magazines to lift the heavy lid. Down under piles of blankets, she withdrew a double-barreled shotgun, and laid it on her lap as she sat down.

''I believe in peace, but I also believe in protecting my children and my shop. We live in a world where sometimes certain things are necessary.''

All three squeezed together and waited.

''I'll only get one . . . only have one shell. The other will get away . . . That's the part I have to leave up to The Universe.''

''Listen, we'll drive Nate over to Claudia's parents . . .'' Wilson's tone was somber. ''I think it's best that we inform the Harris family together. Ramirez, you've just been through this, no need to go through it again. Mario, your boys can go look for Addison, we'll catch up later in the city. My pager has been rocking for the last hour, no doubt somebody's spotted him.''

All nodded, shook hands, and broke ranks in the driveway to carry out their plan.

Nate, held Ramirez's hand and then hugged him. ''Look, if there's anything you need . . .''

''Just find him. I'm going to the office to unearth every contract he ever had, and if he forgot to put a period at the end of a sentence, I'm nailing him for noncompliance.''

McKinney and Wilson patted Ramirez's shoulder and they watched him get into his city-issued vehicle alone.

"Do you know where he might try to go?" DiGiovanni said placidly, issuing a wink to the detectives.

McKinney smiled. "I would try to go to the airport . . . try to get out of the country on my Lear jet, to, shall we say, secure up my investments in the Caribbean."

DiGiovanni nodded. "Yes, I think that would be my direction, too."

"Christ . . . the whole top of the building? Still can't get through traffic . . ."

Nate and McKinney just stared at the radio as Wilson sputtered commands back into it.

"Yeah, that sounds like his work . . . top apartment belonged to a Loretta Harris, now deceased. Could have been additional evidence in there, but we had combed the building earlier . . . yeah, yeah, days before we can start looking for remains. So far only a few minor injuries . . . Okay. We need to dispatch to the airport. Seems like Addison had some investments in the Caribbean, and keeps a Lear out there. Call the airport and ground him. No, me and Mac will go over, we're in Jersey getting ready to swing by the Harris household to tell the parents. Yeah. It's easier for us to hit it from this side. Send the boys out to the building and get back up out to Addison's offices . . . I don't think he'll be foolish enough to go home. Yeah, hold all the rest of the messages . . . we'll pick them up on the Philly side."

Nate let the drone of the police radio numb him. What could he tell the two elderly people who had entrusted their daughter's care to the police, to God, to a world that didn't care . . . ? He would walk in, and he knew Dot would see the looks on their faces and immediately know. Then the sobs and recrimination, and the lack of anything to say that could heal such a gape in the soul. He had been here before, only the last time it was his son. This time felt dangerously close to that precipice where he'd jumped.

"You want to do it, man, or we can?" Wilson's voice was filled with compassion.

"It the hardest part of the job, but it's our job. You don't have to," McKinney said, putting a hand on his shoulder.

Nate just shook his head and stood on the front steps with the detectives flanking him. When Dot opened the door, she almost made them all fall as she hugged and kissed them profusely. Her short buxom frame had filled Nate's arms so fast, that he was forced to step back just to hold onto her.

"Thank you, thank you, Jesus! You found my baby!"

Wilson and McKinney put a steadying hand on Nate's shoulders as he held Dot's hands. Where could he begin? "Miss Dot . . . We should go in and get Mr. Harris. Please."

"Oh, my baby will be so happy to talk to you. I have the number."

Mr. Harris rushed up and shook their hands, then body slammed them with a giant hug. They didn't even have time to open their mouths, and exchanged perplexed glances instead.

"My baby girl sounded good. A little shaken up, but I'm so glad that nice lady is taking care of her."

"You talked to her?" Nate said, now dazed.

"When, Mrs. Harris. A time is critical," McKinney said, anxiety making his cheek twitch.

Dot paused and her once jubilant expression immediately transformed into worry. "About twenty minutes to a half hour ago. Why?"

"Was it well after the fire started?" Wilson asked quickly.

"Oh, God, yes. We've been watching that on the news for well over an hour, more like an hour and a half."

"Where was she calling from? Do you have a number?" Nate cut to the chase and began walking out the door.

"Here it is," Dot said quietly, "it's that nice shop Loretta used to go to around South Street."

"Call Mario," McKinney said turning to his partner. "He may be the most expedient solution."

"Well, you look like you're all out, and I need to save the remainder for any trouble at the airport. Let's say we trade. You keep my dead hit man on the floor there, which will keep you two alive, and I'll take Miss Harris, who is a life insurance policy to keep me alive. Isn't that fair?"

They all looked at Eric Addison as he stepped over the driver's body and moved toward Claudia. Before he reached her, she immediately stood up and turned to Celeste and Nicole.

"Don't. He's dangerous. I'll be a willow."

There was not a cab to be found as they bustled down the narrow traffic jammed blocks, now overladen with detoured vehicles and angry drivers. Going back toward the city, she knew was out of the question for Addison. The gun in her side hidden under his folded suit jacket as they pretended to be a couple, was a constant reminder. He was panic-stricken, therefore out of control and felt all the more dangerous to her. They had no car, everything went up in the building. Ground transportation seemed futile. He had to get to the airport, and she was his only ticket.

A cab caught in the intersection with its lights out, turned them on. Addison smiled at the ON DUTY beacon and pulled her roughly into the back seat, thrust a c-note through the Plexiglas cage into the driver's hand, and slumped back.

"To the airport. Fast."

It took forever to get down a few blocks and over to the other side of Delaware Avenue. They seemed to be going the long way around to I-95 South, but given the traffic, it made sense. She didn't care, and hoped the ride would take forever. She even tried to will her screaming thoughts into the cabby's head. But he just drove stoically, taking unusual twists and turns, stopping every now and then to tell Addison why it was important to avoid this tie up, or that traffic snafu. Claudia sat very still and peered out of the window. She knew that she was surely going to die if Addison ever got her out of that cab.

She needed a plan; a way to make a break once the cab stopped. While Addison slumped back and seemed to be trying to figure out his next move, she worked on hers. But a nagging thought kept haunting her. It was to be still. She could hear Celeste. . . .

"Where the hell are we now?" Addison sat up and banged on the Plexiglas, bullet-proof divider.

The cabby shrugged. "The George C. Platt is all backed up. Thought I'd take a short cut through the refinery . . . I know the service road back there and all. Won't cost you extra. I hate the wear and tear on my vehicle."

Addison relaxed a bit. "Just get us there."

The more desolate the area became, the more Claudia's nerves fractured and severed from her central nervous system. She was going catatonic again. She could feel it. The way her body felt so far away from her mind. The way she could see everything happening from a tiny corner at the top of the cab. The way Addison's grip on her arm no longer hurt. The way she wanted to laugh at his fear, for hers was vanishing quickly into hysteria. When the cab stopped, she screamed.

She covered her head with her hands and accepted blows on her arms and shoulders. The cabby's demeanor seemed out of sync with reality, like her own. But his surreal calmness had a steadying effect on her. Addison's eyes were wild and his gaze darted between Claudia and the driver.

"Why are we stopping here?" he demanded. "The airport's across the river on the ramp above us. I thought you said you knew these service roads?"

Again the cabby shrugged. "The little lady didn't seem right to me, then with you all fighting back there, I didn't want to take no domestic squabble on the highway."

Addison pounded on the clear divider with his fist. "Don't worry about our business back here. Mind your own and get us to the damned airport!"

The driver looked amused. "Well, can't do that at the moment," he retorted, "got a problem with the law. I wasn't supposed to be back this way."

"What?" Addison yelled and brandished the gun. "I'll blow your brains out!"

"Wouldn't shoot a bullet-proof window at short range, mister. Could injure you and the little lady. Me, I'll be fine. Will just have to get new slipcovers."

"Let us out." Addison yanked at her arm and banged on the door that wouldn't open.

The cabby picked up a newspaper and began reading it as Addison banged. "I can't. Mr. DiGiovanni wouldn't like me to break the law. It's Sicilian law. *Capice?*"

Addison went still. His eyes tore around the interior of the cab for an exit. His expression was so full of hatred that she instinctively drew away even though he hadn't reached for her again. But it was coming. She watched every broken dream, every foiled scam, every carefully laid plan in his wealthy wonderland lifestyle crash and burn in his eyes—before his eyes. In Addison's distorted perception, she was part of his failure. She was one of the culprits that had destroyed his empire. And she was trapped in the backseat of a cab with a madman. . . .

"I thought you were the only thing that could get me to the airport alive. I was only worried about the authorities . . . but there is one last thing I need to do before I die, and that's wrap my hands around your throat."

As he lunged at her with both hands, and the gun fell to the floor of the cab, her back hit the door and it flew open. Two sets of strong hands caught her shoulders, and suddenly Addison's weight lifted from her torso.

"And this is how my son-in-law repays me? I am deeply disappointed."

"Don . . . Mario," Addison stammered. "These people," he said sweeping his hands around in empty air, "are all lairs. They've set me up. Ruined my name. I demand justice."

The four men that dragged them out of the cab stood by DiGiovanni. One was dispatched to help Claudia into a long dark sedan. The cab drove off. Three men were left standing with Addison who sobbed.

"Yes. There will be justice," DiGiovanni said quietly, then turned and headed toward the car that she had been helped into.

Dark windows electrically sealed the sounds of hysteria off from the quiet interior of the sedan. Only a brief moment of it filtered into the dimly lit space when DiGiovanni got in, along with the unmistakable stench of burning gasoline. As the driver turned back up the service road, her host gently pulled her chin toward him so that she couldn't see out of the front window. Yet a deep red and golden glow flickered in the glass panels and in the rearview mirror that disturbed her.

"No," he said as though hushing a child after a nightmare. "These are not things for women and children. Let me take you home to your mother and father, and the man who offered his life for your safety."

After a moment he considered her innermost fears, the ones she kept buried as she kneaded her hands in her lap. "You are like your Nate McGregor. An honest woman for an honest man. Hmmmm . . . This is good. So unload your conscience here at this riverside," he said smiling as they crossed the bridge into Jersey. "You shouldn't be haunted by ghosts any more, because of you and McGregor, they can rest. My late son-in-law, God rest his soul, can be added to my list of ghosts to worry about. He won't bother you anymore. I give you my word of honor."

Claudia drew an audible gasp. Then covered her mouth and lowered her eyes. "Forgive me, I just never . . ."

"Never saw anything. My son-in-law will be grieved at a large funeral following his death in the gas main leak at his premier building. Tragic. Such a young man to go up in a blaze. Burned beyond dental plate recognition. But, one must be philosophical . . . This way it was not a suicide . . . So, my daughter's marriage can end without shame, and she can be compensated properly by his insurance carrier. Or, it could have been a lengthy imprisonment that would require a divorce—which is out of the question for the devout. Therefore, we must pray, and I must go to confession to keep all things in balance. And, I will light a candle and give a healthy donation to the church."

Claudia just returned his squeeze when he covered her hands with his thick weather torn palms.

"Sometimes, my child, one must be still . . . to let things work out on their own. I tell my own daughter this all the time."

Epilogue

One Year Later . . .

His kiss melted into her neck like warm butter. She threw back her head and closed her eyes. Surrounded by music they swayed to their own rhythm . . . slower than the soft jazz that accompanied them . . . bare feet sinking into the carpet with sighs . . . the crackle of the fireplace joining Joe Sample's melody . . . Nate's caress down her back drawing their heat to a whimper . . . her touch extracting a breath. . . . Then in the distance, a cry . . . sudden stillness as they prayed for one more moment. . . .

"Nope. He's up." Nate's tone was patient, but held a note of longing.

"Do you think he's really awake, or just fussing in his sleep?" she whispered, his breath still searing her neck.

"Oh, baby, I hope not. Not now . . . You fed him, you changed him . . ." Nate laughed softly against her neck sending new ribbons of desire through her. "It's daddy's turn tonight, boy. Go to sleep."

"I know it's our anniversary, but, can't we just peek at him?" She brushed his mouth with a kiss, and ran her hand down his chest very slowly. "I promise to make it up to you . . . later."

He took a deep breath and closed his eyes. "You drive a hard bargain, Mrs. McGregor."

She chuckled as she pulled him into the room next to their music haven. The baby's whimpers turned to playful squeals as she lowered her face and kissed the brown bundle beneath her. Clasping one of her earrings in his tiny fist, he cooed and smiled as she baited him with a rattle to save her ear. "What chu doin' so wide awake?"

"That boys eyes are wide open, Claud. He's not going to sleep any time soon."

Nate looked down and laughed and scooped the baby up, bouncing the child around, causing giggles of delight. "Isn't he beautiful, Claud?"

"See, and you said I was bad." She laughed. "Now he's really up. I said a peek, not play touch football with him. Give him to me so I can settle him down."

"Aw, girl . . . tell that boy that his mommy works hard all day running the best school in Philadelphia, and his daddy really really wants him to go to sleep because he hasn't seen her in a *long* time." Nate begrudgingly handed her the child and stood close admiring their miracle.

"I see you in the morning all the time, these days," she said with a wink. "That's how he got here, remember?"

"Well you get up so early these days, Madame School Master, the boy's gonna wind up an only child. Plus, I've got some catching up to do after the last six weeks . . . Once the doctor gives the green light, a man can't live by bread alone, even if the Mrs. is an excellent cook."

Still smiling, she found the baby's pacifier and put him up on her shoulder, this time taking her earring out first. She rubbed his back and nuzzled his cheek, rocking him against her until his eyes got heavy and his breathing went deep. "Oh

. . . you're so soft and smell so good, little man. It's so hard to leave you with Dot on the weekends . . . since she gets to have you all day in here to herself.''

Noticing Nate's forlorn expression, she nudged in closer to his side. When he put his arm around her waist, she laid her head on his shoulder and made a funny face and kissed him till he smiled. ''You smell real good too. Maybe next weekend we can get Dot and Daddy to give us a few hours, huh? They love to sit with him, but won't hear of driving him across the bridge. Can you believe it? Maybe we can even spend the night downtown?''

''Girl, if you do for me what you doing for that little one now . . . I'll go along with whatever you say.''

Claudia put the drowsy baby in the crib and kissed the soft down of black curls that covered his head. Lacing her fingers through Nates, she pulled him toward the bedroom.

''C'mon. I can tell when my other baby needs some attention.''

DEDICATION

This book is dedicated to those who give me the truest sense of purpose . . . my family—my soul group . . . which is a wonderful collage of blended textures, forms, personalities, and spirits.

To My Children: Angelina . . . who is full of strength, determination and beauty, Crystal . . . a funny, cheerful delight, Helena . . . who is sensitive, loving and brave, and Michael . . . for his warm hugs, shy smile, and sense of justice. You carry the torch!

To My Fiancé: Al . . . For his ongoing support, strong shoulder, wide arms, and his unfailing belief in me. Thank you for everything.

To My Kitchen Conference Crew: My "Ultimate" Fairy God-Mother—Janine; Saint Patti, The Wise Woman—T.E.; Auntie Mo—and her Bed & Breakfast; Beth, live Soror Jai, Muriel, Isabelle, Debbie Mack, Harriet Garrett, Linda Mann, Jennifer Price, Darlene Atta, Smallszini, Denise, V, Iola, Verna, Ruthann, Kendra, Janice Masud, Asantewa, Asake, Sherylie G, Karen, Marilyn, Carlah, Olivia Abraham, Sarita Kimble, Yvonne Dennis, Melinda Contreras-Byrd, Theo Brown, Suzanne Colburn, and definitely The Psychiatrist—Michelle Parkerson . . . Thanks, crew, there are no words for our friendship!

To My Sisters: Lisa, Terri, Lydia, and Rhonda . . . always.

To My Sister Authors: Lorene Carey, Diane McKinney-Whetstone, Thelma Balfour, and Constance O'Day-Flannery . . . for your light, guidance, support, and encouragement.

To My Sisters Taking Care of Business: Agent, Vivian Stephens, and Editor, Monica Harris . . . thanks for keeping the faith.

. . . and to The Most Recent Angel to light gently on my shoulder, Julia B. Peterson . . . February 20, 1997. I will miss your letters, your laugh, and most assuredly your hugs, but I will always feel your love. Tell Mom and Loretta I love them and said, "Hi," when you get settled into Heaven.

ABOUT THE AUTHOR

Leslie A. P. Esdaile holds a B.S. in Economics as a Dean's List graduate of The University of Pennsylvania's Wharton Undergraduate Business Program, with a dual major concentration in Marketing and Management. She worked as a top ranking Sales Executive for a number of Fortune 100 firms before she became a freelance consultant servicing clients in the microeconomic development arena. Currently, she is pursuing her Masters of Fine Arts through Temple University's Department of Radio, Television and Film, with an emphasis on documentary film-making. She lives in Philadelphia.

Look for these upcoming Arabesque titles:

September 1997

SECOND TIME AROUND by Anna Larence
SILKEN LOVE by Carmen Green
BLUSH by Courtni Wright
SUMMER WIND by Gail McFarland

October 1997

THE NICEST GUY IN AMERICA by Angela Benson
AFTER DARK by Bette Ford
PROMISE ME by Robyn Amos
MIDNIGHT BLUE by Monica Jackson

November 1997

ETERNALLY YOURS by Brenda Jackson
MOST OF ALL by Loure Bussey
DEFENSELESS by Adrienne Byrd
PLAYING WITH FIRE by Dianne Mayhew

ROMANCES ABOUT AFRICAN-AMERICANS!
YOU'LL FALL IN LOVE
WITH ARABESQUE BOOKS FROM PINNACLE

SERENADE   (0024, $4.99)
by Sandra Kitt

Alexandra Morrow was too young and naive when she first fell in love with musician, Parker Harrison—and vowed never to be so vulnerable again. Now Parker is back and although she tries to resist him, he strolls back into her life as smoothly as the jazz rhapsodies for which he is known. Though not the dreamy innocent she was before, Alexndra finds her defenses quickly crumbling and her mind, body and soul slowly opening up to her one and only love, who shows her that dreams do come true.

FOREVER YOURS   (0025, $4.50)
by Francis Ray

Victoria Chandler must find a husband quickly or her grandparents will call in the loans that support her chain of lingerie boutiques. She arranges a mock marriage to tall, dark and handsome ranch owner Kane Taggart. The marriage will only last one year, and her business will be secure, and Kane will be able to walk away with no strings attached. The only problem is that Kane has other plans for Victoria. He'll cast a spell that will make her his forever after.

A SWEET REFRAIN   (0041, $4.99)
by Margie Walker

Fifteen years before, jazz musician Nathaniel Padell walked out on Jenine to seek fame and fortune in New York City. But now the handsome widower is back with a baby girl in tow. Jenine is still irresistibly attracted to Nat and enchanted by his daughter. Yet even as love is rekindled, an unexpected danger threatens Nat's child. Now, Jenine must fight for Nat before someone stops the music forever!

Available wherever paperbacks are sold, or order direct from the Publisher. Send cover price plus 50¢ per copy for mailing and handling to Penguin USA, P.O. Box 999, c/o Dept. 17109, Bergenfield, NJ 07621. Residents of New York and Tennessee must include sales tax. DO NOT SEND CASH.